# Sanctity

Mary Magdalene, Joan of Arc and
Sophie Scholl *with* Jesus the Christ

L CLEMENT MASON

Ark House Press
arkhousepress.com

Scripture quotations marked (NLT) are taken from the Holy Bible, New Living Translation, copyright © 1996, 2004, 2015 by Tyndale House Foundation. Used by permission of Tyndale House Publishers, Inc., Carol Stream, Illinois 60188. All rights reserved.

The textual content in this book is AI-free. No AI has been used at all in the text, but some AI may have been used in forming cover images.

While some tools of the publishing industry such as grammar checkers, design instruments and layout tools have been used to improve the technical fluency of the text, the content is completely original to the author L. Clement Mason.

Indigenous, Torres Strait Islander and Aboriginal people are warned that while no images of deceased persons are displayed within the text proper, references to deceased persons are numerous.

Cataloguing in Publication Data:
Title: Sanctity: Mary Magdalene (of Bethany), Jehanne Darc (Joan of Arc), Sophia Magdalena Scholl, with Jesus the Christ.
ISBN: 978-1-7641051-0-1 (pbk)
Subjects: [HIS031000] HISTORY / Revolutions, Uprisings & Rebellions; [HIS058000] HISTORY / Women; [REL067040] RELIGION / Christian Theology / Christology
Cover Concept by L. Clement Mason & Suzedezigns.
Design by initiateagency.com

*' Mordecai [said] to Esther,*
*"Don't think for a moment that you will escape there in the palace*
*when all the other Jews are killed. If you keep quiet at a time like*
*this, deliverance for the Jews will arise from some other place, but*
*you and your relatives will die. What's more, who can say but that*
*you have been elevated to the palace for just such a time as this?"*
*Then Esther [said],*
*"Go and gather all the Jews of Susa and fast for me. Do not*
*eat or drink for three days, night or day. My maids and I will*
*do the same. And then, though it is against the law, I will go*
*in to see the king. If I must die, I am willing to die."*
*So Mordecai went away and did as Esther told him. '*

- **Esther** 4:13b-17. (NLT)

# Table of Contents

# Prologue

## On Sources.

Mary Magdalene, Jehanne Darc, and Sophie Scholl are intensely beautiful in their extraordinary, striking historical presences. Those are not just pious words – these Christian women are difficult to write about because each is so uniquely radiant in their own ways. I use the adverb 'intensely' advisedly and intentionally – writing about them, and especially their relationship with Jesus Christ, is constantly constrained by my very apparent human limitations, and the sheer calibre of these three disciples. Mary, Jehanne and Sophie cannot be separated from Jesus Christ. This book is about and therefore underlines their experience of and with Him.

How can we see and relate their direct experience with Jesus Christ?

Their relationship with Him is their connecting interface across 2000 years. Even the descriptively abundant English language lacks the semantic colour or grammatical harmony to adequately describe them. Le Francais, avec ses syllabes poetiques et son imagerie prolifique, ne peut mesurer ces reines des ages. Die aufgabe erweist sich auch als zu anspruchsvoll fur die philosophischen, metaphysischen Klauseln des prazisen und wissenschaftlichen

Deutsch[1]. *Mary Magdalene* is broadly known across Christendom, and in popular culture, due to her very visible presence in Biblical sources, as well as in art and film. *Jehanne Darc* is recognized as a warrior, martyr and icon of Christian devotion – the Patron Saint of France, no less. *Sophia Magdalena Scholl* (known generally as 'Sophie') is less widely known, but is gaining much deserved commemoration and attention – Resistance fighter, Defender of truth, Martyr of Christ.

In all ways these were very human and unassuming women, except in their relationship to Jesus Christ. They each had human weaknesses and faults, and while these are important in preventing their romanticization, nor should they be unduly scrutinized. They were human. Their shared exceptionality, in each life, is that Jesus is the catalyst in their greatness. None of them sought greatness for themselves; they shared the quality of humility.

These biographical sketches are derived from evidence, commonsense/ deduction, logic and reasoning. Sources or evidencing vary widely; Mary Magdalene (c. 7 – 90 AD) has bare, specific and limited primary source material, Jehanne Darc (c. 01/1412 – 30/05/1431 AD) has more, and Sophie Scholl (09/05/1921 – 22/02/1943 AD) has most.

Nor is this text an attempt at exhaustive historical narration; there are already many careful and scholarly endeavours at biographical narrative or history, and those are mostly thorough and detailed. This text aims to observe each woman's *relationship with Jesus Christ* (i.e. not only ways in which they resemble Him, although that is obvious at certain points), because in each of their lives they privilege this relationship unto death or risk of death.

---

[1] *French, with its poetic syllables and prolific imagery, cannot measure nor calibrate these queens of the ages. The task also proves too demanding for the philosophical, metaphysical clauses of precise and scientific German.*

Jesus is their Source and Lord, above all others.

They recognize and obey Him, even at lethal risk and heart-rending cost. Each comes from a different time and culture, and historically they are widely separated, while having many commonalities other than their meekness and intrepidity.

We don't know what ultimately happened to Mary Magdalene. Jehanne and Sophie were both martyred, which is to say they were murdered for their faith. In each of them, their commitment to Jesus is front and centre, and this undergirds their courageous willingness to endure lethal persecution and abuse.

Please note that, as emphasized, these were deeply human women. This text is not interested in presenting warped or unhistorical perspectives on any of them; again, there are very good narrative histories and biographies available. This study concentrates as much as possible on the relationships between Mary, Jehanne and Sophie, with *Jesus the Christ*.

Mary Magdalene of Bethany could be naïve and obtuse, Jehanne Darc could be reckless and partisan, Sophie Scholl grew up in a stridently anti-Semitic era and had been tainted by that prejudice. It is also true that none of them are defined by their vulnerabilities. We need to approach them with the Grace we each need, and upon which we all ultimately depend.

## Each woman is a **Warrior of the Cross**.

*Referencing* used in this text is not an exercise or demonstration in citation or lexical probity. Where it is useful, conventional referencing is used, but this work is quite literally _not_ written as an academic exercise.

*Dates* are given in *day-month-year* format, so 10/11/2020 represents 10th November 2020. Gregorian reckoning is applied throughout the book, so even if a day is a Julian day in source documents it is rendered Gregorian.

The primary historical sources for the Person we call **Jesus the Christ** are the *Gospels* of the Holy Bible. (Formal referencing is utilized where needed. Obvious references, and sources that are readily searchable on the internet or in a library, are left to the reader.) This work is history, but necessarily it is highly reflective history. It does not neatly categorize as economic history, political history, revisionist history, feminist history etc.. If it is anything, it is *spiritual* history. As Prof. Regine Pernoud noted, 'History does not exist until it is recorded or told.'

*The Source Gospels* are **Matthew, Mark, Luke** and **John** as recorded in English through authorised and conventional translations from original languages. There are references also in the Biblical book of the **Acts of the Apostles** (commonly referred to just as **Acts**). I accept the historicity of the four Canonical Gospels, and the Divine Inspiration of the Old and New Testaments, as premises for this book. The Gospels are accounts of Jesus' life and ministry written after Jesus left this Earth to enter Heaven. He said very clearly that He would be on Earth in Spirit, until the end of the world (ref. **Matthew** 28:20, **John** 14:17-18). The four Gospels have been skeptically criticized as being only secondary sources, but that is unbelievably hyper-critical. We might as well carp at the documentary sources for Boudicca, or Napoleon Bonaparte. Most written sources for ancient persons/events are secondary. The Industrial/Technological Revolution which began approximately late C18th has generated extensive technological discoveries and changes, which have resulted in chemical testing, photography, sound recording, generation of electricity, filmic capture, DNA analysis, computers, atomic science, forensic methodologies etc., which can be used for and are regarded as primary evidences for object verification. It is also true that Artificial Intelligence (AI) is bringing any and all compositional and recording technology into serious doubt. (This book explicitly does _not_ use AI in any of its text.)

*The Gospels* are documentations of eye-witnesses, and are essentially primary. The historicity of Jesus Christ is better than the historicity of Tutankhamun, but no-one doubts Tutankhamun's reality or regality. Pharaoh Tutankhamun's intriguing tomb, as well as his mummified body, have been found; Jesus' tomb and body have not.

Therein is the story.

Reasons for challenging the reliability of sources demonstrating the historicity of Jesus Christ are just as likely to be politically, religiously or ideologically motivated. Jesus the Christ was inflammatorily controversial in the early C1stAD, and He remains so today. The four canonical Gospels are serious attempts at objective narratives based on accounts and observations of primary witnesses.

The primary source for **Matthew** is the Apostle Matthew, also known as Matthew Levi. **Mark**'s Gospel is generally believed to be the Apostle Peter's recollections and experiences discussed with John Mark, another disciple of Jesus. **Luke**, the only non-Jewish author in the New Testament, is the work of the Greek Physician Luke, who also authored the Book of **Acts**. **John** is the recollections of the Apostle John, and is more reflective than plainly narrative. **Matthew, Mark** and **Luke** are known as the *synoptic Gospels* because they essentially communicate a similar perspective. **John** has differences in emphases and objectives, and underlines Jesus' divinity and His teachings about God. The historicity, authorial integrity, and reliability of the Gospels have been subject to intensive scholarly interrogation, and you can readily delve into this online if you wish[2], or in any University library.

*Old Testament sources* also reference Jesus through prophets such as **Isaiah** and **Micah**. Epiphanies of Jesus are recorded in the Books of **Genesis**, and the prophet **Daniel**.

---

[2]   E.g. ref. James M. Rochford 2024, *Historicity of the New Testament*, evidenceunseen. com

Contemporaneous authors (who are often regarded as objective by modern standards) such as the Jewish *Josephus*, and the Roman *Tacitus*, also establish the historicity of Jesus the Christ.

*In this vein, there are also countless (literally) accounts of/from people who have encountered Jesus in a tangible form by seeing Him, or hearing Him, with their physical senses.* One example is the great English mystic, Dame Julian of Norwich, who very memorably encountered Jesus on 8th May 1373. In more recent times, another is the former Muslim Imam Abdul, who met Jesus by hearing Him, and became a Christian Follower (at great personal cost)[3].

*There are also apocryphal sources*, such as the 'Gospel of Thomas' and the 'Gospel of Mary (Magdalene)'. These are sometimes called 'Gnostic Gospels'; they may be very useful sources, but when the New Testament was compiled in the C4thAD, they were omitted. There are ongoing academic and scholarly arguments about this issue. For the purposes of this text, and especially pertaining to Mary (who is ironically a more central figure in the Gnostic Gospels), I am relying mainly on the Canonical Gospels.

Anecdotal evidence and illustration is also used where helpful. Reader, you can decide whether you find it supportive and credible.

The Qur'ān, the foundational Book of Islam, also references an historical Jesus (named *Isa*), but differs significantly from the Holy Bible.

This book deliberately tries to see Jesus Christ through Mary's, Jehanne's and Sophie's eyes. The Bible is the best place for foundations, but there is much else and more to be seen. In turn, we also inevitably see people as Jesus saw them.

*Supernatural entities* also attest to Jesus.

---

[3]    Voice of the Martyrs 01/04/2023, *The Imam Who Met Jesus*, vom.com.au

Jesus' influence through His teachings and actions, disseminated and propagated through documents and oral traditions, has been profound for approximately 2000 years. Many accounts in those 2000 years attest to the continuing presence and influence of Jesus in relational and tangible forms. Related accounts or perceptions of spiritual or deceased persons are usually designated 'supernatural' and dismissed as spooky bunk, because this designation is now (i.e. AD 2025 atow [at time of writing]) closely associated with negative phenomena, such as the occult (which just means 'unseen', or 'unknown') popularly and invariably presented via cannibalistic zombies, lustful vampires, demonically possessed persons engaged in projectile vomiting etc. - in such a way as to encourage interest, but not understanding.

Jesus, as referenced in the Gospels, gave little attention to occultic beings, referenced in the Bible as *demons* or *unclean spirits*; He did not dispute their reality, in fact He accepted them as being just as real as humans, but He showed no special interest in them. Except for the forty day period when Jesus was tempted by Satan (see **Matthew** 4:1-11; **Mark** 1:12-13), Jesus refused to deal with demons except to compel their obedience, and submission. This is because demons are liars and users. They react strongly to Jesus and fear Him (e.g. **Luke** 4:34-35). Jesus did not go on witch-hunts for evil spirits, but when they manifested, He dealt with them.

When compulsion is used to expel or reject a demon we call this '*exorcism*', but this word has developed negative connotations, mainly due to the literary-filmic horror fantasy genre. 'Deliverance' is a more neutral term. The Bible identifies demons as corrupted and evil angels (**Revelation** 12:9 is the clearest Biblical indication of this). They are always dangerous, malevolent, cruel, destructive, vile, amoral, and *never* to be approached without authorisation from God. If you expose yourself to them, they *will* harm you – guaranteed. Listen to God's protective instruction; do not seek them. Without God's protection and help, humans always come off second-best. We can encounter Jesus (or other spirits) supernaturally, because supernaturality is real. Demons though are totally untrustworthy, and they can no more practice deceptions on God than we can. Their reactions to God are real, and therefore possibly illustrative. They are repelled by God, and they fear Him.

Jesus Himself also encountered people in tangible form who had been long dead, such as Moses and Elijah (although Elijah did not die conventionally). We might call them *ghosts*. Jesus regarded death as an event like a wedding or a pregnancy/birth, not as a permanent condition (a wedding is an event, marriage is the condition; pregnancy/birth is an event, life is the condition). He was able to reverse death, and restore life - something He did on a number of occasions. Instances of Jesus healing and resurrecting dead people have occurred since His time on Earth ended in approx. 33AD. God is *always* the Living God, always pro-Life. The *supernatural* or 'paranormal' was accepted as ordinary by Jesus.

So, a person who returns from death to the present Earth without their corporeal body is designated a spirit, or ghost. All civilizations, cultures and ethnicities record foundational beliefs in spirituality, and in the spirits behind the beliefs. Some are perceived as hostile, some as amicable. We encounter spirits in ancient Australian Aboriginal beliefs, through to C21st Islam. This belief/knowledge about spirits is a belief shared across the range of spiritual metaphysics. Recent religious positions such as Scientism – which is faith in Science as an intelligent capacity, force or energy able to explain all phenomena – are also essentially spiritual. 'Evolution' (a pivotal theory and doctrine of Scientism) is frequently personified and referenced as a guiding power/force ensuring the continuance of life through vivifying adaptation[4]. This effectively attributes spirit or 'life force' to evolutionary

---

[4]    Ref, e.g. Univ. of Bath 2008, *First Rule of Evolution Suggests That Life is Destined to Become More Complex*, ScienceDaily, www.sciencedaily.com. This article identifies

progress. Persons returning from death as relatable beings are features of all religions, from prehistoric animism (e.g. Indigenous Australian account of Birrigun), to scientistic evolutionism (e.g. via cryobiology/cryonics). So, in the Bible text, a dead Moses meeting Jesus on Earth 1500 years later is not so surprising, nor the deceased prophet Samuel returning to rebuke King Saul. People have seen/encountered/heard ghosts or spirits in many times and places. Sometimes they are recognizable as Saints, or as family members and ancestors, or as acquaintances; sometimes not.

Jesus had encounters with the beings we call *angels*. He was in company with angels a number of times, e.g. **Mark** 1:13 details that after He was tempted by Satan (who had once been an angel but tragically and evilly rebelled against God), Jesus was served by angels; and **Luke** 22:43 describes Jesus being comforted by an angel when He was in extreme distress. **Hebrews** 1:4 -14 reveals that Jesus is superior to angels in divinity, authority and power. Jesus knew angels, and they Him. Modern conflations of scientism and animistic beliefs – often called 'new age' – tend to represent angels as personal counselors and/or magic fairies who are spirit guides and can be accessed or summoned through mediations with mediums, crystals and tarot cards etc.. Any spirit encountered this way is likely a kind of spirit very different to the angels who accompanied Jesus at times on Earth. Real angels are not ghosts. They serve God, can still facilitate communication between God and other beings, and will not sin (i.e. wilfully disobey God).

Normal, everyday people have seen/met angels in many times and many places too, from Mary the mother of Jesus in her home (e.g. **Luke** 1:26-38), to soldiers on active service (e.g. the incident reported as the 'Angel

---

evolution as a rule, and as capable of destining. These are intelligent choices implying foresight and rationality, so 'evolution' is a conscious being rather than a neutral force (e.g. like gravity). This article is just one example out of innumerable possibilities.

of Mons' during World War One by both British and German soldiers[5]),
to Corrie ten Boom the evangelist in Soviet Russia (she saw angels shield-
ing her Bible-laden luggage from detection at a Soviet customs post), to
people walking along city streets in Melbourne, Australia (where a man's
integrity was challenged in a surprising way). Their accounts are straight-
forward and, while each was surprised, they had no difficulty identifying
the being(s) they encountered as *angels*, though they appeared in vastly
different guises (e.g. Corrie ten Boom saw large 'light beings', while a man
in Melbourne saw and touched a raggedly dressed old man). Angels do not
appear physically/tangibly very often – and we can't visit them, meet up,
or have a coffee with them, as a rule. They cannot be summoned through
rituals or incantations.

They are servant spirits and act on instruction/direction from God.
They are especially significant in Mary Magdalene's and Jehanne's lives.

Understand this also: the Holy Spirit of God is *not* an angel.

In summary, we can learn about, we can encounter, or we can meet
Jesus in a number of ways:

**a.**

Through historical and documentary primary sources, such as the Gospels
in the Holy Bible (aka 'canonical Gospels'). We can learn about Him this
way, and if practiced with sincere prayer, can open an active communication with Jesus.

---

5    The Battle of Mons occurred late in August 1914 near Mons, Belgium, early in World
War 1. British, French and German soldiers all reported seeing angelic beings during
this battle. For more detail, some research will quickly produce much source material
(and interpretations). One source is: Robert Barr-Smith 2005, *Were the Angels of Mons
in World War 1 Real, or Mass Hysteria?* warfarehistorynetwork.com

**b.**

*Through the practice of prayer*, which is communicating consciously and volitionally with God. Prayer is Earthly communication by humans with God as Divine Being. The Bible identifies Jesus as God, and humans can communicate directly with Him. Prayer is *not* making magic wishes to a fat, old, bearded fellow lounging in the clouds. Jesus is not a cosmic Santa or guru, so performing a ritual or spell is not going to compel His attention. It's really not that hard. If you honestly pray with the intent to communicate with Jesus who is God, then you have already succeeded, and He will listen. Any response is up to Him.

**c.**

*Through secondary and anecdotal sources*, such as e.g. the apocryphal Gospel of Thomas. These are often not reliable narratives as they can present philosophical or psychological perspectives favoured by the writer(s), and they are often fragments of larger missing documents, so context is uncertain. The *canonical Gospels* have far more comprehensive historicity through archaeological and historical evidence and research.

**d.**

*Through other books of the Holy Bible*, such as **Acts** and **Romans** which contain narrative and locational references which are verifiable archaeologically and historically.

**e.**

*Through sources such as the* **Qur'ān** of Islam. Islam calls Jesus 'Isa', and reveres Him as a Prophet. The Bible identifies Him as the Son of God and as having the same nature as God, i.e. Jesus is God. The Biblical Jesus is not the Qur'ānic Isa. (N.B. however, Jesus as the Christ [or Messiah] has often appeared to and communicated supernaturally with Muslim people, whom of course He loves deeply.)

**f.**

*Spiritual beings can be sent by God to communicate with people* who are still alive on Earth. Angels, who are spiritual servant beings, can communicate messages to humans from God. Angels are not humans, but from multiple reliable accounts they can appear like us. They can be invested with powers that humans do not have, such as the ability to manipulate physical objects which humans cannot (e.g. **Matthew** 28:2-4, **Acts** 12:7-10). Angels can use any languages understandable to humans, and they can sing. They often bear witness to Jesus.

**g.**

*Deceased humans can be returned to Earth by God in their recognizable human form.* This can be as an actual apparent materialization in their physical body. E.g. **Luke** 7:11-15 documents Jesus resurrecting a dead boy and restoring him to normal life. (A more recent instance occurred in late 1963 when the recently deceased C. S. Lewis had an important and encouraging conversation with J. B. Philips, who was translating the New Testament into readily readable modern English. They sat in chairs at Philips' home and had a conversation, a very important one for Philips. Lewis looked to be in vibrant health, but Philips knew the situation was supernatural and that Lewis had died a week before.)[6]

There is no viable record of God ever returning a deceased person as a decayed, corrupted body such as we often meet in horror fictions. People can also be encountered as a 'vision'; this means that God gives humans the ability to experience supernatural things with our physical senses. These

---

[6] E.g. see Dan Peterson 2019, *C. S. Lewis And J. B. Phillips: An Unexpected Meeting*, patheos.com

encounters are difficult to verify, and are often dismissed as phantasies occasioned by extremes of imagination, grief or longing. All objectivity is ultimately subjective; what we accept as *real*, depends on what we regard and accept as evidence. Examples of encounters between living and deceased persons are discoverable readily by online and/or rudimentary research.[7] Jesus can and does communicate through people who have died, whether identified as Saints or not.

**h.**

*Jesus can communicate visibly, directly and verbally with people alive on Earth*, if He chooses. A quite recent exemplar of this is recorded by Paula Di Martino[8], who encountered Jesus very presently after the death of her child. There are manifold instances of Jesus meeting people like this, and even cursory research (e.g. online) will discover many examples in which Jesus manifestly meets with people. These communications/instances are mostly anecdotal, but that does not detract from their reliability or truth. Scientific experiments are also anecdotal. What we accept as authentic, is what we are willing to believe. [9] It is important to say here that unfortunately there are

---

7    E.g. see Sheldon Vanauken 1977, *A Severe Mercy*, Harper & Row, San Francisco. N.B. '*The Oxford Dream-Vision*', pp. 221-223.

8    Paula Di Martino 2007, *Life After Loss: Surviving the Death of a Baby, a Story of Hope*.

9    In February 1994, in New South Wales, Australia, I met Ray, who had encountered Jesus directly and physically. Ray and I met at a social barbeque, a common Australian event for sharing a meal with others. He was a Christian Pastor, had been for many years, and was easy to talk with. He related to me how as a young man in the Royal Australian Air Force in World War 2, he had been badly hurt on active service. He was returned to Australia for treatment, but knew that he was expected to die from his condition. He was hospitalised in Newcastle, and his fiancé was in Brisbane. Desperately wanting to see her, he arranged a telegram to be sent, asking her to come to him. She replied that she could not, and was ending their engagement. This was existentially devastating for Ray. He felt totally abandoned by God – at 21 years of age, doomed by mortal injuries, heart-broken that his beloved had rejected him, he wanted to die swiftly - but was unable to even move enough to achieve that. In desperation, he cried out in his hospital room, begging Jesus to help him.

fraudulent people who prey on the bereaved and vulnerable by presenting themselves as mediums etc. and promising contact with the dead. Jesus nor angels can be summoned by ouija boards, astrological charts, tarot cards, crystal balls, palm readings, or meditating with minerals. N.B. <u>These are deceptions</u>. Jesus and angels are not like an online dating app we can download, they do not appear on demand, and they *do not sin*.

To communicate with Jesus, <u>*all you need do is **pray***</u> – just talk to Him. He knows your situation, knows your heart, and hears you, wherever you are, and whatever circumstances you are in.

---

Listening keenly to this story, while enjoying some appetizing barbeque, Ray then said, 'And Jesus came into my room.'

I clarified and said, 'You mean you sensed His presence?' He replied, 'No, Jesus walked into my hospital room – He came in, I saw Him.' I was very surprised at this and could only think to ask, 'What did He look like?' - an almost embarrassingly simplistic question. Ray said that he could not remember all details, other than his room was flooded with light and love, and that he most vividly remembered Jesus' eyes – eyes radiating pure love. Jesus told him he would not die yet, and he had a life to live. This greatly encouraged Ray. He knew he was not hallucinating on drugs, or mentally deranged. The very next day, a Doctor asked if he would be willing to undergo an experimental therapy? That worked, he met the beautiful woman who became his wife, and Ray ministered in churches around New South Wales from that time onwards. He was a completely honest, compassionate and good man, and I came to know him well enough to trust his integrity.

In real-time, he met Jesus during 1945, which is a long time after 33AD.

# MARY

רַבּוּנִי

## Mary, known as *Magdalene*, disciple of Jesus the Christ.

*'She turned toward Him and exclaimed, "Rabboni!" '*
( - Mary Magdalene, to Jesus at His tomb in a
Garden near Jerusalem, **John** 20:16b.)

## Origins.

We know her almost exclusively from the canonical Gospels. There is lively interest in the gnostic Gospel accounts of Mary as well, but this particular study relies solely on the canonical Gospels. Legendary stories tell of her travelling to what is now southern France after Jesus' ascension, but this cannot be verified and is more likely a legend. Mary Magdalene is actually one woman in three representations: she is Mary of Magdala (or *the Magdalene*), Mary of Bethany, *and* the 'sinful woman' who anointed Jesus in **Luke** 7:36-50. Why is she represented this way when the three accounts of her can seem tangled and confusing? Life happens this way for most of us; we have different events and phases in our lives, people perceive us from differing perspectives, and people sometimes change or use multiple names. It is often the perspectives which are complex, not the person being described or indicated. The Bible actually represents and depicts Mary very much as a real person in real ways. (Throughout this text, the acronym initials MM indicate the woman Mary Magdalene + Mary of Bethany + the sinful woman.)

'Magdalene' is a toponym, not a matronym or patronym. By way of illustration, in **Mark** 1:19, James is identified as 'son of Zebedee', or James Bar-Zebedee. The name *Bar*-Zebedee would be a patronymic name, identifying James through his father. In Aramaic and Hebrew, '*Bar*' indicates someone as a son, '*Bat*' as a daughter.

Why then was Mary not identified as *a daughter* (e.g. as Mary Bat-someone)? Orphans did not have patronyms. But, that is also true of many people. Is there any significance in Mary's lack of a patronym?

It is hard to say, but is suggestive. Jesus was/is known as Jesus of Nazareth, and also as Jesus of Galilee, both toponyms – rather than as Jesus Bar-Joseph; toponyms are not unusual/exceptional. Mary Magdalene is identified through her place of origin, or place of residence. In the canonical Gospels, she can also be identified as Mary of Bethany. That she is the same woman with two names is eminently plausible, and does justice to her extraordinary life. What made her life extraordinary was her relationship with Jesus; otherwise, she would have been another person lost completely as yet one more indistinguishable droplet in the ocean of history.

Magdala (*today* Mejdel) is a town in the region of Galilee, equidistant from Tiberias (Rakkath) and Capernaum (Khan Minieh) on the western shores of the Sea of Galilee (aka Lake Tiberias, or Sea of Gennesaret), a large freshwater lake in Roman Judea (Syria Palaestinia from AD135), and now modern-day Israel. The town existed from approx. 150BC to 250AD, and seems to have been a commercial town, probably a centre for fishing and trading in goods which could be transported by boat to the central location from the surrounding regions. In this Greco-Roman period, Magdala remained significantly Jewish, and supported at least two synagogues – a second Magdalene synagogue was discovered recently.[10]

There are also suggestions that the name may be a reference to 'tower', which is apparently the literal meaning of 'magdal' in Aramaic. Mary could have been nicknamed 'Mary the Tower' by Jesus, just as He nicknamed

---

[10] Biblical Archaeology Society 2021, Archaeologists Discover New First-Century Synagogue in Magdala, Israel. Published by Nathan Steinmeyer 15/12/2021, Bible History Daily.

Peter as 'the Rock'[11]. This may indicate Mary's height – she could have been noticeably tall for a woman at the time (something suggested by other evidence). Magdala probably had the meaning of 'Tower-town' in ancient Aramaic.

Was Mary Jewish? Her first/given name suggests so. Meaning 'beloved' in Aramaic, the name indicates a Jewish heritage, but could also have an Egyptian origin, where it would mean 'sorrow' or 'afflicted', as in 'Mara' of the Biblical Book of **Ruth** (1:20). It is impossible to be completely certain. Her brother, Lazarus, had a distinctively Hebrew name, so that is a hint that Mary was likely Jewish. The lack of a patronym could indicate that she was illegitimate, but again, if she is Martha's and Lazarus' sister, their very Hebrew names nudge her ethnicity as Hebrew. This has to be weighed against her startlingly unconventional actions, which defy normative gender behaviours of that era, such as engaging with a man whilst teaching when a meal needed to be prepared – usually a female task. Her sister Martha was chagrined by this, but both Mary and the men present (Jesus and Lazarus, ref. **John** 12:1-3) had no argument with her choice, which was to spend time with Jesus rather than prepare a meal. This is more like the assertive preference of an Egyptian or Spartan woman, and it complicates further as we observe Martha *not* making that same choice. If she shared Mary's upbringing, experience and mores, why is she not spending time with Jesus (ref. **Luke** 10:38-42)? This tends to underline Jesus' significance to Mary. Much of what we can reasonably infer about Mary is conjecture – sensible assemblage of some available evidentiary filaments. What gleams evidently here is that Mary esteemed Jesus over even family, and over cultural expectations. Jesus was the centre of her attention. Her name is not a recondite preoccupation, rather a way of knowing about her.

---

[11] Anne Theriault 2020, *Unravelling the Myth of Mary Magdalene*, Broadview Magazine 16/03/2020, broadview.org

Mary's siblings are our closest clues to her family background. The link between Mary Magdalene and Mary of Bethany is important; it helps explain her attachment and commitment to Jesus - hence the considerable attention to this duality in Mary Magdalene of Bethany. Many people would dispute that these Mary's are the same woman, let alone a tri-unity with the sinful woman in **Luke**. When these are rightly aligned, we see Jesus more vividly, and understand Him more humanly.

## Identity.

Mary Magdalene's identity is controversial. What we know:

1. *She was real.* The primary & secondary documentary evidence is compelling.
2. *She was human.* She is/was not merely a literary or cultural construct, or an AI impersonation (i.e. she is not a mythical persona).
3. *She most likely came from Roman Judea*, from the town of Magdala, and lived in Bethany, near Jerusalem, when she was older.
4. *She was what we would call a 'Christian' – a very early Christian* (early believers and followers of Christ were identified as followers of '*the Way*' – '*Christian*' is a later term), because she followed and honoured Jesus Christ from her conversion (i.e. from some form of paganism/Judaism to 'the Way').
5. *MM was bold in her faith*; she attended on Jesus when He was crucified – something the male apostles did not do (likely out of fear for the Romans), excepting John.
6. *She had key relationships.* As relationships reflect our personalities through engagement with others, her relationships are a fertile source of information about her in an otherwise biographically Saharan environment.

7. *She had been involved in activities regarded as immoral by the Jewish religious establishment.* These activities are not specified, but indications are that they were of a sexual nature. She stopped these activities when she dedicated herself to following Jesus.

8. *She is known in three distinct iterations:* Mary Magdalene, Mary of Bethany, and the sinful woman who anointed Jesus (who is not specifically named) [12]. Having distinct and differing names is not so unusual either: Peter was also Simon, Bartholomew was also Nathaniel, Jude was also Thaddeus, and Saul of Tarsus was also Paul.

*How could one Mary seem to be three distinct characters in the Biblical narrative?*

The sinful woman of **Luke** 7:36-50, and the woman in **Matthew** 26:6-13 & **Mark** 14:3-9, is Mary Magdalene.

This is controversial: is Mary Magdalene really the 'sinful woman' who washed and anointed Jesus?

MM has long been associated with sexual sin, particularly prostitution. This status as a prostitute has been recently challenged and questioned (2025 atow). Consequently and generally, this imputed infamy has been removed from her, more due to feminist prejudice than deduction or reasoning. The historical case may have been the original prejudice, having originated in an early Pope's declaration that she was a prostitute [13]. But available evidence and clues in the Gospels support that she was or had been involved in prostitution – although most likely not by choice.

---

[12]   N.B. A very compact and helpful source regarding Mary's triple identity is: Kent, G. (2010) Mary Magdalene, Mary of Bethany and the sinful woman of Luke 7: The same person? *Journal of Asia Adventist Seminary*, 13 (1), 13-28.

[13]   Pope Gregory 1, c. AD591: ref. S. Gregoire le Grand, *Homiliae in evangelia*, II, xxiii, PL76, col1239C.

**Mark** 16:9 and **Luke** 8:2 (NLT) relate that Jesus cast seven demons out of Mary. It's interesting that both Gospel-writers are quite specific about the seven. Demons are destructive and evil – they are anti-life and will invariably lure people into destructive thinking and behaviours. Reducing a person's value to their sexuality is a lie about the value of a person. Prostitution or 'sex work' is not a harmless or constructive trade or profession. This is true in any ethno-cultural context.

Demons trade in lies.

Biblical accounts of Mary are actually very protective and defensive of her; they are respectful, quite possibly concealing details of her history exactly to prevent aspersions and diminutions being cast on a great woman.

We are not our past; Jesus changes our past.

This is not unusual in the Gospels; when Matthew Levi is called to follow Christ, he is identified as a tax-collector and sinner in **Luke** 5:27-31, but the specific sins are concealed. Jesus destroys sin at the Cross for anyone who places their belief and faith in Him – when Jesus forgives, we are counted *faultless* (see **Jude** 24 & **Colossians** 1:22). Christianly, Mary's past is not a sink of scandal and debauchery; it is a life covered in the Grace of Christ. That is true in terms of accountability and liberation. Jesus made very clear though that He bought our liberty at the Cross with the price of His blood. He forgave Mary before He was crucified and resurrected; His relationship with Mary anticipates Calvary. This is where there is traction: Jesus owns our stories - our history is His. Our testimony is His history. He bought our liberty at huge cost. **Revelation** 12:11 twins the blood of Christ with our testimony; they cannot be separated. We are free to enter eternity with God because Jesus paid the entry fee with the only currency accepted in Heaven – His sacrificial blood. He told us plainly that He is _the_ Way – there is no other way. Jesus is not optional as a way to eternal life in Heaven. Mary's life story, her autobiography, is between her and

God, and completely forgiven, whatever she did in her earthly life. It is not surprising that other disciples and followers who knew her story, concealed identifying details to shield her from unwanted or toxic attention. They did not let her become a sideshow. As in the case of the New Testament epistle **2 John**, it is very possible that John is protecting the identity of a factual woman because early Christians were at high risk of vicious persecution (other explanations identify the 'lady' as a metaphorical reference to a particular church). The controversial but often luminous scholar William Barclay acknowledges that this 'Lady' (cf. **2 John** 1) could certainly have been someone protected by fellow Christians [14]. MM was very probably and similarly covered and shielded from harm.

What the Gospel writers did leave was the essence of Mary's story – her testimony which still powerfully testifies to the universal availability of Grace through Christ.

2000 years on, this is still a blood trail to Jesus.

Luke relates the detail about seven demons trespassing in Mary Magdalene's life immediately after the incident of the 'sinful woman' anointing Jesus' feet with expensive perfume ('spikenard' or just 'nard'). This is a continuous narrative by Luke, especially if we remove the later artificial interposition of Biblical chapters and verses. The narrative moves from the symposium-type meal at Simon the Pharisee's house, to explanation of the main characters involved. Luke's Greek background is very evident here – Jesus is notably Socratic, and the other folk present foreground deep questions for the protagonist's reflection. (Jesus is the protagonist, and Simon is the antagonist, in this Euripydean Biblical scene.) This may account for Luke's marked contextual differences to Matthew and Mark.

---

[14]   E.g. see William Barclay 1970, *Bible Commentary: 2 John*, ch. 1 vv.1-3. (In Studylight. org.)

Luke alone among the Gospel-writers identifies her as a 'sinner', and then explains much of the *why*.

She was demonized.

More recent research in the psychology of trauma and childhood abuse helps us understand Mary's desperation for help and recovery. If her childhood had been abusive, as is highly likely, whether as a slave or as a vulnerable young person, Mary was defenceless to what we understand as mental illness. As now, so 2000 years ago:

> *'Child abuse and neglect during childhood was consistently the leading behavioural risk factor contributing to the burden of suicide and self-inflicted injuries in both males and females... between 2003 and 2019...'*[15].

We can retrospectively and confidently apply modern research findings to the abuse and attendant suffering consistently inflicted on slaves, by noting the levels of this kind of predation among slaves of C19th America:

> *'Some sources estimate that 58% of all enslaved women aged 15-30 years old were sexually assaulted by their slave owners and other white men...* [16]

That is catastrophic data, and it paints a very likely picture of what Mary faced. In relation to sexual abuse victims, we know that,

> *'...qualitative findings show[ed] that a history of CSA [Childhood Sexual Abuse] was a precipitating factor for*

---

[15] Australian Institute of Health and Welfare 2021, *New Insights into suicide and self-harm in Australia, including potentially modifiable risk-factors*, aihw.gov.au 04Nov2021.

[16] Dominique R. Wilson 2021, *Sexual Exploitation of Black Women from the Years 1619-2020*, Journal of Race, Gender and Ethnicity, 10-Spring 2021, 123.

*self-harm throughout different stages of the life-course, and represented a reason for continued engagement in self-harm.'*[17]

Mary's attendance at Simon's meal makes sense as we meet her as a sinner (who was not invited), who interrupts proceedings, and thereby corrects Simon's disrespectful treatment of Jesus. She honours Him, while Simon did not. She anoints his feet. This is peculiar and tense, because *washing* of guests' feet was a common gesture of welcome in ancient Judea and was a service performed by servants/slaves[18]; but, *anointing* of feet was done mainly for the dead. Anointing the head was *a mark of honour*, anointing the feet seems to have been a *death-rite*. Mary here does both. If this **Luke** 7:38 event is the same event as **John** 12:1-3, it makes sense that Mary is anointing Jesus' feet for death – it happens five days before Jesus' arrest and ultimate crucifixion (see **John** 12:1, and note that **John** 11:2 locates this event *before* Lazarus' death, which resolves possible questions about Mary's devotion to Jesus). She also uses her uncovered and unbound hair to dry Jesus' freshly washed and anointed feet; women with uncovered hair were either single, *or* they were 'immoral'. Their mode of dress indicated which. Married women covered their hair, unless they were alone with their families where it was considered safe and appropriate to uncover. The only other women who uncovered their hair were prostitutes (in which case they were considered brazen and shameless), or if they had leprosy. Again, it is worth noting that Luke is the only Gospel author who describes this

---

[17] M.I.Troya, G.Cully et al. 2021, *Investigating the relationship between childhood sexual abuse, self-harm repetition and suicidal intent: mixed –methods study*, BJPsych doi.10.1192/bjo.2021. 962.

[18] This is attested by scholars and researchers from antiquity, (e.g. ref., Like the Master Ministries, *Mary Anoints Jesus in Bethany*, neverthirsty.org, Tucson, Arizona). Slaves *washed*, but they did not *anoint* – this illumines and underlines Jesus' humility in washing disciples' feet: the Son of God positions as a slave. Likewise Mary. Anointings were performed to the head, not to the feet, except for death. Mary's anointing of Jesus' feet is a clear sign of his portending death (see **John** 12:1-3).

woman as a sinner, or sinful. In his account, the woman's hair is definitely uncovered, but she is not identified as a single woman, which would exonerate her (cf. **Luke** 1:26-27 where Luke is careful to identify Mary's [the mother of Jesus'] marital condition and singleness). Simon recognizes MM as a sinful woman. This almost conclusively reveals her occupation/role, without explicitly saying so.

John, Mark and Matthew do not specifically note that Mary was sinful, because to them she was not. She was a fellow disciple, accepted, shriven and respected by Jesus, and they had no business identifying her past sins and afflictions. Luke discussed this because he was not a disciple travelling with Jesus and Mary during Jesus' first three years of ministry, and he had no intention of dishonouring or criticising Mary; he *was* interested in showing the Grace and power of Jesus in any situation. As a physician, he would have seen and dealt with the detritus of sex-slavery and venereal disease; he was obviously very impacted by Jesus' healing powers, both physically and psycho-emotionally. Luke's is a more clinical and diagnostic description of Mary.

Prostitution in ancient Judea has to be contextualized within the dominant (Greco-) Roman governance and culture of that time, as well as within local Hebrew culture. In the early AD30's, Judea was firmly under Roman rule; the Romans tolerated Hebrew customs and culture, so long as the Jews observed Roman rule and law – this was the *Pax Romana*. The Jews were exempted by the Romans from acknowledging their gods as the only legitimate divinities.

Romans were liberal in their attitudes to sex, and sex was available in brothels in any Roman settlement, colony or town. It was also available as an act of homage to the gods Venus/Aphrodite and Dionysus in the fertility cults of Roman observance, adopted from the Greeks. This extended the legitimacy of prostitution, and enlarged its importance[19]. The practice was not regarded as shameful among Romans, and was largely provided by slaves, servants or women who had fiscal interests in brothels. Courtesans (*hetairai* in Latin, fr. Greek) and prostitutes (*pallakai,* viz.) both provided sex for a fee, but courtesans offered a more cultured service, including dance, music, and lyric poetry. Prostitutes offered sex in brothels, courtesans made house calls.

Slavery was a major form of trade and business in the Roman Empire – through both the Republic and the Imperium[20]. Slaves comprised largely prisoners-of-war, progeny of slaves, and abandoned children (a frequent fact in ancient Rome). Slaves were used for prostitution. They often had no background, and no family name (N.B. Mary Magdalene/Bethany has no patronym - just two toponyms). The majority of prostitutes seem to have been female; Romans were tolerant of but contemptuous towards homosexuality – regarding Hellenic pederasty as pathetic weakness.

Hebrew culture prohibited prostitution; Roman culture did not. In Jesus' time, the Romans were the law. The Torah confined sexual relations to marriage, although at many stages in Israel's history they had practiced idolatry and engaged in ritual killings and sexual acts, with prostitutes or with statues etc.. The Hebrew people had frequently ignored their God. They had practised ritual fornication and adultery with prostitutes, human sacrifice/murder, and polygamy. (It is perhaps not so surprising that God visited the Romans upon them.)

Prostitution and sexual sin were not unusual, if only because these were legitimate and cultural in Roman Judea. Prostitutes were identifiable

---

[19] See e.g. F. Mira Green 2015, *Witnesses and Participants in the Shadows: The Sexual Lives of Enslaved Women and Boys*, researchgate.net

[20] Estimates calculate approx. 15% of the population across the Roman Empire was enslaved at any given time.

because they did not cover their hair in public and wore immodest clothing, often featuring transparent fabrics with mauve/purple and gold colourings; that was the red-light of Roman times. Single and unmarried women also left their hair uncovered, but wore modest clothes and also habitually stood with a hand over their left hip, as a sign of protected virginity.

It is certainly possible, even likely, that Mary Magdalene was a slave until she was freed by her owner, or had amassed enough money to buy her liberty. It fits her profile. Someone who could afford 600mls of pure nard, or possibly even receive it in lieu of scrip or as gift, could afford her freedom from slavery. However, what she could *not* do was use money to buy her freedom from shame, guilt, trauma and sin. Shekels and denarii would not erase those.

We can also usefully ask how the 'sinful woman' (almost certainly a euphemism for a prostitute or courtesan) knew the way to Simon's house (**Luke** 7:36-50)?

Possibly, there was such a crowd gathered outside waiting for Jesus that his whereabouts was impossible to miss. However, the Gospels usually indicate when crowds were forming or watching. This incident seems unmarked by a large gathering. To speak plainly, the sinful woman knew where Jesus was, because she already knew Simon's address. (In the account from **John**, she is already there – because the woman in **Luke, Matthew** and **Mark** is both Mary Magdalene and Mary of Bethany. She is the same person.)

In **Luke**, Simon does not seem unduly surprised to see her in his home. He is neither outraged, nor attempted to remove her; we would expect Mary to be expelled forthwith by a clean-living, upright Pharisee. He *is* surprised though that Jesus seems clueless or heedless as to her sinfulness. He expects someone renowned as a Rabbi, who is widely distinguished for performing miracles, to recognize this woman's occupation or reputation

– but Jesus pays no attention to this. He only attends to her humility and sincerity, and is compassionate towards her suffering, indicated by her copious tears. We can only guess at the sources of her sadness, but 'immorality' most likely means sexual impurity, dishonour and misuse – prolonged sexual exploitation and abuse could/would explain the labyrinthine hell-pit of her darkness and remorse. This drew her to the only person who could help her.

Instead of indicating knowledge of and condemnation towards the sinful woman (His subsequent statement of forgiveness for her sins shows that Jesus knew exactly what her problems were), Jesus knows exactly what is in Simon's mind, and answers Simon's private thoughts instead.

Simon himself - the host - is identified as both a leper (**Mark** 14:3 & **Matthew** 26:6) and as a Pharisee (**Luke** 7:40). It would be difficult to mistake him. Could he be both? Yes.

It could be that he was known as a leper, because leprosy was a dreaded disease, and he had been its victim. Is he a leper at the time indicated in **Luke** 7:36-50? Mark and Matthew both speak of the condition in present tense. Why were people visiting at his house for a meal then? Leprosy was a feared disease, and lepers were legally separated from other *un*infected people. 'Leper' could designate many conditions which affected skin, not only the leprosy we recognize today which is caused by the *mycobacterium leprae* (identified by G.H.A. Hansen in 1873). In ancient times, leprosy was any obvious and unhealthy looking skin condition ranging from psoriasis to eczema to rosacea. The Greek word $\lambda\varepsilon\pi\tau\alpha$ ('lepta') covered any scaly or flaky skin condition, and was used generically.

If Simon was a contagious leper with obvious disfigurements and unhealthy skin, he would not have been entertaining anyone at his house in Bethany (ref. **John** 8:1, **Mark** 14:3) apart from other lepers, or such people as had no fear of infection. He would have been banished to a leper colony/compound, and/or in Judea required to comply with **Leviticus** 13 (ref. esp. 13:45-46).

It is more likely that he had been a leper, gained the designation 'Simon the leper', and the name simply stuck, like Mary is known as 'Magdalene', even when she clearly did not live there any more.

No-one would have gone to a leper's house except other lepers – even his wife would have lived elsewhere, assuming he was married. Leprosy was one of the few legal inhibitions to marriage. Any sexual activity Simon may have had would have to have been with another leper. Prostitutes were extremely vulnerable to VD/STD's – there were no effective contraceptives or antibiotics available in 33AD. Infection with syphilis, chlamydia or gonorrhea was a wretched descent into infection, abjection, and rejection.

At this point in time, as a Pharisee, Simon ought *not* to have wanted Jesus at his house anyway – the Pharisees generally wanted Jesus dead (ref. **Mark** 14:1), and the Torah was specific about quarantining leprosy.

Why did Simon make this exception for Jesus? Leprosy was a dreaded, horribly impacting, cruelly isolating condition, and lepers were not permitted to socialize. If Simon was still sick, perhaps the Pharisees thought it could be a useful way to neutralize Jesus – infect Him with leprosy? If Simon knew Him as a healer or miracle-worker, he would not have had any concern for His health. Simon respected Jesus, even though Jesus' indifference (and seeming ignorance) to Mary's obvious occupation and position troubled him. He addresses Jesus as 'Rabbi'.

This begs the question: who would *not* fear leprosy?

We can also ask, who could heal this awful disease at a time when there was no vaccine, no antidote, no therapy, or remedy? Jesus is never recorded as 'sick'. Tired? Yes. Thirsty? Yes. Hurt? Yes. Sick? No. He did not get sick – he just cured it.

Can Simon the leper be the same man as Simon the pharisee?

He can.

In **John**, we know that Jesus, some of His disciples/followers, Martha, Mary and Lazarus were at the meal. We also know that this incident actually occurred *before* the incident of Lazarus' death and resurrection (n.b. **John** 11:1-2). For Lazarus to be entertaining people, he was not sick at this time, so the incident of Mary washing and anointing Jesus happened before its positioning near Passover in **John** 12:1-6. We are not specifically told what killed Lazarus – it is generically described as 'sickness'.

There is no mention or hint of anointing and spices, which were applied to a corpse to mitigate the stench of decomposition. This at least hints that Lazarus was not anointed when he died. He was just wrapped in cloths. Martha was particularly concerned at the stench which would be released if Jesus opened Lazarus' tomb. In ancient times, there was no conception of microbiology, so people thought the contagion of a disease was in the odour, or the flesh itself. Why would a family, which clearly knew the practical and ritual importance of anointing, neglect this attention to a loved family member? Perhaps a sickness which could not be touched? Even bandaging him was fraught, unless his fatal condition had not been a dermatological problem, or if it was, that it was a condition the family were not worried about contracting because they were used to Lazarus having suffered from it without contracting it themselves (e.g. rosacea, or psoriasis). It is possible that Simon the leper is also known as Lazarus, but died from a different ailment.

This would make the narrative an even more interesting story than we know. It is however unlikely that Simon as Lazarus would abhor his sister as a 'sinful woman', or that Mary would have attended uninvited at her own home. They could very easily have lived in adjacent or communal houses, or the accounts could have been altered to protect Mary's identity. Ultimately, the Sanhedrin wanted Lazarus dead (unfortunate Lazarus is one of the only people who had to go through a traumatic death twice), and it requires no great imagination to see that close witnesses, like siblings, would also be inconvenient. So, it would make sense that supporters would protect them through equivocated camouflages.

Perhaps these are two separate incidents, and Matthew's and Mark's accounts are pretty much synonymous, while Luke's and John's are another episode altogether? But, does that add up?

No, it doesn't. The likelihoods are not there. *Balance of probabilities* is a key legal test, and it works generally in life and history.

What are the chances of two (or three) different women crashing 'invitation-only' dinners, coincidentally hosted by two separate Pharisees called Simon, bringing small fortunes in nard both times, and liberally pouring the nard over Jesus both times. (Let alone four times!)

Mary may have been recently sinful in **Luke**, but not by the time of **Matthew** and **Mark** – her sinful past was well past by then. Luke's account positions the incident earlier in Jesus' ministry: Matthew's and Mark's occur very near the time of Jesus' crucifixion. We also need to note that the accounts in **Mark** and **Matthew** can be read as what we would term 'flashbacks'.

**Luke** provides much detail which is not in the other Gospels. How would he know the details if he was not present, or at very least close to Simon? We need to remember that he was a physician, may have known Simon in that capacity, and have received an invitation on that basis. Otherwise, how did Luke know what Simon was thinking, unless Simon told him? Who would Simon trust and confide in more than his physician? Luke the physician would be interested in such a problem as Simon's leprosy. There would be academic contention about whether Luke could have been present while Jesus was active in Judea, but it is not only possible – it would make sense.

**John** is different; we are not at Simon's house here, we are at Mary's, Martha's and Lazarus' house. But what is interestingly coincidental is that their house happens to be in Bethany, like Simon's. The location is the same… another coincidence? But the timing is ambiguous.

In **John**, Jesus is at Mary, Martha and Lazarus's house. They are siblings, and it is an unusual living arrangement at that time. Each of them appears to be unmarried. Jesus knew and loved these people (see **John** 11:5) and this link to the siblings establishes prior relationship, and has to be the case as He previously had contact with Mary (see 11:2). Could Simon have been their father? – this would explain the locational coincidence, and their domestic arrangement? Beyond that, there is no other indication of this. There is no 'Lazarus Bar-Simon', or 'Martha Bat-Simon'.

Simon and Mary were at the same occasion. Both approached Jesus, and both had expectations. Simon expected Jesus to condemn her, to recoil with offended disdain, and to demonstrate His understanding and support for the Law by condemning the woman; Mary did not verbally articulate what she wanted from Jesus - she demonstrated it through her actions. Jesus read Simon's thoughts, and He heard Mary's silent plea. Only one was forgiven. Jesus offers liberal Grace; He is not a fastidious, petty god of perfect and impossible rituals. Mary received liberality in proportion to her generosity and sincerity; Simon received the dry aridity of his censorious austerity.

'Liberality', 'liberation' and 'libation' are close relatives, like the three siblings.

How can **John**'s positioning of the meal at the three siblings' house be the same as **Luke**'s (and by extension **Matthew**'s & **Mark**'s) positioning *differently* in Simon's (or someone else's) house. Surely this is a contradiction? It seems to be a logical impediment. But, remembering that the Gospel authors wanted to protect MM, the alignment of salient facts (e.g. that the event occurred in Bethany, that a woman who somehow knew Jesus' location applied exorbitantly expensive spice over Him, that a Pharisee hosted the occasions etc.) with disorienting information (e.g. that the meal was at different people's houses) makes sense. They accurately record an event, but do not reveal identities. To recap a point, would Mary (of Bethany) go to two separate houses in Bethany and twice anoint Jesus liberally with enormously expensive nard? It is hugely unlikely. The Gospels are histories, not prophecies – they are by definition written *after* the event(s). They record events as evasions, designed to protect someone who belonged to a proscribed and hunted group of people (e.g. see **Acts** 8:1-3), as they happened.

This still leaves the question of the siblings' living arrangement. The house belonged to Martha at the least, and Mary and Lazarus lived with her (**Luke** 10:38 and **John** 11:45 are indicative.) It's unusual – normally the son would inherit at that time, if it was a family house.

Did Mary share ownership of the house? How? If she could afford large amounts of nard, maybe she could afford a house, or at least a share in one? That makes sense. How did she make the money? That remains controversial, but there is a very plain probability - she had been a courtesan. Why was she a courtesan when there is no such indication about Martha? If Mary was a former slave and prostitute, then her sister Martha would surely have been at least a slave also; that would make sense. We know nothing about the siblings' ages, or their ordinality. From the threadbare clues left for us, Mary was the oldest, and it rests comfortably with her other characteristics of charity, courage, kindness and generosity that she spared her siblings from sufferings in any ways she could. We know that she was sufficiently wealthy to contribute to supporting a band of at least thirteen men (see **Luke** 8:2-3), and most likely more. Mary had money. We need to remember too that slaves could not enter contracts (like buying real estate), and if she had been a slave, her socio-economic status is complicated. As a male (though not as a slave), Lazarus could have made contracts. It is possible Mary had been enslaved, but not her siblings.

Why was she so unashamed and free with Jesus – uncovering her head with Him, kissing and wiping his feet with her hair, anointing him with nard – 'anointing' is more than merely pouring, it is active and often includes intentional rubbing or touching? Why is she not reluctant about anointing Him?

Because there is no shame under Grace, and because God does not exploit or abuse people.

Is the anointing and washing of Jesus a description of the same incident from four differing perspectives (albeit that the **Matthew** and **Mark** accounts are very similar)? Is this the same event involving a profoundly grateful and penitent woman who was released from dehumanizing, degrading abuse and suffering?

Mary liked being with Jesus. She felt liked when He stood up for her while her sister berated her, and in turn, she liked Him. She wanted to be with Him, and was willing to spend money to help Him. We see a Jesus here who is likeable. He is not remote in a Heaven we cannot see, not a giant marble statue in a cathedral, not imperious and unapproachable as He can seem in some descriptions (e.g. **Revelation** 1:17). He is likeable, affectionate and accepting, as well as phenomenally powerful (e.g. resurrecting Lazarus). Jesus is definitely not like the men she was used to meeting.

There are between five to seven (5 -7) different women named Mary described in the New Testament, although even this could be contested. Some Mary's are clearly distinct people, e.g. Mary, Jesus' mother is not Mary Magdalene, and Mary wife of Cleopas is not Mary Magdalene.

When Mary the Magdalene needs to be distinguished from other Mary's, the others are always identified for contrast. This never happens re Mary of Bethany.

The chances of four *different Mary's* each featuring in the *four different Gospel accounts* and performing the same events, is an extremely long stretch; this resolves though, if they are the same person.

## Relationships.

Mary has a number of informing relationships.

**Martha**, her sister.

**Lazarus**, her brother.

**Simon**, a Pharisee – a very conservative religious Jew.

**Mary**, mother of Jesus.

**Jesus**, her Lord and Saviour.

*Seven demons* who are not identified other than being 'cast out'.

*Relationships* are generally messy, involved &/or complex, because we tend to be messy and complex as individuals. We are colossally difficult to define and explain: what is the right definition of a *person*? The OED recognizes six variants of definition for 'person', to start with. We are primarily interested in human beings, who have the unique elements of body, soul and spirit recognizable as human.

- the body is physiology,
- the soul is consciousness, intelligence, psychology and emotion,
- the spirit is life-force.

The combination of these in a human being is personhood. We measure/determine *relationship* by gauging the extent of interaction between people in each aspect of personhood. We use a complex, intricate and attenuated spectrum to position relationships in our awareness. Some relationships we describe as intimate, others as nurturing, others as professional, or functional, or negative, symbiotic etc. The possibilities and gradations are almost endless.

Relationships show aspects of our selves – the 'self' is integral to 'personhood'. We are the 'self-system' posited by Harry Stack Sullivan, intricately forming from infancy and processing the ways to optimize satisfaction and minimize anxiety; we develop ways of fashioning interactivities with others, especially significant others, creating self-esteem and appreciation[21]. We are those and more. It is in relationships that we see aspects of a person – aptitude, sensitivity, empathy, virtuosity, flexibility, sexuality, maturity, perception, perspective, honesty, creativity, amiability etc.. As we engage with other selves through our own self, we relate. No two relationships are exactly the same because no two selves are identical, so all relationships are unique. There are similarities between them, but each relationship is particular.

Harry Stack Sullivan postulated and established the concept of the 'significant other' – now an important concept in psychology. These *others* usually accrete to types such as parents, siblings, teachers, close friends etc. We do not know anything about Mary Magdalene of Bethany's significant others, with a few clear exceptions.

Through Mary's relationships, we see more of her as a person. Some relationships are dualities – between two people. Others are collective, e.g. collegial, between people who share close work interests. Others are institutional, between a governing or managerial group and others. We can also distinguish relationships concentrically from the self/ego, to the next circle which is family, to the next circle which is friends, to the next circle which is local community, etc. You can find a plethora of material on relationships. We see aspects of Mary through her relating with others.

---

[21]    F. Barton Evans, *Harry Stack Sullivan: Interpersonal theory and psychotherapy*, pp.82-88.

## Martha is a bold and strong young woman.

We meet her three times in the Gospels of **Luke** and **John**. Martha is forthright and direct in each. In **Luke** 10:38-42 we discover that Martha and Mary lived 'on the way to Jerusalem', but with no clearer identifiers. From **John** 11:5 we know that Martha's and Mary's brother is Lazarus, and from 11:1 that they lived in Bethany, so these facts are readily reconciled. Luke first mentions only Mary in his Gospel, as a 'sinful woman', and recounts her beautiful encounter with grace in 7:36-50; if *Mary's* plotline in Luke's narrative is chronological, then she already knows Jesus in this incident in **Luke** 10:38-42.

And she is happy to sit at His feet - again.

It is Martha who welcomes Jesus and His disciples on this occasion in **Luke** 10, and she immediately busies herself with preparing a meal – it is quite a big task to feed at least 13 men, and possibly Lazarus too. While she gets busy in the kitchen, Mary is sitting at Jesus' feet and listening while He teaches. Martha is unhappy about this; to her it is seriously inconsiderate, and perhaps lazy too. She thinks Mary is being unfair by leaving her to do all the meal preparations. This is her complaint when she fronts Jesus about Mary's behaviour. Again, we see Martha is bold. We also see that she does not confront Mary, quite probably because it would have been useless.

She appeals to Jesus, not to a parent – there are no parents in the picture; these siblings are almost certainly orphans. Mary would just have said 'no' to Martha, and told her to come and sit down. Martha knew that Mary had sat at Jesus' feet before – she knew that her sad, lovely and broken sister had been profoundly changed by this man in her living room. The kitchen was less challenging, she could just default to routine and social mores, so for Martha that was actually the safer place to be, not at Jesus' feet where her life might also be radically changed – He might ask her something? Most of us are like Martha – we don't like change, we are risk-averse.

Mary chose Jesus' feet. She is a disciple first, a sister second. A lot has happened between **Luke** 7 and **Luke** 10, and MM has witnessed at least some of this: did she feel empathy and compassion for the demoniac at Gadara; was she breathless as Jesus looked around for the desperate, anaemic, dying woman whose faith drew power out of Him at the lakeside; as He made totally outrageous assurances to Jairus?

She did not hesitate in choosing to be at Jesus' feet, and she did not make a scene (this time!). Mary is a resolute woman. Her attention was immediately and wholly on Jesus. When Martha questions the fairness of this to the Lord Jesus, who is after all the God of Justice, He says Mary has chosen well. Martha is not rebuked or upbraided, He simply endorses Mary's choice. For at least the second time, Jesus approves Mary's unconventional actions. Mary here shows us Jesus the liberator, and Jesus the eminent.

We see her in her relationship with her sister. Mary doesn't yell at Martha to leave her alone. She doesn't accuse her. She says nothing to Martha – Jesus does that. But we do see composure, confidence, and an assurance in her relationship with Jesus. **John** 20:30 shows us that Mary saw Jesus do many miraculous and amazing things; her brother Lazarus, Jairus' daughter, and the widow from Nain's son were resurrected, blind people received their sight, disabled people received restoration, lepers were healed, demons were banished.

Jesus responds to Martha when she asks Him to reorient Mary's attention by saying,

> 'There is really only one thing worth being concerned about.
> Mary has discovered it – and I won't take it away from her.'[22]

---

[22]  **Luke** 10:42 (NLT)

He means Mary's devoted relationship to Him. If Jesus is not the Messiah, if He is not God incarnate, then He is at best a neurotic narcissist collecting devotees like some magnetic, drug-ravaged rock-star. (It would mean the disciples, including us today, were and are all suckers.)

For Mary here, all else has fallen away, her priorities are sorted out now, and she is on the only path worth walking. Jesus tells Martha that Mary's choice to be with Him is more important than owning a house, doing daily chores, being hospitable to guests, supporting family, living the cultural role expected of her, being in control, and even being right. He is gently showing Martha that she also has a choice to make.

(Returning to marital status and the *likely* ages of the siblings: Mary is not married; she was in her mid-twenties, and likely recovering from intense psycho-sexual trauma from her experience as a courtesan, when she was subjected to evil influences through internalised demonic harassment. She had also chosen to be mobile and follow Jesus in His ministry. Lazarus is not married because he has been ill and is quite likely disabled in some way. Martha is not married because she is youngest – perhaps late teens.)

Martha appears next as she meets Jesus four days after her brother's death. Lazarus has been entombed – Jesus missed the funeral. Four days dead is unarguably dead – he's not just in a coma, or a trance. She has faith in Jesus, but she is also a rational person; she knows about Jesus' other resurrection miracles like the widow's son at Nain (**Luke** 7:11-17), and Jairus' daughter (**Luke** 8:49-56). Mary has told her about what He has done. Martha has seen miraculous changes in her sister.

Jesus was not told about Lazarus' death; He knew because He is God, and He knows whatever He wishes to know. In **John** 11:3, Mary and Martha do send a message to Jesus that Lazarus is 'very sick'. Jesus then waits a few days before telling His disciples that Lazarus is now dead (11:14), that God would do something great, and then travelling on to Bethany. Martha went out to meet Jesus as He came to Lazarus' grave near Bethany, and she both confronts and affirms Jesus: her attitude is different to their last encounter. She is not trying to control or organize the situation; she challenges Jesus on His apparently casual arrival, and affirms that He is not the usual kind of Rabbi. She confesses His power –

'...*Even now I know that God will give you whatever you ask.*' (11:22).

Jesus then plainly tells her, 'Your brother will rise again.' Martha is still primarily an orthodox Jewish believer, and despite what she knows and has seen, she provides a rational response, 'Yes, I know he will rise again when everyone rises on resurrection day.' This is a religious response, not a statement of empirical faith. Jesus now declares possibly the second best-known Bible verse after **John** 3:16,

*'I am the resurrection and the life...'*(11:25-6).

He emphasizes His identity – '*I AM*' is Yah'weh, as well as the subject/verb in the exchange. He asks her, '...*Do you believe...?*'(11:26). Martha's emphatic response is, 'Yes Lord, I have always believed you are the Messiah, the Son of God...' This is not the Martha who got into a twist over organizing a dinner. The dial has shifted for Martha. She both believes in this Rabbi, and that He can overrule death. But, she is still conflicted between the earthly normal and the Kingdom paranormal. Martha has been talking with Mary, and Mary has had an influence, but Mary is the one with the more empirical faith in Jesus. What comes next tests that to shaking point.

Martha goes back to Mary and tells her that Jesus wants to see her. Jesus has now walked to Lazarus' tomb where Mary meets Him; her first words are of disappointment and sorrow. Clearly she believes Jesus could have prevented Lazarus' death, but thinks it is too late now, despite what she has witnessed many times. Her faith is in the past tense. This upsets Jesus; He is deeply troubled (11:33), and weeps. His deepest sorrow is because MM doubts Him, and He obviously wanted her trust. *Our trust matters to Him.* Through Mary, we see Jesus' desire for, and vulnerability to, emotional connection. He is human as well as God. It is possible that Jesus loved Mary in the sense that He was *in love* – Jesus was fully and completely a healthy and vibrant man. That would help explain their closeness.

More on that later.

We are at Lazarus' tomb; Martha is now present, and it makes sense that Mary is there. They are at the cave, with a rock sealing the entrance. Jesus tells them to open the tomb, and Martha objects that it will stink badly of necrosis. Jesus reminds 'them' that they would see the glory of God, and the *them* seems to be Martha and Mary. **John** 11:45 describes a larger number of people present at this resurrection event, but we have no firm idea.

Jesus now speaks to God, praying to Him, thanking God for hearing Him. Addressing the darkness of the sepulchre, He now commands Lazarus to '*Come out*'. Four days after dying, he does exactly that. Swathed in burial cloths, Lazarus walks out of his tomb.

With an almost hilarious understatement, **John** 11:45 records, *'Many of the people who were with Mary believed in Jesus when they saw this happen.'* I bet they did.

It is interesting to note here that the people with Mary believed; there is no mention of the people with Martha. Mary guides them to Jesus. Is it her closeness to Him? Is it His obvious connection with her, a connection that caused Him to cry?

Mary, like Martha, shows belief in Jesus, but prior to Lazarus' resurrection her belief has limited franchise. It is the faith that believes God will make the stars come out tonight, not that He will raise the dead in a few minutes. It is a low-stakes faith – it is like *church*-ianity, not *Christ*-ianity. By physically resurrecting Lazarus in real time, in the present tense here on Earth, Jesus shows immense and overwhelming power; *He does what no one* _else has done in History_. Clever healers and skilled surgeons can lengthen our lives and cure our immediate problems at times, but they cannot resurrect the dead. Mary sees Jesus do just this.

This is an historical event, just as Alexander the Great's conquest of Persia was an historical event, and Neil Armstrong's first step on the Moon, or Rosa Parks' refusal to give up her seat, were historical events. There is no serious dispute.

Jesus proves His claim: _I am the resurrection and the life..._

Martha sees and experiences most of what Mary does, but Mary is the one who very apparently follows Jesus. Jesus loves this family of siblings – He loves each of them (**John** 11:5). Why is there this difference between them? Did not Martha know Jesus? Yes, she did. The difference between them is in _belief_ and _faith_. Martha is not recorded as having people with her at Lazarus' tomb, but Mary did. Mary took people to Jesus when she was going to Lazarus' tomb – she did not have to ask them, they followed her. She was not hesitant about something extraordinary happening; she did not anticipate the scale of Jesus' power though - like most of us today. Why did Mary have this stronger faith? Even when she doubted that Jesus could raise Lazarus, she believed He could do the unthinkable. She had been freed of demons, and she had been liberatingly forgiven for dark and carnal sins. She had heard Simon tell Jesus that the greatly sinful would be more grateful for forgiveness than those who made light of their sins. She directly experienced Jesus' power and grace.

It is more understandable that Jesus cried when Mary still expressed doubt in Him. His tears are described by John as a sign of indignation; He is frustrated with her obdurate vacillation.

Even so, she took people with her to Lazarus' tomb. Martha appears not to have done this – she did not want to look like a fool with her friends and neighbours. Mary was past that point.

The difference between *belief* and *faith* is that faith actualizes what we believe – we act on it. Belief follows Jesus around the Palestinian hills, seeing Him heal people and teach radical truths. Faith goes further; it goes to a tomb, tells people about it, and expects something to happen.

*Faith* is a formerly scared and reluctant follower like Peter confidently telling a dead woman in Joppa to get up (see **Acts** 9:39-41). She does. Faith goes and tells skeptical and disillusioned followers that the impossible has happened, Jesus has resurrected. And He has.

Martha believes in Jesus, but in a religious way; she does not have faith in Him. Jews are still waiting for a Messiah – that is a kind of faith, but a safe one, one which creates God in our image.

Faith acts. Faith goes to the tomb in the morning, on the back of a promise.

## *Lazarus* does not speak.

His sisters certainly can and do, but Lazarus does not speak in the Gospel of **John**, which is the only Gospel in which he figures.

The domestic living arrangements for Martha, Mary and Lazarus are unusual. None seems married, and they are given no patronymic iden-tification like 'son/daughter-of-so&so' etc.. They are toponymically 'of Bethany'. The siblings seem to share ownership or access to the house; **Luke** 10:38 indicates the Bethany home is Martha's, but **John** 12:1 ascribes ownership to Lazarus. John 12:3 pictures Mary displaying wealth – she very comfortably takes highly valuable nard, then sanctifyingly and expensively anoints Jesus. If she doesn't own the house, she is very at home and she has extremely valuable assets.

Lazarus also unmistakably has ownership – even if it's shared.

He famously dies in **John** 11, and is then spectacularly resurrected by Jesus after being dead for four days. Mary of course witnessed this happen, and it is perhaps a little less surprising that she was keen to be at the tomb after Jesus dies, given what she has experienced – she remembers what He could do, and that He said He would also rise from the dead (e.g. **Matthew** 12:39-40, 27:62-64).

She knows the impossible is possible with God (cf. **Luke** 1:37). Mary went to the tomb after Jesus had died; the male disciples only did this *after* they were told the tomb was empty. *MM believed Jesus' words*, she remembered His power with Lazarus, she went to the tomb on the Sunday morning because she knew He was able to defeat death – she had recently seen this. Jesus' famous 12 were almost certainly with Him for Lazarus' resurrection, but Mary's faith is conspicuous and beyond anyone else's at this point. Her faith acts on the impossible; it's no wonder that Jesus makes her the first apostle of the resurrection (see **Matthew** 28:10).

When we meet Lazarus the first time, he is seriously unwell. **John** 11:1-3 describes Lazarus as 'sick' and 'very sick' – three times in three verses. He was in a dangerously bad way. The diagnosis is not shared with us, so we don't know what killed Lazarus. Was it a sudden affliction like snakebite, or a terminal condition like leprosy, or an aggressive cancer they didn't understand in 33AD, or a congenital condition he had suffered all his life like a hole in the heart, diabetes, cerebral palsy, or muscular dystrophy? Lazarus seems to be unmarried, and he seems mute. It is very possible that Lazarus was disabled and unable to speak; that would also explain his solitary station, and that he was cared for by his sisters. He could hear and understand language, so not deaf, but for someone who experienced what very few others have (death, and resurrection back into this world) – he said little or nothing even though we all want to know what is beyond death.

Lazarus actually knew!

Maybe that is why he was chosen for such a display of God's power – the secret was maintained. It remains largely opaque to us. Through Mary's relationship with Lazarus, we see both the humanity and divinity of Jesus. Mary believed in Jesus, but after Lazarus died and Jesus met her at or near the tomb, He was sad and cried. Why? He knew what He was about to do – that Lazarus would be restored. Jesus is upset because Mary's greatest feeling is grief for Lazarus, not trust for Jesus. He sees that she still does not have faith in Him. She believes her brother is dead, and that Jesus failed them.

Jesus never told Mary that He would raise Lazarus; He told that to Martha. Mary meets Jesus at or near Lazarus' tomb because she is torn – she is between belief and faith. Unless Martha told her somewhere between her earlier conversation and arriving at Lazarus' tomb, Mary does not know that Jesus intends resurrection for Lazarus. Martha had more reason to have faith. Jesus' extreme sorrow with Mary is that she thinks He did not sufficiently care, and that He cannot help Lazarus. Jesus is about to show the world that He is not interested in preventing death, because that is futile – we will die. He is showing that He is able to raise us from death. This is His promise: eternal life after death. But earthly death will come.[23]

## Simon the Pharisee is a legalist, a pillar of Judaism, a man of substance.

Pharisees meticulously observed the Jewish Law, and were basically the lawyers of Jewish tradition and observance. They observe Torah, and are punctilious in attending to and demanding detail.

Jesus, Himself a Rabbi, scathingly criticized their attention to legal trivialities while ignoring the desperate needs of the poor and afflicted. He did

---

[23]    See e.g. **Hebrews** 9:27-28 (NLT).

not win, nor attempt to win, the approval or patronage of the Pharisees. Attention to people rather than to Law alienated Him diametrically from the traditionalists. Jesus neither minced words in describing the legalists – He called them 'whited sepulchres/tombs' – externally clean, but inwardly full of death (**Matthew** 23:27). This was both brave and fraught. As today, the lawyer echelon in a society is also the exclusive domain for selecting the wielders of judicial law - judges and justices. These are positions of great power, governance and control. In this field, reward and promotion accrue to capability in trivia, jargon and fastidiousness, not in justice, creativity, and virtue. By exposing the hubris and hypocrisy of the Pharisees, Jesus took aim at the most powerful and influential people in Jewish culture. He offended them deeply, and set smouldering an implacable, spiteful, homicidal vindictiveness.

How did a legalist, and pillar of Jewish law, a member of the elite and privileged, know Mary well enough that he could think and mutter to himself that she is a sinner – a sinful woman, a prostitute? Was it her clothing, or her demeanour, and/or posture alone? Luke paints this scene for us (**Luke** 7:36-50).

How did she know the way to his place? Jesus is very aware of who she is, what her life has been. She says nothing, but in Simon's eyes, she acts shockingly; she touches Jesus, weeps over Him, pours prohibitively expensive perfume all over Him. Simon only notices her sinfulness, her stain, her shame. It is this that he mutters as he thinks about her. Jesus knows his thoughts and actually speaks to them. His concern is for the woman herself; Simon is focused on her reputation, her past. One is grace, the other is law. This dichotomy of grace and law is typical of Jesus' life and ministry. We don't know if Jesus has had contact with Mary before this, it is hard to be sure - but she definitely knows Him. Simon also knows about Jesus and who He is. Simon is offended and apparently disgusted by

Jesus' attitude towards Mary. Mary is purely penitent; the extreme value of her nard perfume mirrors her extreme penitence and genuine sorrow. She reflects a shining illumination of grace; Simon carves a crystalline silhouette of law and condemnation.

Simon's relationship to Mary is muddy. But, he certainly knows her and her immoral reputation. At the very least, he knows what she does. He is in a situation where grace is unfolding before him, and he is witnessing the radical transformation of a life from wretchedness to renewal. All he can think about though is her legal and moral status, that she is unclean, and that Jesus is allowing such a vile woman to touch Him. There are few, if any, such dichroic contrasts between love and law - anywhere.

## *Mary the mother of Jesus* followed Him when it was perilous, and traumatizing.

She is one person who knew the truth of Jesus, like MM did. We know little about her background either. Through her marriage to Joseph after she was pregnant, she connects Jesus to a startling heritage – a genealogy including Josiah, the greatest King in history (see **2 Kings** 23:25), Ruth, and Abraham. Jesus' genetic history is actually half divine, but His human family background is also impressive. Mary ensured Jesus had this by taking a huge risk of faith and acceding to pregnancy before she was married. She had to live her life in a culture which prized virginity before marriage, and which condemned women who were, or who seemed to be, sexually immoral. She figures in a number of episodes involving MM; they understood each other.

Mary His mother had heard direct prophecies over Jesus, and revelations about Him from angels. She had heard Simeon and Anna declare His Messianic nature (**Luke** 2:25-40), that He was the Saviour of all people, and that He would pierce her soul. Mary watched Him grow up, saw Him as a teen and young man, learning Hebrew, engaging and stupefying much older Rabbis with His knowledge and acuity, becoming a carpenter, stepping into the role of supporting her and the family when Joseph was no longer there (we know nothing of what happened to Joseph, except that he was still alive when Jesus was at about legal age, e.g. **Luke** 2:41-47). Mary may have been at Jesus' wedding, if He had one, which would likely have been when He was 16-18. At this point, Joseph is not present (this ambiguity about the wedding is suggested in **John** 2:9-10, although most scholars do not give credence to this event being Jesus' wedding in disguise). Joseph appears to have died during Jesus' adolescence.

Mary Jesus' mother knew that proximity to Jesus could be exalting, and it could be devastating. A further note: the New Testament portrays a number of occasions where unnamed women followed or watched Jesus. These groups very likely included MM because **Luke** 8:1-2 specifically details that MM was part of a group that followed Jesus; it possibly includes Mary His mother, but we cannot be certain.

**Matthew** and **Mark** do not specify that Mary Jesus' mother was at His death and resurrection events. **Luke** (24:8-10) identifies a 'Mary mother of James', who is probably Mary mother of Jesus, at the tomb on the Sunday morning. **John** (19:25) explicitly identifies MM and Mary Jesus' mother at the crucifixion and death of Jesus together. **Matthew** identifies two Mary's at the resurrection; that is all we know.

Staying close to Jesus in the awful circumstances of His killing took not only immense personal, psychological and emotional resilience, but great courage. The Romans were present and could have assaulted them for being close and sympathetic to a criminal. Jewish leaders were concerned that the law be observed and corpses not be exposed on the approaching Sabbath. Their solution was to break their legs so they would die quickly, and then get the corpses off the crosses and eradicated. There was no compassion or humanity whatever in this. They could have asked that instant and more mercifully quick deaths be inflicted (e.g. a javelin to the heart, as one soldier attempted on Jesus); breaking legs is an agonizing and sadistic cruelty. Their concern was law, not people.

Crucifixion was itself a cruel and excruciating death. The stricken victim generally died a painful and often slow death by asphyxiation, hypervolemic shock, and/or heart failure. The trauma to the body was enormous, and always overwhelming; blood loss, dehydration, nervous agony, all contributed to massive systemic breakdown. Victims did not survive Roman crucifixion. If victims did not die quickly enough, the Romans expedited death through stabbing, or as already noted, breaking their legs.

It was also utterly humiliating; not only were victims subjected to agonizing physical punishment, they were tormented with exposure. Most artistic depictions of crucifixion are genteel by contrast to the reality. Victims were naked, not discreetly protected by cloths across their genital area. Apparently, the pain and shock caused involuntary defecation and urination. In men, the penis would often become erect, all of which became the source of mockery and derision. There is not a shred of sympathy. The Romans meant crucifixion to terrify people, which is why they made it extremely public and lined the busiest thoroughfares with crucified victims as a warning to the general populace of the consequences for rebellion or resistance. The message was stark – challenge Rome and there will be merciless retribution.[24]

MM saw this happen to Jesus. She had almost certainly seen crucifixions happen before, and she knew He would not survive. No-one did. When she went to the tomb on Resurrection Morning, she expected only to find a broken and dead body; she did not ask the Groundsman to tell her where

---

[24]    D. Instone-Brewer 2015, *Autopsy of a Crucifixion*, www.premierchristianity.com.

Jesus was having smoko or breakfast. She asked for His body because that's all she expected to find – at best.

## Demons provide perspective on Jesus.

The *seven demons* which possessed/afflicted Mary Magdalene of Bethany are not named or explained; they are only mentioned because they affected Mary. C.S.Lewis wisely counsels us: *'There are... errors into which our race can fall about the devils. One... is to feel an excessive and unhealthy interest in them.'*[25] This book is not about to search for them. But, the Bible shows us how they reacted to Jesus. Biblical examples are many, but one we can examine is **Luke** 4:31-37. In this instance, a demon which has possessed a man, starts yelling out to Jesus, acknowledging that Jesus is the 'Holy One' sent by God. Jesus interrupts the demon, showing no interest in it as an entity; His interest is only in freeing the man. The demon fears Jesus, asking Him if He is going to 'destroy us?' This is not the Gadarene demoniac who was possessed by 'Legion' (see **Mark** 5:1-20), this is another situation, but the demon clearly says it is not alone – it says 'us'. Jesus does not pursue this, or show any interest. He simply ejects the demon(s) from the man, freeing him. Something like this happened with Mary Magdalene. The demons fear Jesus, and He freed her. This happened prior to Mary's meeting with Jesus at Simon's place in **Luke** 7. Demons flee from Jesus; they would certainly not be part of anointing Him with nard.

## Other representations of MM.

Mary Magdalene/of Bethany/Sinful Woman has been depicted and represented repeatedly through various forms and media. She is represented in

---

[25]    C.S.Lewis 1942, *The Screwtape Letters*, p.9.

Art, in Drama, in Music, in Film, in Literature. While often interesting and even beautiful, these creative depictions are not attempts at history or biography. They are responses to her beauty, strength, pathos and inspiration.

MM is portrayed in musical and dramatic depictions like Maurice Maetherlinck's *Mary Magdalene* play, Sal Ponti's *Magdalene the Musical*, the play *Mary Magdalene* in the medieval Digby cycle, a major character in Webber's and Rice's rock-opera *Jesus Christ Superstar* (and the anthemic song *I Don't Know How to Love Him*), Mark Adamo's opera *The Gospel of Mary Magdalene*, Lady Gaga's song *Bloody Mary*, etc.. She has been painted by El Greco, Rossetti, La Tour, Stevens, Da Vinci, Tintoretto etc.. She is characterized and described in fiction from Dan Brown's *The Da Vinci Code*, to C.S.Lewis' *The Lion, the Witch and the Wardrobe* (with elements of both Lucy and Susan), even possibly in Christina Rossetti's Victorian poem *Goblin Market* (as Lizzie *or* Laura). Filmic depictions are many: Rooney Mara in *Mary Magdalene* (2018), Constance Crawley in *Mary Magdalene* (1914), Jacqueline Logan played a courtesan Mary in Cecil B. DeMille's epic *The King of Kings* (1927), Monica Bellucci played her in Mel Gibson's *The Passion of the Christ* (2004).

She fascinates us.

*

Almost as an afternote, we just catch a glancing reflection of MM through **Judas Iscariot.**

**Matthew** (26:8-9 & 14-16) and **Mark** (14:10-11) describe the disciples' indignant disbelief at Mary's liberal application of nard all over Jesus.

Only one disciple is offended enough to act murderously though.

Judas is so infuriated at Mary's attention to Jesus that he reacts viciously – he plans Jesus' betrayal to the Priests. Judas was alert enough to know that this at least could and probably would lead to Jesus' death. What offended Judas so viscerally? So psychopathically?

It was not Jesus' action that affected him so essentially; it was Mary's.

Judas' betrayal of Jesus is revenge, not only because Jesus frustrated Judas' political inclinations and petty criminal enterprises, but because He thwarted his unholy aspirations with Mary.

**Luke** (7:36-50) does not record any disciples' presence with Jesus at Simon's place, except MM (the sinful woman). Interestingly though, Jesus does mention pieces of silver (denarii) in his discussion with Simon; a form of currency later used by Judas.

**John** (12:4-6) also records Judas' confected consternation at Mary's apparent profligacy. John especially notes Judas' hypocrisy in criticising Mary for being wasteful, when Judas himself was a thief. He needed more money than he could earn himself, so he obviously had expensive tastes and a lifestyle he could not afford from his own resources. Given his character, it is very possible that he enjoyed the erotic expertise of an attractive and expensive courtesan. If she was a penitent, she would no longer be available for providing this dark sex. Mary's commitment to Jesus left no room for Judas' scheming and desires. If Mary and Jesus were *in love*, Judas was even more jealous.

So, Judas reacts, furiously and lethally. His behaviour is blankly psychopathic – he is ready to do murder. The trigger for this episode then is Mary's attention to and love for Jesus, which Judas interprets as intrusion and interference. Judas did not want Mary to be saved from sin; he had wanted her to stay as she was, even if that was destroying her. He may have hoped to have her for a long time. Jesus warned that hindering salvation for His children was akin to suicide by drowning (ref. **Matthew** 18:6). Judas coveted and preferred the afflicted and degraded Mary, the woman who was a courtesan and available for the kind of silver that Jesus mentions with

Simon, which Judas later receives as blood payment from the Jewish priests. Had Jesus permanently deprived Judas of more than merely pilfered cash? Judas ultimately died by suicide.

Mary had been *completely freed* from demons, whereas Judas had *opened himself* to that kind of psycho-emotional, spiritual excrement (n.b. **Luke** 22:3).

*

In condensing the facts and deductions, these coincidences are extraordinary.

This unnamed woman in each of the synoptic Gospels is actually the same person named as Mary of Bethany in **John**. It is extremely unlikely that one woman would wash and anoint Jesus' feet using copious amounts of prohibitively expensive nard, two or three separate times – even if she was wealthy. It's the same woman, same story, same event, different descriptions.

Is it likely that four different women did this at three separate homes belonging to different men, who all just happened to be Pharisees named Simon? Again, this would be extremely unlikely.

Mary Magdalene, Mary of Bethany and the 'sinful woman' never appear explicitly in the same incident/scene. If they were individuals in the same incident, they would be differentiated. Further, because MM was a devoted disciple who travelled around with Jesus, she would surely have been at Bethany with Mary of Bethany, if they were different people. Likewise at the crucifixion and resurrection? But these never happened – because they couldn't. They are the same woman.

When the disciples are mentioned in the New Testament, there is often an assumption that this means the 12 disciples who became known as the 12 apostles. This is not true: 'the disciples' was a much larger and murmurating group, and is not precisely numbered. E.g. **John** 12:1-9 makes clear that there was a large crowd at Mary's home, and that Jesus was not alone there for the feast/dinner in His honour. Mary Magdalene was one of his disciples (see **Luke** 8:1-2), and could very possibly have been present, whether inside, or as one of the crowd, but she is not mentioned in this kind of context anywhere in the Biblical accounts. Mary of Bethany is there, of course. Again, they are not mentioned separately, because they cannot be: they are the same person.

'Mary' is a very common female name in Roman Judea – it is estimated that over 25% of girls were named *Mary*. Looked at together, the Gospels identify two different women named Mary who went to Jesus' tomb on the morning of His resurrection. To distinguish the various Mary's, the Gospel writers assigned identifying features to them. One is Mary Magdalene, the other is either 'mother of James', or 'the other Mary'. **Luke** indicates 'several women', but is careful to distinguish Mary Magdalene from 'Mary mother of James' (see 24:10).

Had each Mary anointed Jesus in a prefigurement of His crucifixion and death, in the previous week? No. Jesus identifies this woman as Mary of Bethany in **John** 12:7 and **Mark** 14:8. We know there were two separate Mary's at Jesus' tomb, at His burial and at His resurrection – Mary Magdalene, and most likely Jesus' mother, who had another son called James (see **Mark** 6:3). We know it was not Jesus' mother who applied the nard.

Mary Magdalene is clearly identified by her 'Magdalene' toponym when the Gospel writers mean specifically to differentiate her. Her name is obscured ('Mary of Bethany') or concealed ('sinful woman') where there could be toxic attention if she is identified plainly.

**John** 12:7 and **Matthew** 26:12 combine to indicate that this Mary (of Bethany) was to be directly involved in Jesus' burial, but John later does not record this. He *does* record Mary going to the tomb two days later, as Mary

Magdalene. It can only be the same Mary as Jesus confirmed would be at the burial place, at His tomb.

*

There is a last question which hovers around most discussions of Mary Magdalene of Bethany: *was she Jesus' wife?* There are many theories and speculations about Jesus' marital status. In the 2000's, Dan Brown's novel *The Da Vinci Code,* and the subsequent film, excited speculation about Mary and Jesus as a married couple. The Gospel writers are silent on this, but they are also silent on *any* of the disciples' marital status (excepting Peter, see **Luke** 4:38). Lee Wilson observes that in Jewish culture, especially in ancient times, marriage was the relational default setting – everyone got married (this is plain in the Torah and Mishnah)[26]. Historian Michael Haag notes that in Jesus' time, cultural scruples around both nakedness and burial rites would have precluded any woman touching Jesus' body, except his wife, or a very close relative in her absence or debility[27]. Mary was highly focused on being at the tomb as early as possible to anoint Jesus' body, presumably by touching him in the process. It's food for thought. We know she was not Jesus' genetic sister, aunt or niece. Mary did not end up touching Jesus' dead body though; He was alive by the time she met with Him on the resurrection morning.

MM's reaction at the tomb is revealing – she attends twice. First time, she sees the empty tomb and runs (see **John** 20:2) to get Peter and John. To run and find two people, she must have been fit; this is supported by the leanness and strength characterised by her upbringing. This first time at the tomb could tie with **Matthew's** account, encountering an angel (so

---

[26]  Lee Wilson 2022, *Could Jesus have been Married?,* in Premier Christianity (magazine) 25/04/2022.
[27]  Michael Haag 2017, *The Quest for Mary Magdalene,* p.12.

a second encounter a little later would not have been so surprising), with another Mary. Second time, Mary is outside the tomb after Peter and John have looked inside and noted the grave clothes and folded head cloth. John was the first of the pair to arrive and look inside, then Peter. They then leave, and Mary who has done twice as much running (so it makes sense she got back to the tomb *after* John and Peter) is outside. She is left with an empty tomb – the ultimate futility. Jesus is dead, her faith in and love for Him is now becoming trauma, nothing makes sense. **John** 20:11 emphasises her sorrow by describing her tears twice, as 'crying' *and* 'weeping'. If she could have, she would probably have empathized with W.H.Auden: '...*I thought that love would last forever; I was wrong.*'[28] Like Auden, she is blindsided by the cold reality of grief, a love now irretrievably inconsolable; this intensity of grief drives her to look inside the tomb.

Unlike Peter and John, she meets someone (or two).

Possibly because her life had involved a number of encounters with the supernatural, and because she may already have met an angel, Mary replies to the angels she meets inside who ask her, '*Why are you crying?*', that it is because, '...*They have taken away my Lord.*'

She does not ask 'Who are you?' or 'How did you get in?', or 'Where have you put my husband?' (which would be the natural question, if she was Jesus' wife), nor react with shock and disturbance (as another Mary had when she encountered the angel Gabriel in **Luke** 1:29). Very realistically, MM characterises her relationship with Jesus here on Earth as between Lord and servant, Teacher and disciple. MM is intent on Jesus' missing body, and that she does not know where He is. At this point, for her as for us, body, soul and spirit are fused as 'person'. Jesus' body is still Jesus to her. She is confused, and focused on His corpse. There are two angels,

---

28     W.H.Auden & C. Isherwood 1936, poem in *The Ascent of F6*. Subsequently as W.H.Auden 1940, 'Funeral Blues' in *Another Time,* Random House.

wearing white robes, and they seem to speak in unison. That is what MM saw and heard. She does not seem at all confused about them being ghosts or spirits – they are angels.

She now senses/notices someone behind her and she merely glances over her shoulder. Her bleary eyes can't make out who it is – she knows it's not Peter or John, so she thinks it must be a gardener or groundsman. Interestingly, the angels are of no special interest to her at this point – she is really focused wholly on Jesus. Most of us would be stunned to see or encounter angels! This perhaps underlines just how focused Mary is on Jesus' body and whereabouts. For the second time she is asked why she is crying, and she replies that she only wants 'His body', and asks this gardener to tell her, so she can go and get it. He now speaks her name – '*Mary*'.

(*IF* this account was a Hollywood dramedy, then at this point the cinema would be a symphony of sniffles, sighs, and crumpled tissues. He may as well have said, 'My body's right here, Kid.')

**John** records her response with bare but vivid detail, which is almost certainly Mary's recollection as told to John later. She turns around completely, sees Him, and next thing, Jesus is trying to extricate Himself from a 'cling'! Whatever that was, it obviously involved a wild and emotional embrace, and maybe some kissing. Simple sentences are often the best ones. Mary was happy.

On this resurrection morning, Mary has found the disciples twice, with news of Jesus' whereabouts: the first time, she told them His body was gone. The second time, she told them He was alive and well. Mary is the first person to announce the resurrection of Jesus the Christ – a dead man now alive again, i.e. *an impossibility*. When Jesus told an ecstatically happy Mary not to cling to Him, He was not being a killjoy or condemning her excited love. He was underlining that He wasn't on Earth permanently any more; He was ascending to Father God. She couldn't hold onto Him this way. Permanence happens now in Heaven – where He has come from, and where He is returning. He is saying 'My God is your God, the same Father, and as I have died and yet lived, so shall you die and yet live, for your God is my God!'

God is Life. It's *great News*.

That is still His message today. Have you lost someone beloved? Mary herself is bearing witness to what she saw – she is telling you: <u>There is hope</u>! Jesus has taken responsibility for all sin (i.e. rebellion and defiance towards God) and offers eternal life in Heaven. That eternal life is beautiful, ecstatic, and incredibly exciting.

## *On marriage.*

Jesus may have been married – but not to Mary.

Jesus' empathy with widows is noteworthy (see e.g. **Mark** 12:41-44, **Luke** 7:11-17, **Luke** 18:2-5); it is like he understood their grief from personal experience. In the time of Roman Judea, it was normal for people to marry between 12-16 years. Jesus could easily and normally have married as a young man, and been widowed by his 20's. Why is that not mentioned in the Gospels then? We are not told marital details about any of the disciples, except an allusion to Peter. Jesus' marital status was and is not material to His mission. We have some persuasive and helpful Biblical clues though.

**Hebrews** 4:15 states that Jesus has been tempted in *all ways* as we are. This means He has been tempted to sexual sin - adultery, illicit sex, and dishonesty. It would be very odd if one of our most vexatious areas of vulnerability was excluded from His experience. Sexual temptation and sin is an almost universal foible – if Jesus was tempted in *all ways* as we are, sex must be included, and extra-marital temptations have to be encompassed. For this to be the case, and for Jesus to have experienced temptation in all

ways, He must have been married. Jesus could have been tempted to fornication as a single man, but not to adultery (in its conventional definition
of being sex between married people who are not married to each other).

Were Jesus and Mary Magdalene married? Mary would not have
anointed him publicly in an act of contrition in the way she did, and
Simon would not have wondered about Jesus knowing her history, if they
were married. **Mark** 15:41 specifically indicates that MM cared for Jesus
in Galilee (where MM grew up/came from), along with other women. It
would be unusual for Mark to specify this if Jesus and Mary were married, a
relationship which explicitly implies the partners would care for each other;
it would be stating the obvious.

Were they close? Almost certainly, yes; Mary supported Jesus and other
disciples financially, cared for Him in Galilee, was with Him in Jerusalem
(and nearby Bethany), embraced him on resurrection morning (and Jesus
had to tell her to let go) - He was not angry, and Mary is not depicted here
as being inappropriate; He is just clear – he is saying 'not now!' to someone
He liked very much.

Was MM attracted to Jesus? In her first encounter with Him, was she
thinking that He was a handsome and gorgeous-looking man? She was
certainly not afraid, nor repelled by Him. Did Jesus look at Mary and
know she was an attractive woman? If Judas and Simon could see it, then
other men could as well. Hugging does not seem to have been outside their
boundaries, and MM kissed Jesus many times – if only His feet. (n.b. the
gnostic Gospels tell us that they kissed on the lips.) If she would kiss His
feet, it is unlikely she would have been reluctant to kiss Him elsewhere. We
don't know. The balance of probabilities though indicates that they were
not married, or sexually intimate. If Jesus was married at some stage, then
having a sexual relationship with his wife was of course perfectly normal;
but, to have had a wild affair with a woman who was once a courtesan and

whom He had freed of demons would have been sinful, and made Him a hypocrite.

Jesus was neither.

A man and woman can have a close and cherished friendship without it being sexual. Even if rare, genuine platonic comradeships are honourably intimate and thoroughly virtuous; despite popular assertions, Hollywood does not have the final word on relationships. Friends do not have to end up in bed, or married. Jesus and Mary are comfortably and appropriately close.

There is no mention or suggestion that MM was ever married. The Gospels are descriptive about widows – if Mary was widowed (including if she was widowed from Jesus), it would almost certainly be mentioned. If she was divorced, or separated, likewise it would probably be mentioned (as with **John** 4:1-26). Marriage was the normal relational and legal condition for women in that time and place, so then why is she not?

Slaves could not formally or legally marry. They could not enter contracts. Former prostitutes were not virgins, and not sought as wives.

Every *interaction* between Jesus and Mary tells us about this extraordinary woman.

Why does it matter? Is it important that she is demonstrably represented in three different personas in the New Testament? It matters because by reintegrating MM as one woman, we can see her more closely as a complete person in all her complexity and incongruity, not as three separate people. We instead can see her holistically.

From this point, Mary is reconstituted: normalized as one woman. Three become one.

## Encounters.

We do not know with any certainty about MM's and Jesus' *first* encounter. The most likely Biblical candidate is **Luke** 7:36-50, but this is speculative. The Gospels also indicate that Jesus had had previous dealings with Mary at some stage when he exorcised her of seven demons. Our encounter with MM is 2000 years distant, with scant detail about her; the details we do have are complicated by her representation in three personas, and a paucity of description. We have exactly the same situation with Jesus Himself – we are nowhere given a detailed description of what He looked like, His childhood, or His family life. The clues we have about MM are very limited:

> She is Galilean. Magdala is a Galilean town. Contemporary skeletal evidence indicates that Galilean women of that era were about 155-165cm tall (5'2" – 5'5"). An interesting clue about MM sits in **John** 20:5 & 11. In these verses, both John (assuming he is the 'other disciple') and MM have to *stoop* to enter Jesus' tomb. Other entrants in all four Gospels are not thus described. Why did they need to 'stoop', and why is this detail included? It does indicate that John and MM were taller than normal. MM was probably tall for a woman of her time, which puts her height at very least above 165 cm.

MM likely had dark hair and brown eyes, which is the common colouring of Semitic people in Judea. It is also possible though that if she was taller than normal, she may have been different in other ways. Research into skeletal bone DNA found in archaeological digs indicates that there were people in the Galilean area with blue eyes, at her time [29].MM may have been blue-eyed.

MM was likely of lean physique, if only because children worked from when they were able, so her life was physically demanding. If literacy education was provided at all in Roman Judea at the beginning of the 1st Millennium, it was principally to males. Females were not formally educated, unless the family was wealthy and liberal. Indications are that females were required to maintain a household. Estimates are that in Jesus' time, approx. 5% of Jewish males could read & write Hebrew fluently. The majority of other males could read functionally, i.e. they could read public signs and important names. This also helps us understand why the documentary evidence from Roman Judea is scant, and we are very fortunate to have the Gospels. MM would have learned how to cook, clean, babysit, sew, embroider, dye, tailor, butcher, wash, serve, husband livestock, ensure water supplies, and keep everything kosher. On top of this, her hometown in Magdala would also have necessitated the ability to clean, cook and preserve fish. She was likely not taught to read & write as a child, and any such skill must have been acquired later in life. She was an active girl, with little opportunity to be anything but hard-working and lean. Because indications from her later life are that she had been enslaved, it is possible she did not have family in Magdala, but was bought and owned by people who lived there. Alternatively, her family sold her to cover debt.

**Luke** 8:2b-3 does imply that MM must have been numerate though, which implies at least some literacy.

Linguistically, Aramaic – a Hebrew dialect – was her native tongue, with a Galilean accent. She probably also had a rudimentary acquaintance with Latin – enough to stay out of trouble. (Jesus could speak and understand

---

[29]    Amanda Borschel-Dan 2018, *Anomalous blue-eyed people came to Israel 6500 years ago from Iran*, DNA shows, in Times of Israel 20/08/2018.

Latin – we know he could hold a conversation with a Roman Governor, and speak with Roman soldiers. It is very unlikely that Pontius Pilate bothered to learn anything but baseline Aramaic or Hebrew, if anything; they were barbarian tongues.) MM and Jesus would have communicated through the Aramaic language, with Jesus' Nazarene accent, and Mary's Galilean. What did that sound like to them? For modern-day English speakers, perhaps it was like Australian and American people conversing together - very understandable, but also definitely different.

Mary's first narrated encounter with Jesus in the synoptic Gospels appears to be as the woman who washed and anointed Jesus. As previously noted, Jesus' exorcism of seven demons from Mary is likely their first meeting, but we have no narrative details. Jesus liberated Mary from malevolent and traumatizing torment. That is exactly what it would have been like for Mary. Malachi Martin has dealt with more recent instances of demonic possession and harassment in his work *Hostage to the Devil*, which provides corroboration for a real and continuing problem. Martin cites an old Priest who had striven and battled against evil spirits, describing Hell as, 'Just to be utterly alone and immutably without love. Forever.' [30]. From this grim horror, Jesus spared Mary, giving instead the other 'Forever' – '...*the Kingdom, and the Power, and the Glory...*'

Returning to the washing and anointing, **Matthew** (26:6-13) and **Mark** (14:1-9) are very similar descriptions. **Luke** (7:36-50) has the same incident, but it is described with notable differences to **Matthew** and **Mark,** primarily being that it *seems* earlier. In **John**'s Gospel, Mary first appears in 11:2, but this is a prequel, as Jesus already knew Mary (see 11:5), and a chronologically earlier encounter is described lexically later in 12:3. This is very likely an effort by John to protect Mary from unwanted attention. It

---

[30]   Malachi Martin 1976, *Hostage to the Devil: The Possession and Exorcism of Five Contemporary Americans*, p.451.

raises a slightly digressive but interesting point about Mary: John is widely believed to have been the last surviving of the 12 apostles, but his Gospel must have been written prior to his death in approx. AD90. **John** 21:24-25 indicates clearly that John was very selective in what he wrote, and very careful to be accurate. For John to have been protective of Mary later in his life (approx. AD80-90), she must still have needed protection at that time. She was likely still alive then in the AD80's. I do not have any firm evidence for that, but it is a reasonable deduction.

Mary does appear once more in the Bible in **Romans** 16:6, except we have no way of knowing absolutely if this is MM herself. It could be a different Mary, *but* whoever this Mary is, Paul assumes his contemporary readers will know her. She is someone sufficiently identifiable, and whose whereabouts are known widely enough, that she is recognizable by first name alone in Rome, even when she had an extremely common first-name. She could be Jesus' mother, who must have been in her 90's at this stage (assuming she was approx. 16 at Jesus' birth and adding 80 years), or this could be MM. Scholars generally agree that Paul wrote the letter to the **Romans** in the late AD50's from Corinth. Mary was likely a younger woman in the time of Jesus' ministry on Earth – she was probably just a little older than her siblings Martha and Lazarus, and one thing we are fairly sure about is that Lazarus did not die of old age in **John** 11:14. When Jesus resurrected Lazarus, dotage was not the problem; it was because Lazarus should not have been dead yet – he was young. If MM was alive in the AD80's and still being protected by an old apostle John, she was probably in her early 20's when she met Jesus. Lazarus was likely about 20, and the indignant and bossy Martha was a brat sister in her late teens.

All this together offers some summary clues about her appearance, character and worldview:

**She is tall for her time**. Tall enough that she had to stoop when others didn't.

**She is physically/sexually attractive**. Appealing enough that Judas was psychotically jealous of her commitment to Jesus, and Simon seemed to know about her – reputationally, empirically, or both.

**She is strong**. She grew up in a time when girls worked hard from childhood; later, she did a lot of walking to follow Jesus around - and Jesus had to struggle to shake off her hug.

**She is athletic**. MM ran a long way on Resurrection morning and showed no undue signs of fatigue, even if she lagged a little on her second trip to Jesus' tomb.

**She is convalescent** from psycho-emotional illness and trauma, at least partially caused by spiritual interference; she understands what it means to be mentally afflicted and unwell. Jesus specifically tells accusers to leave her alone; He is protective of her as someone vulnerable.

**She is educated.** Mary had amassed some private wealth and was at least numerate; it is logical that some literacy accompanied numeracy.

**She is intelligent.** MM can observe, intuit, deduce, analyse and reason.

**She is penitent.** Mary does not ask Jesus for Grace with words - her contrition is in her attitude; she trusts Him to know her need, which she signified by acknowledging His authority to forgive sins by kneeling and anointing Him.

**She is faithful.** Jesus is Lord of Mary.

## How does MM present Jesus to us?

She gives us eyes onto some extraordinary scenes where Jesus did incredible things.

We only have two recorded verbal conversations between Jesus and Mary. These are preserved by John, who seemed to be closer to MM than other male disciples. **John** 19:25-27 records John as the only male disciple who followed Jesus even to Golgotha, where He spoke to him from the Cross. There were a number of women in this group, including Jesus' mother and Mary Magdalene.

The conversations (as in words directly exchanged) are in **John** 11:32-33 and **John** 20:14-17. **Luke** 10:38-41 is a situation where Jesus is communicating with Mary, but we do not have any words she spoke. The Bible records Jesus speaking more to Martha than Mary. Again, John may have 'scrambled' this slightly to disguise Mary. (**Matthew** 28:9-10 is not a dialogue, but rather a group discussion.)

The most important blessing and choice Jesus brings for us is forgiveness for sin. In our modern times (2025 atow), *sin* is regarded as an almost obscenely embarrassing, obsolete concept. It is avoided as being a judgmental and intolerant notion deriving from neurotic religiosity. (Islam has no such reservation, but Christianity does – an humiliation for modern Christianity.) The notion that we are accountable to a greater Being for our perspectives and behaviours seems indecent, mainly because we embrace and vaunt our lives as our own unique domains in which we have independent and individual autonomy: 'I am my own'. The Bible does not support this view: we are in fact accountable for all we do – often accountable to others, and always to God. We worship[31] individuality more than we worship God. That is what 'religion' looks like today – the *cult of self.* A reality of sin explicates accountability for objective wrongs. We live in an era when we perceive and accept there are no absolute rights and wrongs – there are only relativities and personal subjectivities. Our moral baseline is 'Do no harm.' But even this is qualified by subjectivities about 'harm' (which implies a fixed moral stasis against which harm can be identified and measured). So long as we are not causing manifest harm to others, we are left to live as we wish. The perimeter of permissibility is competent consent. If we consent to something and we are deemed competent, then we can do it. E.g. If we competently consent to transacting drugs for personal use, that is tolerable, but if our daughter consents to entering a polygynous marriage arrangement with a Mormon or Islamic partner, then will that be tolerable?

In the examples above, a majority of people with western cultural backgrounds and democratic mores would agree that personal drug use is a tolerable area of choice, after all, alcohol has been tolerated for millennia, and tobacco (nicotine) for centuries. There would be more discomfort about women contracting for polygynous marriages. However, even this

---

[31]  *Worship* (as both noun & verb) is understood and utilized in this text as a primary human autonomic necessity like hunger, thirst, relating and breathing, whereby we position rightly towards God. We cannot excise worship from our being; we will worship something. The object of worship is intended to be God, just as fresh-water is the object of thirst. We *can* substitute other objects however, and this often happens. We worship wealth, other humans, intelligence, nature, art, sexuality or power instead of God. Note that each of these entities/principles is good in itself, but are not intended for worship. Water is good for drinking, but not for inhaling. This transference of worship away from God to another object is always harmful to us; when we transfer worship from God to these other phenomena, it becomes idolatry.

barbaric practice would be excused on the basis of cultural history and tolerance (because '*in*tolerance' is regarded ipso facto as negative - strange but true). Western democratic mores are substantially derived from Judeo-Christian legal culture, which in western societies has evolved into a system of governing laws and regulations implemented and maintained by the institutions of judiciary (courts, tribunals, assizes), elected legislatures (e.g. parliaments, councils, congresses etc.), permanent administrative bodies (e.g. departments, bureaux, ministries etc.), and corporate economic bodies (e.g. Apple, IBM, Tik-Tok, SAIC, Tesla, Novo Nordisk etc.). These institutional bodies collectively control: capital (money/wealth), research (creativity/ideas), behaviour (human activity), ownership (primarily of resources/space/land) – known in Economics as the 'factors of production'. Controlling these domains accords significant power to the agents. E.g. Who owns the internet? Someone or something does. We just don't know who is working the levers. The truly powerful are not easily visible.

In AD30 Roman Judea, government was contextually all of the above, and the autocracy. In the democratic West today (AD2025 atow), autocracy is unfamiliar – it existed until the late C18th/early C19th, then autocracy began to diminish as legislatures assumed the powers of the Crown or similar Imperial edifices. Jesus and Mary lived in a time when the greatest powers were actually invested in one person. In Roman Judea this was Caesar. This modality of government still exists today in places like Russia, China, North Korea, Saudi Arabia, and in the corporate sphere of governance. As well as Roman government, Judeans also lived in and under the traditions of Jewish legal culture. The local culture was religious, old and strong.

Sin is offence committed deliberately against God, and it has many masks, variations and degrees. Judeo-Christian culture is premised primarily on the truth and reality of the God described and identified in the Holy Bible. That is our primary source document for God. The bedrock of

Judeo-Christian legal culture has been the 'Ten Commandments' (**Exodus** 20:2-17). Law has developed over time and has covered innumerable facets and instances of legal direction and dispute; this continues.

Jesus the Christ distilled the Law down to two governing precepts:

1. 'The most important commandment is this: *Hear O Israel, the Lord our God is the one and only Lord. You must love the Lord your God with all your heart, all your soul, all your mind, and all your strength.*' (**Mark** 12:29-30)

2. 'The second is equally important: *Love your neighbor as yourself.* No other commandment is greater than these.' (**Mark** 12:31)

In both of Jesus' precepts, '*love*' is the preeminent verb. Jesus uses 'Israel' in the sense of God's Kingdom, which is His Church. By 'church' is not meant the building with stained glass windows and ritualised meetings. Jesus means the community of disciples who follow Him, and live the two commandments (ref. **Ephesians** 2:18-22).

Mary was and is one of these. One of the first.

The reason we meet Mary in each Gospel, weeping over and anointing Jesus' feet, is her contrition for sin. She does not speak words, she speaks actions. Jesus knew what she was doing, and He offered her the gift of Grace and forgiveness. He does this before His condemnation, crucifixion and resurrection; He had not yet died as the universal undoing, atonement and destruction of sin. By forgiving Mary (**Luke** 7:47), He was underlining what He did in **Mark** 2:5 when He forgave the sins of the paralysed man who had been lowered into His presence by some friends. Jesus could always forgive sins – but His death as a sacrifice for sin reverses sin and shifts the initiative to us. We have a frighteningly real choice – we can accept Jesus' gift of reversed sin (i.e. Jesus reverses sin – so our sins no longer exist. See **Jude** 24). This is not mercy, it is **grace**. Otherwise, our forgiveness depends on God forgiving us when we do not deserve forgiveness for our sins of murder, greed, rape, paedophilia, cruelty, fraud, sadism, theft, deceit, slander - each of these deserves punishment, as we in fact do in our legal systems. If God is just, then people who have done these things are doomed to punishment, as are we. A Judge is not merciful and forgiving when s/he passes sentence - even if we weep, cry and beg in remorse. We will go to jail, pay compensation, or end on a gallows. What Jesus did was to reverse sin, so that *it does not exist*. He erases it from time. **Jude** 24 says,

> 'Now unto Him who is able to keep you from falling, and **present you faultless**[32] before the presence of His glory with exceeding joy.'

Mercy refrains from punishing us with a deserved penalty; Grace gives favour to us that we do not deserve. Jesus has eradicated our sins, if we want Him to. *Faultless* means without fault – without the terrible things we did five, ten or fifty years ago. They do not exist. The only way we can be faultless, is if the faults do not exist. That involves changing history, which means changing time. That is why what Jesus did was such a big deal. And it is our choice; our freedom of choice is not impinged or compromised. You can continue to harm others if you choose, but your sin will not be reversed. And sin will be judged. It's not a silly notion explicable by clever psychologists – all they do is describe human thinking and behaviour. Jesus *changes* it. For Mary, this was freedom. If she was indeed a slave at some stage, as very likely she was, she already had emancipation from that; but not from sin. Only Jesus expunges sin forever – so that it never happened. We are free. Like Mary. Her past is no more.

'There is therefore now no condemnation for those who are in Christ Jesus.'
- **Romans** 8:1.

---

[32]    *Emphasis* mine.

That is because the sin does not exist to be judged. Jesus' power (His offer of Grace) is electrifying, breathtaking, and permanent.

When was the last time you wept on someone's feet, or shoulder, or just in front of them, and anointed their feet, or head with $50000 of perfumed oil? Jesus does not ask that of you; He offers *grace*. The reception of grace is acknowledging the gift, which requires ownership and confession of sin through honesty and humility; there is no escape any other way. Jesus is the Way. To what?

To love and to freedom.

It is tempting here to launch into a fictionalized and embellished tale of Mary Magdalene - adding colourful and insinuated imaginings which could increase the allure but compromise the integrity of this wondrous woman. Let's look only with what the Holy Spirit has provided in the Bible.

## Conversations.

Mary M and Jesus had two conversations recorded in Scripture, in contexts already considered earlier. Focusing on their conversations revisits and reorients our perspectives.

## #1

The context for the first conversation is Jesus on the road outside Bethany, within sight of Jerusalem, and what Jesus knew was going to be His greatest and most devastating ordeal.

Martha has met Him there, and after their initial discussion Martha returns to Mary, telling her that Jesus has asked for her. Mary 'immediately' goes to Jesus – the immediacy gilds for us the connection and allegiance betwixt them. A group follows Mary and Jesus finds Himself with Mary, and a crowd.

On seeing Jesus, Mary for the *third time* positions herself at Jesus' feet. (Slightly abridged version of dialogue, from **John** 11:32-34. NLT)

She says to Him, *'Lord, if you had been here, my brother would not have died.'*

She is crying, and the other people with her wailing – characteristic funerary behaviour for that time.

This affects Jesus. He speaks not only to Mary but to all there, and asks, *'Where have you put him?'*

Mary and others reply, *'Lord, come and see.'*

This brings Jesus to tears, and He weeps.

Why now? He knew Lazarus was dead before anyone else. Why is Jesus crying? It's not because Lazarus died – Jesus knows that He is about to change that.

This crowd of people has been consoling Mary, and they follow her, not in faith to see Jesus, but in sorrow to comfort Mary. Even Mary indicates that she thinks He is way too late. Jesus expelled seven demons off and out of Mary, but she does not believe He can do anything about Lazarus.

*This* is why Jesus is crying; Mary does not believe in Him, even after He ejected the demonic infestation, and released Mary from sin, and gave her Grace, and defended her from orthodox condemnation and rejection, and she followed Him and witnessed many gob-smacking miracles. But - Jesus is alone. This is it. It's almost a premonition of what is ahead, He is alone and even Mary does not believe.

> *'... What have I become,*
> *My Sweetest Friend,*
> *Everyone I know goes away,*
> *In the end.'* [33]

---

[33]  Johnny Cash 2002, *Hurt*, from album *American IV: The Man Comes Around*, American Recording Studios. Lyrics by Nine Inch Nails 1994.

Jesus is alone. It is as if His ordeal begins here, the trail of isolation and abandonment leading to Calvary. Mary is simply being rational, being human. She knows empirically what Jesus can do, but she doesn't believe it in the same way as she believes the Sun will rise. Not even Jesus can bring back the dead after four days. Even if He did remove all sin from her, and he healed lepers and gave hearing to the deaf, it was not enough. Mary had at very least heard of Jesus raising the dead, but this was too much, it was too hard. Four days was impossible.

He feels disappointed at Mary's lack of faith, He is about to show His power over death, and even Mary says 'Come and see the grave', not, 'Come and raise Him up.' 'Feels' is the right word; Jesus is emotionally affected.

Jesus now moves to the grave where Lazarus is entombed. There is an audience of a kind, a group of people gathered at the tomb who followed Mary. Martha is already there. Jesus tells some people there to remove the entrance stone, and Martha objects that it will stink. Jesus responds revealingly. He questions Martha, 'Didn't I tell you that you will see God's glory if you believe?'

Jesus reveals:

- God's glory is life. He is the God of life, not death.
- Believing in Jesus <u>is the same as believing in God</u>. Jesus is administering the power to revive dead Lazarus, and this is God's glory.
- Death and corruption are of no interest to Jesus, except that they hinder our belief in God's power. We seem more impressed by death than life, which saddens Jesus.

At this point (**John** 11:40-41a), people remove the sealing stone, and the tomb is open. Jesus now prays – *after* the stone is removed. He has complete faith that removing the stone is warranted – Lazarus is going to walk out. Jesus' faith is absolutely confident. He does not implore God for

Lazarus' resurrection, nor express grief over Mary's or Martha's unbelief. He says basically that He is praying aloud so the people will:

- hear the prayer,
- see the glory of God,
- and believe that Jesus is God's 'Sent One'.

He now speaks into the cave tomb, to the dead man. This itself is bizarre, a perplexing moment for the gathered. Talking to the dead is not in itself unusual – many of us have spoken to loved ones passed. This is not macabre or foolish – it is the residual and often treasured presence of the person in our memories, and in our hopes, for exactly the resurrection of life ahead. God does forbid attempts at compelling a person to manifest again in this world; He does not forbid expressions in love and memory. Huge quantities of art, music and poetry bear testament to the reality of relationships which have been interrupted by death. The great Pyramids of Giza, the Taj Mahal, the Lincoln Memorial, the Burial Ship at Sutton Hoo, what are these? These are monuments in memory of people greatly loved, revered, and/or grieved. They are attempts to defy death by perpetuating knowledge and memory.

Great Rameses II (Gk. '*Ozymandias*'), Pharaoh and Master of Kingdoms and all Egypt, who commanded life and domains, who had his statue set in the midst of his supreme sovereignty … and millennia later found in the desert, a forgotten plinth bearing an eroded and weathered inscription,

> '… *"My name is Ozymandias, King of kings:*
> *Look on my works ye Mighty, and despair!"*
> *No thing remains. Round the decay*
> *Of that colossal wreck, boundless and bare*
> *The lone and level sands stretch far away.*[34]

---

[34]   Percy Bysshe Shelley 1818, *Ozymandias*, poem in *Norton Anthology of Poetry*.

Percy Bysshe Shelley encapsulates the futility of Rameses' quest for immortality – for all the splendor of his reign, he is lost and forgotten in the desert. The great Pharaoh, who likely saw pivotal miracles in his own time, has ended as an archaeological curiosity in far-north Africa.

Jesus spoke into a cave, and a corpse walked out - alive. We've already noted - no dead Pharaoh ever walked out of a pyramid.

What is unusual is that Jesus does not speak to Lazarus like he is a dead man, He talks to a living person and tells him to come outside. Mary is present for all of this.

Even before Lazarus was known to be dead, Jesus said euphemistically that he was asleep (**John** 11:11), and the disciples with Him said that if he was asleep then that was a good sign and he was getting better. To be clear, Jesus says, 'Lazarus is dead.' (**John** 11:14). Because that is how we regard people whose bodies have ceased functioning; Lazarus' heart had stopped. Jesus' first description of him is that he is asleep; to God that state that we call death, in reality is as sleep. Death itself is a euphemism to God; it's not the real state for us.

What was it like for people seeing a man swathed in burial cloths stagger from the dark opening? Interestingly, there is no hint or suggestion of Lazarus replying, speaking, or calling out; he is silent. But he is walking. Jesus' prayer is answered affirmatively, and many people who followed Mary to see Jesus now believe in Him (ref. **John** 11:45). As clearly as we can tell, Mary was going to see this resurrection power *again,* within approximately a fortnight. It also becomes the scene of the second recorded conversation with Jesus.

Both dialogues retained in the Bible between Jesus and Mary Magdalene occur at or near tombs where someone has (i.e. within a short time period) resurrected.

Mary is the apostolic witness to resurrection. Her presence in Scripture, her empirical testimony to Jesus' renewed life after death, is Mary speaking to you. She is sharing with you what she has seen – miraculous power transcending death, something she has seen at least twice.

Is she a liar, or is she a witness?

We are approximately 2000 years advanced in calendar time from then, and there have been other accounts of resurrections through the power of God, from highly credible and evidenced sources, but Mary is the first witness to the eternal life offered by Jesus to those who believe Him, and put their faith in Him.

He presents you faultless.

## #2

After Lazarus' resurrection, Jesus is in mortal danger. Not because of the mission he must fulfil very soon, but a premature death at the hands of Jewish killers. The Pharisees, the Jewish leaders, the Sanhedrin (a Jewish religious council which effectively ruled the Jews), were already wary and suspicious of Jesus. He had been very plain about His poor opinion of them and their psychotic religiosity. They perceived Him as a destabilizing threat to their authority with the Jewish people. (Note, this is prior to AD68-73 when the Romans under Titus destroyed Jerusalem and scattered large numbers of surviving Jewish people away from Roman Judea/ Israel - a great *diaspora* - a separation which was not restored until 1948.) John's narrative connects the event of Lazarus' resurrection with the next few days. Jesus is acknowledged as a remarkable man (e.g. **John** 11:50), but the Jews do not acknowledge His Messianic identity; this would be regarded as a liability. He does so much good, and performs so many miracles, that the Jewish leaders want to kill and be rid of Him due to His popularity with the people. They fear His influence so much that they see Him as a direct threat to their governance. As Judas has concluded, they also decide He is an obstacle.

**John** 11:45-57 narrates an interval between Lazarus' resurrection and Jesus' arrival back in Bethany after he had left the area (Bethany is very close to Jerusalem) due to the Sanhedrin's decision that He should die - rather than the edifice of Judaism collapsing, as they feared. They perceive Jesus not as a fulfillment, but as a threat. The high-priest Caiaphas, the Jewish equivalent of a Pope, decides that Jesus must die in order for Judaism and Israel to survive. John observes (11:52) that Jesus was dying for the whole world, but that the Jews did not perceive this. They thought they were disposing of an agitator, not offering the Son of God as the Lamb of God. Their choice to kill Jesus was a planned murder; we often use euphemisms for uncomfortable or shameful choices and actions – we say 'affair' for adultery, 'incentive' for bribery, 'massaging facts' for lying, 'goss' for slander etc. When a popular or well-known person like John F. Kennedy or Mohandas Gandhi is killed we say 'assassination', when really it is simply *murder* and should be identified accurately. It is dishonest and/or misleading to use euphemisms. The Sanhedrin plotted and ultimately committed murder – shamelessly defecating on the sixth Commandment.

At this point, about a week before the Passover when He would be betrayed, arrested, falsely convicted, tortured and ultimately murdered, Jesus moves away from Jerusalem so he is safer from the Sanhedrin for a short time. He goes to the village of Ephraim, which is about 12 km northeast of Jerusalem. How long was Jesus away between Lazarus' resurrection, and the meal at Bethany where Mary anoints Jesus (**John** 12:1-10)? **John** and **Mark** agree that Jesus was in Bethany just prior to the Passover. John positions this before Lazarus was raised, but locates the anointing after Jesus returns from Ephraim. This is a narrative dilemma; John is quite possibly trying to protect not only Mary, but Lazarus. John realizes that Lazarus is in danger of being killed again (by the Jews – the Sanhedrin) – he remains a living testimony to Jesus' power, to **Luke** 1:37.

When Jesus decides to return to Jerusalem, He travels via Bethany. The narrative of **John** 11 seems moreorless continuous from 11:1 to 11:55 when Passover is close. **John** 12:1 tells us that Jesus returned to Bethany six days prior to the Passover, at which time He was judicially murdered.

He arrived back in Bethany on a Saturday. The days and dates are less important than the events – they just give us an impression of the rapidity with which events develop. When Jesus returns to Jerusalem, He knows what awaits Him this time. He is acting with extraordinary courage in the face of an horrific ordeal and death.

Where does he go? Straight back to Bethany (just to the east of Jerusalem – only 1-2 km) to Mary's, Lazarus' and Martha's home. There is a sense in which this is a refuge for Jesus. He loves this family of seeming orphans. Jesus knows what is ahead of Him – only a few days ahead – and this is where He decides to begin His last earthly journey into Jerusalem, where He is the sacrifice for all sin, for all people who will receive Him in faith, forever.

Christians do not make or need blood sacrifices any more. It is finished.

Jesus begins His Messianic route to Golgotha at Bethany, where He is with Mary Magdalene, Martha, and Lazarus. When He has accomplished His universal purpose, when He arises from death, again He is with Mary Magdalene. She bookends His journey of Messianic atonement. It is at the second bookend that we find their second conversation, as recounted by John.

Their second recounted conversation occurs at Jesus' tomb, after Mary has come back after running to tell Peter and John that the tomb has been opened. After they leave, Mary stoops to look inside the tomb (**Luke** 24:3

& **Matthew** 28:6 indicate she goes inside). She sees the two angels who ask her why she is crying:

> (Slightly abridged version of dialogue, from **John** 20:13-17 NLT.)
>
> **Angels**: *'Why are you crying?'*
>
> **MM**: *'Because they have taken away my Lord, and I don't know where they have put him.'*
>
> She looks behind her and sees someone who speaks to her,
>
> **Gardener**: *'Why are you crying? Who are you looking for?'*
>
> She assumes this is a gardener or groundsman.
>
> **MM**: *'Sir, if you have taken him away, tell me where you've put him, and I'll go and get him.'*
>
> **Jesus** *(whom she thought was the* **Gardener***)*: *'Mary.'*
>
> **MM**: *'RABBONI!!'*
>
> **Jesus**: *'Don't cling to me. I haven't yet ascended to the Father. But, go and find my brothers and tell them that I am ascending to my Father and your Father, my God and your God.'*

Mary is the first human to speak with Jesus after His death and resurrection. What Jesus has done is ground-breaking… or literally and cosmically, death-breaking. The act of *creation* (the posit) implies the possibility of *destruction* (the negate). Ontologically, every positive implies its negative, so life implies death, and love implies indifference etc.. The posit must come first; to compact Hegel, *be*ing precedes *no*thing. Jesus has done the impossible and broken that immutable reality. He is the Lord not only of life and death, but of metaphysics. The reality He has created is that positivity and negativity are no longer necessary/inevitable; it is like removing the negative from the positive in electromagnetism. It seems unthinkable. Life does not imply death – there is only **life** $\infty$.

The consequence of death is a function of sin, which in turn is the negative of holiness. All that God creates is derived from Him and is holy. Holiness is the condition of Heaven, and is superlatively excellent. We were intended for life in this way – the Earth was meant to be holy. The places where negativity has not corrupted the Earth out of recognition (e.g. rainforests and oceans) still seem quintessentially wonderful to us – they are reminiscent of Eden, which was Heaven on Earth. They are places we go for holidays – to refresh, restore and recreate. Jesus squares the circle. It is the nature of eternity - it will not negate - life will not die, love will not end.

In their first conversation, Jesus is the one crying. In this second conversation, it is Mary.

In their first conversation, Jesus asks (about Lazarus) 'Where have you put him?' This time, Mary asks (about and to Jesus) 'Where have you put Him?'

Their second conversation actually begins in company with two angels, who are first to address Mary at the tomb.

Mary answers them, and seems strangely indifferent to having two angels talking to her inside a grave. (Although, when Gideon was himself unexpectedly addressed by an angel, he reacted with similar composure, ref. **Judges** 6:11-13). She appears oblivious to the unusual situation – angels just don't generally visit like this. When is the last time you went to visit a loved one's grave and some angels asked you why you were upset? It is not normal. She is totally focused on finding Jesus, whose body she thinks has been moved or stolen. She thinks He is dead, despite having seen her brother resurrected only a fortnight or so before. Jesus' first question makes more sense in this light – really, she should know better.

His second question has a self-evident answer, but He asks anyway. The answer is right in front of her – she just can't see it, because she needs to turn around.

When she faces Him – her answer is manifestly alive and standing there.

You'd think someone as famous as Jesus, whose Name 2000 years later is on millions of lips in respect and reverence, and on millions of others as a swear word, would be easy to find. But no, His body has never been found – not a corpse, or mummy, or skeleton, or tomb, or bone, or pyramid, or fingernail - anywhere. And that's a point.

They seem to be speaking Aramaic together (because Mary says 'Rabboni', not 'Domini'[Latin] or 'καταγετεσ' [Greek]), which makes sense. It's their language. *Rabboni* means 'Teacher, I respect you, I listen, I believe you.'

All He has to *say*, is her name – 'Mary'.

She is not scared, horrified or reluctant; many of us would be shocked and hesitant about seeing someone walking around whom we knew was dead. Impossibly alive and with her again is the beautiful Jesus, the man she could utterly trust, who never used or abused her, who restored to her the beauty and strength God intends for all people. She saw Him shattered, dead and rejected on a brutal cross, and she sees Him now standing there, right after she threw herself on Him, smiling at her and saying, 'It's not the right time, Mary'. She is not excitedly hugging Him because He is repulsive; Mary shows us Jesus the eternal Redeemer of our souls. She is showing us beautiful Jesus. He's back, and He's beautiful, forever.

Even though John does not record a wild embrace as such, Jesus' next words are basically, 'Don't hug me!', as He has to extricate Himself from her arms (it's hard to 'cling' with anything else). This Jesus is not a remote and austere figure, a guru sitting silently on a mountain and keeping people away. This is a man who ought to be a corpse, trying to avoid being kissed and hugged soon after being resurrected. His explanation to Mary that He has not yet ascended to the Father, makes more sense to Him than to us. (He is likely referencing His role as great High Priest making atonement in the Inner Sanctuary of the Temple, for all time and eternity, and He needs to enter the Holiest of Holies in complete purity – see **Hebrews** 7:24-25.) He is clearly and physically present though, as Mary would have had trouble clinging to an incorporeal phantasm, or ghost. This is flesh and blood. We know He still carried the wounds of his trial and crucifixion (He later exposed them to Thomas), and perhaps that partly explains His reluctance to hug – it may still have been painful? He had sustained horrendously traumatic injuries to His back, face, arms/wrists/hands, scalp, lower legs/ankles/feet, and torso.

Mary is before Him, the first witness, and He is very alive and eternally well.

## #3

This third episode is a harder conversation to track through available sources, because this is the wordless communication – what we would call *body language.* Just as the dialogues between Mary and Jesus are minimal, so also are descriptions of the facial expressions, the movements, and the actions – the conversations without words. They are clear where we can see them though. Mary shows Jesus to us through her non-verbal responses and actions with Him.

Her body language is hard to visualize, certainly, but we have glimpses, and some very clear ones at that. Body language is often more disclosing than spoken words.

Mary's representation through three personas is demanding. Some references are direct, i.e. her name is used. Others are pronouns indicating Mary. Others are associative; we know it is Mary through context and shared reference between incidents. The reason it is difficult to be exact is because there are references to groups of women where the text is not directly and/or unambiguously referencing Mary.

With that in mind, the Gospels mention Mary in numerous contexts:

- as the penitent woman who anointed Jesus,
- as a woman listening to Jesus' teaching,
- as a witness to Lazarus' miraculous resurrection
- as an onlooker at the crucifixion,
- as a witness to the empty tomb and risen Christ.

There are *at least* thirteen (13) references to Mary in **Matthew**. **Mark** and **Luke** each reference Mary fifteen (15) times. **John** references Mary twenty-one (21) times.

Mary finds Jesus at Simon's house. In this **Luke** 7:36-50 incident at Simon's table, Jesus sits down to eat. There is nothing unusual or notable about this, except that at feasts or occasions, people tended to recline with their legs and feet stretched out. As already noted, it's quite Socratic – reminiscent of a symposium, in Greek fashion, with people arrayed around central figures poised to discuss great themes. Jesus 'sat down', but as in reclining for the meal. This is why Mary is behind him (cf. v.38), rather than before Him, or under Him (i.e. under a table). He is not at a raised table, He is reclining and eating the food in front of Him. Jesus knows what Mary is doing as He can feel and see her; He recounts this shortly with Simon.

Jesus does not ridicule, revile, or reject Mary. She is doing this because she knows who Jesus is – she is aware of His deity, and in v.48 she accepts

His forgiveness of her sins, something God alone can do. Like most people at that time, she knew He was a miracle-worker, and He freed people of evil spirits (cf. **Luke** 6:18). He may well already have done this for Mary. By anointing His feet, she is doing something unusual, something done for the dead. Washing His feet is one thing – an act of welcome and hospitality. Anointing them is another. Washing feet was also a task for slaves/servants. Mary is positioning herself as in submission to Jesus. In this whole scenario, Mary is silent. We have no word from her. She is crying, so perhaps some sniffles.

Simon speaks to himself (v.39); he could be speaking under his breath, or thinking inwardly to himself, i.e. silently in his mind. Either way, Jesus knows what he is thinking.

Jesus shows no overt reaction. He is not described as doing anything other than receiving Mary's attention, her tears of gratitude and sorrow, her libations of acknowledgement. She is anointing Him prodigally and regally with prohibitively expensive nard.

Mary is repentant, but she is no impoverished slave.

- *Jesus faces Mary.* In v.44a, Jesus *speaks* to Simon the Pharisee, but *faces* Mary; an unusual dynamic. He asks Simon to look at her too, all while He recounts her kindnesses, her respect, her consideration, her evident love. The last words Jesus speaks are directed to Mary: He says, 'Your sins are forgiven. Your faith has saved you; go in peace.' Jesus forgives sins because He always has that authority – this incident occurs before His death and resurrection. We will all face Him.
- *Jesus accepts her.* His entire demeanour during her attentions to Him is accepting, tolerant and empathic. He does not kick at her, berate her, throw scraps at her etc.. He accepts Mary, her feelings

of guilt, her tears, her anointing, and her kissing his feet. Jesus has been anointed by Mary's actions (cf. v.47), and He anoints her with His commendations. When He speaks of her to Simon, He salutes her offerings of love. Love is as love does.

- *Mary is not ashamed.* She is behaving submissively, penitently, while she kisses, washes and anoints Him, but she is not cringing in shame. Her actions are also grateful and appreciative. Jesus has *released* her, transforming her life; she now travels with Him, and certainly does not engage in the activities Simon describes as shameful. *Guilt* is knowing we have done something wrong and feeling remorse. *Shame* is knowing that we have done something wrong, and believing we are bad. Jesus removes both from Mary. She is free.

**Luke** 10:38-42 describes for us a later visit by Jesus to Mary's home, where she lived with Martha who has invited Jesus to a meal. Mary simply sits at Jesus' feet.

- *Jesus welcomes Mary.* There is a simplicity and naturalness in her quiet positioning at Jesus' feet – an innocence of grace. Jesus is teaching, He is the centre, the λογοσ ('logos'). This is all we see of Jesus here. He is *likely* sitting, as He usually did when teaching and ministering (cf. **Matthew** 5:1 & 15:29). Mary is at His feet again. Jesus accepts her and her position, He does not try to change her. Her sister does, but Jesus clearly and gently corrects Martha. He is characteristically direct and clear.

- *Jesus addresses the core issue.* In the **Luke** 7 and **Luke** 10 incidents above, Jesus focuses directly and centrally on what matters in both situations. When Mary anoints and washes Jesus' feet, He simply allows her to do what she needs to do – she needs to welcome Him.

This is significant; she is a woman who has had little or no free choice in her life over volitional uses of her mind or body; here she freely chooses to *align* and *submit* to the teaching and guidance of the most powerful man in history. *She submits to His authority (or 'Lordship') and dominion* because she wishes this. She affirms that He is the Way, the Truth, and the Life for her, and she emphasises Jesus' absolute welcome in her life. Jesus accepts this, and accepts her welcome – that is the core issue. When she is silently rebuked and rejected by the venomous Simon, Jesus answers him but *He looks at Mary*; He confirms Simon's assessment of her sinfulness, but immediately disintegrates the grounds for any condemnation. He forgives her totally and fully. Grace is the core issue, and Jesus demonstrates total grace with Mary. At her home with Martha, Mary just sits at Jesus' feet. She belongs, and is completely welcomed and comfortable there. Belonging is the core issue, and Jesus confirms to her that she is in the right place. Simultaneously, He tells Martha to pay attention – but gently. He is direct and clear with both sisters.

- *Mary is serene.* She teaches us beautifully and dispassionately from the feet of Jesus; a place of acceptance, belonging, security and growth. Jesus says that she has chosen well; He will not take her choice away. Her simultaneously oxymoronic submission *and* freedom are interdependent. Martha's askant rebuke notwithstanding, Mary is secure and she makes no attempt at justification. There is no need; she is free, and shows us that ultimately we cannot hold this mortal and terrestrial life – we all have to reckon inevitably with death. The only thing that matters is our relationship with God: she trains our attention towards this – as Jesus says, to the only thing that matters (nb. **Luke** 10:42); direct and clear.

*'Though lovers be lost love shall not;*
*And death shall have no dominion.'*[35]

Jesus and Mary were not lovers in the modern sexual sense, but they were lovers in soul, loyalty, faith and joy. Mary knew her source of life and fullness.

**Matthew** (in 26:6-13) and **Mark** (in 14:1-9) don't add much more to our visualisation of Jesus with Mary at Simon's house in Bethany. They do both focus on her anointing of Jesus' head (while **Luke** indicates she also anointed His feet) with nard, and that Jesus openly rebuked His disciples for complaining that Mary had wasted a colossal sum in emptying her expensive jar of nard over Jesus' head. She gave Him everything – to the last drop, shocking many observers, and pleasing Jesus. Luke's additional detail is important because she anoints His feet for death, while anointing His head indicates His royalty as a King[36]. Jesus adds that her prodigality is not excessive and that if anyone feels strongly about what they deem her extravagance, which could have funded charity for the poor, they can provide for the poor in perpetuity out their own goodness and substance.

**John** records that Mary anointed Jesus' feet with the nard; he does not include mention of His head. Nor does John indicate Jesus' position or posture, but he does record Jesus' rebuke to Judas. Each Gospel clearly captures Jesus' *defence* of Mary, and His grace towards her. John adds the

---

35    Dylan Thomas 1943, *And Death Shall Have No Dominion*, in poets.org Academy of American Poets website.

36    N.B. Monarchs across Christendom's kingdoms and states have for millennia sworn fealty and allegiance to Jesus as God and King. There is no doubting that Jesus is acknowledged, regardless of whatever hypocrisies and wrongs are subsequently committed by individuals and governments. From Alfred the Great and Charlemagne to the present, Jesus is historically recognized as the ultimate King.

detail that Jesus foretells He will not be long with these assembled people; He is anticipating His death in six days.

Between the four Gospel accounts, we have a quadrilateral view of this event, and Jesus' actions and behaviour from each perspective.

If, as written in **John** 11:2, we accept that this had already happened when Jesus went to resurrect Lazarus, we are now at the last documented personal encounter between Jesus and Mary Magdalene of Bethany *before* His death. The anointing event happened penultimately, according to this verse. Some of this has already been considered, i.e. Jesus' sorrow that people did not believe He exercised power over death (ref. 11:33 & 38a). He has already told Martha that He is 'the resurrection'(11:25); He does not repeat this to Mary. Shortly, she will see this for herself.

What and who Mary saw before any other human being did, is the impossible fact of the Christian Faith – as Dylan Thomas said – *'And death shall have no dominion.'* She is our witness that Jesus is the Truth.

- *Mary responds immediately to Jesus.* **John** 11:29 describes Mary's response to a request from Jesus to meet with Him. She receives the message via Martha and responds instantaneously; He matters to her, and she prioritises accordingly. It's almost startling, even across the 2000 year gap from then till now - Jesus asks, and Mary complies, making haste to see Him (ref. 11:31a). Not only do we see the fit and strong Mary hurrying to Jesus - as she does later on Resurrection morning - we see her with a following of people. Martha is not depicted like this; Mary attracts people.

- *Mary falls at His feet (***John** 11:32*).* This is the behaviour of a slave/servant, *or* a soldier/comrade-in-arms. Jesus never asks such a sign of deference from her - she is either acting from habit, or from respect and love. You decide.

• *Jesus is troubled by the fear of death He witnesses, and He prays.* He is described as 'indignant' and 'troubled' (**John**11:33b & 38a). He knows this is ahead of Him. He hears people saying that He could heal the blind but He could not save Lazarus from death, and He is perplexed. Death is a phase, a stage – it is not a permanence. As humans, we will inevitably all come to this place of dying & death, but on the whole we avoid the subject through denial and deliberate ignorance. Calling out to a dead man is foolishness, but Jesus does it anyway, after He openly prays to God for attention. Mary witnesses the whole thing; she sees Him crying with frustration at people's obtuseness and faithlessness (including her own), His call to God in prayer, His marching straight up to a tomb and talking to her dead brother, whom she then sees emerging wraith-like from the murk. Jesus does all this so that people (us) will know that God is powerful over even death, and that He cares for us (**John** 11:42). Yet we choose blindness (ref. **John** 9:41), and we fear death, and we will all be as Lazarus eventually; we will all be on the other side of the tombstone. Just as surely, resurrection is this side. The choice is now. Like Jesus, we can pray at any time. He is the Resurrection. He hears you.

• *Mary is sensitive to Jesus.* Almost as a footnote (but I'll include it here), there is a curious little parallel between Mary's response to Jesus on Resurrection morning, and her response to His request to see her before he raises Lazarus.

In **John** 11:28, Martha tells Mary that Jesus wants to see her. Mary's response is immediate, but the way Martha tells her is, *'The Teacher is here and wants to see you.'* (Martha could as easily have said 'Jesus is here…'.) In **John** 20:16, at the tomb when Jesus rises from death, Mary calls Him *'Rabboni'*, and leaps at Him. In the

**John** 11:28 instance, John records Martha using the Greek word *διδασκελος* (Greek for 'teacher') rather than 'Rabboni', but that is how the Hebrew/Aramaic term would translate. We need to remember that Mary and Jesus spoke Aramaic with each other, not Greek. Mary also responds immediately, almost impulsively, to Jesus' presence. It is likely that Martha actually said 'Rabboni' to Mary, which has an electric effect on her. She is very sensitive to Him, and 'Rabboni' is a kind of endearment. It is not romantic, but it is close. She reacts instantaneously to Him.

Mary was the first human to see and witness Jesus resurrected and alive after his death by crucifixion, but Mary was also the first human Jesus saw.

She witnesses to us that everything He said and did was real; He is the Truth.

From Mary's position, Jesus is extraordinarily powerful:

- demons screamed in fear, submitted to Him, and begged to be spared destruction,
- dead children sat up and resumed normal life,
- paraplegics stood up and walked,
- two sardines and five small buns fed 20000 people,
- slaves were as valuable as governors,
- women were equally intelligent and important humans,
- deep water formed a solid footing,
- wisdom formed the foundation of knowledge,
- crowds heard divine truth taught understandably.

Her own life is a testimony to the healing and liberty offered freely by her Rabboni. She had directly experienced demons' hatred and loathing of

Jesus, and she had experienced Jesus' universal power and dynamic love. Her life is compelling; *listen to her.* She reflects and glows with Grace, illuminating Jesus the Christ to us. She is telling us: ***Trust Him.***

Mary Magdalene of Bethany knew Jesus the Christ, Messiah, Son of God, Redeemer of humanity; she knows Him physically and materially; she walked with Him, knew His face, knew His voice.

She is now witnessing to us about Him.

Excepting some oblique references to women in **Acts**, this culminates our seeing Jesus through Mary's eyes. There is one further likely reference to her in **Romans** 16:6; it is debatable, though certainly probable.

She leaves us in history at this point, and aside from distant legends and apocryphal tales, we know nothing more of her life - except that she is now safely and eternally with Him.

∞

# Jehanne Darc.

Also known as *Jeanne d'Ay de Domrémy, Jeannette Darc, Jeanne d'Arc, Joan of Arc, La Pucelle (d'Orleans), the Maid of Orleans*[37], and *the Maid.*

> *'Were it not by God's Grace, I could do nothing…'*
> *– Jehanne, 24/02/1431.*

Her name is spelled in numerous ways prior to C18th. Her own hand-written rendering is **Jehanne**.

So, *Jehanne* it is.

The objective is to see Jesus as Jehanne saw and knew Him. His Name was her last spoken word.

They were in relationship, but please realize from the outset here that Jehanne never explicitly *identifies* Jesus as a Voice or Being whom she sees/perceives with her physical senses, as she does others. Jehanne was often very guarded in her commentary on her own experiences, but she does leave us a trail of breadcrumbs. As an historical figure, Jehanne herself has been studied and written about considerably more than most other well-known historical figures. Estimates at the number of books about her hover around the 20,000 mark (2025 atow). Articles, essays and papers would considerably expand that estimate of this body of work. (And this text, I guess, must then be 20,001.)

Note though, that while there is some detail provided for context, *this is not a narrative of Jehanne's life.* Biographical narratives or histories are available from other authors who have done excellent work (e.g. French historian Regine Pernoud) - you will notice some of the better ones referenced

---

[37] The title 'Pucelle d'Orleans' (which translates to 'Maid of Orleans' in English) was never used by Jehanne in her lifetime. She did call herself 'Pucelle'. cf. Régine Pernoud 1962, *Joan of Arc: by Herself and her Witnesses*, p. 105.

throughout this work, if you are interested to know more narrative history about Jehanne.

This text is history about her life relationship with **Jesus the Christ**.

Whenever Jehanne speaks about God, she is always sincerely reverent, respectful and deferential. In her letter to Philip the Good, Duke of Burgundy, on Monday 17ᵗʰ July 1429, she explicitly identifies Jesus as *King of Heaven* and her '…rightful and sovereign Lord.'[38] On Saturday 3ʳᵈ March 1431, Jehanne testifies during her interrogation before the mercenary and abominable Trial of Condemnation that, 'I do best by obeying and serving my sovereign Lord – that is, God.'[39] It is plain and clear that Jehanne recognizes Jesus as God. Her 'sovereign Lord' is Jesus, who is God. She is not at all confused about the Christian understanding of Jesus' identity as God within a trinity[40]. It is almost impossible to learn more of Jehanne without, as Regine Pernoud observes, finding in ourselves, '…a reason to love her.'[41] At her core (it is a shame that we lose the French emotionality of '*coeur*' or 'heart' from our English usage, meaning 'centre'), Jehanne is a fully realized spiritual being without being remotely priggish or religiously sanctimonious. Spirituality was simply life to her, where love for God was

---

[38]   Willard Trask 1996, *Joan of Arc: In Her Own Words*, p.55.

[39]   Ibid. p.107.

[40]   N.B. the Christian concept of the *Trinity*, wherein God is both One and also Three, is axiomatic. We (humans) are created *In God's Image*, and we are also three – we are *spirit* (the eternal self), *soul* (personality), and *body* (the physical host and temporal expression for the spirit and soul). We are made in God's Image, so of course we reflect His Triune Nature. God is One and only One, in three Persons. Male and Female are equal expressions of God; God is both Male and Female, and created humans as two equivalent genders, which when reunited in sex alchemize the power of God to create life itself. It is shallow nonsense to reject God as Trinity, or misrepresent Him as a pantheon. It is equally nonsense to deny God is two equal genders (ref. **Genesis** 1:27 and 5:1-2). The Bible itself is plain and clear about this.

[41]   Op.cit. R. Pernoud 1962, p.277.

as natural as for her family, or rainstorms in Spring. And she loved Him as she loved all that she enjoyed as good.

If Jehanne could parachute into our present-day, via a time-machine or Tardis, of course she would be overwhelmed in many ways, but it would be interesting to see her response to common language – she was highly intolerant of blasphemy and would be aghast at cheap patois splashing 'Oh My God' and 'Jesus H. Christ' through conversations as if they were inconsequential. She was no wilting violet; and she would loudly confront anyone if they disrespected God, and therefore Jesus. Many a hard and tough French soldier (or earthy Scots highlander) felt her ire when they cursed within earshot. They didn't do it twice. She had pluck by the bucket.

On 17th December 1455, Guillaume Manchon, who had been a prin-ciple notary (i.e. scribe or recorder) at the Trial of Condemnation in 1431, testified to the Rehabilitation (or Nullification) Trial that it had always been the intention of the judges at the Trial of Condemnation to kill Jehanne. A member of the Rouen clergy, Jean Lohier, who was brave as well as scru-pulous, told Manchon in 1431 concerning the court that, '…it was their intention to put her to death.'[42] The trial of condemnation of 1431, which ordered Jehanne be murdered by burning at the stake, was always simply a mechanism for judicial murder, much like the *Volksgerichtshof* centuries later during the Third Reich. Tragically, the trial was instituted and counte-nanced by the Catholic Church, which Jehanne had always revered, obeyed and loved (n.b. in medieval Western Europe, there was only one Church, unlike today when there are many different denominations). The King of France, Charles VII, whose sacring (i.e. anointing and coronation) she had won, was silent; he made no serious attempt to redeem or rescue her.

---

[42]   Guillaume Manchon 17/12/1455, *Third Enquiry, fourth examination,* Trial of Rehabilitation. Retrieved from Jeanne-darc.info

As Dietrich Bonhoeffer observed:

> '*Schweigen im angesichts des bösen ist selbst böse. Gott wird uns nicht als schuldlos betrachten. Nicht zu sprechen ist sprechen. Nicht zu handeln ist handeln.*'

> ('*Silence in the face of evil is itself evil. God shall not hold us guiltless. Not to speak is to speak. Not to act is to act.*')[43]

Even though Jehanne is well-known or 'famous', important aspects and details of her life are generally unknown. For sake of context, some bare essentials of biographical content are included here also; if you know detail about her, you will recognize their relevance.

[*Note on textual translations*: the main primary sources for Jehanne's life and story are the transcripts of her trials in 1431 (*Trial of Condemnation*) and 1455-56 (*Trial of Nullification/Rehabilitation*). The primary texts used as source references in this work are taken from Søren Bie's 2024 website www.jeanne-darc.info. These are eminently credible sources.

A further record of Jehanne's testimony about her life and mission was taken at Poitiers in March 1429, and is known as the *Book of Poitiers*. This document would have been the most reliable contemporary record of Jehanne's own words, and was ordered by the Dauphin Charles who wanted assurance that Jehanne was actually sent from God. At Poitiers there was a College of Theology loyal to the Dauphin where scholars and churchmen could test her credibility. This Book is referenced by Jehanne and others during her trials, but is not extant. It would have been the clearest and most faithfully recorded account of what Jehanne actually said, but it was either destroyed by the Anglo-Burgundians and corrupt churchmen

---

[43] This statement is generally attributed to Dietrich Bonhoeffer, but as a verbal statement, not a publication.

- the same ones who engineered the travesty of her accusation and death - or it has been lost somewhere. The only scraps of testimony from the Book of Poitiers are secondary references at the subsequent trials. There are other sources, such as the Inquiry to exonerate Jehanne conducted in 1449, but these are the most referenced ones. The scribes/notaries at the trials recorded the proceedings in the French language. This French [aka *Middle French*] differs markedly from modern French, in the same way as medieval English [aka *Middle English*] differs from modern English; but, they are somewhat comprehensible to careful readers. The French was then translated into Latin, the language of the Roman Catholic Church. So, Jehanne's actual answers and observations in her own provincial French, are lost. They have to be reconstructed from Latin. Translations never exactly capture the precise meanings of the original languages; nuances and cadences of meaning are missed or unintentionally misrepresented through inexact selections of words and/or syntactic constructions. This must be borne in mind when listening to the source material for Jehanne. What she actually meant may have been considerably changed through translation.]

There is strong evidence that many records were *deliberately omitted, distorted or subverted*, mostly deriving from the Trial of Condemnation. But, exaggerations and convenient omissions tend to happen where incrimination or harm to reputation is possible. E.g. Jean Lemaitre records that in prison on 24/5/1431, Jehanne requested and had her hair shaven from her head after consenting to wear womens' clothes (this after firmly and consistently resisting such until this time, probably because men's clothes gave her greater protection against sexual molestation)[44]. On 5/3/1449 in the First Inquiry to exonerate Jehanne, Jean Toutmouillé recalls that on 30/5/1431 he was assisting Martin Ladvenu, a priest assigned to hear

---

[44] Brother Jean Lemaitre 24/5/1431, *Exhortation made to Jeanne by the Deputy Inquisitor in Prison*, retrieved from Jeanne-arc.info

Jehanne's confession before her death. In describing Jehanne's distress on hearing she was to be burned to death, as an eye-witness he observes that she was, '...tearing her hair...', and crying, '...in a sad and pitiful manner...'[45]. Of course she was. How though, could she tear out hair which was shaven, and not there? The records from the time - even, or perhaps especially, the official ones - are highly questionable. Their accuracy must be held in tension with the ambitions, dissimulations and evasions of people involved in a massive and controversial injustice, in which they wished to avoid any incrimination.

*Lexical note*: Jehanne's native tongue is provincial Lorrainian French, and the written French language uses *written accents* far more than standard English. So, in French, the name of Jehanne's village 'Domrémy' has an *aigu* accent over the 'é' thus. In English, Domrémy would be 'Domremy'. The French word 'forêt' [Eng. trans.'forest'], has the 'ê' thus with a *circumflex*, whereas in English it would normally just be rendered 'forest' without any accent. Unless there is a textual need [e.g. in a direct quotation or proper noun], accents will be used according to *standard English usage*.

## The unusual, supernatural and miraculous swirl around Jehanne Darc.

In the afternoon of Monday 12th March 1431, Jehanne related to the Inquisitorial Court which was persecuting her in the Chateau de Bouvreuil in Rouen, that when she was about 14 years old (i.e. five years previously) her father Jacques had dreamed of her so powerfully, that he was deeply and frantically disturbed.

---

[45]    Brother Jean Toutmouillé 3/5/1449, *Inquiry into the case of Jeanne d'Arc*, retrieved from Jeanne-darc.info

> '... My mother told me many times that my father had spoken
> of having dreamed that I, Jeannette[46], his daughter, went
> away with the men-at-arms ('gens-des-armes'). My father and
> mother took great care to keep me safe, and held me in much
> subjection. I obeyed them in everything, except in the case
> at Toul – the action for marriage. I have heard my mother
> say that my father told my brothers "Truly, if I thought this
> thing would happen that I have dreamed about my daughter,
> I would wish you to drown her; and, if you would not do it, I
> would drown her myself!" He nearly lost his senses when I went
> to Vaucouleurs.'[47]

There are different, plausible ways to interpret this in its English
rendering:

1. That Jehanne was taken away by men-at-arms (soldiers) and sexually abused, e.g. raped and/or forced into prostitution.
2. That Jehanne was taken away by soldiers and murdered through
   some horrific means, e.g. burning.

The dream is not completely explained either by her mother or by
Jehanne, and we only know that the dream so disturbed her parents, Jacques
and Isabelle, that they kept Jehanne very close, which Jehanne experienced
as being 'in much subjection'. Their motive was certainly derived from
love and concern for Jehanne, but she experienced this as control and
constriction. 'Subjection' implies tight restriction. (Interestingly, teenagers'
perceptions of parental concerns don't seem to have changed that much

---

[46]    'Jeannette' is a French feminine diminutive of 'Jehanne'.
[47]    Jehanne Darc testimony 12/03/1431, *Trial of Condemnation: Third Private
        Examination*, retrieved from Jeanne-darc.info.

over centuries.) Jehanne's implication is that she was over-protected, if the translation is accurate. Jacques' reaction to the dream is of profound and abyssal alarm; he even contemplates requiring her brothers to kill Jehanne, or doing so himself, to avoid whatever fate he saw awaiting her. The dream was a nightmare, not a vision of a consecratedly sovereign France ruled by its restored and anointed King.

Most people dream as part of our usual psycho-emotional life, as part of the subconscious interpretation and supervision of our conscious existence. Occasionally we might have a more vivid, or even a profoundly impacting dream. Jacques' was not an ordinary dream; he experienced it as premonitory, and he watched Jehanne carefully thereafter. From Jehanne's perspective, he was overbearing. The dream shook him markedly, distressing him to the point that he considered drastic steps to shield Jehanne; there is clearly more of this dream that he did not share. His preference for her death by water is a possible clue. The men-at-arms taking Jehanne away signifies that Jacques could not prevent this in his dream – that there was disempowerment, and as a manifestly caring father he could not protect his daughter. He could not save her, and this he feared – impotence… and fire.

It could also be that Jehanne is contextualizing her parents' response to Jacques' dream by explaining that they *habitually and always* kept Jehanne in subjection; however, this is mitigated somewhat by other indications that as a younger child Jehanne had considerable liberty in playing with other children and attending church without undue restriction[48].

It seems more likely that the 'subjection' began, or intensified, at about age 14, because of Jacques' dream. Jehanne mentions a marriage proposal/plan, which she had clearly refused to accept (cf. her reference to a court at Toul). That the marriage did not take place perhaps indicates that her

---

[48]    Willard Trask 1996, *Joan of Arc: In Her Own Words*, pp.4-5.

parents *did* listen to her when she refused the marriage they had arranged for her, which had connection to the village of Toul, a significance now lost. It seems that if she was adamant, her mind could not be changed. Arranged marriages in adolescence were quite normal in medieval Europe. It was an arranged and unwelcome marriage plan though. Being mentioned in connection to Jacques' dream, it is likely that the marriage was a further variety of protection that Jacques tried to engineer for his youngest child and daughter. Having a husband would add to the layers of security Jacques and Isabelle attempted to weave around Jehanne.

There is no record of Jehanne seeing her parents again *after* the coronation of Charles VII in July 1429. The six months between February and July 1429 were the most extraordinary period of Jehanne's incredible prophetic and military career. After leaving her home village Domremy for the last time in December 1428/January 1429, she was to see her parents together again only once, in Rheims. Her brother Pierre either accompanies her in her journeys, or he joins her later in Orleans, possibly at the behest of Jacques, who may even have encouraged Pierre's attendance on Jehanne to realize a drowning, should it prove the most merciful option. Pierre was likely a source of news for the Darc family; but, her sister Catherine's death in 1429 elicits no recorded comment or reaction from Jehanne, so if news was communicated, it was probably slow, limited (they could not write to each other because they were illiterate, and had no or extremely limited access to secure mail anyway), or one-way. Someone had told Jehanne for instance, that her father had been stricken with alarm at her leaving Domremy for Vaucouleurs.

Jacques dies in 1431, soon after Jehanne's death.

The dream, his great fear, came upon him – it was not only soldiers taking her away to abuse her, it was fire. The dream portended both. He thought water would be a kinder end.

## Origins.

Scholarly consensus fixes her birth in January 1412. She was born on the eastern borders of France, in the small village of Domremy, a twin village with adjacent Greux, within the Duchy of Bar and the Province of Lorraine, in the Meuse Valley (the *Meuse* River becomes the *Maas* further downstream, e.g. at *Maas*tricht in Holland).

Jacques Darc and Isabelle (aka 'Ysabeau') Vouthon married in around 1400. She was about 15, he was older. Isabelle was also *Isabelle Romée de Vouthon*. They had five children, of whom Jehanne was youngest. The Hundred Years War impacted all aspects of life around Domremy at the time, with brigands and mercenaries roaming the woods and byways. But her childhood seems otherwise to have been reasonably happy and stable. A constant for Jehanne from her infancy was the consolation and centrality of Faith. She grew up in a devotedly Catholic family within a dedicatedly Catholic community in deeply Catholic France.

Her faith was emphatically Catholic, and at the centre of her faith was Jesus Christ. She was not so much religious, as spiritually immersed. Unswervingly.

Without Jesus Christ, we would never have heard of this girl/woman from the eastern borders of France, any more than the other billions of people who pass unremarked through history.

Isabelle had earned the right to add the appellation *Romée* to her name because she had completed a recognized pilgrimage (i.e. recognized within the Catholic Church); it's possible she went to Rome, but there are many pilgrim trails. With brigands in the woods and mercenaries on the roads in the 1390's, wherever Isabelle went, she was courageous, intrepid, and confident. More than likely, this was the assurance of faith in a trusted God. Venturing abroad (remembering that in medieval times, most ordinary people never travelled more than a horizon away from their birthplaces) was extremely adventuresome. Isabelle was a dauntless and strong woman, characteristics she passed on to her daughter. Later in her life, in the late 1440's when she was in her mid-late 50's, she took on the whole machinery of the Catholic hierarchy to attempt some justice for her daughter, who is today a Saint, not a heretic, because Isabelle pursued truth.

Jehanne's life consists of many ironies: she was illiterate, but has generated and inspired over 20,000 books; she never sought wealth or money for herself, yet arranged with Charles VII for Domremy to be exempted from taxes forthwith from 1429; she revered and loved the Catholic Church, which in turn betrayed and murdered her; she refused any connection or interest in superstition or folklore, but was accused of witchcraft; she ensured the dauphin Charles was consecrated and crowned King of France, but was abandoned by him at her condemnation trial and greatest need; she paved the way for France's ultimate victory in the Hundred Years' War, but she lived for only 19 years and five months and did not see the climax of her valour[49].

The border was not merely geographic, but political. Very close to Domremy, slightly to the south, the Burgundians held sway. Northwards and north-westwards was a part of France mostly under English government excepting Vaucouleurs, the fort of Robert de Baudricourt – the only Captain loyal to the Dauphin in the whole area. The Duke of Burgundy (Philip the Good, who was loyal to England, not to the Crown of France) dominated the areas north-eastwards and southwards. To Jehanne, true France was away directly to her west and south-west; in Domremy, she was barely in France at all. To the east was Lorraine, which was Burgundian and not regarded as true France, and the German realms of the Holy Roman

---

[49]  The so-called *Hundred Years War* actually dragged on for 116 years (or - it could be argued - even 221 years if the repossession of Calais into France is reckoned).

Empire were further again, east of the Rhine Valley. It was a politically and culturally fraught area. Jehanne grew up among the tensions between the English, the loyal French (i.e. loyal to the Dauphin Charles and the House of Valois, and also generally known as 'Armagnacs'), and the Burgundians; she knew from personal observation that raids and skirmishes happened around Domremy, even forcing her family to flee from Burgundian forces. Domremy was raided and burned by Burgundians in 1428, possibly in reaction to rumours of a girl in Domremy who was claiming a role in affairs of state. Ironically, they went south for safety to Neufchateau, in Burgundian territory, where there was some sympathy for loyalists[50]. Jehanne lived within general civic stability, peppered with these frequent turmoils.

The Catholic Church exerted influence and pressure across Christendom, which in the C15th was divided into the Orthodox Eastern Church and the Roman Catholic Western Church. The Catholic Church was riven by internal schism, with two serious claimants to the papacy in Jehanne's time: Urban VI in Rome, and Clement VII in France, in Avignon. In Jehanne's brief lifetime, the Church had largely solidified around the Roman Pope, but there was still resistance. The Church had also been loudly rebuked and assailed by reformers who were disgusted by the blatant politicking, institutional hypocrisies, and financial avarices of the Church. John Wycliffe in England and Jan Hus in Bohemia had stirred dissent and disaffection with the institutional Catholic Church. These bold contradictions against the Catholic Church hyper-sensitized the Catholic hierarchy to any popular movements which prioritized personal relationship and responsibility to God, over duty and allegiance to the Church. Wycliffe was controversial

---

[50]  For an account of this, see R. Pernoud & M-V. Clin 1998, *Joan of Arc: Her Story*, pp.17-18. **N.B.** Pernoud's and Clin's text is skilfully adept, and is an engaging account of Jehanne's historical presence.

in England, and the English government had swung behind the Church, mostly because the Church supported the English Monarchy. This had lethal consequences for Jehanne a little later. The Church had already burned Hus to death in 1415 for his opposition; a cautionary event not heeded closely enough.

## Relationships.

- **Jacques Darc,** c.1375 – 1431, her father.
- **Isabelle Darc** (nee **Romee de Vouthon),** c.1385-1457, her mother.
- **Jacques (Jacquemin)** 1402-1452, **Jehan (Jean)** 1404-1477, **Catherine** 1405-1429, & **Pierre** 1408-1467, her siblings.
- **Friends, neighbours and relatives in Domremy and environs.** (Most of these knew Jehanne from her infancy, childhood and adolescence, in and around Domremy.)
- **Companions in arms.** (There were many: they will appear as their perspectives/observations on Jehanne are recounted.)
- **Saint Catherine of Alexandria, Saint Margaret of Antioch, and the Archangels Michael and Gabriel.** (Some of the supernatural beings who guided and encouraged Jehanne; she often called them her 'Voices'.)
- **Officials and Church clergy.** (Most of these were complicit in Jehanne's persecution and judicial/ecclesiastical murder; a very few had the courage and strength to speak in her behalf.)

## Jacques Darc.

Jehanne's father was a farmer, from Ceffonds, about 80km west from Domremy. Little is known of his background, except his own father was a farmer, and like most French peasants, he was Catholic.

He married Isabelle Romee de Vouthon (Vouthon is a small district just north-west of Domremy) when he was about 25, somewhat late for a man in his time, and moved to Domremy. The farm there was substantial and included a stone house – the only one in the village. This property was almost certainly a marriage dowry from Isabelle's family. They also had some money, so while they were peasants, they were relatively well-off ones.

Times were turbulent when he married in about 1400. The Hundred Years War was raging, and Domremy was situated on antagonistic borders – the Royaume de France (the Kingdom of France), the territories under control of Burgundy, and territory under English rule. Tensions here could and did manifest as marauding and bandit attacks. In about 1420, after France's Royal House and Kingdom suffered cumulative, withering defeats from the English (e.g. Agincourt 1415), Jacques was made Dean (*Fr.* 'Doyen') of Domremy, a post which involved protecting the village and enforcing the laws (similar to being a Sheriff). This implies that Jacques knew how to fight and wield common weapons such as sword and arbalest (crossbow), and how to organize people. Jehanne showed familiarity with weapons – she learned some of their use while young.

For anyone, the father-child relationship is formatively essential, emotionally nourishing, and cognitively instrumental; it is meant to be (and the 'meant' is understood as 'meant by God'). If this positive, paternal presence is missing from a child's life, it has consequences later, which begs the question – when is one a *child*?

Legal definitions of this vary from one culture to another. It could be between birth and 18, or it could be nuanced somewhere between 3/4 and 12/13 years? God's definition would be a constant, but God does not provide an exact formula. He does indicate that adulthood begins at approximately 13 years; from this adolescent age, we graduate steadily into mature people who are fully functional as independent humans by about

18 years. David was about 13 when he took on Goliath; Jesus was about 13 when He taught the scribes and priests in the Jerusalem Temple. Josiah was still a child when he became King of Judah at age 8, and needed advisors (principally his mother Jedidah); at 18, Josiah (who is Israel/Judah's - and the world's - greatest King[51]) made independent decisions and restored Judah to the Way of God. Biblically, childhood seems to be from conception through to about 12 years. Adulthood develops from about 13.

Children are very impressionable – we learn the essentials of life (from the same word stem as 'essence') and develop our fundamental values in this phase. While still needing guidance, we are becoming capable at about 13, and we are basically mature at 18 when we make independent and responsible choices.

In about 1424/1425, aged 12/13, Jehanne began receiving guidance and tuition from Heavenly spiritual beings. Her relationships with them are fundamental to her brief life. Remember that at 17/18, she was actually commanding French armies in the field - in combat.

Think on that.

It is stupendous. The Dauphin (King-in-waiting of France) gave active command in his army to a teenage girl with no aristocratic preferment, military experience, or governmental connections. Among many of her other exceptionalities - this simply does not happen.

Otherwise, her childhood/youth seemed quite normal.

Jacques was a busy man. As well as ensuring the farm was productive, as Dean he had responsibility for the village when threats of livestock theft and robbery arose; and these were regular hazards. Did he have time for

---

[51] Ref. **2 Kings** 23:25. Josiah is history's greatest exemplar of a King/Monarch; greater than David, Charlemagne, Elizabeth I, or Abraham Lincoln (US Presidents are republicanized versions of monarchs). At 18, Josiah was independent – an adult. So was Jehanne.

close relationships with his children? Did they need him? It may explain some of Jacques' close supervision of Jehanne that she acted unusually for a young woman of her position – she prayed when bells rang, she went to church at any opportunity (including when she was meant to be working in the fields), she distanced herself from the play of her peers, and she heard voices. We do not know if Jacques was fully aware of all this, but it would have been difficult to live with Jehanne and not catch glimpses of her spiritual encounters/relationships – seeming to talk to someone not there, regularly and frequently attending church when not required, praying lengthily for people's needs, emphatically asserting herself in defiance of his wishes. And this all applies equally to her mother. Jehanne was bold and certain beyond her years. For Jacques, his daughter was probably in most ways a normal French farm-girl for that time, but with definite and disturbing differences; her spiritual devotion, her determination, and her occasional defiance - and the dream. That he loved her is actually most apparent from Jehanne's own perspective: '... *he nearly lost his senses when I went to Vaucouleurs.*'[52] Indifference or nonchalance would not '*lose their senses*' over perceived danger to someone.

We know that Jacques saw Jehanne in Rheims on/around 17th July 1429 at Charles VII's sacring as King of France. This was the apex of Jehanne's achievements: did Jacques realise what was happening – just how extraordinary and strange it was that his youngest child and daughter, a peasant girl from the borders, had paved the way for the sovereignty, renewal, and growth of France into a European and world power, which despite many upheavals, revolutions and assaults it has remained to this day? In ways

---

[52]     Op.cit. *Trial of Condemnation* 12/3/1431.

this can be seen as the watershed in Jehanne's life – she had prophesied to Charles the Dauphin that through her God would:

- Drive out the English from France
- Clear the way for Charles to be crowned and consecrated King of France
- Rescue the Duke of Orleans from the English
- Deliver Orleans from the English siege [53]

Jehanne triggered and set in motion each of these. They happened directly due to Jehanne's actions, over the 12 years or so from 1428 to 1440. *Look at her*.

Do you doubt that God operates in history? Open your eyes and look.

The Person and power of Jesus Christ are not immediately obvious through Jacques. From his perspective, if anything can be gleaned, it is that Jehanne was different to other children due to a strong connection to Jesus, and that this manifested from her as an irradiation of mystique. Not in any romantic or sexual way, but in that she was attuned and sensitive to the spiritual dimensions of life – to prayer (which is direct communication with God), to the holiness of Christ, to the sovereignty of God first and foremost [54], and to the importance of maintaining the standards and patterns of a dedicated life. Even if Jacques did not know of Jehanne's Voice(s) and Vision(s), he did know she was unusually devout. Her vocation and

---

[53]   Trask, p.27.

[54]   Jehanne always understood, better than theologians and academicians, that the ultimate King and Lord of France is God. The earthly King (i.e. Charles VII) is God's chosen temporal King, who holds the Kingship in trust. This is why the sacring at Rheims mattered so deeply to her. She emphasized this many times, such as witnessed by the Knight *Jean de Novelemport* (aka *Jean de Metz*), ref. his deposition before the Church Court conducting the Trial of Nullification 1455. Ref. also the deposition of *Bertrand de Poulengey*. From, *Depositions at Domremy* 1455, retrieved from Jeanne-darc.info

determination echoed prophecies of a Maid from Lorraine who would save France – prophecies deriving from Merlin no less. She not only honoured the rites and practices of Catholicism, she sought any opportunities to partake in Mass. In Catholic observance, the Mass is the direct reception of the Body and Blood of Christ into the supplicant believer, and is a mystical interaction. In this way, Jehanne had mystique, as distinct from mystery; her faith was sacrosanct. Jehanne loved Mass and preferred it to any other activity – other kids loved playing, Jehanne loved Mass; this Jacques saw. He nightmared of her removal by soldiers, and quailed at her treatment by them. He even tried to arrange a marriage so that her husband would control her and keep her safely in or near Domremy. He saw her at Rheims, with the King. He knew she was killed by fire, alone and abandoned by all who had been blessed and helped by her, including the wretched and craven Charles VII.

Jacques knew; Jehanne walked the same way that Jesus had walked.

## Isabelle Darc (*nee* Romée de Vouthon).

Jehanne acquired her faith principally from her mother. Isabelle was deeply Christian, faithfully followed the paths of Catholic spirituality, and taught these to her daughter. Her name is witness to her dedication – the 'Romée' in her name is because she had taken pilgrimage. How often or how far is unknown, but she could claim 'Romée', indicating that she had possibly even traversed the Alps and reached Rome. This is a woman with dedication and resolve. It is likely that she gave birth to Jehanne at around age 27, her fifth child. Late medieval Europe has complex demographics for many reasons – epidemic diseases, desolating wars, economic depressions, socio-political instability. The Darc family was average, even large, for the early C15th. As well as keeping a home, Isabelle had to divide her attention six ways; there is no reason to believe Jehanne was a favourite, or given special treatment. Only after Jacques' dream was there heightened vigilance.

Isabelle was illiterate; whatever she taught to Jehanne was what she knew from memory, such as the Lord's Prayer (the '*Pater Noster*').

Jehanne never had books read to her at bedtime; she may have heard stories such as fables, or some Bible stories, as heard and recounted in Church from the village Priest. In Domremy, history was oral, and knowledge was familial, localized and cultural. She never read the Bible, because she could not. Something that stands out in Jehanne's life is that she does not quote Scripture or recount Biblical passages to support herself and shame her tormentors, even later in her Trial. She is consistently Catholic in her faith, so she can sound peculiar to a Protestant ear, but remarkably often she speaks with the full support of Scripture without having ever read any words of it. She did not know them through study; she could not read them. How then did Jehanne, as an illiterate and uneducated farm-girl, testify and engage with such doctrinal and exegetical certainty to hostile and murderous academics and scholars at her trial?

As you reflect on Jehanne's exceptionality, keep in mind that Jehanne never once read the Bible.

> *'And when you are brought to trial in the synagogues and*
> *before rulers and authorities, don't worry about what you*
> *are to say in your defense, for the Holy Spirit will teach you*
> *what needs to be said even as you are standing there.'*
> **- Jesus of Galilee, the Christ**, Luke 12:11-12.

Why hammer this point? Because she begs the question, 'How could she debate, explain and contend faithfully and eruditely against extensively educated antagonists without thoroughly knowing source documents?' How? *Because she knew the Author.*

If she had committed doctrinal or Biblical errors in her trial testimony and addresses, her persecutors would have seized on them immediately and loudly.

Like Isabelle, Jacques was also illiterate, even though he held a municipal position. Probably the only literate people Jehanne knew were clergy. All her knowledge of Jesus, Faith and Scripture came through them, and from her own relationships through prayer and vision. To Jehanne, to be close to Christ required observance of the rituals of Catholicism, and obedience to the Church. This is what she knew.

Mass always meant much to Jehanne; for her, reading the Bible was not an option, and she could not ask the Holy Spirit to speak to her through her reading of Scripture (as many millions of Christians can and do today) except via priestly mediation. For Jehanne and the vast majority of Christians in the early C15th, hearing from God meant direct communication, or believing a Priest – reading was unavailable. 'Sola Scriptura' as chanted by some later reformers, was not much help to ordinary people. Isabelle could ensure Jehanne received solid Catholic training, but she could not open new experience through literacy and books. Another layer of impediment to accessing Scripture and doctrine was the Church's insistence on using Latin in the rites/sacraments. On the one hand it ensured the Church could communicate across ethno-cultural divides, but it was an extremely select and homogenous literacy. Again, this restricted access to the central documents of Christian Faith (including the Bible, which had so galvanized John Wycliffe, and later Martin Luther) to the ecclesiastical few. Jehanne had no Latin, except the few memorized prayers and responses needful for Mass.

How could Jehanne learn more of God, how could she draw closer to Him, how could she know His purpose and plan for her life? What were her options? The answers are: through *ritual* (and therefore memory), through *prayer* (direct communication with God, although this was partly formulaic), through *direct inter-personal relationships* (with family, friends and acquaintances), through *artistic representations* and *interpretations of Biblical stories and truths* (e.g. Stations of the Cross, sculptures, paintings, glasswork etc. in churches), through the *guidance and help of the Priests* (e.g. through sermons, confession and absolution), through the *intercession and counsel of Saints* (great Christians from past times, and therefore strong examples and role-models), and through *obedience to the instruction of the Church* (God's government for Earth [the Church Militant] headed by the Pope).

For most C15th Catholics, nothing could be checked against Scripture for verification, and nothing could be challenged or disobeyed without present and eternal consequences. Notwithstanding these, Jehanne loved the Church, its rituals, and its ways of teaching truth – through art, homilies, and music (mainly singing). Many Catholic Churches (to this day) feature the 14 Stations of the Cross – a way that Catholic people can learn and follow the sufferings of Christ to and after the crucifixion. The Churches had art. There were sculptures representing Biblical truths such as Mary the mother of Jesus holding Him as a child, Christ on the Cross (i.e. the Crucifix), Christ in prayer. There were murals of Bible scenes, such as Jesus at the Last Supper (the origin of the Mass), and Jesus healing the sick. There were windows of stained glass in some churches, showing Jesus ascending to Heaven, and angels in the sepulchre speaking to the Magdalene, all in striking and glorious colour. These artistic representations were further ways Jehanne could access her Lord and God. In all of these, the initiative was Jehanne's, *except* for counsel of the Saints/Voices.

Generally, Christian people do not have regular, temporal, sensory communication with spiritual beings; but Jehanne did. Angels and Saints did communicate with Jehanne, and while Jehanne was illiterate, she was certainly not inarticulate. She could speak very plainly, expressively and cogently. Literacy is not of itself an effective indicator or measure of intelligence or ability.

One further point pertaining to communication worth noting here is that Jehanne had no apparent difficulty in distinguishing the counsel of Saints and Angels from her own thoughts and wishes. She was firm in identifying and hearing the advice and directions of spiritual beings, even when these led her to seeming disaster. Christians across the world and throughout history have wrestled with discerning divine guidance; Jehanne heard this unambiguously.

Isabelle taught her daughter the ways of Catholicism. Jehanne learned these manners of belief, and that in the heart of Christian faith is enthroned Jesus Christ. When she told the Dauphin Charles that he needed to honour and obey his Lord, she spoke boldly, and she meant Jesus[55]. Her knowledge and familiarity in faith had grown from Isabelle's diligence. Of Jehanne's faith Isabelle remembered, in her appeal to the Church to rehabilitate Jehanne's name and reputation,

> 'I succeeded so well that she spent much of her time in church
> and after having gone to confession she received the sacrament
> of the Eucharist every month… she had a great compassion
> for [the people] in her heart and despite her youth she would
> fast and pray for them with great devotion and fervor.'[56]

Her description is of a young girl – a kid of 9 or 10. So, this is not a sage, practiced and mature old Nun, who has had a lifetime to contemplate Christ's teachings and example. One of the outstanding qualities of Christ

---

[55] See e.g. R. Pernoud & M-V. Clin, *Joan of Arc: Her Story*, p.23.
[56] Isabelle Darc 7/11/1455 appeal to *Procès de condamnation et de réhabilitation de Jeanne d'Arc, dite la Pucelle, Trial of Nullification*, retrieved from Jeanne-darc.info

Himself is His compassion. He often went out in solitude to pray, and He loved people - despite our sins and afflictions. He did not recoil from lepers – He actually touched them; he did not heap rejection or vilification on a woman caught in adultery – He showed compassion and wisdom. Jesus reflects the love of God. When searching Mary Magdalene's life, we meet her with Christ, anointing Him, at the same time as Simon - who was both Pharisee & leper - was recoiling inwardly from, and condemning Jesus for, touching her (if you *allow* someone to touch you, you are passively touching them back). Jesus kept company with both, He showed compassion and acceptance to both Simon and Mary M., but only Mary reciprocated love. Genuine compassion derives from love.

Jehanne at a very early age is showing love for and from Christ through compassionate prayer – Jesus is active in Jehanne's soul from early childhood. We cannot pray genuinely without sincerity and love (for example, praying for Christ to assist us with greed, lust or murder would be spiritual insanity).

Jehanne was a prayer warrior by age 10.

One of the fundamental, primary motivations and needs in our lives is *attention*: we seek, yearn and long for it. We give and offer attention. In all our relationships (and if we are without them, then we desire them) we seek *attention*, the attention of the other, whoever the other may be. It could be a great crowd, or it could be one beloved person. We expend great effort, intelligence, resources and ingenuity to obtain the attention we require or wish. Sometimes we need or we seek attention from people who are indifferent to us, such as public officials, politicians, journalists, people who have abused us. We see today that in a world with a far larger population than in 1425, and after six centuries of progress, people are transfixed by the internet, stare yearningly at social media, trust and hope in AI, and meditate their lives through technology. We can now imitate attention such that the illusion is more pleasing than reality. Attention from a chatbot is preferable to attention from a less predictable real human. Isabelle and Jehanne knew nothing of this. The only art or images Jehanne saw were in churches, and the attention she received from God was refracted through Mary's changeless love for infant Jesus more attractively than the very limited and usually didactic attention she herself received from others.

Attention from people who genuinely love us is strengthening and nourishing, but we may also need to be heard or seen by people who are cold and/or Laodicean (i.e. lukewarm or indifferent). Attention is implicit to relationship, to life. Isabelle seems not to have expended lavish attention on Jehanne, but she did educate her thoroughly in Christian Catholic faith, and Jehanne found through this the present and eternal love of God in Christ.

We need also to note that Jehanne's family did not seem to aid her against her captors in 1430, nor her trial adversaries in 1431. This could be for many reasons, from simply being unaware of her true situation (unlikely), to fear and/or intimidation (more likely). It must be remembered that Jehanne was doomed from her capture (23/5/1430), and it is even likely that she was betrayed into captivity – treachery was something she always feared. Once captured, she was never going to be free again in this world, and murder was the ultimate way to silence and afflict her for daring to assail, embattle and terminally disorganise the Anglo-Burgundian Plantagenet regime.

That Jehanne was a loved young girl and member of her family echoes through Isabelle's grief as she demanded posthumous justice for her daughter. Time does not heal all wounds. Despite being illiterate and a peasant,

Isabelle had prepared a careful appeal to the Church Doctors of Notre Dame Paris in 1455. Speaking powerfully of Jehanne, she averred:

> *'She never thought, spoke or did anything against the faith. Certain enemies had her arraigned in a religious trial. Despite her disclaimers and appeals, both tacit and expressed, and without any help given to her defence, she was put through a perfidious, violent, iniquitous and sinful trial. The judges condemned her falsely, damnably and criminally, and put her to death in a cruel manner by fire....I demand that her name be restored.'*[57]

After this appeal to the assembled court, Isabelle had to be helped from the plenary area to the sacristy of Notre Dame to recover – she had become so distressed and emotional. 24 years had not in any way reduced or ameliorated the emotional trauma experienced by Isabelle after Jehanne's murder. Jacques had died soon after Jehanne, later in 1431. Perhaps this signals to us that Isabelle and Jacques were normal parents who loved their kids, and like all parents, were not perfect. They were ordinary people, with understandable and distracted lives, often more busy than they wanted to be, but with an extraordinary daughter. Jehanne was lovable, and she was special to her parents. Most people with children can empathise with this.

Jacques and Isabelle in their own ways fortified Jehanne with immovable faith. Behind such faith was Jehanne's capacity for loyalty and trust, developed within her family, and behind all was the person of Jesus Christ as the cornerstone of not only the Christian Church, but the very Kingdom of God itself, which in turn authorized the source of Law and governance, of power, sanctified and protected in the soul of a prayerful young girl in the borders of France.

---

[57]    Isabelle Darc, ibid.

*'For Thine is the Kingdom, and the power, and the glory...* [58]

Words that we know Jehanne spoke frequently, and perhaps meant more purely and sincerely than anyone else in Christendom at that time. Her relationship to Jesus, as enabled by her parents, particularly Isabelle, formed her perspective permanently and agelessly. France today (2025 atow) is still Catholic France, despite the Reformation, the Revolution, Vichy, and the rise of Islam & the Ummah.

## Jehanne's siblings.

There is little material about Jehanne's siblings. Her brothers Pierre and Jean are best attested, mainly because they engaged in a strangely macabre exercise after Jehanne's death, in which they pretended that an impersonator was Jehanne, and invented a tale wherein she survived the death sentence in Rouen. They profited from her by passing off this woman, whose real name was Claude des Armoises, to counterfeit Jehanne. It is a bizarre exploitation of their sister's incredible achievements, hallowed faith, and rapidly spreading fame that they behaved like this. It does provide a quirky glimpse into some aspects of Jehanne's life and person we might not otherwise catch. The woman who impersonated Jehanne managed to even gull some people who had known Jehanne well, so there must have been a very strong resemblance. In fact, even Charles VII, who had known Jehanne closely, only detected that Claude was a fake because he asked her to recount something that only Jehanne could possibly have known, from their first meeting at Chinon on 6/3/1429. Claude couldn't, of course. After this, the whole ruse was exposed. Charles forgave Claude; Pierre and Jean seem to have evaded disgrace. There is a contemporary representation

---

[58]   See Bible (KJV) *Matthew* 6:13.

of Claude; we can be confident this is a face very like Jehanne's, although the likeness of Claude was likely made when she was aged about 40 and is only a profile, so perhaps not *very* like her?

Even ontologically, this charade of duping good and ordinary people testifies to Jehanne's character – she would never have entertained such a fiction for pecuniary advantage. The only way her brothers could profit illicitly from Jehanne was to misrepresent her, and for her to be really dead. The genuine Jehanne would never have engaged in such conduct. Jehanne la Pucelle would not *perform*. If there had been any place for that, it would have been in Rouen during February – May 1431, but even in that lethal and psychopathic atmosphere, she was completely transparent. Her Lord Jesus refused to *perform* (e.g. miracles) for the entertainment of Pharisees and Jewish notables[59]; when He did anything miraculous, it was because there was genuine need.

On one rare occasion when Jehanne expressed anger by hitting someone, the hapless miscreant was a Scottish soldier (Scotland allied with France during the Hundred Years War) who had got hold of some stolen meat and brought it into camp. Jehanne was incensed and let this perhaps naïve (or extremely hungry) soldier know all about her expectations of troops. We gain insight into her as much by what she excluded, as what she included.

What were Pierre and Jean doing with their strange scam? Did they not know their own sister sufficiently well that they could not detect a replica? Jehanne had seen her family ennobled by Charles VII in December 1429, the village of Domremy exempted from taxation in perpetuity (this concession lasted until the Revolution – 360 years), and she was made Countess du Lys[60], though she never alluded to this honorific in any

---

[59]  E.g. Bible (NLT) *Matthew* 16:1-4.
[60]  Patricia Nell Warren 2008, *What Did Jeanne d'Arc Look Like?*, retrieved from Essays & Articles, Jeanne-darc.info

way. The Darc family had benefited very practically from Jehanne's life and legacy, although Isabelle and Pierre seemed to have moved away from Domremy to Orleans in the late 1430's. (The Municipality of Orleans cared for Isabelle until her end.)

Pretending that Jehanne was still alive, and parading a living effigy as the real Jehanne, is perplexing, even today. Were they also tricked by Claude? It seemed not; more probably, Pierre and Jean simply saw a chance to make some money. We know very little about Jesus' family of origin either, only that He had a mother, a unique version of step-father, and siblings. Jehanne's emergence from an anonymous provincial French peasant family is not especially surprising or unusual.

In late July/early August 1429, as Jehanne was inching slowly from Rheims towards Paris with the King's procession after his sacring/coronation, she declared her personal wish to return to Domremy and engage in family farm-work , '...*taking care of the flocks with my sister and my brother, who would be so happy to see me again!*'[61] This speaks either to a deeper connection and affinity between the siblings, indicating that they had enjoyed happiness together, or to a wishful yearning that was not her real home situation. Whichever is true (likely a bit of both), it is a simple and endearing comment from Jehanne the teenager, rather than from the *Pucelle*, the Maid of Orleans, Avenger and Deliverer of France.

Pierre at least seems to have been with Jehanne throughout 1429 -1430. He was captured alongside Jehanne at Compiegne on 23/5/1430, but was then puzzlingly released. He says little, and even in Jehanne's nullification trial in 1455-56, Pierre does not depose. His is a strange silence.

Of her eldest brother Jacques (Jacquemin) little is known. He married and had some children, but his wife died in childbirth in approx. 1430.

---

[61]    R. Pernoud & M-V. Clin 1998, *Joan of Arc: Her Story*, p.73.

Of Jehanne's only sister Catherine, even less is known. She died also in childbirth, in 1429; she was only in her early 20's.

Jacques and Isabelle had suffered grievous loss through Catherine's death, and the loss of her baby, as well as Jacquemin's wife's death. Losing Jehanne in 1431 was a further and devastating assault on their emotional reserves and resilience.

## Self & Others.

> *'I will only be with you for one year...'*
> - Jehanne, to Dauphin Charles, after the
> victory at Orleans in May 1429.

She was uncannily right. She knew this, and delineated precisely her year of living dangerously. How did she know?

We have all sorts of explanations for prescience, or foreknowledge – we call it logic, magic, prophecy, sight, prediction, luck, hallucination etc. None of these can be asserted as definitive about Jehanne. What is certain is that she could and did foresee events in ways most of us simply cannot.

These are not the makings of an entertaining fiction; they are facts of history.

> *'How long will you fools fight the facts?'* – **Proverbs** 1:22c (NLT)

Facts are not contestable. The world, as Ludwig Wittgenstein asserts, is the quotient of all facts[62]. If I could dare a paraphrase of one of his propositions, it could be thus: 'The world divides into realities', (a 'reality' being parallel and equivalent to a fact). Then all that is actual is composed of realities, where each reality is a divisor or dividend contributing essentially

---

[62]    Ludwig Wittgenstein 1921, *Tractatus Logico-Philosophicus*, p.5

to a total which is the quotient we call the world, or possibly the cosmos, or Creation. Facts are as they are – parts of a greater whole reality we call the cosmos or universe. The sum, difference, product or quotient of facts is infinite.

As **Proverbs** teaches us early in its precepts, it is foolishness to fight or contest facts - they are the elements of reality. The Bible tells us that fighting facts *identifies fools*; we need to take note. Why? Because fools are dangerous. They do not deal in facts, but in something else. What are non-facts? They are not reality. We might call them misconceptions, deceptions or illusions in some contexts - lies or frauds in others. If a fact defies the customary patterns and behaviours of nature, then what is that fact? It is a fact anyway. It just may be a difficult one. We have names for this kind of fact – miracle, wonder, omen, marvel, spell, weird, fantastic. Call them what we will, these kinds of facts concentrate around Jehanne. Explain them away if you like, but remember that those who fight (deny) facts are fools.

The facts of her, the truth of her, still speak very clearly today: *listen*.

It is temptingly easy to romanticize our heroes, to paint their lives as other than they were. We prefer George Washington with a cherry-tree, than George Washington the slave-owner; we prefer Hirohito the great emperor, rather than Hirohito the depraved war-criminal.

Jehanne was likely unaware that the lethargic procession of the King's retinue to Paris after the coronation was *intentional and calculated*, and was a political tactic to ease diplomatic maneuvering between France and England. Henry VI, King of England, was not even 10 years old; intrigue and conspiracy suppurated around him through the likes of Lords Bedford, Suffolk and Gloucester. Charles VII had parleyed away all the significant military advantages Jehanne had won him, and was not eager to 'liberate' Paris; by the time Jehanne arrived at Saint Denis, on Paris' outskirts, with her army in early September 1429, the task was infinitely harder than it would have been a month earlier. Her gormless King had undermined her extraordinary strategic gift of popular support, numerical strength, and political momentum. She nearly succeeded anyway. On September 10, the King ordered that the attack on Paris be ceased; on September 21, he disbanded Jehanne's army. This was probably the last practical moment Jehanne had for retiring back to Domremy. Charles is revealed as desperately incompetent and vacuous. She had had clear directions from God - almost a blueprint - via the Voices to liberate Orleans, and to lead Charles to Rheims for consecration and coronation. These she had accomplished by this stage. Other signs involving the rescue of the Duke of Orleans (an English captive) and the complete restoration of France through the complete ejection of the English, took longer, but began with Jehanne's consolidation of the Royaume (the Kingdom of France). Jehanne had no spiritual guidance from her Voices to attack Paris[63]. We cannot know why this happened, but we know from Jehanne herself that her military strategy after Rheims was not a divinely ordained campaign, as Orleans had been. She was acting on her own.

A demoralizing puzzle for Christian people across generations and history is why God seems often to disappear in our most challenging and traumatizing moments?

Jesus cried out, *'My God, My God, why have you abandoned me?'*[64] from the Cross.

God was not present in Jesus' worst extremity. God was silent as Jehanne slowly crept along the road to Paris, agonizingly constrained and delayed by the King. Even though she did not have divine directions, had she been allowed to prosecute her plans after Rheims, France would have comprised

---

[63]   R.Pernoud 1962, *Joan of Arc: By Herself and Her Witnesses*, p.134.
[64]   **Mark** 15:34 (NLT)

Paris and probably Normandy far sooner than happened. Many things would have happened differently.

It is true that the brighter and more radiant the light source, the deeper and sharper the shadows. There were very few genuine Christians around Jehanne after she left Domremy in late 1428/early 1429. Being religious and being Christian are totally different things. She is quite singular in her devotion and adherence to Jesus Christ; Charles VII had no conception of this. Jehanne was moved and connected by Mary the Madonna, and Jesus; Charles and His court were impressed only by the influence of the Church and its personnel, its symbols, its political and diplomatic influence, its wealth – its power. Note that both the English and French Courts supported the Church.

Within the black shadows circling her were void maws of corruption – spiritually, psycho-emotionally, and physically. Their intent, from the beginning of their involvement, was murder. Jehanne never had any earthly chance of a fair trial, let alone an acquittal.

Even well over a century later, we can taste some of the poison directed at Jehanne, via Shakespeare's Anglo-Burgundian combatants in *Henry VI pt. 1*. In his play, Shakespeare takes enormous liberties with fact, including an invention that Jehanne (called *Pucelle* in the play – a rare accuracy in the text – Jehanne did in fact call herself '*Pucelle*') takes the city of Rouen for the Dauphin Charles through stealth and trickery (something that never in fact happened). The English Lord Talbot rails thus,

> '*France, thou shalt rue this treason with thy tears,*
> *If Talbot but survive thy treachery –*
> *Pucelle, that witch, that damned sorceress,*
> *Hath wrought this hellish mischief unawares...*'[65]

---

[65]   William Shakespeare c.1590, *Henry VI Part 1*, Act 3 Sc.2.

And his accomplice, this fictitious Duke of Burgundy follows up, addressing Pucelle with,

> '... *Vile fiend and shameless courtezan,*
> *I trust ere long to choke thee...*'[66]

(Charming aren't they?)

Did the Bard believe this blather? Or is he describing Establishment sentiment? (There is some scholarly misgiving that he wrote the play at all.) Jehanne obviously still rankled in English consciousness far beyond her lifetime; this is the tenor of English perception over 160 years later, and the hatred still throbs palpably. Even so, the killers and careerists in the Anglo-Burgundian faction and Church hierarchy interacted with Jehanne, so that their exchanges with her still highlight aspects of her nature and personality.

Our enemies tend to foreground what we are. Jesus' enemies hated Him for revealing and reminding all Humanity that God is their Parent/Father and <u>loves them</u>, that we are all sinful beings needing His/Her Grace and healing, which S/He will freely give through Christ. So, demonic hatred of God actually accentuates His love and beauty. Jehanne understood this at a molecular level – she was deeply spiritual... in a way we most often glimpse among Indigenous peoples. The religious hierarchy wanted exclusive control of access to God (or at least the construct they offered as 'God'), because this gave them power over others. Something Jesus showed us is that Faith is a personal relationship expressed through Love. Religious belief systems reduce faith to objectifications of deity as a demand or attainment: Judaism deifies law, Islam deifies submission, Scientism deifies progress, Paganism deifies nature/forces, Hinduism deifies reincarnate

---

[66]  Ibid.

determinism (i.e. as caste), Churchianity deifies legalism etc. If we do not receive attention gifted through love, we will seek and steal it through control and coercion. By removing Jesus and asserting the monolith of Law instead, the Pharisees/Sanhedrin thought to control Israel, and universal perceptions of God. As it turned out, that did not work. (Jesus has more followers even today than any other Faith movement, completely eclipsing the Judaism which persecuted Him.) By murdering Jesus, His mission was actually accomplished.

Jehanne had interpersonal access and communication with God in ways most of us do not, mainly with beings she called *Voices* (saints and angels). She was feared and rejected because she was successful in reshaping the government and realm of France, restoring it to independence, and to centrality in Christendom. Jehanne is not Jesus, but she was careful to listen through prayer, and to respect through attention. She was hated, because she was like Him. Ultimately, she resembled Him mortally and terminally, an imitation which underlines her faith, and her courage. She became His image.

C. S. Lewis canvases this reflectively on Christ's universal sacrifice:

'...*Then He faces the Church; the very Church that He brought into existence. It condemns Him.*'[67]

It also condemns people who follow and are thereby like Him. Jehanne shares much in common with *Martin Luther King Jr* [d.1968, Memphis, USA, aged 39], *Dietrich Bonhoeffer* [d. 1945, Flossenbürg, Germany, aged 39], *Betsie ten Boom* [d.1944, Ravensbrück, Germany, aged 59], *David & Natalie Lloyd* [d.2024, Port-au-Prince, Haiti, aged 23 & 21] and the

---

[67]   C. S. Lewis 1963, *Prayer: Letters to Malcolm*, p.45.

millions of others who have followed Christ even to death[68]. Many of these inspiring believers were criticised and abandoned by the Church to what was called the 'secular authority' in Jehanne's case. Jesus warns His followers that they will likewise be reviled and despised because of their commitment to Him[69]. We do not know whether Jehanne knew of Jesus' warning (we remember that her illiteracy blocked ready access to the Bible), but she certainly experienced the fact of it. She walked with Jesus even to the Cross.

Always courageous (some would say 'reckless' after the way she was captured at Compiegne on 23rd May 1430), Jehanne followed her Voices, and her best instincts. Her greatest demonstration of courage was not in military combat or guiding the King to his coronation. Theresa Aletheia Noble in a reflection on Regine Pernoud's work says,

> '...[Jehanne's] greatest act of heroism lies in her behaviour during
> her unjust trial... Seeing the reality of her situation and the
> clear hopelessness of stating her case, she nevertheless responded to
> learned theologians with astounding clarity and firmness.'[70]

This is her. This is a way that she shows Jesus to us – He also did not rail viciously against injustice and declare condemnation and abuse upon those who wished to murder Him. Jehanne follows Him, and in her following, we see Him.

We see her through the Saints and whom she calls 'Voices'[71], through her prayers, through her human relationships, through her persecutors,

---

[68] These Christian believers died due to their direct and courageous obedience to Jesus Christ – each is a martyr.

[69] Bible NLT, *Matthew* 10:22.

[70] Theresa Aletheia Noble 2020, *A Chapter that Changed My Life: Joan of Arc and the "One Thing"*, Wordonfire.org.

[71] Jeanne-arc.info, *Trial of Condemnation* see *Second Public Examination* 22/2/1431, Jehanne testifies, '...my King and many others have also heard and seen the Voices which came to me...'

through her actions, through the ways people responded or reacted to her. Just as she also understood Jesus through His mother Mary's love for Him, so we see Jehanne through her love for those who love Jesus, and her compassion for those who do not.

**Many people had acquaintance, friendly, or neighbourly relationship with Jehanne. Many were her adversaries or enemies.** The majority were comrades-in-arms or acquaintances.

Because her Trial of Condemnation was documented at the time, we have records about her, through people who actually knew her, in uncommon numbers for a medieval event. Sometimes, Jehanne herself is the most efficient witness.

Compiled below are events both in and because of Jehanne's life which are surprising because they are marvels. Both the events themselves and the pattern they form are incredible. The people who recalled and knew these qualities and actions in Jehanne's life are noted. With the exception of some later historians, sources cited knew Jehanne in some degree. These events and incidents directly indicate Jesus Christ's closeness to Jehanne.

*'Just believe that I am in the Father and the Father is in me.*
*Or at least believe because of what you have seen me do.'*
- Jesus the Christ, **John** 14:11.

Summary order of some wonders and miracles:

1. Jehanne has singularly profound faith and exceptional trust in Jesus.
2. Jehanne experiences spiritual visions.
3. Jehanne is notably different to other children and adolescents.
4. Healthy young soldiers could not think sexually/lustfully about Jehanne.

5. Jehanne recognized Dauphin Charles in a crowd, despite having no idea whatever of his identity.
6. Jehanne is both humble and assertive in an era when chauvinism was normative.
7. Sword at St Catherine de Fierbois.
8. At 18 years of age, with no military experience, Jehanne is given field command in the French Army.
9. Weather and tide changing at Orleans.
10. Jehanne passes the stronghold at Saint Loup without the English knowing.
11. Predicting her own wounding, leading and succeeding in the assault on the Tourelle at Orleans.
12. Routing and decimating the English at Jargeau, Meung & Patay.
13. Sacring of Charles VII at Rheims.
14. Resurrecting a dead baby at Lagny, late April 1430.
15. Grace in extremis, like the Apostle Paul, Dietrich Bonhoeffer, Manche Masolema.

What these instances also do is underline that Jehanne had direct help and power from God. Independently, these are extraordinary; together they point to one objective conclusion – God did these things. To assist in evaluating this, as well as noting that Jehanne was central to spiritual as well as ordinary activity, each event is positioned on a spectrum. Any *spectrum of the unusual* can range from 1 to 5 possibilities:

1: Unexpected/unlikely sequence of events.
2: Coincidence.
3: Improbability.
4: Wonder.
5: Miracle.

Normal or natural likelihood *decreases* from 1 to 5. This spectrum is not supported by experimental research or peer reviews etc., which are the the normal apparatus and habitat of science, mainly because each level of hyper-normality is subjectively defined whether we regard ourselves as scientific thinkers, or new-age crystal-diviners (and these are often not far apart).

A *miracle* is defined as an event that does occur but which is not possible in general nature (excluding areas developed through human ingenuity like aeronautics, micro-surgery, hydroponics etc., as human ingenuity is natural). A *wonder* is an event that has occurred but which is highly unlikely or unusual in general nature, though not impossible. (A *wonder* would be to ask God for food in the midst of famine and to then unexpectedly receive provisions from an enemy – it is extremely unlikely, but not impossible. A *miracle* would be to ask God for food in the midst of famine and to then experience one small crust of bread expanding into a tonne of bread – it cannot happen ordinarily.)

N.B. If you only read the summary list below, you will be left with questions. Wonders and miracles are integral to Jehanne's life. Also note that this is an *evidenced selection*.

Many more wonders and miracles occurred around Jehanne than are arranged here.

Wonders and miracles did swirl and constellate around Jehanne. She honoured God mightily and faithfully. As we know, she eventually suffered agonizing rejection, abuse and death because she maintained loyalty and fealty to Jesus as her High King. She was absolutely serious about that, and for us living in an age which minimizes and ridicules royalty, we need to recall that royalty is God's most effective and efficient form of government. It is not God's fault that we exploited His gift through selfishness and lust. Jehanne was untroubled about this, and understood the chivalry of Heaven.

The selection outlined here is only to honour what God did in and through her. This is absolutely not exhaustive, definitive or complete. *Many* other extraordinary events happened in her life.

Remember that Jehanne is rare because she actually and daily sought to follow Jesus.

He was and is her true Liege Lord and King. She was only 18-19 when most of these happened.

## 1
## *Profound and exceptional Faith in Jesus.*

*'I look to God, my creator, in all. I love Him with all my heart.'*
- Jehanne, 2/5/1431, Trial of Condemnation, Rouen.

Feeling betrayed or devalued by a beloved person is unutterably difficult for any of us. In ways, it is the unthinkable wound; that the person we trust and love deeply and wholly, commits treason against us. The lie, the rejection, the toxic criticism, the abandonment, the adultery, the mockery - things we describe with words like 'shocking', 'destructive', 'appalling', 'obliterating', 'devastating', 'annihilating', 'iconoclastic', 'abusive'.

*'I fear nothing but treachery.'*
- Jehanne, 14/7/1429, to Gérardin d'Épinal.

Jesus felt abandoned by God. He knows how painful, how excruciating this is. That very word 'excruciating', derives from the Latin *ex crucis,* 'of the cross'; we use it for the most extreme pain and suffering. Is that because Jesus felt cheated, deceived, betrayed by God? He said God had *forsaken* Him; another very strong word. As with Jesus, Jehanne was maneuvered into circumstances where strong words are required. Was she also forsaken?

She did not verbalise her feelings of fear and abandonment by complaining to and of God; she went to the stake in terrible distress, but also praying for the people who had treated her so murderously.

*'Jesus, Jesus, Jesus, Jesus, Jesus, Jesus.'*
- Jehanne, 30/5/1431, Site of Execution, Old Market Place, Rouen.

She answered treachery and betrayal with blessing and mercy. She very accurately accused Bishop Pierre Cauchon of her murder, but was even very restrained in addressing that vile man (she didn't call him a 'vile man'; but I have no such reluctance). There is no word raised against God. Who would have blamed or accused her if she had cried out as Jesus had? *'Why have you abandoned me?'* But there is nothing like this. Her equanimity is miraculous. Eyewitnesses remembered her asking forgiveness from anyone she had offended or treated unfairly as she was taken to the stake. The eyewitnesses do not record any of the people accepting this from her[72]. The people she had offended deserved the offence, and were mostly nearby, watching a 19 year-old girl being murdered by judicial calumny. Gathered at her killing was a crowd of some 600-800 English/Burgundian soldiers, approximately 8000 townsfolk of Rouen, clerics and churchmen of the Inquisition, and officials with some role to play in the perfidious and cowardly charade taking place before them. It may as well have been Golgotha. Why did nobody help her? We could ask the same about Jesus Himself. A combination of conformity-bias and the 'Nuremberg Defence' is the most human explanation – that everyone was *just doing their duty*. The conformity-bias, derived from fear and intimidation, accounted for the pusillanimity – rampant cowardice. Jehanne is still challenging, compelling us to ask 'Would I do differently? Would I cry out 'STOP!'

---

[72]   Ref. e.g. Maitre Guillaume Manchon and Maitre Jean Massieu, *First Inquiry* 1449, Jeanne-darc.info.

Would I try to wrestle her off the gallows? Jehanne holds up a painful mirror to us.

She loved and trusted God. Literally.

> *'If God commanded, it was right to obey. If God commanded it… I should have gone.'*
> - Jehanne, Second Private Examination, Trial of Condemnation, 12/3/1431, Rouen.

His name was her last word. In itself, that is extraordinary, in the sense that all reason and logic indicate she ought not to have followed the instructions given her. When first she encountered a spiritual entity directly, she was 13. This led ultimately to her early death – 19 years and five months is a short life span. Her faith was miraculous – so very like Jesus Himself. At the end, Jesus had no-one with Him. Neither did Jehanne. Ultimately, at Calvary, Jesus called on God to receive His Spirit. Jehanne called on Jesus. In heeding God, Jesus ended at the Cross. In heeding God, Jehanne ended at the stake - staying the journey with Jesus to the end.

5

## 2
### *Spiritual visions.*

> *'When I was thirteen, I had a voice from God to help me to govern myself. The first time I was terrified. The voice came to me about noon: it was Summer, and I was in my father's garden. I had not fasted the day before. I heard the voice on my right hand, towards the church. There was a great light all about.'*
> - Jehanne, 22/2/1431, Trial of Condemnation, Great Hall of Rouen Castle, Rouen.

The great Jewish Prophet and Leader Moses had a similar experience. He also saw a great light in the form of a burning bush which was not being consumed by the flames[73]. Curiosity gripped him, not fear or terror. The encounter was radically transformative for Moses though – God spoke to him from the bush and sent him on a mission to free Israel from oppressive slavery and despotism. Moses was less enthusiastic once he understood what was being required of him. Jehanne heard a voice also, but had quite likely never heard (and certainly had not read) the narrative of **Exodus** 3; there was no precedent she could draw upon. The similarity of these encounters would most probably not have been apparent to her, and a feeling of terror is very understandable; she describes this first encounter as engaging her auditorily and visually. The visual experience was of 'great light', and from her right side, but having no form. It could not be the Sun, which was overhead at noon. She had not fasted, so the experience could not be intelligently dismissed as a consequence of hunger – there were no quick sugar hits to distort her senses or behaviour either; sugar was not an ingredient in the medieval peasant diet. Knowing that the Voice came from her right is an interesting aspect; God indicates that 'the right hand' is a sign of His favour and power[74]. We tend to remember significant details in important moments; again, it is unlikely that Jehanne knew the Biblical importance of the right hand, but she was in that position regardless. The Voice did not set out her mission straight away. Moses did not see a form either. He became afraid as his discussion with God continued, and by the time his staff had become a serpent at God's behest, he was terrified. Jehanne moved in the other direction; her fear abated.

---

[73]   Ref. **Exodus** 3:1-15.
[74]   Cf. **Matthew** 22:44-45, **Psalm** 110:1-2.

*'I believe [the Voice] was sent to me from God. When I heard it for the third time, I recognized that it was the Voice of an Angel. This Voice has always guarded me well, and I have always understood it. It instructed me to be good, and to go often to Church; it told me it was necessary for me to come into France. You ask me under what form this Voice appeared to me? You will hear no more of it from me this time. It said to me two or three times a week "You must go into France."'*
- Jehanne, 22-2-1431, Trial of Condemnation,
Great Hall of Rouen Castle, Rouen.

Jehanne's reluctance to explain much of her knowledge about the spiritual visitor who spoke with her makes sense. She is a prisoner, and is treated with hostility and disrespect by her inquisitors. The remark about going to France makes sense if her home location is remembered – France for Jehanne was where the French had authority – the *Royaume*. She lived on the borders of this, where the Burgundians and English held sway. France was away to her west when she was growing up in Domremy.

Interestingly here, Jehanne indicates that the supernatural being did have a visible form – she could see him; she refuses to describe him to the judges though.

'God' and 'Light' are often juxtaposed and admixed. In **John** 8:12, Jesus says that He is the 'Light of the world'. **1 John** 1:5 is unambiguous – God is Light. Intriguingly, **James** 1:17 entitles God as 'the Father of Lights' – this is frequently taught as meaning that God is the Creator of the stars, but is this also that He is the Father of Angels, the Creator of the Seraphim and Cherubim, the Father of Jesus the Light – is this why Jehanne saw great light? Even those she would have regarded as infidels, the Muslims, acknowledge that God is Light[75]. She saw Light and form, and from it

---

[75]    Qur'ān, Surah *An-Nûr* (XXIV) 35.

came that which she henceforth called her 'Voice(s)'. She does not say that the voice and the form were the same person or entity, only that they were simultaneous.

A great Light also shone upon the Pharisee Saul as he hastened to Damascus to persecute Christians. **Acts** 9:1-2 tells us that he was bent on chaining and destroying Jesus' followers – Saul was a murderer and victimizer of Christians. Until, one day he was literally knocked off his feet, sprawling on the ground by a 'brilliant light'. Saul heard a voice, replying to his question, 'Who are you?' - *'I am Jesus, the One you are persecuting'.*

Jehanne never specifically identified the particular Voice at this time (i.e. she did not say it was the Archangel Michael, or St Catherine, as she does later); but perhaps we can guess.

Saul became Paul the Apostle, and was instrumental in taking the Word of God across the known world – he obeyed Jesus and followed to the end. Like Jehanne, his end was martyrdom; he most likely died by beheading, ordered by Roman emperor Nero in approx. 67AD.

Another great Martyr, Dietrich Bonhoeffer, teaches us:

> *'...the Cross is not the terrible end to an otherwise God-fearing and happy life, but it meets us at the beginning of our communion with Christ. When Christ calls a man [person], he bids him [her] to come and die.'*[76]

> *'There is no day that I do not hear the voice. And indeed I need it. I have never asked it for any other reward than, in the end, the salvation of my soul.'*
> - Jehanne, 22/2/1431, Trial of Condemnation,
> Great Hall of Rouen Castle, Rouen.

---

[76]    Dietrich Bonhoeffer 1937, *The Cost of Discipleship* [*Nachfolge*], p.79.

Is it really this plain? The judges wanted to know the form or identity of the Voice whom Jehanne is referencing. This is part of her answer, '...I have never asked it for any other reward than, in the end, the salvation of my soul.' Clever, innocently simple, and profoundly truthful: who alone can save our soul?

Jehanne speaks of seeing and communicating with spiritual beings who are Saints and at other times with Angels; this was not unusual in her experience, but for most other people, it *is* unusual. She identifies the Voice as an Angel, but she saw many Angels and she does not say they are always the same Angel, in fact she says she could see many. She does not indicate gender, but uses neuter pronouns. One thing definitely known, both by Jehanne in 1429 and us today, is that Angels themselves cannot save our souls – there is no point asking them. There is only One who can save our souls.

5

### 3
## *Notably different to other children and adolescents.*

*'From her early youth, Jeannette [Jehanne] was brought up*
*with care in the Faith, and in good morals; she was so good*
*that all the village of Domremy loved her. ... She had modest*
*ways, as beseemed one whose parents were not rich. ... when she*
*heard the Mass-bell, if she were in the fields, she would go back*
*to the village and to the Church, in order to hear Mass.'*
- Jean Morel, labourer, deponent at Domremy
for the Trial of Nullification, 1455.

*'She was a good girl, simple and gentle; she went willingly and*
*often to Church, and Holy Places. Often she was bashful when*

*others reproached her with going too devotedly to Church. ... I*
*loved her dearly for her goodness and because she was my friend.'*
- Hauviette, wife of Gerard of Syonne, childhood friend
of Jehanne, deponent at Trial of Nullification, 1455.

*'From my childhood I knew the parents of [Jehanne]; as to [Jehanne],*
*herself, I knew her in my youth... She was very hospitable to the poor,*
*and would even sleep on the hearth in order that the poor might lie in*
*her bed. She was not fond of playing, at which we, her companions,*
*complained. She liked work; and would spin, labour with her father,*
*look after the house, and sometimes mind the sheep. She was never*
*seen idling in the roads; she was more often in Church at prayer.'*
- Isabellette, wife of Gerardin, labourer of Epinal,
deponent at Trial of Nullification, 1455.

These people all knew Jehanne personally in her early years. There are
many more deponents who gave sworn evidence at the Trial of Nullification,
attesting to Jehanne's unusual devotion to the cycles and patterns of
Catholic piety, that she was good and generously kind, remembering that
Catholicism was the only face of Christianity Jehanne had ever known. The
term 'protestant' had not even been coined at this time.

What stands out is Jehanne's profound dedication and devotion to God
despite her young age. This we hear in the depositions. She was compassionate, loving, and loveable; even the poor and destitute received care
and compassion, in Jehanne's own bed, while she slept on the hearth – a
hard place to sleep. This speaks to a generosity of faith rare in any time or
generation.

And something happened in her youth which separated her from the
other young people in Domremy. They knew she was different – she did not
play or frolic as the others did. She prayed and went to Church, often and

without being told. Encountering the Voice changed her – noticeably, but beneficently (and her peers had no idea of her supernatural relations). The tone is that her friends missed her, not that they resented her. If not miraculous, Jehanne's devotion was at very least remarkable. She was different.

**3**

## 4
### *Healthy young soldiers could not think sensually/sexually about Jehanne.*

*'Sometimes in the army I lay down to sleep with Jehanne and the soldiers, all in the straw together, and sometimes I saw Jehanne prepare for the night and sometimes I looked at her breasts which were beautiful, and yet I never had carnal desire for her...'*
- Duc John II d'Alençon, deponent, Trial of Nullification, 1456.

*'Every night she lay down with Jean de Metz and me [on the journey from Vaucouleurs to Chinon – approx. 10 days/nights], keeping on her surcoat and hose, tied and tight. I was young then and yet I had neither desire nor carnal movement to touch woman, and I should not have dared to ask such a thing of Jehanne, because of the abundance of goodness which I saw in her.'*
- Bertrand de Poulengy, deponent, Trial of Nullification, 1456.

*'They said that in the beginning [i.e. of Jean de Metz and Bertrand de Poulengy planning the journey from Vaucouleurs to Chinon] they wanted to require her to lie with them carnally. But when the moment came to speak to her of this they were so much ashamed that they dared not speak of it to her nor say a word of it.'*
- Marguerite la Touroulde, deponent, Trial of Nullification, 1456.

*'She heard Mass in the morning and remained long at prayer. I
have seen her beneath the vault of that church on her knees before
the Holy Virgin, sometimes with bowed head, sometimes with her
head raised. I believe her to have been a good and holy girl.'*
- Jean le Fumeux, Priest at Notre Dame de
Vaucouleurs, Trial of Nullification, 1456.

*'All the soldiers held her as sacred. So well did she bear
herself in warfare, in words and in deeds, as a follower
of God, that no evil could be said of her.'*
- Maitre Jean Barbin, King's Advocate, deponent
at Paris, Trial of Nullification, 1455-56.

Aside from indicating that Jehanne was an attractive young woman,
we also know that she was powerfully and transformingly good. Jean de
Dunois expressed it thus,

*'There was in her something divine.'*[77]

There was in Jehanne a quality which caused lusty men to regret and
repent of their carnal desires. This is very unusual; it does show us that
an attractive 17/18 year-old girl was safe from an army of sexually active
and desirous young Frenchmen. We do know that the soldiers were not
transformed into virginal celibates by her presence - Jehanne on a number
of occasions physically exiled prostitutes and soldiers' girlfriends from the
army camps, even chasing them away with the flat of her sword[78] - so we
know the men were certainly interested in sex if they could get it. It also

---

[77]  Jean, Comte de Dunois, Bastard d'Orleans, deposition before Trial of Nullification,
Orleans, 1455. Jeanne-arc.info
[78]  Louis de Contes (Jehanne's Page) deposition, Trial of Nullification, Paris 1455-56.
Jeanne-darc.info

perhaps in part explains Jehanne's insistence on her army being regular at confession with priests. They needed renewals of penitence and absolution. She may have been disapproving, but Jehanne was realistic.

Jehanne's physical appearance was obviously desirable; yet when soldiers thought of her sexually, they actually felt shame about objectifying her that way. Guy de Laval, a young nobleman who joined Jehanne's Army after Orleans, comments on a sense of the divine when seeing and hearing her, which is an unusual description[79]. She had a beauty which affected people. There is a long distance between knowing a woman is beautiful, and thinking of going to bed with her; Jehanne herself gives no indication that she thought herself sexually desirable – she is nowhere recorded as using cosmetics, beauty treatments, laser surgery, or generally wearing out the mirror. She did not seek to enhance her feminine allure. She may have been naïve to think her exposed breasts would not be particularly noticed by young men, but that was innocence, not teasing. She was probably used to seeing and being seen by her brothers and sister.

She did like nice clothes though. She had what we might call 'fashion sense'. Her wearing men's clothing is indicated as a pragmatic measure for both ease of movement and as protective disguise from bad men who would not have scruples about a woman's right to her own body. While not vain or conceited, Jehanne was aware men could be attracted to her and therefore of her vulnerability as a woman. (This did become a problem for her, but more towards the end of her life in Rouen. She seems to have remained unmolested however.) The first indications of her wearing men's clothing are at the outset of her mission from Vaucouleurs, and the clothes were given to her then, at her request. Until then, she wore women's

---

[79]     Guy de Laval, in Regine Pernoud 1962, *Joan of Arc*, pp.111-12.

clothes, and she had a marked preference for a red dress[80]. The dress shows up repeatedly in the memories of people who knew her in Domremy. Red hose (i.e. socks or stockings) or a red skirt of some kind features in a mural in the Chapel of Notre Dame de Bermont, probably Jehanne's favourite place of worship within walking distance of Domremy. It is most likely a contemporary picture of Jehanne by someone who actually knew and remembered her. As an amateur artistic effort, it is rough, but the only one we have. And she has fair hair - she dyed her hair later when she was in military service. Many early artistic representations of Jehanne (i.e. within a century of her lifetime) show her with fair hair, not the black hair insisted by more recent historians. The mural sketch in Notre Dame de Bermont is most likely the only detailed contemporary representation of Jehanne in existence. In it, she is shown accurately with the red hose, and with fair/ yellow hair and blue eyes. The artwork has been carefully dated to early C15th. She is described after she began her mission for France as having dark hair, and we must remember that it was in Jehanne's interest to be disguised when possible. A very good black dye apparently derives from walnut husks, and walnut trees were and are common in rural France. If Jehanne could dye things red, she could also dye them black.

Wearing feminine or attractive garments proved costly. An English soldier was able to unseat her from her horse by getting hold of a long golden tunic. Had she been only wearing practical men's gear, that would not have happened.

Is it 'miraculous' that men did not feel sexual desire for Jehanne, seeing she was an attractive young woman? The answer has to be no – people see other attractive people daily, and appreciate their beauty - without sexual

---

[80]   Jean de Novelemport (aka Jean de Metz), deposition Trial of Nullification, Domremy 1455. Jeanne-arc.info. In this deposition he attests to Jehanne's clothing. This detail later becomes a mortal theme for her.

desire. The context in Jehanne's life exposed her to very concentrated attention among an army largely of young men, but these men could see her
femininity without desiring her sexually. The men themselves experienced
this as unusual though, as if surprised at their own contained concupiscence.

The best summary of this quality in Jehanne is cited above: '*There is in
her something divine.*'

3

## 5
### *Jehanne recognized Dauphin Charles in a crowd, despite having no idea whatever of his identity.*

*'The Kingdom of France is not the Dauphin's but my Lord's.
But my Lord wills that the Dauphin shall be made King and
have the Kingdom in custody. The Dauphin shall be King
despite his enemies, and I shall lead him to his anointing.'*
- Jehanne, to Robert de Baudricourt, Captain
of Vaucouleurs, February 1429.

Jehanne's certainty and relentless dedication to her mission never wavers.
The narrative does not change in its essentials for her – she does not adapt,
or change her plans. She knows that God is orchestrating the survival and
restoration of France, bringing the Crown Prince (the 'Dauphin') Charles
to the throne, and liberating France from English rule and occupation. Her
specific instructions are to free the geopolitically vital city of Orleans from
English oppression (it was under crippling siege), and to take Charles to
Rheims for his sacring as King.

*'... [Jehanne] said in addressing the king, "God give you life,
gentle King," even though she did not know him and had
never seen him, and there were many pompous lords there more*

*opulently dressed than the king. Wherefore he replied to Jehanne:*
*"What if I am not the king, Jehanne?" Pointing to one of the*
*lords, he said: "There is the king." To which she answered, "In*
*God's Name, gentle Prince, it is you and none other."* [81]
- Jehanne, first meeting Charles Dauphin of
France, Chinon Castle, 6/3/1429.

*'Most Noble Lord Dauphin, I am come and am sent to you*
*from God to give succour to the kingdom and to you.'*
- Jehanne, meeting Charles Dauphin of France, 6/3/1429.

Gaining access to the Dauphin of France seemed ludicrous for a peasant girl from the borders. The Voices directed her, so that through the help of the Captain of Vaucouleurs, and the Duke of Lorraine, she journeyed safely from Vaucouleurs to Chinon – an 11-day journey of approximately 530km, often through hostile territory into the heart of France. She seems to have been cautious and wary (she only attended church for Mass twice in that time – normally she would seek Mass every day or two) - but not afraid. Her guides, Bertrand de Poulengy and Jean de Novelemport, both squires of Robert de Baudricourt, found the experience of proximity to Jehanne profound and edifying. It is another small wonder that she inspired them to accompany and guide her to the Dauphin of France, at a very long distance in those days.

The best known aspect of her meeting with Charles, Dauphin of France, is that she knew him, despite never having seen or heard him before. She had no way of recognizing him by sight nor sound, yet she walked straight up to the disguised Dauphin in a large crowd of bombastic aristocrats and court sycophants, addressing him with '...*the curtsies and reverences*

---

[81]    R. Pernoud & M-V. Clin 1998, *Joan of Arc: Her Story*, pp.22-3.

*that customarily are made to a king as though she had been nourished at the court...* [82]. She made an impression wherever she went, but this introduction to Charles was spectacular. He had positioned and dressed himself so that he simply blended as a member of the crowd. The impossible identification was not all; she then spent 30 minutes with Charles privately, in which time the illiterate teenage peasant from remote Domremy won the confidence of the future King of France by sharing with him a secret only he and God could know. At this point, Charles knew she was, at very least, unique.

All Jehanne has done thus far is to be obedient to God. She is not following the Bible, because she is illiterate, and could not read it. She is not following a particular creed, because she does not know one. She is not following an eloquent demagogue – and the Dauphin Charles certainly does not fit that category: he was by most accounts an unimpressive man, and not a distinctive leader. His eminence was hereditary, not heroic. Jehanne is following God directly, through prayer and her obedience to the Voices.

5

## 6
### She is both humble and assertive in an age when chauvinism and elitism were normative.

*'I'm not one of your professional prophets. I certainly never trained to be one. I'm just a shepherd, and I take care of fig trees. But the LORD called me away from my flock and told me, "Go and prophesy to my people in Israel." '*
- Amos, Prophet of God, **Amos** 7:14-15 (NLT).

---

[82]    Ibid. p.22.

*'He picked up five smooth stones from a stream and put them
in his shepherd's bag. Then, armed only with his shepherd's
staff and sling, he started across to fight Goliath.'*
- Description of shepherd boy David, **1 Samuel** 17:40 (NLT)

*'... I saw her when she presented herself before the royal majesty,
with much humility and great simplicity, the poor little shepherdess,
and I heard the following words which she spoke to the King: "Very
noble Lord Dauphin, I am come and am sent by God..."* [83]
- Raoul de Gaucourt, on Jehanne first meeting
Dauphin Charles, 6/3/1429.

Shepherds feature significantly in the Bible, and in Jehanne's life. As a young girl she shepherded her family's flock, among many other farm chores. She would have had, at best, limited awareness of Biblical references to shepherds. But that aside, she was like some of the greatest figures in Scripture, who were shepherds: Abel, Abraham, Rachel, Zipporah, David, Amos – all shepherds. This was one of the most menial and working-class jobs in the ancient world, up to and beyond medieval times. God honoured all working people by designating humble, proletarian shepherds as primary witnesses to the advent of Jesus, the Prince of Peace, the Messiah. Shepherds are honoured in the Bible, and Jehanne is identified with Biblically stellar company.

Her gender is unimportant in working as a shepherd of sheep, and a shepherd of men – as military commanders are. God appoints her to be both. Nothing she says presents her as a feminist, but she neither limits herself concerning her femininity – she is a disciple, obeying God's leading wherever it takes her (ref. **Galatians** 3:28).

---

[83]    R. Pernoud 1962, *Joan of Arc*, p.48.

Jesus said, *'I am the good shepherd; I know my own sheep, and they know me, just as my Father knows me and I know the Father. And I lay down my life for the sheep.'*[84]

Jehanne loved and trusted Jesus implicitly. She knew Him.

3

## ϡ
### *The sword at Saint Catherine de Fierbois.*

*'...I had a sword I had taken at Vaucouleurs. Whilst I was at Tours, or at Chinon, I sent to seek for a sword which was in the Church of Saint Catherine of Fierbois, behind the altar; it was found there at once; the sword was in the ground and rusty; upon it were five crosses; I knew by my Voice where it was. I had never seen the man who was sent to seek for it... I wrote to the Priests of the place... and they sent it to me. It was under the earth, not very deeply buried, behind the altar so it seemed to me... As soon as it was found, the Priests of the Church rubbed it, and the rust fell off at once without effort...'*[85]

- Jehanne, 27/2/1431, Trial of Condemnation,
Great Hall of Rouen Castle, Rouen.

This matter of Jehanne's sword is about the closest we come to a fairy-tale event. It really does sound like a kind of magical spell! It involves a mysterious sword, found buried behind a Church altar, on the guidance of Jehanne's voices. It is a case of angelic guidance to God's provision. But, it is not magic, or a spell. Lance Bernard points out that the sword is mentioned only once during Jehanne's inquisition. That is in itself interesting; the inquisitors spent dreary long hours examining Jehanne about wearing

---

[84]  **John** 10:11-12 (NLT)
[85]  Retrieved from Fourth Public Examination, 27/2/1431, Jeanne-darc.info

male clothes, but they barely register the miraculous sword. Clearly, the inquisitors wanted this left alone and without emphasis; their thunderous silence has however ensured some attention.

> *'If we take Jehanne at her word, she had this sword retrieved for no other reason than that her voices had told her about it. Presumably, they also suggested she fetch it. If this is so, why did they indicate this particular sword? No doubt they led the search to the Church of St Catherine because one of the voices allegedly belonged to this Saint, and Jehanne had great devotion for her. But why did her voices lead her to that particular sword and not another? …*
> *Clearly, there must have been something unusual about it.'*
> - Lance Bernard 2001, *The Sword from Heaven*, stjoan-centre.com

Why did Jehanne mention the salient facts that:

a.   The sword was buried in a Church.
b.   It was rusty, but the rust wiped off easily.
c.   The sword had five Crosses on it.
d.   The sword went missing after Saint Denis, in September 1429.

Lance Bernard suggests that the sword could have been Charlemagne's. It was concealed in a Church because it was blessed and used by a Christian King. The effortless rust removal could be because it was stainless steel, *or* because it was made of meteorite metal. Stainless steel is very unlikely – it *is* remotely possible that a medieval armourer or smith experimented with iron and chromium to make the sword, but stainless steel is generally too brittle for combat weapons, and it would have been an exceptionally experimental sword at that time and place. Japanese swords of the same era were made from meteorite metal, and did not rust either. The story of the sword being 'sent by God' to Charlemagne would make sense if it came through the air.

Five Crosses on the sword are intriguing; were they Crusader symbols? Or do they recall the five piercings of Christ at Calvary? Or five stones for slaying a giant?

It is likely that Jehanne gave her sword into her brothers' (i.e. Jean's and Pierre's) keeping after the Army was disbanded at Saint Denis. It disappears.

A last consideration is that the disappearance of the sword coincides with Jehanne's decline as a military leader.

> *'At Tours, she was offered a sword, but insisted the one she needed could be found at St Catherine's Church at Fierbois. The Priests who were sent on this errand did what they were told, and found the sword.... . [Jehanne] was understood to have prophetic gifts, and the sword was a symbol of her approval by God. Later, it would be understood by the English as a sign of her demonic power.* [86]

In medieval piety, no demonic item could have endured in sacred ground, such as the environs of a Church altar. But Jehanne knew there was a sword where no one else knew there was one, and it was an unusual sword. It would not corrode, and it bore symbols which hinted at its use as a weapon in Christian/Crusader Arms. Jehanne had other swords, but this one was revealed and gifted by her voices, who were ultimately messengers of God.

The evidentiary question of this incident/event being raised only once during the whole trial, and that Jehanne could have heard of the sword while she was at Fierbois prior to reaching Chinon and Charles, leaves the

---

[86]    Mary Gordon, *Joan of Arc*, p.42.

question of why she did not retrieve the sword earlier than she did to use as further evidence to convince the tremulous and suspicious Dauphin?

Jehanne's testimony before the trial is characteristically honest and plain. She refused to answer questions pertaining to spiritual entities, or matters she regarded as private to Charles VII, but all her other testimony is plain-spoken and transparent. All witnesses at the Trial of Nullification reiterate her goodness and honesty.

There is no reason at all to doubt her testimony here.

5

## 8
### *At 18, Jehanne is given field command of a French Army.*

'+ *JHESUS MARIA* + *King of England, and you, Duke of Bedford, who call yourself Regent of the Kingdom of France; you, William de la Pole, Earl of Suffolk; John, Lord Talbot; and you Thomas, Lord Scales, who call yourselves lieutenants of the said Duke of Bedford: do justice to the King of Heaven; surrender to the Maid, who is sent here from God, King of Heaven, the keys of all the good towns you have taken and violated in France. She is come from God to uphold the blood royal. She is ready to make peace if you will do justice, relinquishing France and paying for what you have withheld. ...'*
- Jehanne, letter sent to designated English
nobles and officers, 22/3/1429.

18 year-old Jehanne writes (via dictation to a scribe) a letter addressing the King of England (Henry VI, aged 8 at this time). Gently and ironically, a youth addresses a child, over the fates of two increasingly powerful European kingdoms. The English side had appeared to be dominating the

French and succeeding in its quest for preeminence. English royal authority was actually vested in the Regent of France, Bedford, aka Duke John of Lancaster. What is an 18 year-old woman doing by this? Her boldness, her equalising with people normally regarded as far above her station, her confidence and faith, all speak as from an ordained leader.

She warns them, 'Surrender to the Maid.'

> *'You Englishmen, who have no right in this Kingdom of France, the King of Heaven sends you word and warning, by me Jehanne the Maid, to abandon your forts and depart into your own country, or I will raise such a war-cry against you as shall be remembered forever.'*
> - Jehanne, letter shot by arrow to the English forces at Orleans, 4/5/1429.

Only a few days later, on 8/5/1429, the English abandon their siege and they retreat. This is a phenomenal victory for the beleaguered French; a win against all odds.

A widespread legend/prophecy in medieval France was that a maiden ('une pucelle') would rescue France from its oppressions and troubles – some versions even specified a maiden from the borders of Lorraine. The source of the legend is attributed to Merlin himself, the Celtic seer, and/or the Venerable Bede, devout and saintly churchman and chronicler. Jehanne's sudden emergence in the national consciousness in early 1429 is salient; she was widely reputed to be the fulfilment of the prophecy. Her own insistence that she was first and foremost a servant of the King of Heaven, and a servant of the earthly King second, only solidified her reputation. She had authority, both from Heaven and from the Dauphin of France. In late April 1429, after thorough checking by Charles' appointed investigators, she left Blois for Orleans as a leader of the French Army.

Jehanne is the legend who came true:

> *'But people, I have never heard*
> *A story of equal mystery,*
> *For all the champions who lived,*
> *As one goes back through history,*
> *Could not compare in prowess to Jehanne*
> *Who strives our enemies to ban;*
> *For God who counsels her gave her*
> *A greater heart than any man.'*
>
> - Christine de Pisan, Ditié de Jehanne Darc[87], July/August 1429.

This translated excerpt from the only poem/lyric published about Jehanne in her lifetime, expresses the widespread wonder and incredulity about her presence and accomplishments. She is extolled as a great-heart, a champion of prowess, and a mystery. It sums up her effect on people. What it misses, because at the time of composition Jehanne was celebrated, alive and well, is the hatred and fear accumulating against her. Great leaders are usually deeply reviled, as well as deeply admired.

Her leadership in the French Army from April to September 1429, effectively as General, reads like a superhero comic - except Jehanne's military career is demonstrably real.

Medical researchers have sifted the evidence for signs of efficient pathological or psycho-active causes for Jehanne's extraordinary achievements as a military leader, but they were unable to provide an explanation.

> *'In attempting to answer the achievement question, we end up*
> *with a surprise conclusion – we do not have an answer. Although*
> *it has not been difficult to dismiss the medical and psychiatric*

---

[87]    Christine de Pisan 1429, *Ditié de Jehanne d'Arc*, stanza *XXVI*.

*diagnostic claims, the achievement question has left us with empty*
*hands. All efforts to provide an explanation have failed.* [88]

Not quite. Believing Jehanne *is* an explanation – the best one. Ignoring her is to be willfully obtuse.

4

## 9
### Weather and tides change at Orleans.

*'But to reach Orleans it was necessary to sail against the stream [Loire*
*River], and the wind was altogether contrary… Then Jehanne said to*
*me, "… I bring you better succour than has ever come to any general*
*or town whatsoever – the succour of the King of Heaven. This succour*
*does not come from me, but from God Himself." At that moment, the*
*wind, being contrary, and thereby preventing the boats going up the*
*river and reaching Orleans, turned all at once and became favourable.'*
- Jean, Comte de Dunois (Bastard of Orleans),
deponent at Orleans, Trial of Nullification, 1455.

*'[On the sudden change of wind… the witness… added only this:*
*Jehanne had expressly predicted that, before long, the weather and*
*the wind would change; and it happened as she had foretold. …]* [89]
- Raoul de Gaucourt, Grand Steward, deponent
at Orleans, Trial of Nullification, 1455.

---

88    J. Phillips MD, B. Fallon MD et al. 2023, *Undiagnosing St Joan: She Does Not Need*
      *a Medical or Psychiatric Diagnosis,* Journal of Nervous and Mental Disease, *211(8)*
      *pp.559-565.*
89    Retrieved from Jeanne-darc.info : Trial of Nullification, Orleans 1455.

*'The French had with them a convoy of supplies; but the water was
so shallow that the boats could not move upstream, nor could they
land where the English were. Suddenly the waters rose, and the boats
were then able to land on the shore where the French Army was.'*
- Jean Pasquerel, Priest & Monk, Trial of
Nullification, deposition at Paris, 1456.

*'My Lord has sent me to succour this good town of
Orleans. Hope in God. If you have good hope and faith
in Him, you shall be delivered from your enemies.'*
- Jehanne, entering Orleans, 29/4/1429.

Jehanne had openly maintained for six months that God had sent her to help France through military aid and the restoration of the rightful French government (i.e. Charles VII of the French House of Valois, as against Henry VI of the English House of Plantagenet). The military aid was in the form of Jehanne herself, and the government was in the form of Charles VII. Neither of these appeared propitious to observers and stakeholders. Then, to Charles' evident amazement at Chinon, the Lorrainian peasant who had never seen or heard him previously, walked straight up to him in a crowded room in which he was also disguised, and identified him. (*See event 5 above.*)

When asked by examiners at Poitiers, who were tasked with ascertaining her validity as a messenger from God and what kind of aid she was offering, she basically told them to stop wasting time so she could get on with liberating Orleans, which was at the point of capitulating to the English. The capture of Orleans would have opened all of southern France to English invasion, occupation, and incorporation into the realm of England. It was a big deal, and France's sovereign existence was on a knife's edge.

Charles accepted what he already knew, but had fumbled due to his characteristic timidity, suspicion and caution. He sent Jehanne to Orleans with the French Army. She arrived just after the French had suffered another exhausting, debilitating defeat (the 'Battle of the Herrings') and were barely hanging on. The French could not re-supply their army because the River was their only realistic way in, and the water level was too low, with the wind blowing the opposite way; it was desperately, depressingly inauspicious.

Then Jehanne arrived. The wind suddenly turned 180°, the river level became navigable, and the French position favourable.

4

## 10
### *Jehanne passing the Saint Loup tourelle without the English knowing.*

*'Even if their numbers were not large, the Saint Loup soldiers were probably sufficient in strength to keep the small French force, with its slow-moving supply train, from entering the city until reinforcements could arrive. Again… witnesses claim, a miracle occurred. Jehanne and her company passed the boulevard of Saint Loup seemingly without any incident at all.'*
- Kelly DeVries, *Joan of Arc: A Military Leader*, p.68.

*'And we passed beyond the Church of Saint Loup despite the English. From that moment, I had good hope in her, more than before; and I then implored her consent to cross the river of Loire and to enter into the town of Orleans where she was greatly wished for.'* [90]
- Jean, Count of Dunois (Bastard of Orleans), Deponent at Orleans, Trial of Nullification, 1455.

---

[90]    See R. Pernoud 1962, *Joan of Arc*, p.82

This is a miracle easily bypassed. Miracles are generally celebrated and fêted, but this one is commonly swept into the bundle of astonishing events we call the *Raising of the Siege of Orleans*. Jehanne's presence at Orleans initiated vital weather and water-level changes, which allowed the French Army and the City of Orleans to receive desperately needed supplies. Saint Loup was a robust and well accoutered fortification on the outskirts of Orleans, with a Church nestled next to it; the English could see any enemy approaches, and shoot lethal projectiles from relative safety if needed. Getting past Saint Loup was moreorless impossible, hence the French yearning to sail up the river, even though that was also an exposed route – it was less risky than the road that ran past the front gate.

Jehanne carefully led a supply train (i.e. long wagon convoy) past the Fort, on the road/track, and the English seemed blindly oblivious, despite their commanding position and substantial interest in preventing exactly what Jehanne did. Like the Sword at St Catherine de Fierbois, and the weather and tides changing instantaneously adjacent to Orleans, this event has an almost mythic quality. It is the kind of thing we read in fantasy fiction; but, not with this. It happened.

5

## 11
### *Predicting her wounding, and successfully leading the assault on the tourelle.*

'When evening fell, Jehanne ... went to the bridge and thence spoke
to Classidas [William Glasdale, an English Commander] and to the
other English who were in the Tourelle [bridge fort] and told them
that if they would yield themselves at God's command, they were safe.
But Glasdale answered basely, insulting her and calling her a 'cow-
girl', shouting very loudly that they would have her burned if they

*could get their hands on her. At which Jehanne was much enraged and answered them that they lied, and then withdrew into the city.'*
- Jehanne at Orleans, about 30/4/1429, from
*Journal of the Siege of Orleans*[91].

*'Keep close to me all day, for tomorrow I shall have much to do and greater things than I have had to do yet. And tomorrow blood will flow from my body, above my breast.'*
- Jehanne, to Jean Pasquerel (Jehanne's
Chaplain), Orleans, 6/5/1429.

*'... Jehanne went to the attack of the bridge-fort, in which was the Englishman Classidas [Glasdale]. ... At this assault, after dinner, Jehanne, as she predicted, was struck by an arrow above the breast. Some of the soldiers, seeing her severely wounded, wanted to 'charm' her*[92]*, but Jehanne would not, saying she would rather die than commit what she knew to be a sin. Oil of olive and lard were applied to the wound. After the dressing, she confessed herself to me, weeping and lamenting. Then she returned... to the attack, crying: "Classidas, Classidas! Yield thee, yield to the King of Heaven! Thou hast called me 'Whore' - I have great pity for thy soul, and for thy people!" At this moment, Classidas, fully armed from head to foot, stumbled into the Loire River, where he was drowned. Jehanne, moved with pity, began to weep for the soul of Classidas.'*
- Jehanne, at Orleans 7/5/1429, deposition of Jean
Pasquerel, Trial of Nullification, 1456.

---

91    Ibid. p.84.
92    i.e. use folk magic – some kind of talisman.

How did she know that she would be wounded, and the specifics of the wound?

Jean Pasquerel, Jehanne's Chaplain and an eye-witness, describes Jehanne's wound as 'severe', which makes her subsequent return to the fight just a little more remarkable. Other soldiers who saw her wound were sufficiently alarmed to suggest she needed something magic, indicating they thought she was beyond merely human medical agency. Smearing congealed animal fat and olive oil over the wound might seem like hocus-pocus to us in the C21st, but to those soldiers, that was clearly normal practice, and they believed she needed extra (supernatural) help. They were right, but it came not in the way they anticipated. She rebuked them for their suggestion (because it invoked pagan practice), but left it at that – she obviously understood they meant well. After this, she went back to the battle.

This action to eject the English from a fortified bridge-tower ('tourelle' in French) was dangerous and high-risk. The fighting lasted all day, and only in the evening did the French make progress. When Jehanne was wounded, the French believed she was severely wounded, possibly a mortal wound, and this was as disheartening to them as it was encouraging for the English. Soon afterwards she re-entered the fray, inspirationally planting herself with her banner in front of the English on the French frontline, which greatly unnerved the English, who thought she was mortally wounded. Their defences thence deteriorated rapidly - not helped by Glasdale dramatically drowning as he hurled abuse at Jehanne, leading to renewed assault by the French. And a formidable victory.

Jehanne's deeply felt pity for 'Classidas' (her French rendering of 'Glasdale') underlines again her capacity for compassion and grace. He had yelled obscenities at her, threatened her with an agonizing death by fire if he caught her (as Regine Pernoud noted, a threat the English later fulfilled), and mocked her with sexist insults. He had shown no gallantry or respect for an unlikely and formidable opponent, only dismissive disdain and contempt. Why did Jehanne pity him? Pity arises from compassion; this very compellingly shows Jehanne's real self. There is no pretense or pretending. She knew that it was pointless to oppose her at Orleans, and she felt sorry for even the witless Glasdale, whose hardness of heart and lack of faith were his doom.

This action effectively ended the Siege of Orleans. A victory believed impossible only a week before.

5

## 12
## *Routing the English at Jargeau, Meung and Patay.*

*'After the deliverance of Orleans, the Maid, with myself and the
other captains, went to seek the King at the castle at Loches, praying
him to attack immediately the towns and the camps on the Loire,
Mehun, Beaugency, Jargeau in order to make his consecration at
Rheims more free and sure. ...the King... sent, for this purpose,
the Duke d'Alencon, myself and other captains, as well as Jehanne,
to reduce these towns and camps. All were reduced in a few days
– thanks alone, as I believe, to the intervention of the Maid.'*
- Jean, Count de Dunois, deponent at
Orleans, Trial of Nullification 1455.

*'... [the English] who survived (i.e. the fighting at Orleans) retreated
next day to Beaugency and Meung. The King's army followed them,
Jehanne accompanying it. ...on the day of combat, the English
retired again; and the (French) army began afresh to pursue them...
the King's army was victorious: nearly all the English were slain.'*
- Louis de Contes, deponent at Paris, Trial of Nullification 1455-56.

*'On the day that the Lord Talbot (English General), who had been
taken at Patay, was brought to the town of Beaugency, I arrived at that
town; and from thence Jehanne went with the men-at-arms to Jargeau,
which was taken by assault, and the English were put to flight.'*
- Gobert Thibaut, Squire to Charles VII, deponent
at Paris, Trial of Nullification 1455-56.

*'On the French side, three men were dead; on the English side, the
Burgundian chroniclers estimated the casualties at two thousand.
... "Thus the French gained great victory at the place called
Patay, where they spent the night, thanking Our Lord for their
fine adventure... because of its location, that battle will forever
be called the 'The Day of Patay.' " The unexpected outcome of this
encounter provoked panic all the way to Paris... But it was not
against Paris that Jehanne intended to direct the royal army... In
the aftermath of combat, the dauphin agreed to head for Rheims.'*
- R. Pernoud, M-V. Clin 1998, *Joan of Arc: Her Story*, pp. 61-62.

The success of French military actions in 1429-30 prevented the Anglo-
Burgundian subjugation of France under the English Plantagenet dynasty.
The Armagnacs (French loyal to Charles VII and the House of Valois) were
positioned to resume and extend French sovereignty over all France. The
ending of the siege at Orleans, and the subsequent and incredible victories
in places like Jargeau, Beaugency, Meung and Patay, opened the way for the
loyal French to defeat English attempts at invading all of France. In 1428,
this looked hopeless; by the end of 1430 it looked both feasible and likely.

The French claimant to the throne Charles VII, neither a great King
nor an inspiring one, was a very different person to Jehanne, who did not
understand his reluctances and deep-seated suspicions of others' motives.
Jehanne trusted God; Charles trusted prejudice, pragmatism and dealing

(aka *diplomacy*). We see the same pattern of maltreatment towards other great Christians like Martin Luther King, Dietrich Bonhoffer, and Manche Masemola. People who do not trust or honour God will seek to exploit, emaciate or eliminate those who do.

Jehanne established her fame as a (teenaged) military commander in 1429-30, especially as she campaigned along the Loire Valley to escort Charles to Rheims where he would be consecrated King of France. The battles she won are extraordinary. There are comprehensive and excellent histories that already detail these events (see *bibliography*). One startling example of Jehanne's closeness and connection with God occurred at the battle of Jargeau, where she told Jean, Duke d'Alencon, to move away from a particular position because he would be killed if he stayed there. D'Alencon listened to Jehanne and moved away, only to note shortly after that another man was killed in that exact spot[93]. That precise foreknowing is prophetic – we cannot know such things by our own surmisings.

Jehanne initiated the liberation of France and ultimate success in the Hundred Years' War through the military movement from Orleans to Rheims.

4.5

## 13
## *Sacring of Charles VII at Rheims.*

*'Many times in my presence Jehanne told the King she would last but one year and no more; and that he should consider how best to employ this year. She had, she said, four duties to accomplish: to beat the English; to have the King crowned and*

---

[93]   K. DeVries 1999, *Joan of Arc*, p. 98.

*consecrated at Rheims; to deliver the Duke of Orleans from
the hands of the English; and to raise the siege of Orleans.'*
- Jean, Duke d'Alencon, deponent at Paris,
Trial of Nullification, 1455-56.

Jehanne is very clear that her ultimate duty and loyalty is to God. Her secondary duty and loyalty is to France, and the King who is the Head of Government in the Kingdom, under God. It was not a complete appointment until Charles the Dauphin submitted to God's Authority, which was done through anointing and oaths made to God's Sovereignty at Rheims cathedral on 17/7/1429. When this was done, Charles was both appointed and consecrated as King and Ruler of France, under God. His sacring was Jehanne's most pressing and motivating objective. It made Charles VII God's rightfully appointed Sovereign.

' *"How did the angel carry the crown? And did
he place it himself on your King's head?"*
*"The crown was given to an Archbishop – that is, to the Archbishop
of Rheims – so it seems to me, in the presence of my King. The
Archbishop received it, and gave it to the King. I was myself present.
The crown was afterwards put among my King's treasures."* '
- Inquisitors and Jehanne, Fourth Private Examination,
Trial of Condemnation, 13/3/1431, Rouen.

It is apt and contextualizing to remember that the notations and records of the Trial of Condemnation were prone to embellishments, omissions and distortions through the conveniences of the criminally biased Inquisition which formed the Trial. The record was also written in French, then translated into Latin, and then had to be translated back into French (or whichever language is/was needful) to be understandable. Precision and nuance are always lost in translation, however carefully done.

This item is both puzzling and intriguing. For an account of a plainly supernatural incident, it is strangely overlooked in many histories which very carefully describe and depict other Jehanne miracles. Jehanne is recalling an episode in which an angel provides a crown for Charles. She recounts the incident as if it was just another day, but this time other people are noted as having seen the angel. Generally, Jehanne alone saw the angels, or the Light with the Voice, but not this time – others also perceived something supernatural (Biblically, this is not so unusual, cf. **Acts** 9:3-7).

Jehanne describes an angel delivering a crown for Charles' sacring. This occurs well before arrival in Rheims, alluding to Chinon, which would date the event in March 1429, not July. Jehanne indicates that Charles also saw the angel, and the Archbishop of Rheims, but that others present did not see him (she uses masculine references). This incident underscores the divinity of God's establishment of the government of France, and Charles' perception of Jehanne as an authentic messenger of God.

> *'At the core of the rite was the anointing itself... The King prostrated himself on the steps of the altar, while litanies of the Saints were chanted. The Archbishop who had prostrated himself at the King's side, marked the King with holy oil... The crown was taken from the altar and placed on the new King's head... It was then that, as depicted on the seals of the time, the new King appeared in royal majesty. ...During the aforesaid mystery, the Maid was always at the King's side, holding his standard in her hand.'*
> - Regine Pernoud & Marie-Veronique Clin.[94]

---

[94]    R. Pernoud & M-V. Clin 1998, Joan of Arc: Her Story, pp.65-66.

Jehanne was warmly and devotedly close to Charles during the sacring; she was next to him in the cathedral. With her was the banner she had carried throughout the Orleans and Loire Valley campaign[95]. Her remarkable battle-sword was not flourished about, but she often carried and waved her banner, on which Jesus and His Dominion were artistically depicted. From start to finish, Jehanne ensured Jesus was central to the King's position. A peasant girl from Lorraine, the prophesied Maiden to liberate France, a teen who defeated the English army, standing quietly beside the Dauphin as he became King.

4

14

### *Resurrecting a dead baby at Lagny, late April 1430.*

*'But Peter asked them all to leave the room; then he knelt*
*and prayed. Turning to the corpse he said, "Get up, Tabitha."*
*And she opened her eyes! When she saw Peter, she sat up.'*
- Luke, and Peter (aka Simon), Apostle
of Jesus the Christ, **Acts** 9:40.

*' "How old was the child you visited at Lagny?"*
*"The child was three days old. It (or 'he') was brought before the*
*Image of Our Lady. They told me that the maidens of the village*
*were before this image. I wanted to go and pray to God and Our*
*Lady to give life to this infant. I went and prayed with them. At*
*last, life returned to the child, who yawned three times, and was*
*then baptized; soon after, it/he died and was buried in consecrated*
*ground. Three days had passed, so they said, during which no life*

---

[95]    R. Pernoud 1962, p.125.

*had appeared in this child; it/he was as black as my coat, but when*
*it/he yawned, the colour began to return to it/him. I was with*
*the other maidens, praying and kneeling before Our Lady."* [96]
- Inquisitors and Jehanne, Trial of Condemnation, 3/3/1431, Rouen.

*'… she moved on to Lagny, where another miracle occurred. A baby*
*believed dead was brought to her… "As black as my cloak," she*
*reported at her trial. When she took the baby in her arms, he drew*
*breath, and lived long enough to be baptized before he died.'*
- Mary Gordon 2000, *Joan of Arc*, p.72.

*'By 29th March [1430], she was in Lagny, dated there by the miracle*
*of her restoring the life of a baby long enough for it to be baptized…'*
- Kelly DeVries 1999, *Joan of Arc: A Military Leader*, p.162.

The significance of Catholic doctrine is important for context here. The medieval Roman Catholic Church believed and taught a perspective on sin in which the sacrament (ritual) of baptism is essential to a child's eternal condition. This view, which commends infant baptism, is still current although its authority may have changed; it is also believed and practiced in many Protestant Churches, with their own variations and distinctives (e.g. the Anglican, Lutheran and Calvinical Churches all baptize babies). Our interest is in what the people of Jehanne's time in Catholic France believed.

*'…children who did not live long enough to be baptized… were*
*believed to spend eternity apart from God in Limbo, separated*
*from their families in both burial and the hereafter.'* [97]

---

[96]    Retrieved from Jeanne-darc.info, *Trial of Condemnation*, Sixth public examination & R. Pernoud 1962, *Joan of Arc*, pp.147-8.
[97]    Crow M. et al 2020, *Doctrinal and Physical Marginality in Christian Death: the Burial of Unbaptized Infants in Medieval Italy.*

This explanation derives from work on belief and practice in medieval Italy, but the beliefs and practices of the Catholic Church were similar across medieval Europe. The common Catholic belief in 'original sin' implicates all of humanity in sin, for which all are separated from God. So, providing the sacrament of baptism to babies was important for the very basic reason that a child's eternal status and situation depended on reception of the sacrament, such that the original sin of Adam which tainted the child was removed by the cleansing atonement of Christ. The sacrament was intensely important. People believed this firmly and deeply. Only baptized babies could be buried in consecrated ground, guaranteeing their admission to Heaven. Otherwise, their souls would spend eternity in *Limbo* – a kind of perpetual, spiritual suspended-animation.

The branch of Protestantism which is today widely called '*evangelical*' neither believes nor commends this theological position (E.g. Baptist, Church of Christ, and most Pentecostal Churches).

Catholic doctrinal reasoning is that *original sin* is the sin we inherit through Adam, and it implicates all humans in sin because sin is characteristic of humanity, just like consciousness is characteristic of humanity. Original sin is not volitional sin, it is inherited sin – but any sin separates us from God. The Catholic Church basically taught/teaches that original sin is expiated in young children through baptism. So, the sooner one is baptized, the better one is covered by the Grace of God. Without baptism, original sin condemns us to separation from God.

Evangelical Christians do not believe this; they do believe in original sin, but not that it condemns babies or infants. That is a doctrine held by the Catholic Church. Disagreement on this point was a significant spark in the ignition of the Reformation. Early evangelical Christians were known as 'Anabaptists' ('re-baptisers') who preached that baptism was required only once a person could make a volitional (informed and deliberate) profession of individual faith; very young children cannot do this, so evangelical Christians believe that young children will be received into Heaven without baptism because they cannot commit sin as responsible people (Jesus is very clear about this, e.g. **Luke** 18:15-17.) In medieval France, the Catholic Church was the sole source and arbiter of doctrine.

Jehanne certainly believed infant baptism was true and necessary.

If infant baptism is actually *unnecessary* to salvation of someone's soul however, then why did God revive this 3-day dead baby? This little child only revived for a short time – long enough to be baptized by a priest. Why bother?

Because God is understanding and kind; He often allows eventualities which help us, but may not be effectively necessary. Why did He feed 20000 people with just five buns and two fish (see **Mark** 6:30-43)? Those people could all have gone and found food, or survived a few more hours. God did that because it helped those people – it echoes the manna that God provided through Moses (see **Exodus** 16). It helped people believe and know that Jesus is both powerful and good, as God is powerful and good. Jehanne had no personal access to the Bible, but she would have known some of the fundamental facts of faith, e.g. that Jesus was dead for three days. Connections like that were given to help Jehanne, who also carried a heavy Cross.

This baby boy (the child's gender is immaterial really, but a quirk of French grammar is that the pronoun 'il' can be understood/translated as either masculine or neuter, so where context provides no key, the baby could be indeterminate, or male) revived long enough to be prepared for Heaven. Jehanne would have firmly believed this Catholic doctrine. It was regarded as essential for salvation to be baptized at or close to birth. God seems to do this for Jehanne's benefit, not for the baby boy's.

It is, in any sense, a staggering display of God's power. God resurrected Tabitha through the Apostle Peter's agency. God alone can do this. Jehanne is reminded graphically that God is greater than death. This newborn baby had turned black, a description of rigor mortis, and had shown no signs of life for three days – i.e. no movement, no breathing, no heartbeat, no excreta, no cooing or crying. The child's corpse is what they have. Then, when Jehanne joins some girls praying for the baby (remember that these uneducated medieval French girls believed this baby was doomed to separation from God unless the baptism happened), he revives, yawns, gets colour, and is baptized. Then he dies. That is sad, but for those people, it was now acceptable. He was destined for Heaven.

Jehanne is shown incontrovertibly that God is beyond death.

5

## 15
### *Grace in extremis (like the Apostle Paul, Dietrich Bonhoeffer, Manche Masemola).*

*'Do you remember what I told you? A servant is not greater than the master. Since they persecuted me, naturally they will persecute you. And if they had listened to me, they would listen to you. The people of the world will hate you because you belong to me, for they don't know God who sent me.'*
- Jesus the Christ, **John** 15: 20-21.

*'I think Jehanne died as a Catholic, for, in dying, she cried on the name of the Lord Jesus. She was very devout, and nearly all present were moved to tears. After she was dead, the ashes that remained were collected by the executioner and thrown into the Seine.'*[98]
- Laurence Guesdon, Advocate in the Civil Courts, deponent at Trial of Nullification, Rouen 1456.

---

[98]  Transcript sources of Jehanne's Trials retrieved from Jeanne-darc.info

*'Jehanne was put in irons; ... thus fettered [she] was given over to the custody of four English, although the Bishop and the Inquisitor had stated and sworn that they would themselves faithfully keep her. Jehanne was treated with cruelty, and towards the end of the Trial, was shown the torture. ... she put on man's clothing and lamented that she dare not doff these, fearing that at night the guards might attempt some violence. I, as notary, wrote Jehanne's answers and defence. Two or three writers who were secretly ensconced near, omitted, in their writing, all that was in her favour. ...* [99]
- Guillaume Manchon, Notary of the Trial of Condemnation, Second Examination rescript on authority of Pope Calixtus III, 2/5/1452.

*'I do not know whether she asked for Counsel, but I think no one would have dared to counsel or defend her, nor would they have been permitted. ...* [100]
- Brother Pierre Migier, Prior of Longueville, Second Examination, 2/5/1452.

*'... [Jehanne] was led to the Old Market-Place... accompanied by more than 800 soldiers, with axes and swords... she evinced her contrition, penitence, fervent faith... devotions, lamentations and true confession of faith, she besought mercy also, most humbly, from all manner of people whatever condition or estate they might be... begging them to pray for her, forgiving them the harm they had done her...'* [101]
- Maitre Jean Massieu, Priest, First Inquiry 1449, Rescript on authority of Charles VII, King of France.

---

[99]   Ibid.
[100]   Ibid.
[101]   Ibid.

The Inquisitorial Court organized to kill Jehanne was as corrupt as the depraved and cowardly men who conducted its business. Even though Jehanne very rightly and justifiably asked to be taken to Rome for judgment by the Pope, this was denied her. The putrid case of confected 'evidence' assembled by Bishop Pierre Cauchon and his accomplices to condemn Jehanne was a diseased fabrication – it would never convict anyone in a just and fair court. She was judicially murdered by the Catholic Church, treacherous French dupes, and the amoral government of England. The actual King of England was only 10 years old, and had no capacity to conduct or supervise the affairs of the judiciary, nor parliament. Jehanne was condemned and killed because she had won the liberation of France against the English and all humiliating odds, and because she followed the will and purposes of God, at 18-19 years of age! As with Jesus Himself, her devotion and faith took her to terrible death.

She prayed forgiveness for them.

5

## Voices, Angels and Saints.

### 1. Jesus and spirits to Jehanne.

Jehanne was equally guarded and open about whom she called *Voices*.

These voices taught, directed and encouraged Jehanne in her life from about the age of thirteen, inspiring in her great respect and pleasure with their company and guidance.

She identifies them plainly as **angels** and as **saints**. She does not say this is an exclusive description.

> '...I could easily hear the Voice which came to me... I believe it was sent me by God. When I heard it for the third time, I recognized that it was the Voice of an Angel. This Voice has

*always guarded me well, and I have always understood it….'*
[102]

Jehanne identifies Saint Michael, Saint Catherine (of Alexandria) and Saint Margaret (of Antioch) explicitly as voices, in the Trial of Condemnation (4th Public Examination, 27/2/1431).

(N.B. Other conjectures and theories about the Voices are accessible and available in libraries and online. Pathogenic causes [e.g. tuberculosis] and psychiatric conditions [e.g. schizophrenia], have been thoroughly canvassed too. For more about this, please see the bibliography at the end of this text and read some more specific material.)

Overall, the explanations investigated and offered by science are more mystical and unlikely than the explanation very simply and consistently provided by Jehanne. Recent scientific and medical research (2025 atow) has decided that Jehanne was exactly who she said she was, and that all of her astounding and miraculous achievements were/are exactly what she says they are[103].

The Bible teaches that *Angels* are intelligent and relational beings different to humans and God, and able to manifest in human form. They are a separate and distinct order of created Beings. Angels themselves refuse any association or attribution as God or gods. Of Mary Magdalene, Jehanne Darc and Sophie Scholl, only Jehanne has/had consistent/regular relationship with angels. Mary Magdalene did see and communicate with angels, but so far as we know, that was only one occasion. Sophie Scholl does not share any such experience(s) or relationship(s).

---

[102]  Jehanne, 22/2/1431, 2nd Public Examination, Trial of Condemnation, Rouen. Retrieved from Jeanne-darc.info
[103]  J. Phillips, M. Fallon et al. 2023, *Undiagnosing St. Joan: She Does Not Need a Medical or Psychiatric Diagnosis*, Journal of Nervous and Mental Disease.

Saint Michael is a curious case; he is an angel[104], but also designated a Saint in the Catholic and Orthodox Churches. How can an angel be also a Saint, because Saints are exemplary Christians recognized and reverenced for their outstanding devotion and piety? They are <u>humans</u>. Catholic and Orthodox piety believe Saints can convey prayers to God (an area of belief which, among others, separated them from the Protestants like the Reformed and the Anabaptists) so have a prominence they do not have in Protestant traditions. Protestants understand the word 'saint' simply to mean a committed follower of Christ; there is no hagiographical aura. Michael as angel *and* saint is then a Catholic, High Anglican and Orthodox conflation.

In the Bible, angels are invariably identified as male, whereas saints are naturally both genders/sexes. There is speculation by some people which advances the idea that femininity or femaleness was only created by God at the final event of Creation in Eden. This is a serious misunderstanding of **Genesis** 1:27, and is more of a 'fringe' position. The male (masculine) and female (feminine) are equal representations of the Image of God, and therefore God is both genders. God is fully male, and fully female; S/He is not a non-binary confusion, but simply, completely and discretely both. While angels always manifest physically as males when they appear in human form in the Bible, that does not in any way preclude the existence of female angels. Not seeing something does not mean that it does not exist. Nobody has ever seen or touched *time*, but no rational person would say it does not exist.

Jesus alludes to angels *not marrying* (**Luke** 20:34-36), which has led to further speculation that angels do not have gender. Obviously, they do. We cannot ascribe masculinity to a creature unless it carries the obvious

---

[104]   See **Daniel** 12:1, **Jude** 9.

imprint(s) of masculinity, and is objectively different to the feminine. Jesus only said that angels do not marry; he did not say there were no female angels. (N.B. excepting Peter, none of the Apostles are specifically identified as being married either, but we can be confident that if only for cultural reasons, they certainly were. It is not mentioned because it is not material to their commitment to Christ [our commitment to Christ is the one relationship which takes precedence even over marriage]). Jesus teaches us that in Heaven we will not marry, just like angels don't marry, but it will always be the case that humans *can* marry. 'Not marrying' is not evidence of no females. We can also remember that Adam and Eve did not marry either. There was no wedding in Eden – marriage was their commitment to each other, and marriage as an institution actually came with the Fall, as did predation. It seems very normal to us now, but neither of these practices were given in the Beginning – probably because they were not necessary. Jesus does not teach that angels *cannot* marry, which would mean it was not possible; He teaches that it *does not* happen. God has not created it to them, and God will have reasons.

Genesis 6:4 alludes to creatures identified as *nephilim*, a Hebrew word translating most plainly as 'fallen ones', who were attracted to human women. The mention of the *nephilim* immediately precedes and connects to God's statement of regret at creating humanity, because they/we became so wicked (**Genesis** 6:5-6). The presence of the nephilim had obviously been disastrous – they were not meant to be here, but they came anyway – there was a way for them to further corrupt the Creation. The nephilim, if they are angels, or a kind of fallen angels, are clearly sexual. If fallen angels are male, and can have sexual intercourse with human women, then the direct implication is that female variants of angels must exist, otherwise their sexual capacity is pointless, and nothing that God creates is pointless. They can desire and cohabit with human women, so they are not asexual/

neuter. (That is not what God says anywhere either.) They had the capacity for sexual union, but the Bible does not indicate any kind of intimacy or family, only that they found human women attractive, could conceive children with them, and such children were unusually strong, with the peculiar characteristic of having extra fingers and toes.

The Great Flood follows, and purges all people/humans except Noah and his family from the Earth. We are not told what happened to the nephilim or their children with human mothers. These are identified as 'giants' (*nephilim*, or *anakim*). **Genesis** 7:21 indicates that all *people* died in the Flood. The children born of the nephilim and women are not called 'people'.

As Jehanne had no capacity to read the Bible herself, she likely knew nothing of the Biblical passages about angels, except that they were holy and servants of God. She most likely had never heard of 'nephilim', 'anakim', or 'Seraphim' for that matter, and indicates that she often saw angels as if she was seeing people. There is no hint of revulsion or fear. Nor does she describe anything like the angels we know as 'Cherubim' (see **Ezekiel** 10:12) who do *not* look like typical humans; they are other and different. When she was asked about angels during the Trial, some were described as wingéd, and some not; this is Biblical – some angels have wings, but not all. She did describe her first experience of encountering the Voice in her father's garden as 'terrifying'. In describing the Voice, she does not say the Voice and the Light are the same being or phenomenon – but that she saw great light, *and* heard a Voice. We have to be careful to read the facts, not jump to constructions!

The Saints identified by Jehanne are *Margaret of Antioch* and *Catherine of Alexandria*, both of whom were martyred in the early Church. Catherine was a particularly adored and precious Saint to Jehanne, so her appearance is understandable, as Jehanne would trust her.

We cannot overlook the magnitude of what God asked of Jehanne. She needed reassurance. That these two Saints were both martyrs, seems not to have disturbed Jehanne.

## 2. Jesus as sacrifice and martyr to Jehanne.

Christians are accustomed to knowing Jesus as the *Lamb of God* – the sacrificial Lamb whose blood is atonement for our sins.

In this we also see Jehanne. While we know that Jehanne was not a perfect person, she did live with purity of intent and purpose, and she achieved this to a high degree. She followed Jesus not only geographically and doctrinally, but attitudinally and behaviourally. Her degrees of integrity and purity separate her from the great majority of us. Jesus reveals Himself to us as Truth (see **John** 14:6), and sincere followers will seek to imitate this in their faith.

> '... she was so good that all the village of Domremy loved her. Jeannette knew her **Belief** and **Pater** and **Ave** as well as any of her companions. She had modest ways...* [105]

> 'Often, when we were all at play, Jeannette would retire alone to "talk with God"... she was simple and good, frequenting the Church and Holy places...* [106]

> 'She was a girl of good disposition, devout, patient, loving the Church, going often to confession, and giving to the poor all that she could.* [107]

---

[105] Jean Morel, Trial of Nullification, Deposition at Domremy 1455. Retrieved from Jeanne-darc.info

[106] Jean Waterin, Trial of Nullification, Deposition at Domremy 1455. Ibid.

[107] Durand Laxart, Trial of Nullification, Deposition at Domremy 1455. Ibid.

Contact with the Voice(s) was at their (i.e. God's) initiative, not Jehanne's. She describes them as coming to her, not as visitors/visitations on summons, though they did come to her if she prayed to God for their help. Almost invariably, the contact was delightful, and she wished she could go with them when they left her[108]. A consistent facet of her interaction with the angels and saints is that she is very careful in the detail she shares with her trial Inquisitors, who try to extract information about the voice(s) from her[109]. That she maneuvered through webs of deceit and guileful ensnarement as adroitly as she did is miraculous in itself; she was a young woman, isolated and alone, despicably treated for a fell year in cold and grim prisons, and denied all natural justice. (Eventually, she was sentenced to death - for wearing men's clothes.) She most often tells them that she does not have leave or permission to share detail about the Voices, but communicates openly when she perceives no obstacle. The source of guidance and instruction through the Voices is a mixture of 'from God', and attribution to the Voices themselves; ultimately her source is always from God.

Jehanne's life and experience serve to mirror the Biblical record. For instance, the Apostle John is not permitted to publish what he hears in **Revelation** 10:4. Zechariah was struck mute and prevented from communicating in **Luke** 1:22. Jesus directly tells people in **Mark** 5:43 not to share the news of a miraculous healing He has given (but this time they

---

[108]  Jehanne, 27/2/1431, 4th Public Examination, Trial of Condemnation, Rouen. Retrieved from Jeanne-darc.info

[109]  The Inquisitors, like Pierre Cauchon, Nicolas Midi and Jean Beaupere, were seeking means to incriminate Jehanne. Their motives are malevolent, murderous and destructive, so their questions to Jehanne on the subject of Voices, Saints and Angels are never honestly interested; they are only hoping for something whereby to condemn her. They did not succeed.

disobey Him). Jehanne is not unusual in keeping hidden what she knows. If anything, she is quite transparent.

She lived on Earth as if she was in Heaven. The standards she applied and lived are universally high principles of truth and integrity. In this she reflects a normality we identify as Heavenly, where there is no corruption or darkness. The Voices spoke to her from this dimension, and she applied that hegemony to herself at all times. Jehanne knew the prayer we call 'The Lord's Prayer'. She knew it in Latin (i.e. the *Pater Noster* - memorized by all Catholics from an early age), and knew its meanings. '*Thy Kingdom Come. Thy Will be Done…*' is a powerful call to actualize God's immanence and guidance in all our life, and Jesus taught us that the Kingdom of God is within us[110] – we are the ones in whom the Kingdom is realized. Jehanne did this. Where she was, the Kingdom was with her and in her. The demarcation of sanctity against abomination is rarely so stark as the Trial against Jehanne. **Hebrews** 11:35b-38 speaks eloquently to the situation in which Jehanne found herself from May 1430 to May 1431. As Jesus was treated, so was she. Her identification with Jesus was close and identical, in that she endured cruel torment, and undeserved death. She followed Jesus to the end.

Jesus was despised before the Sanhedrin, and cast before Pilate. Jehanne shows us what Dietrich Bonhoeffer calls 'costly grace'[111]. She walks with Jesus, reminding us through her suffering that He and His Way are the antithesis of the world's way.

We so easily forget.

---

[110] See **Luke** 17:21.
[111] Dietrich Bonhoeffer 1937, *The Cost of Discipleship*, ch. 1.

### 3. Jesus as Voice to Jehanne.

> *'... I sent for the first time to the Castle of Chinon, where the King was... After dinner I went to the King who was at the Castle. When I entered the room where he was I recognized him among many others by the counsel of my Voice, which revealed him to me...'* [112]

The Voice is a guide. Jehanne does not identify the Voice in this instance, which is consistent with her approach until later at the 4th Public Examination at Rouen.

This is also consistent with Jesus' promises to us; *He guides*. He incarnates the Kingdom of God within us so that where a Christian is openly and obediently following God, *there* is the Kingdom. That was certainly so with Jehanne. When Jesus calls people to *follow* Him, there are no lavish guarantees of a comfortable and coddled life featuring large property portfolios and boutique-label wardrobes. He explicitly says _not_ to expect or seek that (see **Matthew** 19:21-24). He says, 'Follow Me', and eternal life with God is the blessing we receive (**John** 10:27-28). He says that following Him is to take up a cross – i.e. that there will be suffering. A direction that we should *follow* directly implies that there shall be *guidance*; Jesus says He will guide us. He is our Guide.

It is also all that Jehanne asked of the Voice(s) – that her soul would be in Paradise.

> *'But never have I asked of it any recompense but the salvation of my soul.'* [113]

---

[112]   Jehanne, 22/2/1431, 2nd Public Examination, Trial of Condemnation, Rouen. Retrieved from Jeanne-darc.info

[113]   Ibid.

Jehanne is referencing the Voice in the past historic sense. She is reflecting back to prior positions and describing it/them from within the memories. She is narrating communication with the Voice, and is speaking of 'it' in the singular and neuter. As already noted, French relies on context to differentiate the masculine and neuter persons represented by 'il'. So, the above reference could be speaking of a 'him' (naturally, I defer to those with far more fluent mastery of the French tongue than I). Either way, the object of the clause is a being – a Voice. We are left with the question: why is she seeking salvation of her soul from an angel? Medieval Catholic theology and piety may have had peculiarities, but Jesus is always acknowledged as Saviour. *Saviour* as in 'One who saves from sin unto eternal life in Heaven'. Who is Jehanne speaking to? Who is the singular Voice she seems to identify as an angel, but also avoids identifying as *one* being. At no point does she say the Light and the Voice are the same being/entity. Lest you are thinking, 'That's a bit of a stretch!', bear in mind that she could very clearly differentiate St Catherine and St Margaret from the Archangel Michael, who is a mighty Angel. (If he was the one advising Jehanne, it is no wonder she smashed the English all the way from Orleans to Rheims.)

Jehanne would not ask an angel for salvation; *nor* would Michael allow her to make that error.

When she speaks of Michael, she uses his name; likewise when she communes with Saints Catherine and Margaret.

Who then was she talking to?

## 4. Jesus as Light to Jehanne.

*'The light comes at the same time as the voice.'*[114]

---

[114]   Jehanne, 24/2/1431, 3rd Public Examination, Trial of Condemnation, Rouen. Retrieved from Jeanne-darc.info

*Light* does seem to attend angels and divine beings. Jesus identifies as the 'Light of the World' (**John** 8:12). To us this seems figurative, but in Heaven perhaps it is purely a fact.

Light is a common metaphor for the divine, across cultures ancient and current. J.R.R.Tolkien, who is famous for imagining the prehistoric context of languages, and shaping a past we experience as very distant echoes or movements (e.g. the nephilim), equated God (Whom he named *Eru* in his Middle-Earth cosmology) with 'Imperishable Flame', and the Creation of Life as beginning with angelic beings, still created, but older than Earth[115]. Flame is light.

Jehanne nearly always experienced light with the Voices, which is commensurate with Biblical descriptions of divine and supernatural experience. Jehanne could not have fabricated any such description as she *could not read* to know the parallels, quite aside from her manifest integrity.

> *'Suddenly there was a bright light in the cell and an angel stood before Peter…'* (**Acts** 12:7)

Like the Apostle Peter, Jehanne met angels/voices in her prison.

> ' *"Has not the angel, then, failed you with regard to the good things of this life, in that you have been taken prisoner?"*
>
> *"I think, as it has pleased Our Lord, that it is for my wellbeing that I was taken prisoner."* '[116]
>
> *'I heard this voice to my right, towards the church; rarely do I hear it without its being accompanied also by a light. This*

---

[115]  J.R.R.Tolkien 1977, *The Silmarillion*, AINULINDALË, pp.15-22.

[116]  Jehanne and 7 assessors, 12/3/1431, 2nd Private Examination, Trial of Condemnation, Rouen, Retrieved from Jeanne-darc.info

*light comes from the same side as the Voice. Generally it is a great light.'*[117]

Even under the hostile interrogation of 55 assessors - that is 55 church-men and lawyers dedicated to her prosecution and murder, while she, a 19 year old girl, was refused any counsel - she explained the presence of light,

' *"When you saw this Voice coming to you, was there a light?"*
*"There was plenty of light everywhere, as was seemly."* [118]

Jesus was and is to her as He declared of Himself – Light! And she de*light*ed in Him.

He is her **King Jesus.** [119]

## 5. Jesus and angels as strength and comfort to Jehanne.

Jesus suffered, and was comforted by angels (ref. **Mark** 1:13. **Luke** 22:43. **Matthew** 4:11).

The year of imprisonment from 23/5/1430 to 30/5/1431 was an appalling time for Jehanne. Conditions were deplorable; we know she was subjected to intense verbal and psycho-emotional abuse, and attempted physical/sexual abuse, by her guards and inquisitors. We know that they tormented her with threats of harm – most likely telling her they would rape and otherwise torture her. Only the direct intervention of the power-ful English Lord Bedford secured her from this fate temporarily, and only because he wanted her death to be in fire, not by the suicide he feared she

---

[117]  Jehanne, 22/2/1431, 2nd Public Examination, Trial of Condemnation, Rouen. Retrieved from Jeanne-darc.info

[118]  Jehanne and Inquisitor, 4th Public Examination, Trial of Condemnation, Rouen. Retrieved from Jeanne-darc.info

[119]  W. Trask, *Joan of Arc: In Her Own Words*, p.52, 'Letter to the people of Troyes'.

might engineer if she was pushed too hard. She was locked in a cage, and chained by her feet to a huge block of wood.

Once the Trial began, there was unrelenting pressure from the 55 assessors (which means *prosecutors*). These were academics, clerics, lawyers and bureaucrats from Universities, Courts and Colleges connived together with the webs of the Catholic hierarchy, purposing to punish and destroy the brilliant woman who had defeated and terminally bled the English Army and Government in France; all these ranged against an illiterate 19 year-old young woman, who was denied legal counsel or representation.

She affirmed questions about her contact with saints and angels, but only very occasionally with detail.

A repeated theme from witnesses of her conduct during the trial is that she consistently endured antagonistic, technical and complex questioning, responding with unprecedented intellectual flexibility, clarity and integrity.

None of the assessors are described this way.

At the end of her life, when she was close to murder and she knew this on 30/5/1431, Jehanne seems to have been alone. In her greatest need, the Voices seem silent. This is hard to understand - it seems cruel and unnecessary; and the Inquisition with its controlling English puppeteers wished to ensure Jehanne died painfully.

In this way, she walked with Jesus Christ to the end.

*'Eloi, Eloi, lema sabachthani?'* (**Matthew** 27:46)

We do not know exactly what happened in Jehanne's experience at her death; we do know she called out Jesus' name multiple times. There is no report that she called to Michael, Catherine or Margaret at this point. Witnesses at the execution/murder-scene saw a dove fly out of the flames, some who were literate saw the word 'Jehanne' in letters of fire, and the

English executioner who had mocked her up until her death, swooned and babbled that he was '...*damned because he had burned a holy woman*'.

## *Jehanne is great* - in history and in life.

Many of us struggle in our daily lives to see meaning, let alone the Hand of God, in purposeless jobs, repetitive futilities, hours gazing at screens, consuming items we do not need, amassing wealth we cannot use beyond our brief life-span, confusedly trying to distinguish truth from illusion. Regret, anxiety, disillusionment, hope, fear, wonder, desolation – all aspects of being human.

She lifts our eyes from these, and her own Voice of Grace says to us - '**Look!**'

She fixed her eyes on God, showed us what Jesus looks like to a faithful medieval French teenager, and followed Him. Jehanne does not specifically recall or relate an encounter with Jesus; but she does directly communicate with Someone who could bring her soul to Paradise (Heaven).

She also experiences and witnesses events typical of Jesus' presence and power. Imagine what it was like for her to see a baby revive after being dead for three days; to feel the wind swing at Orleans; and to hear a voice saying '*There is the Dauphin*' as she stood in a hall of 300 bombastic, arrogant aristocrats - all utter strangers.

Jehanne prioritised Jesus over the Catholic Church while simultaneously honouring her own Christian faith and principles; she very innocently challenged the corruption of court and church politics, while cementing stability into French governance for 350 years. Honouring the Catholic Church was deeply important to her, but ultimately she honoured Truth more. She recognized Christ as the Lord over the Church Militant (the Kingdom of God on Earth), and as the Way to the Church Triumphant (the assembly of all Christians in Heaven). Jesus is pre-eminent in her faith; believing such, she is one of the earliest sparks of the Reformation[120], esteeming Christ over Institution[121].

There is yet little to comfort us in imagining this beautiful and extraordinary young woman treated so appallingly by toxic, corrupt weaklings. Only that many witnesses recorded that Jehanne cried out, *'Jesus,'* in her final moments; notably, what they do *not* record is what we might have expected – screams of agony or terror.

Jehanne knew Jesus as the story, as the child with the Madonna, as the name in her prayers, as the Voice who offered her forgiveness, who sent guides and helpers to her. She knows Him as the Light and Lord above Michael the Archangel, Catherine of Alexandria, Margaret of Antioch. She still speaks to us, assuring us of Jesus the Christ: ***Listen to Him.***

I suspect, that as Jehanne lost consciousness on the stake at Rouen, as in her last breath she called out Jesus' Name - which was her last word - He lifted her up and away. He is the Promise-keeper.

∞

---

[120] John Wycliffe, Jan Hus and Martin Luther were also Catholics, but who honoured Christ above Church.

[121] Jehanne has been cited as writing a letter to early Reformers/protestants known as 'Letter to the Hussites' (i.e. followers of Bohemian Reformer Jan Hus). In fact, she did not write such a letter; a letter attributed to her was composed by her priest Jean Pasquerel, and addressed to the Hussites. Jehanne did not compose or sign this letter. For the text of the letter see, R. Pernoud & M-V. Clin, *Joan of Arc,* pp.258-9.

- Sophie Scholl, 22-2-1943

## Sophia Magdalena Scholl.

We have more primary source material about Sophie than either Mary M or Jehanne. A frequent letter-writer, and regular communicator with her family and friends, she has bequeathed us a fertile repository of her original perspective, reflection and opinion. Many people who knew Sophie personally did survive the Second World War and shared their recollections in various textual formats. A factor highlighted by the *Center for White Rose Studies* is that some of the sources have been obscured by what they call 'gaps', meaning that custodians of primary sources about Sophie and her family may have effectively redacted or concealed some matters. Some possible evasions and/or distortions are encompassed within this text, others would need to be pursued through other means.

There are considerations we need to understand early in this observation of the relationship between Sophie and Jesus Christ.

*Firstly*, Sophie speaks frequently of God and to God, and like Jehanne, has an intuitive sense of Jesus' divinity as part of the Godhead. She expresses no confusion about this. For her, Jesus is God.

*Secondly*, Sophie was a part of the German Resistance group known as **White Rose**. There were numerous other courageous people involved in White Rose, and they each and all deserve attention and honour for their resolve and fortitude in the face of one of history's most evil and depraved regimes, but this study is particularly of *Sophie Scholl*. To learn more about other White Rose activists and supporters, there are numerous texts, history websites, and online biographical sources; consulting the *select bibliography* for this section of the text could provide some helpful references[122].

---

[122]    E.g. see Center for White Rose Studies at www.white-rose-studies.org , a website with a broad spectrum of pertinent resources.

*Thirdly*, Sophie herself had been enmeshed in the perverse propaganda and recruitment apparatus of the National Socialist State (known commonly as the 'Third Reich' or 'Nazi Germany'). She was active in the Nazi Youth Movement for Girls (*Bund Deutscher Mädel* – BDM – translates to English as 'League of German Maidens')[123], and had training/instruction in Nazi ideology. We can assume that Sophie had experienced the anti-Semitic indoctrination applied energetically across Germany through the education system, and the concomitant racial theorizing which resolved 'Aryan-Nordic' people as the apex of human evolutionary perfection. She seems not to have succumbed to this though, and even found it ludicrous. It is well to remember that Sophie was only an adolescent during the beginning years of the Third Reich (1933-37); she was only 11 when Hitler became Chancellor of Germany in early 1933.

*Fourthly*, Sophie is a Christian; it is difficult to pin down her point of commitment to following Christ. For many people, their faith develops with them organically through childhood and so is a form of continuous spiritual development (e.g. this more continuous spiritual development accurately describes Jehanne's pathway), rather than a transformative and definite decision. Sophie seems to identify openly with Christ later in her teens. At this point it is notable that Christians are often held to higher standards than people who do not make such a commitment, and are then judged more critically by those people who never make that life-changing choice. If you are reading this with a judgmental lens, then please put it down. You will see Sophie more clearly if you accept her as she was and is: a young Christian woman in a violently anti-Christian environment.

*Fifthly*, as noted, Sophie was a child during the 1930's in the Third Reich, and she was subjected to the relentlessly prevalent and lethal racial

---

[123] The male equivalent was *Hitler Jugend*, or HJ, which in English is *Hitler Youth*.

theorising of that time. So far as I can determine, Sophie does not directly address anti-Semitism in her diaries or letters; racial discrimination was inherent to National Socialist ideology, which idealized the supreme Germanic *Aryans* while demonising Jewish people as inferior and parasitic[124]. In between was a poisonous, scientistic spectrum of racial status supported by and deriving from eugenics and evolutionism, both branches of science. 'Racial science' (German: '*rassenkunde*') was not exclusive to Germany by any means. 'Eugenics' and 'racial anthropology' in English-speaking countries was espoused widely in America and across the British, French and other European Empires where it found support in evolutionary theory and corrupted interpretations of the Christian Bible. White Rose condemned anti-Semitism; Sophie was deeply involved in producing and disseminating the White Rose Leaflets[125] which manifestly *did* condemn the crimes against Jewish people which were sadistically brutal on a scale difficult for normal, humane people to conceptualise.

For its victims, the Third Reich was barbaric anarchy; unrestrained savagery reigned.

This is what Sophie, her brother Hans, all of White Rose, the German Resistance altogether, were combating, exposing, denouncing. The following accounts of anti-Semitic persecution are graphically illustrative, direct memories of inhumanity from Nazi Concentration Camps. We must not forget how vile, sadistic and amoral the institutions of German government were at this time, nor that such cruel and violent regimes can still happen. This is what White Rose stood against:

'...*like wild dogs the two [Nazi guards] lunge at the wounded,*
*badly bleeding old man, and beat him indiscriminately with their*

---

[124] N.B. cf. Adolf Hitler 1925, *Mein Kampf*, p.263 & p. 277.
[125] For the text of a White Rose Leaflet condemning anti-Semitic practice, see A. Dumbach & J. Newborn 1986, *Sophie Scholl and the White Rose*, pp.190-92 (2nd Leaflet). Alternatively, see www.white-rose-studies.org where many White Rose documents are readily available online.

*heavy, tube-like rubber truncheons, so that he again sinks down,*
*and tries in vain to protect his head with his bloodied arms... he*
*manages to get up, but the blows keep raining down on him... he*
*walks, is dealt one last blow across the right side of his face, and then*
*walks alone, completely alone, accompanied only by eight shots, and*
*then nothing, absolutely nothing. Peace and quiet, and God.* [126]

'*... Me and a Jewish American... were subjected to medical*
*experiments. SS German Shepherd dogs belonging to the SS*
*Obersturmfuhrer Rosenbaum, with a special poison on their*
*teeth... we had to run and the dogs chased us. Afterwards they*
*examined our wounds, the blood. A doctor... ripped the flesh of*
*my legs and examined it. After some time... I was able to escape*
*to some friends of mine in Krakow. There my wounded legs started*
*healing. As a result of this experiment (the dog bites and poison), my*
*whole left foot was ripped apart... and during the course of years*
*I developed wounds and cancer... My good parents were shot in*
*the Summer of 1942 under the supervision of SS Obersturmfuhrer*
*Rosenbaum and were buried in the mass grave in Rabka.*' [127]

Likewise, Hans Scholl, Sophie's elder brother, truth-speaker, and in many ways role-model, provides primary testimony to the tragedy and calamity befalling and engulfing Jewish Europe. As a medical student, he was in late Summer 1942 seconded to the Wehrmacht[128] as a junior officer, and sent as a medical orderly to the Russian Front. Hans later related an

---

[126]  S. Zámečník 2002, *That Was Dachau 1933-1945*, p.121.

[127]  Testimony of Mr G. (age 82) recalling medical experimentation forced upon him at Rabka bei Zakopane, Poland, 1942. Recorded by, *The Conference on Material Claims Against Germany (Claims Conference est. 1951),* New York, claimscon.org.

[128]  The *Wehrmacht* was the German regular Army, as distinct from the *Waffen SS*, which was the Nazi combat branch of the armed forces.

experience from his train journey to the Front to his elder sister Inge, which she remembered:

> *'During the transport to the Front, their train had stopped for a few minutes at a Polish station. Along the embankment he saw women and girls bent over and doing heavy men's work with picks. They wore the yellow Star of David on their blouses. Hans slipped through the window of his car and approached. The first one in the group was a young, emaciated girl with small, delicate hands and a beautiful, intelligent face that bore an expression of unspeakable sorrow. Did he have anything that he might give to her? He remembered his Iron Ration – a bar of chocolate, raisins and nuts – and slipped it into her pocket. The girl threw it on the ground at his feet with a harassed but infinitely proud gesture. He picked it up, smiled, and said, "I wanted to do something to please you." Then he bent down, picked a daisy, and placed it and the package at her feet. The train was starting to move, and Hans had to take a couple of long leaps to get back on. From the window he could see that the girl was standing still, watching the departing train, the white flower in her hair.'* [129]

Hans was in training to become a Doctor, which was leading him into the chamber of horrors that was the medical profession in Nazi Germany. Medicine was militarized in the Nazi State so that Doctors were regarded as 'biological soldiers' simultaneously protecting the *Volk* from racial contamination by *untermenschen* (i.e. subhumans), and ridding the Reich of those sources [130]. Members of the German medical profession supported the

---

[129] This account related by Inge Scholl has at least two sources. 1. Spartacus Educational, www.spartacus-educational.com - Hans Scholl, 2. A. Dumbach & J. Newborn 1986, *Sophie Scholl and the White Rose*, p.110.

[130] M. Scharf 2020, *'Biological Soldiers': War and the Nazi Euthanasia Killings*, pp.51-52

Nazi State by joining the NSDAP[131] in large numbers – by end 1933, only nine months into Hitler's Chancellorship, more than 50% of Doctors were Party members. Part of their work was euthanasing/murdering the racially and hereditarily unfit ('euthanasia' is a euphemism for *imposed killing* – in the Third Reich it was a diabolical, silent policy of homicide inflicted upon the physically and intellectually disabled - simply a form of murder). Did Hans know about this appalling devaluation of human life? The Bishop of Munster, Count Galen, was quoted in a pamphlet that Hans certainly read, revealing that ,

*'... many unexpected deaths among mental patients have not been due to natural causes but have been deliberately arranged ... and that it is permissible to destroy "life which does not deserve to live".* [132]

It would have been difficult for Hans *not* to know, and this perhaps further explains his sense of metaphysical offence at the Nazi regime. Hans had a very strong, even profound, influence on Sophie. (This influence was noted later and suggested as a possible legal defence to save Sophie's life; but, she would not allow this.)

The psychotic violence inflicted on people who fell victim to the insane evolutionary racism of the Nazis is now history to us. It has become words on pages, and depictions in cinema such as *Schindler's List* and *Sophie Scholl: Die Letzte Tage* [133]. These narratives and representations are important as graphic reminders, and the history is necessary; but, we were not actually there. Actual survivors of the Nazi persecution are dwindling rapidly (2025 atow). The impact of hearing, seeing, meeting the perpetrators and vic-

---

[131] NSDAP, acronym for *Nationalistische Sozialistische Deutsches Arbeiter Partei* – the Nazi Party.

[132] Inge Scholl 1970, *Students Against Tyranny*, p. 19.

[133] S. Spielberg 1993, *Schindler's List*, Universal Pictures & M. Rothemund 2005, *Sophie Scholl: Die Letzten Tage*, Zeitgeist Films.

tims, is now mostly documentation. Even so, the connections back into the Shoah (i.e. the Hebrew term for 'Holocaust') remind us of just what Sophie had taken upon herself. When she prayed, knowing the Lord's Prayer, she asked,

'*...sondern erlöse uns von dem Bösen. Amen.*'[134]

A prayer she made, willing to offer her own life in its answering. She likewise prayed the words,

'*Dein Reich komme.*'[135]

These were fervent for Sophie, and for clear-eyed Christians around her; the political Reich manifesting in Germany at the time was *not* God's Reich (Kingdom/Empire).

Simone Weil describes this part of the Lord's Prayer (or '*Pater Noster*') as,

'*We can only invite Him... we must just invite Him purely and simply, so that our thought of Him is an invitation, a longing cry...*'[136]

We often pray '*Thy Kingdom come...*' more as a declaration, or a fond wish, but Sophie more likely agreed with Simone. She certainly had a remarkable sense of peace in the worst of circumstances; her invitation was accepted.

Sophie loved and honoured God. Hatred of Jewish people was to hate all people – as Hannah Arendt observed,

[134] **Matthew** 6:13b, in English, '*...but deliver us from evil. Amen.*'
[135] **Matthew** 6:10a, in English, '*Thy [Your] Kingdom come.*'
[136] Simone Weil 1951, *Waiting for God*, p.144.

*'... the Nazis were in principle, of course, as anti-Christian as they were anti-Jewish.'*[137]

Dissent against the Nazi government had to be covert, so Sophie's apparent silence on anti-Semitism is really just pragmatism. Open rebellion or dissent courted death – literally.

As Mary Magdalene's and Jehanne's lives do, so Sophie's brief life mirrors Jesus Christ's. The comparisons are quite clear, quite early.

- Mary Magdalene knew Jesus closely and personally. Her prior belief system is unknown – it could have been anything; when she commits to following Jesus, she is a disciple of 'the Way'.
- Jehanne Darc knew Him through saints, angels, and Himself. Her belief system is what we call Catholicism.
- Sophie describes no supernatural visions of Jesus, no meetings with spiritual beings, no lights or voices, no prescient and prophetic indications of mission. Like Jehanne, she commits to truth and refuses compromise. Sophie's belief system is what we call Protestantism (Lutheran).

Sophie is closer to us; she is less than 100 years away (2025 atow): historically, that is not far at all. Jehanne is much further away, and Mary much further again. Jesus was only about 33 when He was judicially murdered by the Roman-Semitic state, which is certainly not old.

Mary M is an unknown – we can hope that she died of old age, in a lovely villa somewhere in Gaul, supported by caring family and loyal friends. Her chances of that are low, however. Christians were violently persecuted across the Roman Empire until the C4th A.D.. Catherine of

---

[137] Hannah Arendt 1963, *Eichmann in Jerusalem*, p.202.

Alexandria and Margaret of Antioch, both inspirations to Jehanne, died horrifically for their commitment to Jesus.

In taking up her cross, Sophie was taking the way of Golgotha. She already knew that the German government was diametrically opposed to Christ.

## Family.

1921 was a turbulent year in Germany; the vengeful Versailles Treaty, which formally ended World War 1, was starting to bite deeply into the socio-economic fabric of Germany, spreading the venom of resentment, mediated through dramatically corrosive inflation. The Weimar government was trying to maintain a solvent republican German State while paying punitive war reparations to Allied nations. The German populace was generally still wondering how the war had been lost so disastrously, and how they had lost swathes of formerly German territory from the Rhineland (to France), from Schleswig (to Denmark) and from east Prussia (to Poland and Lithuania)? People wanted reasons for Germany's sufferings, and they wanted someone to blame. The Jews were as good scapegoats as anyone, and anti-Semitism was already historically entrenched across Europe. Post-WW1 Germany was a fertile petri-dish for political extremism, which initially leaned towards communism, before lurching to the hard right, especially after the Great Depression smashed into the susceptibly fragile German economy in 1929.

Stability was not a hallmark of Germany in the 1920's, and into this volatility Sophia Magdalena Scholl was born on 9th May 1921.

Her parents, **Robert** and **Magdalena Scholl**, had six children: **Inge** (1917-1998), **Hans** (1918 -1943), **Elisabeth** (1920-2020), **Sophie** (1921-1943), **Werner** (1922-1944), **Thilde** (1925-1926).

Her mother is **Magdalena Scholl,** *née Müller* **(1881 – 1958)**; we have limited insight into her as a person, wife and mother. She worked as a nurse in German military hospitals during the Great War, and tended wounded troops for almost the entirety of the conflict. Her husband Robert entered her life at this time, as he was a medical orderly, being a pacifist, and refusing combat service. He was ten years younger than Magdalena; they married in 1917.

We know that Magdalena held Lutheran values, but she seems not to have been an actively evangelical Christian. Evidently, she held deeply Pietist views and quietly emphasized the centrality and reality of Jesus Christ to her children. Sophie's older sister Inge describes their mother as having a 'tranquil heart'[138] – not easily disturbed. Available nuances of context indicate that Magdalena's husband Robert was a strong personality, and expressed his perspectives rather dominantly. Magdalena was the submissive, complementarian wife expected in Lutheran and Calvinical circles. When the Nazis came to national power in January 1933, Magdalena also shared her husband's distaste for Hitler. Her influence in the family was more backgrounded and gentle, but eventually very impacting.

When Magdalena saw Sophie for the last time, just prior to her death at Stadelheim Prison in Munich, her last words were, '*Sophie… remember Jesus…*', to which Sophie replied, '*Yes, Mama, you too.*' [139] If nothing else, we know that Jesus had been discussed and honoured between them.

We cannot remember what we have not known.

Deep concern for her mother troubled Sophie, especially the stresses Magdalena was experiencing. There is indication of this in a conversation between Else Gebel (Sophie's prison cell-mate) and Sophie on 21/2/1943, the day before her death, in their shared cell in Munich. Sophie expressed

---

[138]   Inge Scholl, *Students Against Tyranny*, p.51.
[139]   A. Dumbach & J. Newborn 1986, *Sophie Scholl and the White Rose*, p. 160.

selfless, moving concern for her mother and how she would cope with hers and Hans' sentences, while also having the worry of a son on active service in Russia[140] (Sophie's younger brother Werner went missing-in-action on the eastern Front in early 1944; it is not known what happened to him. Most likely he was killed-in-action and his body never identified).

Sophie's father **Robert Scholl** (1891-1973) was a man of firm convictions and political interests, whose views were slightly left of centre. He was a lawyer, and also successful in local politics; he served as Mayor of Ingersheim in 1917-1920, Mayor for Forchtenberg 1920-1930, and Lord Mayor of Ulm 1945-1948. Robert also took interest in the West German political sphere after 1948, but without electoral success. His involvement in politics passed to Hans and Sophie as awareness and acceptance of each individual's civic duty to be engaged in governance and justice.

An incautious assertion about Hitler being the 'scourge of God' landed him in prison in 1942, and he was disbarred from practicing law – a serious financial consequence for the Scholl family. He had been concerned and disappointed by NSDAP success, particularly after 1933 when President Hindenburg appointed Adolf Hitler as Chancellor of Germany. Hindenburg largely gave Hitler a free hand, and even more so when he obligingly died in August 1934, enabling Hitler to merge the offices of Chancellor and President to become overall *Führer* ('Leader') of all Germany. The Nazi Reich was underway; Germany was a dictatorship.

Initially, in 1933-34, as the Nazis established themselves in power and control, there was a sense of national unity and progress which had not existed for 20 years. Sophie grew up in this heady time of national resurgence, when the perceived disgrace of the 1919 Versailles Treaty was being torn up by a strong demagogue who believed in a supreme Germany and

---

[140]  Ibid. p.152.

who was very effective at preaching his message. He told Germans what they wanted to hear about the salvation and future of Germany, and they responded enthusiastically. Sophie grew up in a redeemed Fatherland where Germans, '… *find the embodiment of that salvation in the messianic leader.*'[141]

Magdalena and Robert disapproved of Hitler from the outset, but along with her older siblings, Sophie was attracted to the pageantry, preaching, power and persuasion of the Nazi message. Hitler was cannily aware of the potential of technology for propaganda purposes via radio and cinema, and used it effectively. His appeal to youth was particularly systematic, methodical, alluring and affirming. Hitler may have been wicked, but he was also a mesmerising orator. Close to two million German servicemen had been killed during the First World War: a colossal number. This left a generation of fatherless young Germans who lacked guiding masculine influence and protection in their lives, something which every child needs. Hitler knew this, and how to exploit the vacuum in a generation of young hearts, to tragic effect.

The relationship between Robert and Sophie seems not to have been emotionally close, which we can discern through her letters to him, but there is respect, affection, stability and trust. Sophie's letters are a cache of enthusiastic communication. To her mind, a friend was a treasure infinitely worthy of investment in the time and effort required for writing letters. In this alone, we see the qualities of this girl/young woman. Her letters and diary entries are a prime window into her thoughts and feelings.

## Siblings.

Inge and Sophie were four years apart.

Of their family, Inge said,

---

[141]  J. P. Stern 1975, *The Fuhrer and the People*, p. 96.

'... *we were comrades, our father and ourselves ... our family was a small, stable island in the ever stranger, incomprehensible swirl of events.*'[142]

On Hans, Inge observed that he,

'... *was aware that beauty, esthetic pleasure in existence, and his passive growth to manhood were no longer enough, that these could no longer insulate him from the dangers of the times... The Bible took on a new and startling meaning; a sense of immediacy broke through the old and apparently worn-out words, giving them the authority of persuasive reality.*'[143]

Hans' questing intelligence sought answers to the contradictions around them; Germany was experiencing welcome economic growth and affluence, but had also become a place where philosophers and poets were now proscribed if or because they were Jewish. Sophie was closely attuned to her older brother.

Elisabeth and Werner completed the complement of siblings, excepting a baby sister, Thilde, who died shortly after birth. Elisabeth lived until 2020 and provided empirical recollections of Sophie until late in her life.

Whereas Mary Magdalene kept physical company with Jesus in Israel/Palestine, and while Jehanne was frequently and verbally guided directly by God, Sophie was guided by the more familiar means of human discussions and encounters:

- engaging with others through their ideas and writings in conversations, books and correspondence,

---

[142]    Inge Scholl 1970, *Students Against Tyranny*, pp.12-13.
[143]    Ibid. p.16.

- reading the Bible (which for Christians is a direct way to hear the Holy Spirit's guidance, teaching and wisdom),
- engaging with people through their art and creativity, whether painting, music, poetry or prose,
- perceiving God through Creation (e.g. forests and animals),
- identifying evidences of God's presence through intellect (e.g. ontologia, theodicies),
- communicating with God through prayer, receiving help and inspiration through images, ideas, impressions and insights.

She grew up and lived in southern Germany all of her life, although she greatly enjoyed travelling and exploring new and different places. Adventure appealed to her, and she was not a hesitant or irresolute person; this was a key feature of her personality all her short life. There is a point at which adventure can become hazard, and even when this crystallized into immediate and dangerous threat, she displayed resolve and determination. Her courage is palpable and powerful - like a pulse coursing through her thoughts and sentences; Sophie refused compromise or rescue. Her ideals of integrity and faithful relationship within comradely friendship impelled her to walk with Christ to the most difficult and dangerous of places, when the *Volksgerichtshof* (Nazi Peoples' Court) sentenced her to death on 22/2/1943. She was 21.

## Objective faith.

In the present Western world (2025 atow), the most advertised, assumed and visible worldview is the secular and atheistic one. This is being dispersed widely and torrentially through social media, universities, cinema, and popular music. Education and the Arts are the media of personal and cultural worldview. It must be said that science has permeated the space which was once the almost exclusive preserve of faith systems like Islam, Buddhism or Christianity, and it often exactly requires faith to believe in its doctrines/branches like evolutionism or cybernetics/AI. These require immense leaps of faith. *Evolutionism* because it requires faith in the evolutionary cosmology. Cybernetics/AI because these are humanity creating *humanism* – minds and creativity we can shape in our image. Accordingly though, the accepted standards for truth and factuality are science and mathematics. From Prime Ministers to Influencers, the mantra is that '*we trust the science*'.

In the early 1940's, Sophie knew there was a fundamental shift – in Germany, racial science demonstrated the inhumanity of Jews and Roma (i.e. Gypsies). She was young and accepted the beneficences of science, but was more interested in relationships, artistic creativity (in all its various modes of expression), and the dynamics of love; that simply made her a normal young woman, who had some exceptional qualities. One of these was her *faith in Truth*. Christianity teaches that truth is not only a process of experimentation and/or validation in science, logic and mathematics, but that _Truth is a Person_. It is through relationship with Jesus Christ that *objective truth* can be understood (Jesus identifies Himself as Truth, see **John** 14:6). The capacities of science and mathematics to interpret the cosmos and the mind are limited to observations, experimental processes, algorithms and formulae. Generally represented using Latinate terminology and ancient Greek lettering, the designations and equations are accessible only to that demographic who have studied modern science, which is now become a priesthood, complete with its own exclusive hieroglyphics. Even this fortified monastery of cabalistic elitism is now endangered by Deep Learning and Artificial Intelligence; the servant is becoming master. Science and Maths are useful and helpful at many levels, but they are still not the metaphysical core of reality.

Jesus said, 'I [pronoun subject] am [verb]… the [article] Truth [noun object].' Sophie has said, as does any genuine disciple, 'I believe You.' Truth for her is a 'You' - an objective Person.

Infants do not learn through science, mathematics, lab experiments and logic. Our infantile mode of learning is through nurturing and loving relationship. A scientific lab experiment will not prove love, however carefully designed. Love involves higher and more complex reflection. The Bible tells us that 'God is love' (e.g. **Psalm** 136:1-26 [n.b. the antiphon to each verse NLT], **1 John** 4:16), that love is His/Her nature. This Sophie believed and defended. We cannot have a relationship with a theory, formula or algorithm, but we can with a person.

Humans are the only terrestrial creatures in the physical cosmos who understand and think about creation and reality. The animals can perceive these things, but they can explain nor manipulate them beyond nature and instinct. Animals, for example, do not know that they will die, so they do not worry about preparing their futures. They do understand threat and danger, but they do not understand that the danger is unto death (e.g. canines do not take out doggy life or health insurance policies.) Humans know this very well, once we are beyond infancy. How do we know? We observe and deduce; all organically living creatures cease autonomous life eventually. There are no exceptions. Our awareness of this obsesses us insofar as our own species is concerned, and most of us are fearful of death, if we are plainly honest. It is final, inevitable, terminal. We observe that it is also irreversible (so, if death ever *is* reversed, we know immediately that something/someone has intervened with power which is not in the normal/natural way of the physical cosmos, e.g. Mary M with Lazarus, and Jehanne with the baby at Lagne).

All of which is to say that humans have an awareness and consciousness which is greater than any other terrestrial life-form, and we are confronted by our own mortality. Do we learn this awareness? Are we born with this? Is this given/imparted/bestowed to us? These are questions which have interested philosophers for millennia.

Sigmund Freud addressed death and religion almost obsessively, especially in his last years. In his metaphysical exertions over mind and psychology, he studied anthropological observations of non-westernised Indigenous people to whom the dead are perceived as hostile (i.e. as demons and angry ghosts) and to be combated through religious placations (e.g. rituals such as sacrifices and communion, calculated to pacify resentful spirits [who are resentful because death has robbed them of terrestrial life])[144]. This fearful and reactive perception of death evaporates in Sophie's case. Her personal knowledge of imminent dying and death was something she accepted in peace and with equanimity, exactly because she trusted that her life was within relationship with God through Jesus Christ. There is no anger or vengeance against her judges and murderers, who were in fact amoral and brutal misanthropes. Jesus Christ is Sophie's worldview and truth.

Humans also learn in *multiple ways*. We do not develop in agar and then at age 5 head off to school where we learn from edu-bots (although that could easily become a reality). Integral to learning is *relationship*. Our development begins at conception, which itself derives from intimate heterosexual human relationship. In a common dynamic, male and female parents engage regularly in sexual intercourse and this will normally and eventually lead to conception/pregnancy. From conception, the new human embryo/child is in close relationship to his/her mother; it is a healthily dependent relationship, which continues to and through birth. The father typically and directly supports the mother during pregnancy, and by doing this indirectly but importantly supports the child. This is a strong and secure relational

---

[144]    Sigmund Freud 1913, *Totem and Taboo*, pp.76-79.

triangle. Triangles also happen to be the strongest geometric shape; they may also form the strongest relational template (ref. **Ecclesiastes** 4:12).

A question today (2025 atow) is whether Sophie is a peace activist and human rights leader, or a disciple and martyr for Jesus Christ? She can of course be both, but what was her objective, her motivation?

We could as easily ask the same question about her White Rose brother Hans. Recent inquiry about Hans' work in White Rose evinces more pre-occupation with his sexuality than his opposition to Nazism. This is a sad development, as it distracts from his principal objectives and purposes, and shadows the achievements of White Rose. Jesus makes clear that every human being has a problem; the problem is *sin* (e.g. see **Romans** 3:23). Sin is disobedience to God, and there are infinite variations on how we do this. For example, one form of sin is *gluttony* (i.e. excessive and selfish food consumption) which gets very little attention in general society or in churches. By comparison, *murder* is regarded as a worse sin, and is con-demned more severely, although that depends very much on the prevailing definition of murder, which was an active issue in Nazi Germany. Another form of sin is *homosexuality*, which gets besetting attention from its pro-pagandists, proponents and interest groups. But to God, these are each equally dire behaviours because they separate us from Him, which is His greatest concern. Hans Scholl has been positioned more recently as a gay icon, almost more than as the Resistance fighter he was. This is disturbing, because Hans never advocated homosexuality as far as I am aware, and if he was inclined to homosexuality, then all it means is that he is a sinner like the rest of us. It is no different to highlighting his support for Nazism at one stage; such an emphasis is dishonest. He did not want his vulnerabili-ties or personal life, homosexual or otherwise, paraded as justifications for a cause he never advocated. It is dishonest to do that to him, or to criticize his sister Inge who after his death tried to protect his legacy in this way by covering any perceived homosexuality. Why is there not equal attention to his attachment to Nazism, to telling lies, or to joining the Wehrmacht? Surely they were bad choices, wrong choices – but perhaps understandably poor choices given his socio-cultural context?

Leave him alone.

He should neither be vilified nor aggrandized for his sins, whatever they are. Those are between him and Jesus; they are not playthings for LGBTQI zealots, gender extremists, or puritanical moralists. He was a profoundly courageous and humanly normal young man, who had human problems with human vulnerabilities, like anyone else. Emphasising his sexuality is prurient (and by way of balance, he did have a girlfriend - Rose Nägele - to whom he was very close, so depictions of a 'gay Hans' are likely just nonsense). Hans' attention was on revealing the terrible truths of the Third Reich's criminality and xenophobia. That was his interest and commitment.

Sophie and Hans ask confronting and existential questions to those of us who profess Christian faith, perhaps the principal of which is, *'Is Jesus Christ the most exalted and important person in my life?'*

The next might be, *'Do I walk the talk?'*

They're simple and direct questions, but also strangely difficult to answer, because while we may want to say *yes*, most of us will have to make excuses and avoid the raw truth. Sophie, Jehanne and Mary all treated and honoured Jesus as the most important person in their lives; they refused to compromise, which is something most of us do, time and again, day by day, minute by minute. We lean heavily on *grace* - on Christ atoning for us over and again for sins we often really don't try very hard to overcome. These three young women also lean heavily on *integrity*. They confessed their sin to Jesus, and then really tried to walk with Him, wherever that took them. That is a rare quality.

Perhaps that is what makes each of them so admirable, so beautiful - and also so awkward for us. They are not fictions, they are real historical people, and they all happen to be young women. None of them were aristocrats, pop stars, business barons, prime-ministerial or presidential candidates, Hollywood legends, sporting heroes, billionaires' heirs, media moguls, etc. – far from it.

Most challengingly unpleasant is that they *search* Christians, or those of us who call ourselves 'Christians'; they make us deeply uncomfortable. We know that we compromise daily; we may talk about Jesus occasionally, perhaps in or after a church service or some form of church activity, or in a meeting if we work within a sector like welfare or a charity. On the whole, we do not treat Jesus as the most important person in our lives; we lie, we lust, we betray, we accumulate, we flatter, we cheat, we gossip, we assault, we manipulate, we dishonor. Very often we do these things to ourselves more than others, but we do them, and we think of Jesus as an afterthought maybe at the end of the day, or when we are afraid that we might actually be exposed for our substance addictions, our sexual obsessions, our criminal neglects, our diagnoses, our hubris. We fear these things, we fear discovery. Turning to Jesus, whom we treat like a little idol that may help us in our worst moments, is more a panacea – that's certainly not a relationship. Then we proceed to ignore Him until another drama disturbs us. We have made Jesus into a convenience, a psychological therapy. He is our pacifier, our treatment, our anodyne. And then we wonder why our desperate prayers for resolution disperse and disappear with no miracles, no radical interventions, no resolution. We want to feel better, so we pray, we promise to attend to Him in future. (**Matthew** 14:36 presents us with an image of desperate people reaching for and touching Jesus' clothes – these three women walk next to Him; proudly and unashamedly. Perhaps we find MM, Jehanne and Sophie difficult for this reason: they mirror our real self.)

But, He will not be used like that, like a genie. We cannot manipulate Him for magic wishes.

How do we *know* Nazism was wrong? Are Nazis not entitled to their beliefs and cultural mores? Weren't there some good Nazis – like Martin Heidegger, Leni Riefenstahl and Ferdinand Porsche? We could even make a case that Sophie was a Nazi at one stage.

Isn't it desperately intolerant and judgmental to condemn the Nazis just because they were different to us? Because they killed people who they did not even recognize as people?

For example, we tolerate Islam's oppression of women in places like Afghanistan, Nigeria and Saudi Arabia – our position is that our beliefs are our own, and there is no absolute standard against which we can measure and test our beliefs. We tend to be disapproving and contribute a 'yes' or 'no' in an opinion poll on television if oppression looks nasty (e.g. if someone gets hurt, or armed thugs attack someone), but that is the extent of our engagement. Our position is that it is their business if people want to act like that, and if they want to believe that women's evidence has only 50% of the value of men's[145].

Sophie did not accept that view. What then was her measuring standard? Was it a notion of humanity? Or the Shariah? Or the Bhagavad Gita? Or Gottfried Leibniz? (whom Sophie did like.)

We comfortably destroy unborn children because they cannot defend themselves against the violent and murderous brutality of abortion. Huge sums are made in the blood-trade of this inhumane practice. How are we better than Nazis, who are infamous in their brazen disrespect for human life, by assenting to this with our silence?

Prof. C. S. Lewis studied ancient world history and found that across early religions (i.e. belief systems which tied facts, evidence and the dimensions of naturality and supernaturality together, such as Christianity, ancient Aboriginal

---

[145]   Qur'ān, 2nd Surah *Al-Baqarah* 2:282.

Dreaming, and ancient Egyptian religion etc.) there is extraordinary congruence between these geographically disparate ancient worldviews[146]. They all featured clear codes which promoted care and help to others, and forbade murder or lying etc.. His question was 'Why is there such congruence?' It can only be that these principles are either innate to humans, *or* they have been revealed to our forebears for our ethical education. Then of course the question is 'Revealed by whom?' Lewis was interested in the congruence between these creeds, when the cultures themselves were far apart and often completely isolated from each other, yet contained essentially the same edicts.

Sophie would have agreed and been interested by this, but she was murdered in the same year as Lewis published his study. She had principles which refuted Godlessness, and she did not adopt a tolerant, live-and-let-live approach to Nazism (which was an antithesis to Lewis' congruent worldwide ethical principles). Where did she get such absolute truth, and such certainty that Nazism was wrong and had to be actively opposed? Lewis was not suggesting a syncretism, he was suggesting a common source. We know right from wrong because positives are first: peace precedes violence, life precedes murder, love precedes indifference, strength precedes weakness, Creator precedes creation. Sophie did not articulate this, but she enacted it.

Jesus Himself accuses us of being hypocrites:

> *'Hypocrite! First get rid of the log from your own eye; then perhaps you will see well enough to deal with the speck in your friend's eye.'* (**Matthew** 7:5 NLT)

No-one enjoys being called a hypocrite, but when it comes from Jesus, we have to face it, or deny Him. We are generally happy to listen to Jesus from an object position as His Disciples, *but* not as Pharisees. We interpret the

---

[146]   C. S. Lewis 1943, *The Abolition of Man* (see section titled *The Tao*).

words He spoke to the Pharisees as censures for bad people – other people, not ourselves, not *me*. (Those excoriations are for nasty old Jews in the olden days, not for the centre of the Universe we meet in the mirror.) Jesus was speaking to all of us when he castigated the Pharisees and priests. Such is the power of His grace that He can heal our hypocrisy if we repent before Him.

He is kind.

In turn, the mostly young White Rose members deserve grace and understanding, partly because we all have logs in our eyes (ref. **Matthew** 7:5), and partly because few of us have been subjected to Gestapo interrogations. Why did Sophie or Hans or the others make errors and inadvertently provide information which compromised other people? I do not think we can condemn them for mistakes or naïvities under conditions like a Gestapo scouring. They were under pressures most of us have never known. There is evidence that Sophie was carrying a debilitating leg injury after Gestapo attention; she didn't have that prior to 18-2-1943[147]. We need be respectfully careful in judging those who have been subjected to harsh and extreme persecution.

It is noteworthy that Mary Magdalene was physically with Jesus every day for about two years, but we have only few of her words. Jehanne was frequently in company with spiritual beings, and One she refused to identify but Whom we glimpse through her reverence, was Jesus Himself; we have more of Jehanne's words. Sophie does not share any accounts of encounters with spiritual beings, but we have a relatively large volume of her words, even glimpses into her personal prayers.

The physical, sensory presence of Jesus correlates inversely to the records of communication. Sophie's relationship with Him was entirely through prayer and spiritual communion; Jehanne's was a mixture of prayer and presence; Mary's was almost all presence, and only limited prayer – at least

---

[147] Holocaust Historical Society 2018, *Hans and Sophie Scholl*, holocausthistoricalsociety. org.uk

until Jesus' ascension. Sophie is the most understandable to us – she is a modern Christian; but, she is also a disciple like the early believers who walked into arenas, who stood up to speak the Name of Jesus, to obey Him despite vilification, assault, imprisonment, torture and death. In the West today, we generally do not face those challenges. In Nazi Germany though, for those 12 years, we were back in Nero's Rome.

Relatively few Christians did identify wholly with Jesus Christ in the crucible of the Third Reich; some who did are well-known, like Dietrich Bonhoeffer and Maximilian Kolbe. But, on the whole, across Germany and its territories, very few Christians resisted Nazism - nor its cellular militarism, and virulent anti-Semitism. Eminent social historian Richard Grunberger records Gerhart Hauptmann, a Nobel-Prize recipient for Literature, declaring very honestly when asked in 1938 why he stayed quietly in Germany,

> '… because I'm a coward, do you understand?
> I'm a coward, a coward!'[148]

He was truthful, but certainly not alone.

People like Sophie are silhouetted so starkly because they actively opposed the evil around them. She is courageous where most of us will yield to fear. And that's the question about Sophie; where did she find the strength and composure to resist and fight? Sophie found very practical and empirical strength in Jesus Christ – even unto death.

With her siblings, Sophie knew a young school teacher who refused to join the Nazi Party[149]. He would not compromise by affiliation (unlike the vast majority of teachers in Germany, who capitulated in gelatinously large numbers! Sadly, Teaching was not a particularly courageous profession in the Third

---

[148]  Richard Grunberger 1971, *A Social History of the Third Reich*, p.42.
[149]  Inge Scholl, *Students Against Tyranny*, pp.10-11.

Reich[150]). In consequence, he was blackbirded by the SA (*Sturm Abteilung* – a militant street-fighting wing of the Nazi Party) and positioned in front of a squad who all marched past the teacher and spat in his face. He then disappeared, apparently to a concentration camp. The Scholls were stunned at this event. His 'crime' was to refuse identification with Nazism. The totalitarian Roman state did the same to Jesus; **Isaiah** 50:6 (prophecy) and **Mark** 15:19 (fulfillment) describes Jesus' persecution by the Roman guard, which included the despicable act of spitting into Jesus' face. It is intended as a gesture of utter contempt and loathing, but in this instance it outlines radically just how craven and pathetic we humans can be in preserving ourselves, for the prize of cowardice. Spitting on someone who has objectively done no wrong is a pathetic act of debasement in order to demonstrate allegiance to some despot or gang. Sophie knew about this teacher - this happened before she was actively involved in White Rose, but she went ahead and supported White Rose anyway. Sophie is here willing to identify with Jesus in His suffering and sacrifice, something He had warned His disciples would happen (**John** 15:20). Sophie meets and experiences Christ in identification.

*'It is no shame to suffer for being a Christian. Praise God for the privilege of being called by His wonderful name!... if you are suffering according to God's will, keep on doing what is right...'* (**1 Peter** 4:16&19a)

Sophie had unaccountable peace in identifying with Jesus, unaccountable except that Jesus specifically promises *peace* to his followers (see **John** 14:27).

Sophie's knowing and perception of God is an objective faith, not wishful thinking. Aside from His time on Earth as a human, God is Spirit. To relate with Him, we have numerous ways.

She knows God through:

* prayer,

---

[150]  Op.cit., p.364.

- reading the Bible,
- listening to other people's perceptions and experiences of God,
- following the ideas and insights communicated to her spirit by the Holy Spirit,
- God's reality as deduced from the patterning and evident cause & effect design in Nature.

God's presence and reality to Sophie are objective, based on her recognition of Him as He is, not as we want Him to be. She knew Jesus through her objective faith and experience of Him in prayer, in truth, and spiritual communication. Relationship with Him was pre-eminent.

> '...I believe a person can be a Christian without belonging to a church. Besides, a Christian isn't compelled to be anything other than what his principal commandments require of him.'[151]

The primary requirement of a Christian is not formalities or rituals, but honouring and obeying Christ.

Sophie knew that people needed to be established and grounded on the value of *beauty*, not the value of *capital*. God does not create ugly, disgusting things; those are distortions caused by disobedience to Him. Even the very creatures we think of as fearsome or grotesque (e.g. poisonous spiders and stone-fish) are perceived that way because of their characteristics and behaviour. If aggressive, venomous spiders were as playful and harmless as butterflies, we would not think of them as ugly and grotesque (n.b. these aggressive, predatory behaviours are consequences of the fall, meaning the fall of humankind from harmony with God to chaotic disobedience). She valued life and love, over wealth and power. This is a transformational

---

[151]    Sophie Scholl (Inge Jens ed.) 2017, *At the Heart of White Rose*, p.98.

alignment which is implicit to following Jesus. Through this, Christians are completely freed to live in truth and love - and Sophie did. She shares this with Mary and Jehanne; it is their sistering together in Christ[152].

## Relationship with God through Jesus.

Our perception of Sophie's heart and motivation clarifies once we understand Sophie's admiration, sympathy and trust in Jesus Christ. To reiterate, she was deeply committed and connected to Jesus Christ, knowing Him through:

- ❖ the close and intimate practice of prayer,
- ❖ reading the Bible (which for a Christian is listening to the Holy Spirit),
- ❖ speaking about Jesus verbally and in writing (like Paul, John and Peter, she wrote letters frequently),
- ❖ sharing/communicating ideas and inspirations about God (via various forms of art),
- ❖ living by Jesus' values and priorities,
- ❖ the Holy Spirit's presence and counsel in her life,
- ❖ sharing community in faith, ('…where two or more are gathered…')
- ❖ perceiving God through the beauty of Creation/nature.

*

- ❖ **Prayer.**

> *'O Lord, I need so badly to pray, to ask.*

---

[152]  **Matthew** 12:50

*Yes, one should always bear in mind, when dealing with other*
*people, that God became man on their account...* [153]
(Sophie, diary entry, 12/2/1942)

*'My God, I can only address you falteringly. I can only offer you*
*my heart, which is wrested away from you by a thousand desires...*
*Help me to be singlehearted and remain with me... Teach me to*
*pray... Better to be parched with thirst, than to feel empty and*
*to feel so without truly feeling at all. That I mean to resist.* [154]
(Sophie, diary entry, 29/6/1942)

These are beautifully sincere, soulful prayers - sentences rising as incense to her God, and because they were not intended for anyone other than God, there is an immediacy and realism difficult to mirror in fiction. We feel Sophie's pain and guilt over condemning others for whom God died as the sacrificial lamb, Jesus at Calvary. We feel her hesitant trust in feeling parched and knowing that this means there is drink, for thirst tells us there must be water, as loneliness tells us there must be companionship, as the impulse to pray tells us Someone must be listening.

Every aspect, every tone, every syllable of prayer is a way God communicates with us. Sometimes it is plain and clear; sometimes we need to wait, watch and reflect.

And her final brief sentence on 29/6/1942,

*'I mean to resist.'*

Resist what? The temptation to settle for an empty feeling, and not to examine it? Or a resolve to resist the Third Reich?

---

[153] Sophie Scholl (Inge Jens, ed.), *At the Heart of White Rose*, pp.209-210,
[154] Ibid, p.228

Does a *resolve* to resist criminal corruption tell us there is exquisite life? *Resisting* for Sophie meant certain pursuit, and real peril of death. Reflecting on resistance is critical and fraught for Sophie – but she listens. This comes through prayer.

Just over two weeks prior to this, another young woman in another corner of the Third Reich began, like Sophie, the practice of being a diarist. She wrote,

> *'Vrijdag 12 Juni … ik jarig was…Het was in de*
> *eerste plaats jou die ik te zien kreeg…'*[155]
> *('Friday 12th June… it was my birthday… and*
> *it was the first time I got to see you … ')*

Anne Frank's 13th birthday, far from Munich in Amsterdam, is her first mention of 'Kitty', who has become perhaps the most famous diary in history. Both Anne and Sophie are afflicted within the same evil regime, and their writings are equally searching and penetrating, as if the crushing weight of ochlocratic tyranny compresses a purity from the overwhelming mass of criminality, cruelty and compromise that assails them. They share many qualities, differences, and afflictions – up to and including their last moments. Being writers, being different ages, being righteous women in lethally dangerous positions, both liking flowers, being both deeply aware of and devoted to God, equally sensitive and spiritually receptive, Anne and Sophie share much in common regarding what matters: love, justice and truth. They live unto eternity, not mere temporality.

> *'God heeft mij niet alleen gelaten en zal me niet alleen laten.'*[156]
> *('God has not left me alone, and will not leave me alone.')*

---

[155]   Anne Frank 1942 (1985), *Het Achterhuis: dagboekbrieven*, p.23 (14 Juni 1942)
[156]   Ibid, p.204 (31 Maart 1944)

Anne's relationship with God is not always made clear in literature written around and about her, but she is a spiritually alive Jewish girl. By the time Anne wrote this in her diary, Sophie was already in Heaven. Within 12 months, Anne was with her.

('But… she was not a Christian', might be an objection. The unreached, those people who have not heard the Gospel plainly and clearly, are not 'hell-fodder'. They are before God, He will do the judging, and we ought remember that He is **love**. *Love* is God's primary colour. Will some people go to hell? I am sure of that, yes, because Jesus told us that hell is real; but it is a real choice people make. If people reject God and the Grace of Christ, then God will allow them their choice – even if it is an awful one, a tragic pride. There are two paths we can choose to walk – the path of Christ, or the path that leads to hell, but that path entails choice and knowledge. People can only choose responsibly if they understand the options. Any Christian should be ashamed of wishing people into hell, even the ugly and awful, and ought better concentrate on the Gospel. That is our calling. The Gospel is not *bad* news; on the contrary – the very word comes from the Anglo-Saxon *gōd* + *spel* = 'good tidings'.)

For Sophie and Anne, God is present, not leaving us alone, but beside us in prayer.

Sophie's prayers are a glimpse into the heart of a martyr; a privileged and hallowed space. What do we see? Depth of seeking, depth of courage, desire for communion, and help from Christ so she can follow Him. We see a determination to resist evil, a determination which will be expensive. Defeating evil always entails cost,

> 'Cheap grace is the deadly enemy of our Church. We are fighting to-day for costly grace.'[157]

---

[157]    Dietrich Bonhoeffer 1937, *The Cost of Discipleship*, p. 35.

Anne does not leave her prayers transcribed for us, she blesses us simply with evidence of the transforming power of God.

When Sophie faces us with the challenge of understanding that being *parched* is actually a logical step towards *therefore water must exist*, she is not only corresponding to one of C. S. Lewis' well-known and well-made arguments for God's reality, she is challenging us to see as she did. It is difficult to follow those who are above us, whom we recognize as our luminaries. If we apply Sophie's logic though, she is helping us – she is showing us that our desire and hunger for Heaven, for eternal life with God, which is to say eternal present relationship with God, is the difficult way, but the only worthwhile way. As Lewis helps us see, so Anne and Sophie help us –

'... *if I find in myself desires nothing in this world can satisfy,
I can only conclude I was not made for here...*'[158]

Every seeming loss here on Earth is restored exponentially in Heaven.

How did God's Word in prayer help Sophie, or Anne? They both faced the murderous hatred of very real, violently ruthless predators; their value and dignity as human beings was merely incidental to Nazi killers. This has happened many times across history, but the Third Reich remains starkly vivid and putrid – a warning beacon.

'*Wij jongeren hebben dubbele moeite onze meningen te
handhaven in een tijd waar alle idealism vernield en verpletterd
wordt, waar de mensen zich van hun lelijkste kant laten zien,
waar getwijfeld wordt aan waarheid en recht, en God.*'[159]

---

[158]  Brooke Fraser, referencing C. S. Lewis, in her song, 'C. S. Lewis Song', Track 6 in album *Albertine*.
[159]  Anne Frank, *Het Achterhuis*, p.264 (15 Juli 1944)

*('The younger generation have double difficulty in*
*maintaining our viewpoints in a time when all idealism*
*is destroyed and crushed, where people show their ugliest*
*sides, where truth is undermined, and law, and God.')*

Anne wrote this about three weeks before the Achterhuis (i.e. literally the 'behind house') was disclosed to the Gestapo. Her family was betrayed, and they were among the remaining Jews in Amsterdam to be sent to German death camps in 1944; Anne was sent to Belsen, and did not survive.

How did she remain confident in goodness, in 'truth, law and God' among the oppressions and calumnies inflicted upon her and the people she loved, and lost? There is something greater here than optimism, or positive thinking.

Sophie struggled with similar questions, with feelings of spiritual claustrophobia. What would she say to Anne and people in her position?

*'Sometimes when I utter God's Name, in fact, I feel like*
*sinking into a void. It isn't frightening or dizzying, it's nothing*
*at all – and that's far more terrible. But prayer is the only*
*remedy for it, and however many little devils scurry around*
*inside me, I shall cling to the rope God has thrown me in Jesus*
*Christ, even if my numb hands can no longer feel it...* [160]
*(Sophie, 18/11/1942, letter to Fritz Hartnagel [her boyfriend]*
*a Wehrmacht soldier, at that time in Stalingrad, Russia.)*

At this stage, Sophie is involved in White Rose, actively sabotaging the Nazi regime, and prioritizing the Kingdom of God. We meet this in the leaflets distributed by White Rose, which of course Sophie had read and disseminated – declaring awful truths to the German public, such as,

---

[160]    Sophie Scholl (Inge Jens ed.), *At the Heart of White Rose*, pp.282-3

*'...since the conquest of Poland **three hundred thousand** Jews have been murdered in that country in bestial manner... Here we see the most terrible crime committed against the dignity of man... May God grant that this program has not fully achieved its aim as yet...* [161]

Hans Scholl, and fellow White Rose activist Alexander Schmorell (aka 'Schurik'), were via their leaflets addressing the present and planned persecution and genocide[162] of Jewish people, as well as a systematic campaign of murder against educated Polish men.

Sophie was thrown into the confronting knowledge that her country was perpetrating these repulsive crimes. How could she balance this with her faith, as a German woman, of German family, with German history and relationships, whose own brother - a Wehrmacht Medic - is telling her his eye-witness experiences. Her need of prayer and her dependence on Christ alone allows us to see Him in Sophie's life. Jesus is not an abstraction or hallucination to her, He is her relationship with God, her security in tenuous and threatening conditions, her ground. Being actively involved in White Rose was simultaneously dangerous and unavoidable for Sophie.

She obeys Jesus – this is her 'costly grace', as Dietrich Bonhoeffer expressed it. For him, his encounter with the Black Christ in New York

---

[161] From *Leaflet 2* of White Rose, written in June/July 1942 by Hans Scholl & Alexander Schmorell who were in Poland at about that time on their way to Wehrmacht duty in Russia. The leaflet was subsequently distributed mainly in southern Germany late in 1942 by Sophie and other White Rose activists.

[162] *Genocide* is a specific description of intent by commission or omission to mass-murder an entire ethno-racial type of people, so actual genocide is historically rare (a tragic example is the genocide of full-blooded Tasmanian Aboriginal people in c.1800-1876). The Nazi intention to eradicate/murder all Jews under German jurisdiction was genocidal. The word is misapplied now, often for political motives, to mean lethal persecution of particular types of people in particular places. This is evil, but is not genocide; a better term might be 'xenocide'.

had been transformative. For Sophie, Christ is the truth - the suffering she is now seeing.

The dilemma she faces is between historico-scientific knowledge and objective faith (a variation on philosophical *objective morality* but also independent, as *objective faith* requires living and real relationship between Jesus Christ and the follower/disciple): science could mean whatever scientists interpreted results and data to mean. The Word of God however is true eternally – it does not change. It is reliable. Where He says, 'You shall not murder', it means *ever*. It is not conditional on race, ethnicity, gender, age, ability, wealth, appearance, time, or evolution. It is solid rock, which Sophie could depend on, but it also required exceptional courage to stand there, and uphold the truth.

God's direct presence is overwhelming to us; if we experience it (i.e. in our earthly dimension – it may be different in Heaven), it can affect us powerfully for what it is – supernatural. On an occasion preserved in the Old Testament, the prophet Daniel was with other human men when he saw a Heavenly 'man'; the others did not see this man, they felt only a profound fear, so they hid, while Daniel lost strength and actually fainted when he heard the man's voice (ref. **Daniel** 10:7-8). We experience God as God wishes us to experience Him; some may see, and others may only feel, at exactly the same time. The holy supernatural is overwhelming in Heavenly form, and Daniel only recovered when the 'man' lifted him up. For reasons we do not fully understand, Heavenly agents can be hindered by evil supernatural beings (i.e. demons), as with Daniel in this instance; the 'man' (probably an angel) was delayed by the 'spirit prince of Persia'. **Daniel** 10:13 provides insight into the territoriality of demonic entities. These entities seem to have assignation and authority corresponding to earthly socio-political boundaries. It is more than likely then that a demonic prefect of some kind had authority or locus in or over Germany, as with all other nations. The Apostle Paul indicates this in **Romans** 8:38-39.

Sophie's security was in Jesus. She interacted with Jesus functionally, in prayer and Bible-reading. Prayer is the 'rope' between them; He does not let go. Sometimes, Jesus felt uncommonly close however, and Sophie sensed His presence through His 'selfless love'.

> *'...I only feel really secure when I recognize the presence*
> *of selfless love, and that's comparatively rare.'*[163]
> (Sophie, 16/2/1943, letter to Fritz Hartnagel.)

There was no predicting this, but Sophie knew Him when He was there.

A facet of her relationship with Jesus was deep confidence that she was secure with Him. Like anyone else, she lived in expectation of a future on Earth and that she would have a family of her own with her boyfriend/possible future husband Fritz. But, even before her arrest and judicial murder, she perceived Earthly life as transient and mutable.

> *'... I keep on having colourful, innocuous dreams about the future.*
> *I realize how innocuous and trivial they are, thank goodness, or*
> *I might easily become immersed in them, like so many people,*
> *and rejoice on their sole account that the war will soon be over.*
> *But they aren't my grounds for rejoicing – far from it.'*[164]
> *(Sophie, 13/2/1943, letter to Fritz Hartnagel who had*
> *escaped Stalingrad just days before the decimated German 6th*
> *Army surrendered to the Red Army in February 1943.)*

Sophie speaks as if she knew that her Earthly future was insubstantial. This could be because she understood that involvement in White Rose was

---

[163] Sophie Scholl (Inge Jens ed.), op.cit., p.308.
[164]   Ibid. p.302.

extremely fraught and something was almost certain to go wrong, sooner or later. It could also be that Sophie is assessing and separating what is eternally worthwhile from what is temporarily pleasing. Any dreams of a predictable, colourful future seem trivial and innocuous to her. (Sometimes when working with translations from German to English, direct comparisons may not work – the word 'innocuous' seems unapt. Sophie's meaning does not match the intention; 'innocuous' means unimpressively inoffensive, and probably intends as 'ordinary', a subtle difference.) She anticipates an ordinary and happy life ahead, yet she knows that to achieve that would mean avoiding anything risky (or capable of harming her ordinary future). She cannot continue with White Rose and retain an ordinary, colourful future, because the war will not soon be over in such a way as to facilitate an ordinary life. There will not be German victory. The war must end, but it must be made to end with the defeat of Nazism, which meant the defeat of Germany. As a deeply German woman, she faces anything but innocuous choices towards an ordinary future; consonance with her relationship to Jesus means she must actively work for the defeat of her own country – the same dilemma faced by Dietrich Bonhoeffer, and the rest of White Rose. In the immediate aftermath of Stalingrad, and with the North African campaign going badly for Germany after El Alamein, Sophie knows that rejoicing in a colourful and ordinary future in a victorious Germany is delusional. She is intelligent, and pragmatic. If there is to be rejoicing, it will not be in the global Reich led by an autocratic and vindictive Führer. *Rejoicing* is in the inevitable, continuous and ultimate victory of the Kingdom of God, like the Church Militant and Jehanne, a victory won by Christ with martyrs' blood. In T. S. Eliot's words,

> *And the Son of Man was not crucified once for all,*
> *The blood of the martyrs not shed once for all,*

*The lives of the Saints not given once for all:*
*But the Son of Man is crucified always*
*And there shall be Martyrs and Saints.*
*And if blood of Martyrs is to flow on the steps*
*We must first build the steps...* [165]

It is amazing that Sophie rejoiced at all! The pressures she was under were momentous – her boyfriend (a deeply conflicted relationship for her) had been both lost then found in the decisive battle of Stalingrad, her father had been arrested and imprisoned for insulting the Führer, her younger brother Werner was fighting in Russia, Hans was deeply involved in anti-war activism, as was she secretly (an activism which was regarded as treason and attracted the death penalty) - and she was profoundly disturbed by the reality of German defeats, atrocities and war crimes. Yet, in this, she managed to *rejoice*? How did she retain composure and steadiness? Not once does Sophie even hint recognizably at the existence of White Rose in her diaries or letters; she was extremely careful – more careful than Hans. On the same day as her arrest for distributing White Rose Leaflet 6, the Nazi Propaganda minister Joseph Goebbels screeched his way through a speech in Berlin in which he rails against 'International Jewry' as '...a contagious infection'[166] responsible for the world's problems, while he implored Germans to wage *total war* in the cause of Hitler and the Reich.

What is called the *Führerprinzip* – meaning 'leader principle', the basis of authority in the Third Reich – aggregated all authority upwards and all responsibility downwards. It is very like governance in executive hierarchies globally today (2025 atow), excepting that in western democracies the authority is often elected or is a committee where one person does

---

[165]  T. S. Eliot 1934, *Choruses from 'The Rock'*, VI.
[166]  From Joseph Goebbels, 18/2/1943, *Nun, Völk steh auf, und Sturm brich los!*, see English translation Randall Bytwerk 1998 at research.calvin.edu

not have exclusive authority (although in practice, there is often a political imbalance in committees). These hierarchies are little different structurally to the Third Reich ones, except that they do not have the same capacities to punish or manipulate others (e.g. murder and torture) – they are usually more subtle or collective. Sentiment against truth-tellers in 1943 Germany was rabid. The anti-Semitism endemic to fascism/national socialism is on clear display in Goebbels' speech – how can we calculate the effects of virulent discrimination like this on young University students? Sophie grew up with this in her schooling and BDM, she witnessed at very least the pogrom of *Kristallnacht* (and her family's silent complicity), and she was close to Hans: she would have known the story of his encounter with the Jewish girl in Poland for instance, and the immediate evidence it bore to murderous Nazi anti-Semitic hatred.

How does Sophie see Jesus in this, and how is it prayer, or even like prayer? She sees the vivid reality of evil. And how do we know evil? Because we know truth and beauty first. Positives imply negatives, not vice-versa. The removal of death is not life, but the removal of life is death: the removal of darkness is not light, but the removal of light is darkness. Death and darkness have no meaning without life and light. Sophie hints at this:

*I've become aware that we would starve to death if not sustained by God, and that not only one long thread attaches us to God through the creation, as I used to believe when I still didn't know what a life is, especially a human life.*[167]
*(Sophie, unsent draft of letter to her friend Otl Aicher, approx. January 1942)*

---

[167]  Sophie Scholl (Inge Jens ed.), *At the Heart of the White Rose*, p.209.

Her imagery is graphic – we would *starve to death* if not sustained by God. The solution is prayer, where she knows she will receive soul-food from Jesus Christ.

> *I've decided to pray in church every day, so that God won't forsake me. Although I don't yet know God and feel sure that my conception of him is utterly false, he'll forgive me if I ask him. If I can love him with all my soul, I shall lose my distorted view of him.*[168]
> *(Sophie, 12/2/1942, diary entry.)*

In her constantly growing and evolving relationship with God, we see Sophie's intense desire for closeness with Him, and her very typical conflation of *relating to God* with *human relationships*. She perceives God as distant and officious here, regarding prayer as a way to avoid rejection (i.e. 'forsaking'). This is probably more a glimpse into her relationship with her father Robert, a strong and principled man, a man who loved his family, but who was also distant. This is how Sophie struggles with knowing and understanding God. (The ways we are parented leave imprints, and those colour our perceptions of God.) Simultaneously, she understands that view is distorted. Even her desire and resolve for prayer is in fact a response. She knows that prayer is her first place of connection, however she is feeling.

> *'The only remedy for a barren heart is prayer, however poor and inadequate.'*[169]

**Philippians** 4:6 invites Sophie (and anyone) into prayer[170]. Prayer is practiced globally in all religions, from atheism (where the deity is self), to animism (where the deities are organism and/or energy); some form of

---

[168]  Ibid.
[169]  Ibid. p.282
[170]  See also **Psalm** 91:15-16.

submission is established, and a force is recognized and interconnected. Christianity has accessible and minimally ritualized form(s) of praying – in His blueprint for prayer (the *Lord's Prayer*, or *Pater Noster*), Jesus shows us that we are speaking to our Father. A loving, kind and attentive Father.

❖ **Bible-Reading.**

Like Jehanne, who prayed at every opportunity[171], prayer was a part of life, not only a thoughtless recitation in a memorized creed. Sophie was a pray*er*, and knew the value of prayer. She had a favourite Bible verse apparently - a verse which she lived and honoured.

> *'And remember, it is a message to obey, not just to listen to. If you don't obey, you are only fooling yourself.'* – **James** 1:22 (NLT)

> *'But be ye doers of the word, and not hearers only, deceiving your own selves.'* – **James** 1:22 (KJV)

Communication can be one-way, or two-way. One-way communication is limited by its monophonal nature; there is no reciprocity. There is a speaker, and a hearer: that is all. Message goes out; nothing returns. That is very unsatisfying communication, unless there is a particular purpose such as in a computerized guidance system, in which case we are receiving communication from a machine, not a person. Much of our communication *is* like this though – we are passively receptive, not reciprocally engaged. Sitting in front of a television is like that – we watch stories, we receive news, we digest advertising... all totally passive. The same happens with books – we read the text, we might love the story, or be deeply interested

---

[171] See e.g. Regine Pernoud 1962, *Joan of Arc* , pp.90 & 110 etc.. N.B. Regine Pernoud is an excellent and accurate historian who chronicles almost exclusively from primary sources; her narrative is highly indicative.

in the subject matter, but we cannot communicate with the author or characterizations within the text. We cannot *converse*. Telephones are different; technology allows engaged communication over distances. Technology both facilitates and regulates our communication.

We like to hear voices, to see expressive body-language, to read writing. Sometimes we are content to be passive hearers, and sometimes we want reciprocity. AI (i.e. Artificial Intelligence) is now allowing machines to communicate with humans in ways such that an illusion of humanity is almost complete. We can *converse with* and not only *talk to* images on the screen. But we know it is not a human we are conversing with; it is an illusion – a program. When we read books or print matter, we are in the same situation – we are communicating with something created and developed by people (or, increasingly and rapidly, AI machines) but it is one-way. We can't *converse* with the author, even if his/her ideas are stimulating or engaging. It is like a screen of print. We are now not even certain if the text/print is human, or if it is generated by AI. Robotic technology is generating ever more convincing androids, capable of imitating human characteristics, including speech (and body language). The inorganic reaches into the organic, and *I, Robot* and *Blade Runner* become plausible; it is AI generated by deep learning that is creating programs where people are *not* behind the program – another machine has done it. Increasingly, these are called 'algorithms', but they are not algorithms people have developed or discovered, in the sense that an algorithm is a logical pattern which resolves multiplication of numbers, or division of volumes, or calculation of the area of a semi-circle etc.. In these kinds of algorithms or programs, there is ultimately human intelligence behind them, but not in command of them. AI, as with all textual construction from books to online data, traces back to human intelligence.

But, when we read what God has done, from God's perspective, we are not tracing back to humans. We are looking into the Mind of God.

People who are simultaneously both cynical/skeptical *and* familiar with the Bible may say, 'No, you are reading the words of the human who wrote the Bible – whether Moses, Solomon, or someone else.' The question is then that the Bible presents history and cosmology such that it provides coherence and explanation from a unique perspective which humans could not develop, because they were not present. It is like conceiving a colour not on the electromagnetic spectrum.

Harper Lee penned,

> *'When he was nearly thirteen my brother Jem got his arm*
> *badly broken at the elbow...'*[172],

and then proceeds to explain in narrative detail how that came about in one of the most popular novels ever written; but she is not positioning as an omniscient Intelligence describing the origins of space and time. The Bible is unique in that way. How could Moses (who is generally suggested as the human scribe of the Decalogue or 'Torah') write of the cosmic creation that,

> *'In the beginning God created the heavens and the earth.*
> *The earth was empty, a formless mass cloaked in darkness.*
> *And the Spirit of God was hovering over its surface'*[173],

*unless* he knew the cosmos could not spontaneously self-generate? How would Moses have conceived of emptiness having surface? Using Simone Weil's concept of decreation, the way that a 'formless' earth could exist is as the space caused by God removing Himself to form the space for our world.

---

[172]  Harper Lee 1960, *To Kill a Mockingbird*, p. 3
[173]  **Genesis** 1:1-2 (NLT).

(The earth was 'empty' because it had not been filled, or formed, but God created the space/locus for it by removing Himself from that area.) Why did Moses not imagine a pantheon of humanoid or fantastical animistic beings to populate cosmic palaces, mountains or trees? Or conceive a system of self-creating beings beginning with a detonation in vacuous nullity? The Islamic Qur'ān does not present a compact or sequenced creation account, instead describing creation events in different parts of its text.

Why is the Bible different?

We hit limits. The Bible describes creation, but does not facilitate participation in creation power. We cannot create new previously unconceived primary colours, nor new life forms, nor new elements, or dimensions. What we call 'science', can only *describe* - it does not create anything new. Creation was completed progressively *in situ*, not as a subatomic stew left to *somehow* produce the organic from the inorganic. God first created the inorganic (space, light, water, rock/ground), then the organic (plants, seeds, animals, microbiology, macrobiology, humans). The Bible is a boundary, as well as an account. Did Sophie meditate on boundaries, on **Genesis** 3:24?

I bet she did.

The Bible-author here is positioned prior to humans, prior to even the most fundamental originations, and it positions Intelligence (remarkably like ours, but on an infinitely larger scale) to provide a principle prior to material, cosmological existence. How do we separate *Creator* from *created* without syntactically separating first from second from third person; is not this the essence of communication, that there must be two similar creations with communicative compatibility? A problem that other texts and theories have is that the origins of matter and life are reduced to a magic explosion (i.e. 'big bang') at some indeterminate point. But the next question of course is quite logically, 'Whence did the space and energy originate for this magic bang?' Energy in our universe comes from friction of some kind, which requires movement, but how can there be movement before anything exists? Atomic theory breaks down. Atoms and subatomic particles are inherently impossible in that case (i.e. motion must begin with motion, but original motion requires motion etc.), and then so is the physical universe. The Bible resolves this: creation (or 'origin') occurred when an Intelligent Being created energy and matter. God initiated motion. (There must be an eternal Being, or else all matter & energy must take its place without dimension or time: those are the options. Either the physical cosmos is eternal, or there is Someone causing its existence.) What are 'the Heavens' referenced in the Bible, but time and space? And what is the earth but our physical locus in that time and space? Behind the text, behind the idea, is exceptional Intelligence. A principle behind all that exists. The Bible tells us this is *God*. When we read the Bible, we are looking into the Mind of God.

Is this extraordinary, yes. Hard to believe, yes. Ridiculed and rejected, yes. Coherently rational, yes.

Sophie did not have a problem of confusion. She *did* have the same problem as any Christian when reading the Bible. What are we engaging with? Is it like a print book which is one-way, or is it conversing through a text-screen with Someone on the other end? Is the Holy Spirit of God listening as we read and engage, speaking back to our spirits? This is both beautiful and unsettling.

Is the Bible a type of zoom with God? Has it always been? (No, the Bible is a relatively recent initiative from God, and really fired up when literacy accelerated in the C19th & C20th). Questions… Sophie engaged and wrestled with these, as all Christians do.

Sophie knew the value of prayer as direct communication with God. She did not confuse it with Bible-reading or study, and she did not pray to the Bible or turn it into an idol, a fetish, or a votive object. God never tells us to pray to nor venerate the Bible, but does guide us to read it and listen to inspiration provided through reading it. When we open the Bible, God the Holy Spirit is with you (ref. **John** 1:1, **2 Timothy** 3:16).

Prayer and Bible-reading/study operate mutually. The Bible gives us firm explanations, reasons, guidelines, laws, and principles. Prayer contextualizes these in our situations. The Bible will not guide you to your future spouse by name (well, not usually), but it does set parameters for moving successfully towards him/her eventually. Prayer will be more personal, and of course God knows about you and your circumstances; through prayer, S/He speaks personally with us. We may not get the answers we want, but we will receive Truth and Wisdom. Sophie knew that God approved her dedication to the Way, Truth and Life because it is an unambiguous teaching of and about Jesus Christ. How did she remain committed and resolute in applying that Truth where it could harm and even kill her? Here, she is where Jehanne found herself.

When Sophie felt that God was distant or silent, she knew the Bible was accessible and near (this is not the case for all Christians – where Christians are persecuted, there is usually also Bible-burning).

She could seek God there,

'*I'm still so remote from God that I don't even sense His presence when I pray.*'[174]

This is both a mature assessment of her spiritual situation, and a child's cry for attention. Sophie knows that when there is no directly discernible response from God by way of prayer, written communication is always a good option – if a Bible is available, so is God.

---

[174]   Sophie Scholl (Inge Jens ed.) 2017, *At the Heart of White Rose*, p.283.

*'And read the wonderful words at the beginning: "For the law of the Spirit of life in Christ Jesus hath made me free from the law of sin and death."* [175]

For Sophie, the Bible is listening to God, as it can be for anyone. *'Wonderful words'* are there and waiting. Scriptures she meditated upon inspired and guided her, using the Word of God to enhance both her mind and her understanding of others. When challenged by others' ideas and impressions she went to the Bible, as with a response to Hans' ideas on poverty; she turns to **Ephesians** and **Colossians**.[176]

She is not only reading, but God is speaking to her, in 'wonderful words'.

The Word of God led Sophie to extreme discipleship, following Jesus even to death.

*'Sophie surely knew and understood the implications of the Biblical passage which calls Christians to "...give justice to the weak and the fatherless; maintain the right of the afflicted and destitute." Sophie used this and other Scriptural commands as a launching point into her life of rebellion.'* [177]

She doesn't look like a 'rebel', at least not a militant one – she isn't a Ché Guevara, a Stonewall Jackson, or an Emmeline Pankhurst – other historical people who engaged in rebellions.

Her rebellion was with words, deriving from the Word. Sophie was a pray-<u>er</u>, a read-<u>er</u>, and a do-<u>er</u> of the Word.

❖ **Speaking/conversing about Jesus.**

> *'The first service that one owes to others in the fellowship consists in listening to them. Just as love to God begins with*

---

[175] Ibid, p.277.

[176] Ibid p. 197.

[177] Jake Johnson 2019, *Christianity, Rebellion, and Sophie Scholl: The Final Days*, 171 p.2

*listening to His Word, so the beginning of love for the brethren is learning to listen to them.'* - Dietrich Bonhoeffer.[178]

Sophie was a practitioner of Dietrich Bonhoeffer's advice (although she very likely did not know of him, at least not until 1942). Conversation is inherently two-way/mutual/interpersonal/shared; it is not a lecture/discourse/dumping. There is a place for preaching and soliloquy, but not at the centre of conversation and relationship.

We know that Sophie liked company and contact with people. As a priority, she communicates with Jesus Christ every day through prayer and Bible, and frequently writes letters to friends and family. As indicated by the majority of books in the New Testament, epistolary contact is next best to physical presence. Today, we have email and a variety of online memo and message services as well – electronically mediated letters. In whatever way the letters are mediated, they are parts of communication – the correspondence of speaking and listening. If we cannot be with someone, and if we care, we will communicate, we will write to them, using the means at our disposal.

'Speaking' can happen in many ways.

Voice is the obvious one, less consciously through body language, also via writing, and through creative expressions such as music, dance and art. The essence of conversation is mutuality – we speak, and then we listen to the other. We are not always very good at listening – generally we are better at speaking.

Jesus repeatedly calls people to 'Listen' (e.g. **Mark** 4:3, 7:14, 11:24) as to remind them; if speaking alone without expectation of reply were sufficient to a conversation, we could be satisfied with speaking to a tree.

---

[178]  Dietrich Bonhoeffer 1939, *Life Together*, p.75.

Conversation mandates intelligent response, which must come from a person.

Why is a baby's learning to speak such an important step in the human developmental journey? Why is the baby's first intentional word (often 'Mum' or 'Dad') so exciting? Because communication is not only a function, it is our purpose, and language exponentially facilitates relationships. It is elemental. *If* humans as a species began with a solitary evolving organism developing the capacity to communicate, or if by some colossal coincidence two humans developed the capacity and impulse for language at the exact same time, and sexually heterogenous maturity at the exact same moment – then we could conclude that evolution uses language to refine human primacy in the history of life. It is the capacity for syntactic language and the expression of abstraction that separates us from the animals. Alternatively, *if* the human was first made by an omnipotent and omniscient God Being/ Entity, and enabled by the God/Creator Parent to converse with God from the beginning, and then separated into the two elemental genders of God, sharing a language they could use together to effect communication, then the extraordinary coincidence of simultaneous evolution is removed. Fundamentally, we have an inherence which is to speak to the Being God who created *all* – we yearn for this, and for the intimate recombination of the male/female essences enabled through language and closeness. Prayer is not a behaviour confined to Judeo-Christian peoples, by any means. Humans long for relationship and communication with God as with other humans. Sophie seeks both; she does not herself meditate on these aspects, but she engages through them, and she notices them.

People move from 1st Person utterance, which is our speaking about and from self, to 2nd Person utterance (direct conversation/address) which encompasses response, to 3rd Person utterance (indirect discussion/commentary) which is observation without direct engagement. We shift adeptly and unconsciously through these points of view in our communications every day. Each type of communication implies relationship from and with our personhood.

In English, the basic forms are:

1st Person: e.g. 'I love you.' (subject/verb/object)

2nd Person: e.g. 'You are loved.' (implied subject-object/ verb/direct elaboration)

3rd Person: e.g. 'S/he is loved.' (implied subject-object/ verb/indirect elaboration)

In 2nd and 3rd Person the subject is implied (i.e. self), because it is redundant to state the self repeatedly.

When we speak in the 3rd Person, we could be speaking about a living person, or a dead person. Is that person less real because of their condition? (We can speak of a corpse [as object] in the 1st Person, but it is now inanimate and implicit that the communication is not mutual – it cannot now become 2nd Person.) When we speak of our parent who is now deceased, are they a lesser person? The difference is that we cannot now engage in the 2nd Person with them, but we have 3rd Person. Their reality is now our memory, but also their enduring character eliciting our feelings and attitudes (we can love or hate a dead person). Can we have 3rd Person unless there has been 2nd Person? Yes, I can speak about Martin Luther King, even though I have never had 2nd Person experience of him – others have. The 2nd Person has to have been possible though, whether we ever actually engaged with that person or not. Can we have 3rd Person unless there has been 1st Person? No, I cannot speak my perspective about Martin Luther King unless I have knowledge of him. That knowledge can have two sources – 2nd Person or 1st Person, but three expressions (1st, 2nd or 3rd Person). That source knowledge indicates the ontological reality of the object (e.g. Martin Luther King). Its reality can be denied, e.g. someone could deny the existence of Martin Luther King, and it then falls to us to either accept that ignorance or correct it through evidence. However that might be done, Martin Luther King remains real throughout. Our perception is not necessary to his reality. His reality is contingent on being an evidentiary form of a self.

Sophie speaks about Jesus conversationally,

> *'Only one person has ever managed to go straight to God, probably, but who still looks for him nowadays?'* (Sophie Scholl, 29/5/1940)

> *'…this thoroughly un-Christian attitude is especially common among self-styled Christians. If it were so, how could one expect fate to make a just cause prevail when so few people unwaveringly sacrifice themselves for a just cause?'* (Sophie, 22/6/1940)

> *'Once, when I'd lost heart because I kept backsliding, I didn't dare pray any more. I decided not to ask anything more of God until I could enter His presence again. That in itself was a fundamental yearning for God.'* (Sophie, 10/11/1941)[179]

Each time, Sophie is speaking about God to either a friend or to herself (via a diary). These are 2nd Person utterances, in which she is talking about a 3rd Person object. In the 10/11/1941 excerpt though, she alludes to her 2nd Person communication. Either she is delusional, or she is speaking to a real Person.

---

[179]  Sophie Scholl (Inge Jens), *At the Heart of White Rose*, p. 190

Ontology allows Sophie to speak about and to God; however, she cannot introduce a colour which is not on the spectrum. She communicates within the boundaries of space, time and intellect, but cannot exceed them.

Her wishes/hopes are simply human – she yearns for the love which is God, also knowing that S/He is other, not self. We cannot yearn for something which is not possible, or converse with something which is not a person (whether anthropomorphic or human). A heroin addict yearns for heroin because it is possible, a baby yearns for his/her mother because it is possible. 'Yearning' *ipso facto* indicates the existent object.

Conversation requires speaker and listener; without either, the other is redundant. In conversation, the speaker implies the listener. And vice-versa. Sophie conversed with Jesus through prayer, and some would contend through reading (in which case there is an author to complement the reader). Sophie's speaking implies a listener. (As prayer implies a respondent.)

Why does God not manifest Himself to Sophie, as He did with Jehanne? Would that not make a difference? It didn't with Charles VII and Jehanne; Charles saw supernatural phenomena too, and reacted very differently to Jehanne. Presence, reality or manifestation are not guarantees of change, growth or maturation. Sophie never records any such experience. She does indicate awareness of God as a Self, as Other and Being, and she records due changes in her thinking and acting.

> *'Weariness... keeps me silent when I ought to speak out...*
> *I put it off until later... I know what I'm like, and I'm too*
> *tired, lazy, and bad to change.'* (Sophie, 22/6/1940) [180]

---

[180]  Ibid, p.85.

Even allowing this to be true (she does seem quite hard on herself), it is not permanent; there is significant, active and extremely courageous change in the ensuing two and a half years.

❖ **Inspiration through Art.**

Sophie is a poet. Certainly in the sense that she loves communicating creativity, excellence and beauty. All of our creativity, our appreciation of flair, genius and virtuosity, is a direct function of imagination and inter-pretation. To create, we imagine (i.e. form an image/concept/impression in our mind), and then realize the imagined concept via media which enable communication of the concept to others, whether through writing, paint-ing, sculpting, composing/singing, dancing/moving, designing etc.. Art is a form of language, of communicative expression. Sophie was herself a painter, musician and philosopher, if we allow these all to be art-forms. She was actually in the process of illustrating an edition of J.M.Barrie's *Peter Pan* when WW2 broke out. Music and literature were probably her deepest interests. But, God was her inspiration, and she wondered at His selfless love, and her need of it[181]. She presents us with questions and musings – is philosophy art? She does not ask in those words (so far as I am aware), but she flirts with theodicy and then shies away with a sense of incapability which appears to derive from her anticipations or interpretations of oth-ers' perceptions of her thoughts. She is a deep thinker on her own, and if philosophy can be art, then Sophie is an artist at that level, as well as with musical manuscript, pen, ink and brush.

Alexandra Lloyd asks,

---

[181] See her letter to Fritz Hartnagel 16-2-1943, 2nd last paragraph (in Inge Jens [ed.], *At the Heart of White Rose.*)

*'...How was it possible for [White Rose] to be apparently immune to the indoctrination apparently perpetrated by Nazism, and furthermore to act on this knowledge?*

*There are many possible answers to this... They all suffered losses or difficulties in their early life; they were all open to discussion or debate with others; they all had some form of personal faith, or at least an openness to Christianity and/or Christian thinkers. They also shared a serious interest in and engagement with culture and the arts.*[182]

It's an excellent and focusing question, and Lloyd broad-strokes some possibilities;

- family of origin issues & possible trauma in childhood,
- curiosity and intellectual engagement,
- faith and openness to Christian worldviews,
- receptivity towards and exploration of art and culture.

Sophie was interested in each of these.

Do we see her relating with Jesus in any direct way? In her letters and diary entries she alludes to great composers she enjoyed – Bach, Beethoven, Schubert. Writers like Goethe, Rilke and Bernanos are mentioned (but these are likely more of a homage to Hans' influence than a direct line between Sophie and Jesus). She does seem to have a taste for French literature, specifically referencing Victor Hugo's poetry.

In prayer, Sophie is directly connected to Christ. In reading and reflecting on Scripture, she is directly connected. In appreciating artistic creativity is there any direct connection?

---

[182] Alexandra Lloyd (2023), *The Arts, Culture, and the Evolution of the White Rose Resistance.* Oxford German Studies 52(1), 1-14.

In some ways, she is a radical contrast to her environment. Even though as a young teen she was involved in Nazi organizations (i.e. BDM), as she grew older, she outgrew the antagonistic racial narcissism of National Socialism. In this she showed growth into truth and wisdom, leaving behind the carapace of collective irrational prejudice. She herself became an art-work, a beautiful masterpiece of courage, intelligence and vibrancy. Beauty attracted her – in nature, in human artistry, in relationships, in God. In the visual arts she enjoyed and appreciated Bertl Kley, Wilhelm Geyer, Paul Klee, and Auguste Rodin[183]. Oppositely and equally she was repulsed by ugliness, psychotic hatred, cowardice, vilification of the helpless, injustice.

It is against her own beauty – her valour and strength – we see the reality of corruption as a contrast to her goodness. Despite her self-abnegation as a sinful human, she yet shines as a Christian woman. The narrative of Sophie's activism, her capture, interrogation, prosecution, conviction, and judicial murder between June 1942 – February 1943 is well told in other texts[184], yet some incidents and events have been screened, or evaded.

We need to remember that toxicity and corruption are often most clearly illustrated when contrasted to the beautiful and pure. It is also well to recall that holiness and evil have similarities which can be confusing: neither exhibits guilt or shame.

Just days after Sophie's murder by guillotine, large gatherings of out-raged students - a sample of Germany's brightest and best - protested deliberately, loudly and passionately at Munich University. The White Rose activists were passionately condemned for their treachery against Reich and Führer. Indications from late February 1943 are that hundreds of Munich University's brilliant minds slavered their loyalty to the Nazi State,

---

[183]    Ibid.
[184]    See e.g. A. Dumbach & J. Newborn 1986, *Sophie Scholl and the White Rose* for written narrative, and M. Rothemund 2005, *Sophie Scholl: Die letzten Tage* for filmic narrative.

abandoning Sophie and White Rose as 'degenerates'. Sophie had predicted and believed in student revolution, but not of this type[185].

This was the crowd screaming for Barabbas. Other White Rose activists who were arrested and subjected to Gestapo treatment were also judicially murdered over the ensuing months. Alexander Schmorell *(Schurik),* Hans' close comrade and fellow Wehrmacht officer, was most likely betrayed 2-3 days after Sophie's and Hans' murders, and was murdered by guillotine on 13/7/1943.

A few survived.

How does this connect to Sophie through art?

If there is an ideological, existential and ethical theme woven through the White Rose activists' backgrounds, it is their commitment to *Freiheit* (Freedom). Where did their ideas and ideals come from?

Jesus said, '... *You are truly my disciples if you keep obeying my teachings. And you will know the truth, and the truth will set you free.*'[186] Freedom is a frequent and elevated aspiration of the creative mind, and is a high form of art in any society if it can be achieved for all peoples and citizens. Freedom of artistic creativity is a metric for the quality of freedom in a society; it is a significant measure of civility and the freedom of will granted us from our creation.

Many people in Germany privately longed for personal and civic freedom, but relatively few were prepared to fight for it against the Nazi State. Hitler was astutely sensitive to the hegemonic power of collectives and alliances; he moved swiftly and ruthlessly to destroy unions and organizations which were either independent of or opposed to National Socialism, when he acceded to government in January 1933. He knew that his control over Germany had to sweep away the collective opposition of

---

[185]  Ibid, Dumbach & Newhorn, p. 163.
[186]  **John** 8:31b-32 (NLT)

the Left (i.e. Marxists and Socialists), the Centrists (political liberals and Christian allegiances), and the geo-politically and religiously aligned (e.g. Catholic Bavaria). Preferably, he could appropriate their tacit support or passive acceptance - at minimum. Hitler knew it was essential to redirect their collective strength into acceptance of, or at least acquiescence towards, National Socialism. Unions, alliances and collectives were key to Hitler's accession to and of power. Where/if he could not tame or sway them, he destroyed them, through infiltration and redirection, or dissolution through law and fragmentation. Conversely, he assembled huge and hierarchical institutions within which roles and positions were structured and supported with rewards and prestige. The *Deutsches Volk* was the principle and goal of all effort and striving, maintaining and extending the supremacy of the racial pyramid, undergirding the apex of the Aryan.

This pursuit of the perfect human became the Topheth of Germany.

In the end, to achieve this, street-fighting and intimidation were acceptable if other means failed. From the late 1920's-1934, Hitler had the Sturm Abteilung (SA)[187] as a private Nazi Army dedicated to installing a National Socialist state under the Führer. When the SA had served its purpose, it was in turn bloodily subordinated in the 'Night of the Long Knives'[188]. Whichever policies and tactics worked were satisfactory. Hitler was both a pragmatist and a strategist. Total power was the ultimate Nazi end - the corrupt and dark treasure that Hitler most desired.

Its demonic culture sketches out plainly from people who fell as its victims:

---

[187]  *Sturm Abteilung* translates literally to English as 'Storm Department' – it was an earlier, militant wing of the Nazi political movement, by 1934 rivalling the Wehrmacht. Leaders of the SA tended to believe in the 'socialist' aspect of 'National Socialism', which was not Hitler's pre-eminent interest or goal. The *Night of the Long Knives* disposed of that socialist faction in the National Socialist movement.

[188]  For an account, see W. Shirer, *Rise and Fall of the Third Reich*, pp. 267-283.

*'My anxiety grows with each minute. The car [locomotive carriage] doors open with a grating sound. Men in striped uniforms tell us: "Come out fast. Leave everything here, take only something to eat! Fast! Fast!"*

*They are Jews, they don't look bad. A thought occurs: "It must be better here than in the ghetto." Sentries have been posted along the train at each car... the SS officer waves his hand and orders: "Women to the right! Men to the left!" I hold my son's hand tightly and walk as if hypnotized. I hardly see anything. All my attention is concentrated on the SS man, and more specifically his power-wielding hand... a terrible noise rings in my ears. He tears my boy away from me: "Children go with the women."*

*I look dumbfounded after my son, until he vanishes into the crowd. Utter despair... I ask a man in a striped tunic, "Where are we going?"*

*"You will see," he says. "To Heaven."*

*Especially upsetting is the fact that... Jews like us, who have evidently been here for some time, are no less vile than the SS men.'* [189]

White Rose was a relatively tiny and delicate wildflower, by comparison to the noxious fields of poisonous weeds engulfing it on all sides with sewers of megalomania, angry hatred, conformist acquiescence, mindless subservience, and amoral brutality: an aggressively toxic list.

---

[189] Abram Kajzer, in A. Adelson & R. Lapides 1989, *Łódź Ghetto: Inside a Community Under Siege*, pp. 461 & 464.

Again, there are ready answers in other texts to where their ideas and ideals came from, but in all their reading, exploring and discussing as prelude to White Rose, these young students drank long and deep draughts from the likes of Immanuel Kant, Georg Hegel, and Gottfried Leibniz, all philosophers who meditated on the extent and possibilities of human freedom. They listened to Handel and Mozart, and read Thomas Mann, Jacques Maritain and George Bernard Shaw. They spoke and shared together, reveled with Russian farmers, absorbed the folk-songs and balalaika music in the Ukraine, wrote many letters, and reflected in diaries - and of course in leaflets.

It is very notable that Sophie's writing and expression often have a poetic cadence and quality, although she did not write them with deliberate scansion. Her articulations nevertheless meander with currents both of grace and determination. She compares very interestingly with some recognized poets, even though Sophie did not intend comparison, nor to write poetically.

Adrienne Rich, a celebrated poet with a large oeuvre of work, a poetry which is characterized by rich imagery, uneven syncopation and irregular rhythmic schema. The example below is from her poem,

I Dream I'm the Death of Orpheus (1971)

*'I am walking rapidly through striations of light and dark*
*thrown under an arcade.*
*I am a woman in the prime of life, with certain powers*
*And those powers severely limited*
*By authorities whose faces I rarely see.*
*I am a woman in the prime of life...'*[190]

---

[190]   Adrienne Rich 1971, *I Dream I'm the Death of Orpheus* (poem), in *The Will to Change.*

Sylvia Plath wrote more stylistically, cradling her poetry in recognizably rhythmic forms. She is a chronicler of life through a lens of depression, close observation and stark realism – she noticed hypocrisy and falsehood. Going further, Sylvia meddled with what was beyond death, attempting to contact spirits from another dimension (God warns us emphatically not to do this, as it exposes us to spiritual chaos and darkness[191]).

She enjoyed and appreciated art as poetry, exemplified by this excerpt from her poem,

Tulips (1962)

*'I didn't want any flowers, I only wanted*
*To lie with my hands turned up and be utterly empty.*
*How free it is, you have no idea how free –*
*The peacefulness is so big it dazes you …* [192]

The Tsitsistas people, an Indigenous American nation known better by their French demonym *Cheyenne*, sang/chanted their lyric poetry, and while the melody is somewhat preserved in the Bureau of American Ethnology Collection, the original harmonies and syncopations are lost and gone. But they also had poetry, of a type we would regard irregular,

*' The old men*
*say*
*the earth*
*only endures.*
*You spoke*
*truly.*

---

[191]  See **Deuteronomy** 18:10-11.
[192]  Sylvia Plath 1962, *Tulips* (poem), in *Norton Anthology of Poetry, p.1283.*

*You are right.*'[193]

And a sample of Sophie's own writing; from a *letter to Fritz Hartnagel* on 16-2-1943; less than a week before her murder.

> '*But being on my own does me good,*
>    *even though I sometimes feel ill*
>    *at ease because people spoil me so much.*
> *However, I only feel really secure*
>    *when I recognize the presence*
>    *of selfless love*
>    *and that's comparatively rare.*'[194]

Can we reduce poetry to dexterous word arrangement? In some styles, perhaps; but the point here is that the words must be chosen and deployed for their semantic richness and musicality as arranged with others, to form rhyme and meter. Sophie's words held those qualities; she often immerses her expression alliteratively and onomatopoeically (or, at least, it presents so in English translation).

Each of the above poems is verse. They are intentionally poetic (Adrienne's and Sylvia's), and lyrical (the Tsisistas/Cheyenne lyric); each recognizable as poetry. Sophie's expression is often artistic and creative in itself – she achieves a similar poetry of expression, without consciously trying at all.

Proximity to Jesus is inspirational – it is not possible to be positively close to Him and not be inspired, energized, enhanced, elevated. Jesus renders all his followers' lives into poetry.

---

[193]   Dee Brown 1970, *Bury My Heart at Wounded Knee*, p.447.
[194]   Sophie Scholl (Inge Jens ed.), *At the Heart of White Rose*, p.308.

(*Negative* closeness would be the experience of people intent on sin and desecration, e.g. deliberate blasphemy of the type practised by leaders of the *Deutsche Christen* [Nazified Church], or people legalizing/legitimising murder [i.e. abortion] as 'reproductive freedom' [2025 atow]).

People close to Him, when He was travelling around Judea/Israel in approx. 30-33AD, started doing extraordinary things – literally. They did things that were not normal – healing people with terminal conditions, with incurable diseases, even resurrecting the dead. They were brought before the equivalents of Premiers and Popes. They communicated the Gospel of Jesus wherever they went, and thousands were engaged and transformed. But they were also hated, reviled and persecuted, sometimes to death. The disciples and apostles of the early times were incredibly creative, but that was because God's power through the Holy Spirit enabled them. Jesus promised that power for all who follow Him, not just for the 1st Century folk. (E.g. It helps us understand how Jehanne resurrected a dead baby.) It is not really surprising that Sophie spoke and wrote eloquently and poetically, at 19 – 21 years of age. Certainly, she was intelligent and creative, but she also had Christ's inspiration. Even that word 'inspiration' stems from '*spiritus*' – Latin for 'breath'; He breathes into us.

Is art *anything* which is created/developed purposefully by humans? No – that would then encompass toxic chemicals (like Zyklon B) as art. In the English language, *art* can have two meanings: 1. it can mean clever and subtle skill, and 2. it can mean creative expression of perception, beauty and idealism. Art is the creative expression of human experience and conceptualisation.

Creativity + Love = Art!

From whence Sophie's dedication to *freiheit/freedom*? It turns out to be highly visible and deeply soulful: we relate to Truth – we actually have relationship with Truth... it is not a remote ideal, meditative mantra, or philosophical construct. *Truth is a Person.* Jesus said, *'I am the way, the **truth**, and the life. No one can come to the Father except through me.'*[195] Jesus is the Truth. When we relate to Jesus, we relate to God – He is the Way. How did Sophie experience direct connection to Jesus through art? She sought truth and beauty in art, and in the finding of truth, she inevitably met Jesus. Ontologically, the highest creativity has to be God's. What did Sophie see?

> *'His oath, His covenant, His blood,*
> *Support me in the whelming flood.*
> *When all around my soul gives way,*
> *He then is all my Hope and Stay.'*
> ( - Cate Williams)[196]

And for Sophie, He seems to have been exactly that.

It is not exactly clear when Sophie was apprised of White Rose, and/or when she began her active involvement. Very likely it seems to have been around June/July 1942. She was probably aware of Hans' and Alexander Schmorell's resistance stance and activity before this.

Sophie was freely artistic to the end! Her very last flourish on this earth was a doodle on a legal notice – her formal conviction and sentence.

On its back, she wrote *'Freiheit'* ( i.e. *'Freedom'*) - calligraphically, winsomely, artistically. Even amidst the ugliness and evil of her deplorable treatment by the Nazi State, she knew that she was free.

The Truth was with her.

❖   **Living Jesus' values and priorities.**

---

[195]   **John** 14:6 (NLT)
[196]   Cate Williams 2014, *My Hope is Built,* from album *Dance of Life* CD, lyric excerpt Track 10.

Sophie's doctrinal upbringing was Lutheran – she knew the creed and expectations of Lutheran observance, so the basics of Lutheranism are fixed in the context of Sophie's childhood. She knew the Augsburg Confession, and had undergone baptism as a child, followed by confirmation at the Ulm Cathedral (albeit in her BDM uniform as an adolescent – this alone emphasizes the rift between walking with Christ, and formal religiosity!).

Churches are not the primary indicator of Christian faith. They are intended as the collective expression of commitment to Christ, the gathering of Christians together as the Kingdom of God, as the Body of Christ, to honour, worship and serve God in Jesus' Name, as His Redeemed people. Jesus nowhere says, 'The Church is the way, the truth, and the life.'

He does say that He is (see **John** 14:6 per above).

Magdalena followed *pietism*, a holiness movement within the Lutheran Church which emphasized personal accountability for sin, living confessionally before Christ, and living a life centred in the holiness of God. There is no evidence that pietism was a central feature of the Scholls' family life, but Magdalena was definitely a pietist and her devotional manner of living would be visible within the family. The emphases were on prayer, confessional living, owning absolute dependence on the atoning Grace of Christ, devotion to reading Scripture, personal holiness in conduct and outlook. Robert was not a pietist, so the home functioned as a family with a strong father figure, a submissive and meek/gentle mother, and intelligent, curious children. It sounds like a supportive, comfortable, orderly home. There is no indication, other than Magdalena's pietism, that the home was particularly spiritual or religious. But, it was Sophie's milieu, her environment; she grew up in and with Jesus' influence.

Through *freedom*, Sophie's connection to Jesus in the arts is visible, especially in literature, philosophy and music. The opposites that the White Rose activists saw juxtaposed between the beauty of creativity and the corruption of evil, was a primary motivation for them, including Sophie. In White Rose Leaflets 5 & 6 particularly, freedom is articulated and prized as a fundamental element of life which defines human independence and volition. Nazism has at this point so debased and compromised freedom that it is become a virtue and condition which must be and needs to be restored – it has corroded away such that it is effectively non-existent in Germany.

Late 1942 sees Sophie undergoing a kind of crisis. Her long-term boyfriend Fritz is displaced in Sophie's heart by Alexander Schmorell (aka 'Schurik' – a Russian-born [and good-looking] highly intelligent, close friend of Hans'), and even though this is a momentary infatuation or attraction - it shakes her. She speculates on her affections, and where this vacillation positions her with God? Schurik persists in her heart, and she determines to pray her way out of the tension she finds in herself, first resolving to '...*tear him out of her heart...*' and then doubting it is needed – perhaps sensing an over-correction to an over-reaction?

This happens during a time when Hans, Schurik and Fritz were all in Russia (though not all together) at about the high-water mark of the Nazi empire, and Sophie was in Germany. (Sophie's younger brother Werner was also a soldier serving in Russia, but there is no indication that he was involved in White Rose.) The importance of her confused feelings for Schurik, and her uncertainty about Fritz, consists in her growing resolve to support and act within White Rose. Schurik was White Rose – a righteous man. Fritz was just Wehrmacht – a German combat soldier. Fritz was fighting with an infantry unit in the Wehrmacht; Hans and Schurik were medics, not combatants. Her attraction to Schurik resolves and illustrates any conflict in her allegiances/commitments. Loyalty bound her to Fritz, captivation and attraction bound her to Schurik. Jesus' values sometimes present us with dilemmas, and Sophie certainly experienced this.

Her faith parallels her activism; and her relationships mirror her choices. She has moved away from Fritz emotionally[197], and closer to Schurik. Her quandary also edges closer to God, and more deliberately aligns her choices with her deepening faith. This is reflected in the focus and tone of her diary entries and letters from August/September 1942. When did Sophie discover the composition of and the personnel involved in White Rose, such as Hans and Schurik? Probably mid-late June 1942. They had been exceedingly careful to conceal their activities, but Sophie unraveled their anonymity[198]. It has to be said, that if Sophie could uncover them, they ought to have redoubled their efforts and complicated their camouflages. They did not. By 23/7/1942, when Hans, Schurik, Willi Graf, Jürgen Wittenstein and Hubert Fürtwangler took their train to Russia, White Rose was an active, committed and growing, if embryonic movement.

Hans, Alexander Schmorell, Christoph Probst, Jürgen Wittenstein, Willi Graf, and their teacher Kurt Huber were involved in creating and composing the Leaflets. Sophie knew about this at least from the time of Leaflets 3 and 4, and was probably involved from this time. Sophie herself was meticulously careful not to leave any detectable hint of White Rose. Hans unfortunately seems to have been the slightly reckless one.

*'In the ten years of destruction of all material and intellectual freedoms, of all moral fibre in the German people, they have sufficiently demonstrated what they understand by freedom and honour...'*[199]

This language is both articulate and inflammatory; it clearly describes National Socialism (Nazism) as:

---

[197]  See Sophie Scholl (Inge Jens), *At the Heart of White Rose*, p.194.
[198]  See Dumbach & Newborn, Ch.7.
[199]  White Rose Leaflet #6.

- destructive to fundamental freedoms (e.g. faith, belief and association),
- reducing Germany to moral bankruptcy,
- a rejection of freedom and honour.

They speak freely, exactly as intended – thereby ensuring they would be hunted.

Thus is the ideology of Nazism critiqued, repudiated and condemned by White Rose. Sophie is not credited anywhere as an author of any of the Leaflets, and she may not have been a direct contributor or writer, but the tenor of Leaflet 4 conveys an intimately profound respect for God, and a remorseful sorrow for Germany's wicked disobedience. The 4th Leaflet quotes the Bible, the only Leaflet to feature Scripture (**Ecclesiastes** 4:1-2). Sophie was reading her Bible in 1942[200]. The language of the Leaflets at this time (i.e. Nov/Dec 1942) is saturated in Godly ire.

> *'Every word that comes out of Hitler's mouth is a lie. When he says peace, he means war, and when he blasphemously uses the name of the Almighty, he means the power of evil, the fallen angel, Satan. His mouth is the foul-smelling maw of hell...* [201]

This language and content is distinctively Biblical, it even resonates with direct inspiration – words fresh from the mouth of the Holy Spirit. Not lyrically beautiful words, but incisively true ones. I would suggest that Sophie had spoken to Hans and Schurik, and by so doing ensured Biblical truth as words from Jesus were featured in this dynamic and gripping Leaflet. *Leaflet 4* is a little different to the others; it is not written with academic quotations from philosophers and classical seers like Lao-tzu,

---

[200]  See Sophie Scholl (Inge Jens), *At the Heart of White Rose*, p.197.
[201]  White Rose Leaflet #4.

Goethe and Aristotle, which were unlikely to resonate much with ordinary people. They do crackle with indignation and righteous anger that most people will readily understand though. The language and imagery is vivid.

This is Jesus with His whip (cf. **John** 2:15-16). The Holy Spirit can be insulted and enraged by disrespect to the Grace of Christ (cf. **Hebrews** 10:29).

The Leaflets persevere in condemning the Nazi regime with all its hatreds, septic lies, and misdirections.

Jesus never says *anger* is wrong, but He does plainly say to be *very careful* with this emotion. In **Matthew** 5:22, He delineates anger as a short spectrum:

1.  feeling the emotion of anger (i.e. victimization),
2.  expressing the anger as personal attack (i.e. reaction),
3.  wishing and intending harm to the person with whom we are angry (i.e. vengeance).

He is clear that anger will bring us to God's judgment, and it is far better to resolve anger by going to a person you have offended and asking their forgiveness before we ask God to visit judgment on anyone else. We ought also ask God to forgive us as we self-righteously cling to our own vengeful, self-pitying melodramas. Even if we have every right to be angry because of an injustice, bring it to God.

Anger is the right response to injustice; Jesus is not saying that we ought not to feel anger, simply that we have to be wise and careful in responding to the emotion. If we have wronged someone (i.e. therefore they have a right to be angry with us), go and apologise *before* we ask God to forgive us. Don't ask God to do what we refuse to do. It's all psychologically sensible of course – Jesus is the Lord of Psychology. He knows us, He gets us. Take responsibility where we need to, and seek restoration.

If we have wronged no-one and there is no hypocrisy in our own anger, we are advised to reconcile the relationship and avoid the recriminations of anger. Restored and healed relationship is preferable to vented resentment, which will likely only result in harm.

In **Matthew** 5:26 & 6:21, Jesus warns us that stored anger will end up robbing us of all our treasure. He teaches us that where our treasure is, there shall our heart be also, and therefore make sure our hearts are aligned with His. Treasure the right things, not just the things we like, or are used to, or that maintain our pride or reputation. Treasure truth, love, peace, justice, holiness.

White Rose's anger at the evils of Nazism reflects Jesus' hatred of sin. Sin is *destructive*, which is why God rejects it. God is *creative*. God is life and love, not death and indifference (which is the true opposite of love; *hate* is usually love that has gone wrong). Their anger was righteous indignation,

*'I ask you as a Christian who is wrestling to preserve his greatest treasure, if you are hesitating and playing games of intrigue and procrastination in the hope that someone else will raise his arm in your Defense? Has God not given you the strength and will to fight? We must attack evil where it is strongest, and it is strongest in the power of Hitler.* [202]

These are strong and courageous words; words which eventually led to death sentences upon these brave young White Rose Truth-speakers. Jesus asks us to follow Him wherever He leads, which implicitly involves carrying our own crosses, and can and does include difficult suffering – from rejection by people we love and value, to physical torment and assault by Christophobes, and those who sin against the Holy Spirit. Christians face these every year, every century, every day. Sophie was absolutely right to be

---

[202]   Ibid.

implacably opposed to Nazism, and she was in company which chose to express their hatred of evil in manifest ways (n.b. like anger, *hatred* is not inherently bad if it is directed righteously… e.g. God <u>hates</u> sin because it is destructive and corrupting). It was a costly determination.

So, anger itself is not wrong; when we experience it, our obligation is to channel it according to Jesus' directions. We need to be thoughtful about what has angered us (i.e. triggered our anger). In late Summer 1942, Germany stank with putrid depths of blood guilt, and was also at the zenith of its powers – the Nazi German Reich stretched from North Cape in Norway to the Ukrainian plains east of Crimea, and from the deserts of Tunisia to western Egypt. Wherever it ruled, Germany victimized innocent people, leaving a trail of foul murder and cowardly persecution from Heraklion to Trondheim. German government was practicing systemic, sadistic cruelty wherever the Reich ruled, leaving babies to die for lack of basic care, torturing people who dared to speak truth against them, and violating the Law of God written onto the human conscience from Creation. Jesus says that when we help someone in need, we are actually helping Jesus Himself (see **Matthew** 25:40). He did not say that would be easily done – Dietrich Bonhoeffer is right about *costly grace*. In this her resistance, Sophie is living by Jesus' precepts, and upholding His standard; she is here most visible as a Kingdom warrior, and illumines Jesus Himself in her obedience to Him.

To this day, Sophie is calling and leading people to Christ. She follows and shows to us the radical Christ, whose road is love, and whose victory is unchangeable. It is already achieved, and it is we who carry it wherever we are and go. Sophie did this bravely and intelligently.

When Sophie speaks her truth through White Rose leaflets, when her voice is present and audible (as in the 4th Leaflet), she is testifying to Christ in a very dangerous space. When Christians refuse to deny Christ, or to compromise His truth, we are testifying; He warns us there can and will be consequences. Sophie offers hope and opportunity to any who will listen, opposing and fighting evil as they can. They are not alone. There are others who also resist, and Jesus is with them in such situations, to the end of the age.

❖ **Creation & Nature.**

Being outdoors in the beauty of the wild, among infinite varieties of landscapes and night skies, was a source of both excitement and serenity for Sophie. She was anything but a fainting damsel. **Romans** 1:19-20 very clearly encourages us to perceive God in the intricacy and eternity of Creation – if we are open to seeing and receiving it. Our prejudices arising from acceptance of scientific method as the sole source of reliable knowledge, vastly limits our access to other sources, such as history and philosophy. This Scripture from **Romans** is actually more definite – maintaining that evidence of God's reality is inherent in Creation. Sophie was very open to this. She was traveler, climber, walker, rider, watcher – all of these.

> 'One sees so little at night, and all we saw was the beauty of the place
> [on the Danube River, in southern Germany]. We could make out
> the reflection of Orion in the water, and plenty more stars besides.
> We headed west along a path of some kind, and saw dark forest and
> the stars above it. It was really lovely.' (- Sophie, 3/4/1940) [203]

Sophie was a night-walker - out exploring along the banks of the Danube in the dark, marveling at stars reflecting in the water. While she could see little detail, she could see the immensity of beauty over and around her.

---

[203]   Sophie Scholl (Inge Jens), *At the Heart of White Rose*, p.70

Darkness only reflected and accentuated the beauty of Creation and light – the contrast enhances our perception.

> *'Trees and flowers and animals were created too,*
> *after all, and possess a hint of spirituality.'*
> ( - Sophie, 10/12/1941) [204]

**Romans** 1:19-20 is more emphatic, but underlines the same point; the cosmos as an extensively intricate eco-system, functioning as a network of interconnected balances and suspensions. All aspects of the cosmos have function, and function implies purpose, and of course purpose implies intelligence. For instance, *eyes* evolving spontaneously over countless millennia from original atomic nurseries in a magic-bang, are a difficult proposition to entertain. The micro-design alone involved in the pairing of dimension with vision is monumental. So much else is involved, not least the parallel existence of light. That two eyes on a level (such as the sockets in the skull) enable depth perception through autonomic trigonometry is staggering – it works so spectacularly well, with a brain functioning as a super-computer processing the constant streams of data. One eye is sufficient for visual perception; two are needed for ready depth perception. Creation/Nature is a teleological wonder. Sophie's conclusion is that nature was created, and in this she sees God the Architect of Life, and His eternal spirituality.

> *'... when all else falls away, he alone [i.e. God] will remain.*
> *How terrible to be remote from him... My sole sustenance*
> *is Nature, the sky and the stars and the silent earth.'*
> ( - Sophie, 12/12/1941) [205]

---

[204]   Ibid p.193
[205]   Ibid p.194

'*When all else falls away...*' implies something from which the falling can occur.

Something immovably permanent.

'*...sole sustenance...*' directly indicates that there is one primary source of support and nourishment. Sophie sees the permanence of God in Nature, that He endures when 'all else' does not. This homeostasis is within God, is His/Her essence and stability, and He will not fall in any way. It is more likely that when we fall, we fall *to* Him.

> '*... I'm delighting once more in the last rays of the sun and marveling at the incredible beauty of all that wasn't created by man: the red dahlias by the white garden gate, the tall, solemn fir trees, the tremulous gold-draped birches whose gleaming trunks stand out against all the green and russet foliage, and the golden sunshine... It's all so wonderfully beautiful here... My sheer delight in all things beautiful has been invaded by a great unknown, an inkling of the creator whom his creatures glorify with their beauty...*'
> ( - Sophie, 10/10/1942)[206]

Beauty reflects the essence of beauty *within the Creator*. Could something exquisite and beautiful be made by something destructive and wicked? No. The beautiful can only derive from a beautiful conception. In all the beauty that Sophie sees in Nature, she perceives in this a glimpse of Almighty and beautiful God. As a bird must come from a bird, and as colour must come from light, so beauty must come from beauty, motion from motion: Sophie teaches us the elemental truths she herself is seeing.

---

[206]  Ibid, p. 276

As she is enfolded in the beauty of God through the Creation around her, His/Her presence impresses her as a 'great unknown' – an exact description echoed 25 years later, also about God:

> *'Hold my hand all the way, every hour, every day,*
> *Come here to the great unknown*
> *Take my hand, let me stand,*
> *Where no-one stands alone.'*
> ( - Elvis Presley, 1967)[207]

These are perceptions about God that Sophie forms through observing/ experiencing Creation:

- That S/He is visibly and beautifully manifest through beauty in the created order
- That God is absolutely reliable and steadfast
- That darkness or contrast accentuates the beauty of God rather than extinguishing it
- That God is self-evident in Creation through principles of reproduction and motion.

❖ **Presence of the Holy Spirit.**

The Holy Spirit has many qualities and essences, but above all is **a Person**. The Third Person of the God-head is first recorded in the Bible long before Jesus is mentioned. In **Genesis** 1:2, the Spirit is present over the Creation of the material universe at a proto-creational phase. This was a period of intense activity and beauty (because God is beautiful and does

---

[207] Elvis Presley 1967, *How Great Thou Art* (album), Track 12 *Where No One Stands Alone*, RCA.

beautiful things), but one for which we have no records other than the imaginations we can generate of a primordial cosmos.

For Christians, 'God' is a generic term, encompassing the three Persons of God: Father and Creator Yah'weh + Son Jesus Immanuel + Holy Spirit. Each is equally God and each is individually God. These are not three different gods, but three elemental Persons of God, as there are three elemental states – solid, liquid and gas. We understand that people are complex and intricate, yet God is greater and incalculably more sophisticated than any concept we can envisage. Our clearest manifestation of God's Trinitarian (i.e. three-way) nature is that He created us (humans) *in His Image*. And humans have three equally human and equally individual persons: we have body + soul + spirit. It makes sense: like our Creator, and as He explained – we are made in His Image. As well as being tri-une, God is also bi-gendered – male and female. Human beings – made in God's Image – are therefore always spirit, soul and body *and* either male or female.

(Because God's gender is fixed and/or controversial for some Christians, please find here some clear indications. This ought not be vexing when the Bible is itself transparent. **Genesis** 1:27 & 5:1-2 explain that God is both genders, or the equal source of both: male and female. The Spirit underlines this in **Galatians** 3:28. God's dual-gender Nature is restated in **Deuteronomy** 32:18 [only a mother can give birth, despite recent attempts to confuse or muddy the delineation between genders], and **Isaiah** 66:13 describes God as female. Sophie expresses no confusion or perplexity about God's nature, from which we can probably deduce that she simply accepted the Bible's description of God as authoritative – including the female descriptions.)

The Holy Spirit, whose Personal name we do not know yet (unlike the Father and the Son, Yah'weh and Jesus), is the *Spirit of Truth*. **John** 14:17 and 15:26 make plain that the Holy Spirit blesses us with ultimate and complete truth. Knowing truth means that we cannot be deceived; it is a tremendous quality to bestow on us as Christians. It means that like Jesus Himself, we know and speak truth. We need also to hold that in tension with the reality that truth is hated, and as Jesus was hated, so shall we be as Christians. There are many signs which indicate the Holy Spirit's active presence – from the effect on our senses, to deep awareness of God's holiness, to appetite for God's Word and prayer, to miracles – but a converse way we can know He is active is that we will be targets of hatred because we follow Jesus.

Jesus promises the Spirit will be with us because He has asked the Father to send and provide His company, counsel and comfort in perpetuity (ref. **John** 14:16 and 16:7). Jesus knew this is better for all His disciples across time, because He cannot be with us simultaneously – He has an humanoid body. But a Spirit has not those confinements, and can be present wherever and whenever S/He chooses. Jesus assures us that when we are persecuted for His Name, the Holy Spirit will speak for us and through us, even in the most abject and extreme circumstances (**Mark** 13:11).

Sophie's sister Elisabeth described her in about 2008 to Frank McDonough, who wrote a movingly expressive, colourful and requiemesque narrative of her life; Elisabeth said,

> *'[Sophie] had a distinctive personality; she had her own opinions and was very independently minded. She was very religious, read the Bible regularly and prayed to God each night.* [208]

What was she like? Her sister remembered independence, religious dedication to Scripture, and prayer. It is a condensed description, but vivid. 'Religious' is often used as an *accusation* today (i.e. 2025 atow) – it has negative overtones of hypocrisy and irrationality, but the truth is that every human is religious, just as every human is conscious. Saying that Sophie

---

[208] Frank McDonough 2009, *Sophie Scholl: the real story of the woman who defied Hitler*, p.158.

was 'religious' is like saying she was 'oxygenated'. Did Elisabeth mean that Sophie was *spiritual*? That is how I read her observation.

Sophie accepted life gratefully, lived consciously and intentionally, sensed her own spirit's needs, which were always her deepest needs.

Ultimately too, Sophie is astonishingly pragmatic and calm about her own death. Why is this? Where does this composure come from?

Jesus promises that the Holy Spirit will speak through us in all circumstances.

Light, as example, accompanies energy. When we look at the night sky from Earth, we see an array of stars every clear night – the light reaching our retinas may have originated 100000 years ago according to astronomy. Light appears not to be deflected or diverted by other light particles or waves as they stream through space – they are stopped only by dense masses like planets, or human eyes. What we actually see as we gaze at the stars is *the past*; all those stars and planets are emitting light constantly but by the time it reaches our retinas, it could be 100, 1000, or 100000 years since it left the energy/light source. We are seeing the past. Clever trigonometry allows us to calculate some of the stellar distances, but there comes a point where even computer assisted trigonometry cannot calculate the spans. Parallax has limits. Somewhere, according to scientific theorizing, all of this began with a colossal explosion, or 'bang' - a magical bang in a dimension we cannot describe because whatever it was, it had to have energy, and energy derives from friction, or motion. How could anything move *before* there was space? It is oxymoronic. And where did the thing we call 'space' come from? Questions multiply. It is difficult to imagine anything which does not exist in a space of some kind. But space is comprised of particles. The next question is obvious, and does not resolve.

Jesus identified *Himself* as Light:

*'I am the light of the world...'* [209]

In saying this, He is refuting the Gnosticism of His contemporary culture, which was the New Age Movement of the early 1st Millennium. He states plainly that He is the Light: it is not a spiritual force we generate within ourselves, or through having sex with many different partners, or seeking guidance for destiny from stars (which are large balls of burning gas in space – they are not intelligent any more than rocks on mountains) - it is the gift of a loving God, the Holy Spirit who lives in us, the Spirit of Jesus.

For Sophie this is her experience of Jesus, in the fullness of His promises. His Truth resolves for her what ultimately matters in life – her relationship with Christ, the way that He illuminates truth for her, and her obedience to Him.

*'...If you follow me, you won't be stumbling through the
darkness, because you will have the light that leads to life.* [210]

Jesus does not say that darkness is not real, He says that light (which is Him) will prevent our stumbling and will bring us through to life. Darkness though, is real enough.

*'...then did he turn his eyes to me and I came face to face with the
Beast of Belsen. The evil authority showed on his arrogant face.'*
( - Hetty Verolme, prisoner, age 14, Belsen Concentration
Camp, January 1945. The Belsen Camp Commandant was
Jozef Kramer, known as the 'Beast of Belsen' - a sadist and
murderer [hanged by a British Military Court later that

---

[209]  **John** 8:12 (NLT)
[210]  Ibid.

year]. Hetty escaped death on this occasion apparently on Kramer's whim. She could see evil in his expression.)[211]

Hetty was a Dutch Jewish captive, who was sent to Belsen in 1943 - a place of drastic darkness. Unlike Anne Frank, also a victim of Belsen, she survived. Hetty did not know Sophie. But Sophie did know of the evil and horrific maltreatment of innocent people by the Reich government and its forces (Hans had written of this in *Leaflet 2*), and she reacted strongly and purposefully. The White Rose activists can possibly be accused of naïveté and rashness, but not of indifference or docility; they did not sit and whimper over noisome evils - they actively opposed them. She recognized darkness, and brought light against it.

> 'Then he began: "You pig, I have been watching you the whole
> time! I'll teach you to work, yet! Wait til you dig dirt with your
> teeth – you'll die like an animal! In two days I'll finish you off!"…'
> ( - Viktor Frankl, a Jewish-Austrian Doctor and Philosopher,
> recounting an Auschwitz Kapo's invective when Viktor was
> so deprived and brutalized he could barely walk. [*Kapos*
> were prisoners seconded by the SS to guard duty – they
> were often more cruel than the regular SS guards].)[212]

The therapeutic practice of logotherapy and existential analysis was developed by Viktor, who was a Doctor and Psychiatrist. After the Second World War, in response to afflicted people's experiences of cruel and depraved abuse under the Nazis, logotherapy helped victims to reframe and renew their lives within the context of trauma. He never met or knew Sophie, but her response to knowledge of the systemic and systematic

[211]  Hetty Verolme 2013, *The Children's House of Belsen*, p.160.
[212]  Viktor Frankl 1946, *Man's Search for Meaning*, p.23.

persecution of Jews and other targets of the Nazi regime was to *actively resist*. Conformity and hiding were not options for her. Sophie evidently believed that honouring Jesus Christ involved loving people who needed help by actively defending and supporting them in dangerous and costly circumstances.

> *'Somebody, after all, had to make a start. What we wrote and said is also believed by many others. They just don't dare express themselves as we did.'* [213]

( - Sophie Scholl, testimony in Volksgerichtshof Session, Munich 21/2/1943, presiding judge Roland Freisler, [who was a Nazi lackey and sycophant – Sophie never had any chance of a just trial].)

Had Hans Scholl not been murdered by the German State on 22/2/1943, he would very likely in the next week have met with Dietrich Bonhoeffer. White Rose was just beginning to connect with other Resistance groups/ activists at this time, and a meeting had been planned. As it was, Hans was killed, and Dietrich was soon arrested, imprisoned and eventually murdered by the Nazi State in 1945.

Dietrich spoke words of piercing acuity,

> *'...Not to speak is to speak, not to act is to act.'*

Sophie and White Rose lived and honoured this aphorism: they spoke, and they acted.

**Holiness** is characteristic of Jesus Christ, and an ultimate standard of right and wrong.

---

[213] This is an unsourced recollection of someone present in the courtroom. The trial transcript is destroyed or lost.

How can we assert the morality of a position when others hold that wrong is right? They can easily dismiss our objections as 'subjective' moral opinions which apply only to holders of that view.

In Nazi Germany, the law classified and identified Jewish people as non-citizens, as *untermenschen* (sub-humans) – these legal impositions and categorisations are usually referred to as the *Nuremberg Laws,* nationally enacted in 1935. Jews had no legal rights under these racialist laws and therefore no human rights in Germany. Their legal and human position was extremely tenuous and fragile. Crimes against them were legally void, as they did not have human or civic status. Jews could not make contracts, and so could not own or purchase property, nor apply to courts for enforcements. They could not legally marry, so could not enforce familial wills nor inherit. Jewish people could not vote, send their children to school, attend public hospitals, or expect civility from neighbours and other people designated Aryan and/or Germanic.

Darkness blanketed Germany.

The violent and virulent anti-Semitism demanded and implemented by Hitler was modeled on an existing system which had fulsomely tutored the Führer in effective legal discrimination and prejudice – the *Jim Crow* system of segregation in the USA[214] (Hitler had also admired white American destruction of Native American culture and population). From the end of the American Civil War in 1865, Southerners in particular and large numbers of white Americans in general, had ensured the newly freed slaves were subjected to harsh legal oppressions, and excluded from access to the rights and privileges of American citizens. This intricate and foetid web smothered any possibilities African-Americans had of active citizenship,

---

[214] References for this are numerous and readily searchable. A useful one is: Alex Ross 2018, *How American racism influenced Hitler*, New Yorker (magazine) 23/4/2018, newyorker.com

and used a ruthless, unofficial and widely supported policing network - the Ku-Klux Klan.

This taught Hitler valuable lessons in how to impregnate governance with hatred, hostility and dominance. His endeavours were supported by the science of eugenics, a popular ideology embraced under scientism at that time, which was abandoned after WW2 when the full horror of Godless racial science became apparent.

It is reasserting itself now, under different names and guises (e.g. 'reproductive health', 'genetic editing', 'cloning'). Charles Darwin's evolutionary theory is an iron-clad foundation for disposing of designated weak or deficient children; the 'survival of the fittest' is an obverse way of saying the weak and disabled are better off eliminated. So, we abort the most helpless and vulnerable small children, salving our increasingly armour-plated and diseased consciences with arguments and excuses about preventing pain and suffering. We hypocritically condemn capital punishment for murderers, but inflict it on our smallest and most defenceless children in utero, adjusting our language to accommodate the killing.

If Nazis and American segregationists choose to believe that there are people who are in fact inferior to themselves in value, and if that belief is their genuinely held view, then who are we to tell them they are wrong? They can equally accuse us of being wrong. People who are devalued and dehumanized because of their skin pigment, their ethno-cultural background, their designation as disabled, their age and level of perceived development, their gender, their economic status - these are ways in which people have been and are deprived of human rights. African people have been enslaved, Indigenous people have been dispossessed of land and environment, people with physical disabilities have been refused access to education and adapted housing, women in particular have been compelled to wear restrictive clothing and denied equal opportunities to men, young children *in utero* are brutally and horribly killed deliberately in abortuaries, people in economic poverty are denied education and work opportunities. It is a painfully long, and sadly incomplete, list.

How does this connect to Sophie and her relationship to Jesus?

When law contradicts God, then stand with God. The problem is that doing this attracts ferocious reaction and rejection. A Christian who refuses to compromise will typically be attacked. Sophie certainly was.

> *'If they believe that might must prevail, ask them if they think that man and beast should be placed entirely on a par, or that man additionally shares in a world of the spirit.'* [215]

Before the Fall in **Genesis** 1:30, the Earth was a totally harmonic and non-predatory system. Animals did not prey on each other. They ate grass and green plants. No exceptions are noted. **Genesis** 1:28 recalls that humans were to rule all animals, birds and fish. After the Fall in **Genesis** 3:14, animals became either wild or domestic, and the nutritional harmony of living things was ruined – thrown into chaos. Predation appears.

(N.B. Varying translations of **Genesis** 1:25 can be confusing; **Genesis** 3:21 indicates the animals being subjected to death for the use of humans.)

Where the Will of God operates harmonically, there is no predation, as in **Isaiah** 11:6-9.

Sophie references 'man and beast' above, and asks if they should be placed on a par? It's a strange question until we see that Sophie is contrasting peace and force (might).

Feeding on other creatures is the way of predatory beasts, which is exactly what she saw around her. The Nuremberg Laws, Kristallnacht, Belsen, Dachau, the Lødz Ghetto, Auschwitz – all predatory and lawless.

---

[215]   Sophie Scholl (Inge Jens), *At the Heart of White Rose*, p.277.

Legalism values law over justice, as algocracy values formula over wisdom.

The highest form of law is the Rule of Christ: His keys are Grace, Love and Wisdom. Animals are ruled by instinct – survival necessities, like territory, food, water and procreation. These are the same for humans, *but* we choose and plan with intelligence and intent. We are not instructed to imitate the animals, we are to rule them. When we revert to bestial attitudes and behaviours (as in the Reich), we compromise the mandate implicit in Creation which is that we emulate God's creative authority and rule with intelligence and grace. God's original mandate excluded violence – there was no predation. Humans were not initially carnivores. The Rule of Christ does not exclude predation, but it does forbid cruelty and greed. Sophie saw this contrast between the Rule of Christ and the rule of depraved mankind very clearly; it was around her.

We expend enormous effort and attention in delaying death for as long as possible – large sums of our treasure are devoted to the governance of Health, and protection from harms which could hasten death. *Why?* Death is inevitable, so why expend huge quantities of time and money in researching ways to prolong life for a few months? Our fixation on life, and reaction to death, is because death is unnatural – we know it is wrong. It is primal, instinctive, to cling to life. In Eden, Adam and Eve, the proto-parents, knew that it was *possible* to die, but there is no indication they feared it as inevitable. It was a consequence which *might* occur. Only however if sin – deliberate disobedience to God – was introduced. Death was not inevitable. But, it is an enemy – it blocks our access to other people's spirits and souls which we recognize are different to the physical body and world. We do not mourn the loss of a body – that is an agglomeration of tissue which temporarily houses the soul. We do lament *the person*, who is the intelligence, the conscious being, the lasting persona, the soul, or in Greek, the ψυχε (psyche).

To revisit this point, most societies or civilizations have recognised the *essence of life* as consisting in the person *within* the physical body, and that the physical world is the interface which allows connection and relationship. Relationship is the dynamic which sustains and energises soul-life. The spirit alone cannot relate to another spirit in this physical world; it requires the body. But we know the spirit is more lasting than the body; if we speak to a corpse, there is no response – relationship is not possible via the dead body. The person is in the soul, which has no physical body in this physical world any more – there is either another dimension - or extinction. The spirit is the eternal self – it is the part of us which is the immortal, and reacts to death because death is not meant to happen (see **Genesis** 3:3; like predation, death is a consequence of the Fall). We are eternal beings – death is annihilation, but only of the physical body. There is a second death, but only God can kill or destroy the spirit. Physical might/power prevails only over the physical body. There is a world of spirit as well. The ancient Egyptians and Aztecs built towering edifices to commemorate and expedite the souls of the physically dead to another world. The pyramids are monuments to physical death and spiritual life: they recognise both. We do not build pyramids today, we arrange funerals and farewell the dead. The spirit moves on to whatever is next – we speak of the 'hereafter' or 'heaven' or 'nirvana' or 'svargaloka' or 'reincarnation' or 'jannah' or 'eternal rest'. We have names and concepts. Some believe in extinction or permanent ending, but most human history and culture anticipates a continued form of life after death.

Sophie was in a position where the physical world around her was ruled by physical force, with primitive and brutal cruelty. She understood this, but chose to pursue the beauty and truth of the spiritual over the immediate force of physical dominance - the soulful over the animal. The concepts of dominance and coercion derive from understanding freedom and independence. The negative force can overwhelm the positive, but only in the physical world. Its power is contained to the physical universe.

It begs the questions, 'What is the negative to the positive which positions as compromise?' and 'How is compromise identified?'

In White Rose's case:

1. The negative is evil.
2. This is identified by its exact opposition to God.

How could Sophie know and contend that respect and peace are right and that violence and cruelty are wrong? Are these not simply personal value choices? Are not Nazis equally entitled to despise Jewish people as to adore Aryans? It is their choice. Are not anti-Semites in modern-day Palestine and other places equally entitled to despise Jews and extol Arabs?[216] If they express their hatred with murder, rape and kidnap – is that not their personal choice?

Holiness is around, within and over Sophie, as with us. In its most literal form, holiness is a separation or uniqueness unto God. The holy is sanctified to His uses. Everything created by God contains His/Her holiness; sin can disfigure, obscure and damage this, but it cannot eradicate it entirely. The loyalty of Sophie to Christ is holy; but in even the misdirected and tragic loyalty of German soldiers to Hitler, loyalty itself is still admirable. Their immoral and atrocious behaviour is sin.

---

[216] E.g. In Sydney 2025, two Muslim nurses employed by an Australian public hospital threatened to kill Jewish patients under their supervision. Anti-Semitism is virulent, violent and vicious. ref. BBC News Simon Atkinson 12-2-2025, *Australian nurses suspended over 'vile' antisemitic video.*

When we come to the end of Law, we come to God. Many nations still derive ultimate legal authority from the Crown, but where does Crown derive its authority? From God. Other nations might derive authority from 'We, the people...', but where do 'the people' derive their authority? From God[217]. The ultimate source and arbiter of Law is God. Otherwise, we come merely to human beings, who can be evil as well as righteous. Hitler made legislatively and constitutionally approved laws; Abraham Lincoln made legislatively and constitutionally approved laws. Should we observe and obey both?

We know laws are wrong if/because they contradict the positive. They negate the good. The positive and good value:

- Freedom
- Relationship with God: worshipping, honouring, respecting Him/ Her
- Constructive work and regular rest
- Relationship with family
- Life, and the right to life
- Loyalty and fidelity
- Honesty and integrity
- Truth
- Love for others
- Generosity and boundaries[218]

---

[217] See United States of America *Declaration of Independence*, opening paragraph reference to 'Nature's God'. The DOI does not have legal force, but it created the nation, and has moral force. Sadly, its pivotal '...all men are created equal...' was not transplanted into the Constitution, until Abraham Lincoln embedded the 13th Amendment in 1865. (He was also subsequently murdered – evil hates righteousness.)

[218] See **Exodus** 20:1-17. Each of these positive values is derived from the Ten Commandments. Jesus refined these in **Mark** 12:30-31 to 1. Loving our God and, 2. Loving our neighbours.

When a nazi, islamist or paedophile seeks to legitimize his/her particular misanthropy, we can counter with the positive even if it is only in our own mind. The *negative has no meaning* without the positive. It is essentially destructive. Murder is meaningless unless first there is innocent human life. Treachery has no meaning unless first there is loyalty, etc.. It is not legitimate or right to assert that all value positions are equivalently valid. The positive is always pre-eminent: no positive = no negative. The negative is always subject and inferior to the positive. Negatives cannot exist unto themselves. The Nazi view that Jews are *'untermenschen'* directly negates the command to love other people, and is therefore negative and morally destructive in any context.

Jesus Christ died equally for all people. He did not die more for Australians, and less for Chinese people. Jesus' Blood, often symbolized in the Cross, is the great equalizer of history. Every person's value is equivalent to the Blood of Jesus Christ, regardless of wealth, age, heredity, talent, family, intelligence, or ideology. Jesus is our God of Equal Value.

God is always *creative*; S/He only destroys when the negative has expanded or threatens to expand, as cancers do. Excising cancer is positive.

This is exactly how God utilized/directed White Rose; S/He used White Rose to expose Nazism for what it was – utterly evil and totally unjustifiable. Profane and accursed.

In the physical world, electro-magnetics and gravity obtain; in the spiritual world, justice and truth obtain. Forces and powers have their natural domains.

*'Obey the government, for God is the one who put it there. All governments have been placed in power by God.'* – **Romans** 13:1

*'Remind your people to submit to the government and its officers. They should be obedient, always ready to do what is good.'* – **Titus** 3:1

*'So [the Government Council] called the apostles back and
told them never again to speak or teach about Jesus. But Peter
and John replied, "Do you think God wants us to obey you
rather than Him? We cannot stop telling about the wonderful
things we have seen and heard."'* – **Acts** 4:18-20

Plainly, Peter and John disobeyed the government. In **Acts** 5, the apostles were out teaching, preaching and miraculously healing against the direct instructions of the authorities. What they were doing was dangerous because the government abominated the power and success of the apostles' ministries. They were jealous of their effectiveness and the expansion of the Way. God's Word, declared with the Holy Spirit, is always powerful.

*'And more and more believed and were brought to
the Lord – crowds of both men and women.'*
– **Acts** 5:14

When Christian people stand on the Gospel and declare Jesus' truth and sovereignty, whether in words, deeds or both, the Kingdom is incarnated in them. The Kingdom of God is within us (**Luke** 17:21) – so the Kingdom is not only geography or topography, it is heart and spirit, and *wherever we are*, is the Kingdom. Where Sophie stood in the Volksgerichtshof - of all unclean and evil places - antagonized, derided, insulted, impugned and assaulted; she was the Kingdom. She brought Christ into a Nazi courtroom, into the core of Reich government. She spoke compelling and enduring truth – after all, you are reading her words and observing her actions as you read this book, more than 80 years later[219]. Those words were composed,

---

[219] The transcripts of Sophie's courtroom event (it does not deserve the term *'trial'* which implies impartiality and justice) are most likely destroyed, so we do not know exactly what was said. We can guess judge Freisler's haranguing invective from other surviving

calm, and truthful. Exalting Christ while exposing the corruption and poverty of those accusing and condemning her, evinces the steel of her faith and the depth of her compassion.

By printing and disseminating material which corrected lies perpetrated by the government, Sophie was definitely disobeying that government; she was though obeying the higher Kingdom government. Willingly following God to the point of death is either a tragic and sad delusion, or it is a courageous choice to assert the truth of God over the fall of humankind.

The seeming contradiction between **Romans** 13:1 and **Acts** 4:18-20 is not so. There is no contradiction here. Christians are to honour God first, and humans second. If the government of man requires you to act against the Government of God, love God as a first principle. Most people in Nazi Germany did not do this. If they had, there would not have been a Nazi Germany in the first place. Nor would European colonialists have dispossessed and disenfranchised Indigenous peoples across the Americas, Asia, Australia, New Zealand and Africa. Nor would Indigenous peoples have inflicted devaluing sexism on women, nor Islamic cultures have subjected women to polygamy, nor Hindu Indians have discriminated so cruelly against Dalit peoples ('untouchables'). There is a price for ignoring God. The equalizing Blood of Christ removes all of these miserable prejudices.

In **Esther** 4:16, a young Jewish girl (whose real name was Hadassah), asserts the truth of God over the human laws of Persia.

Hadassah has been through a personal hell; both her parents had died, and she was brought up by her cousin Mordecai in Persia, a land of exile for vast numbers of Jews. He was like a father to Hadassah[220]. What actually happened to her has often been whitewashed to appear as an exem-

---

transcripts. The tenor of Sophie's and Hans' statements and responses can be fairly reconstructed from letters and contents of the White Rose leaflets.

[220] The principle Biblical events in Esther's life occurred c. 479-473 BC.

plary romantic fairy-tale, but to put it plainly, she was abducted from her adoptive family because she was a very attractive young woman, and along with many others, placed in a harem of women who were at the King of Persia's disposal. We do not know her age, but she was probably mid-teens. These young women, all sexual virgins, were prepared for King Xerxes with 'beauty treatments' over a year, and he then had each girl for a night. He took a different woman to bed every night, had sex with them, and then they were discarded back to the harem where they lived out the rest of their traumatized lives, unless the King wanted them again. Women in that position were a type of sex-slave, and became captives. It's a very wretched story. Esther was chosen by King Xerxes to become his Queen, because she pleased him – that means she was sexually attractive to Xerxes, and probably also impressed him with some dancing, pleasant conversation, and recitation of poetry and/or singing. Becoming Queen made her a powerful woman, and Esther would have been keenly aware of the fate of her predecessor Vashti, who had been exiled to the harem for refusing to follow the King's demands.

Esther knew that Haman, who was Xerxes' Prime Minister and a mindless anti-Semite, was plotting the deaths of Mordecai and as many Jews as possible. The only hope for averting a cataclysmic mass-murder was for Esther to intervene by approaching Xerxes and enlisting his help. She had to do this subtly and carefully because Haman was a very powerful man – the Prime Minister – and Esther could not approach the King without his explicit invitation. Even she as Queen was subject to capital punishment if she approached Xerxes and he declined her request for an audience/ meeting. She was scared by this possibility – a distinctly plausible outcome. Vashti had once been a beautiful and favoured Queen as well, and now she was entombed in the sterile quarantine of a harem for the rest of her days. Esther's risk was even greater – she could be killed.

Her ultimate choice was to take the risk, and approach Xerxes. She understood that her options were to attempt an intervention to save countless lives, or to remain silent, live a while longer, and eventually be caught herself in the webs of Haman's psychotic anti-Semitism.

If Esther obeyed and followed existing Persian law, she might live a while longer, but the anti-Semitic law that Haman engineered will catch up with her. If she defies the law and approaches the King, she is immediately and mortally vulnerable. Her choices seem between the devil and the deep blue sea. Esther's calibre is plain: her decision is,

> '... then, though it is against the law, I will go in to see the King. If I must die, I am willing to die. [221]

Sophie's choice was similar. She could have settled into her University studies and awaited the war's end, then married Fritz, raised a family, deplored the evils of the Third Reich over coffee, and rebuilt a satisfying life - while along with 99% of Germans, she had watched while it all happened, saying 'What could I do?'

It was to be a fair question. How many Americans, Australians, Canadians, Saudis, Palestinians, Japanese, Indians have actually done anything effective or courageous to redress or remedy injustices imposed on Indigenous peoples, on Dalit, on Manchurians or on Kafirs/Infidels? How many Indigenous peoples have apologized and redressed millennia of repression, polygyny and polygamy against women? How many people anywhere have protested and redressed the appalling harm and discrimination visited on children in utero through the practice of abortion? Sophie and White Rose were exceptional – most people at any point in history

---

[221] **Esther** 4:16c (NLT)

avoid being spot-lit over human rights. Unlike Esther, Sophie's choice was unto death.

Sophie does not see God quite as Jehanne and Mary did. She *does* follow Esther's patterning in some ways, through her awareness of God, and His presence through Prayer, Scripture, Creation and Nature, and by prioritising Jesus' values.

The Book of **Esther**, Hadassah's story, is also the only Book of the Bible that does not mention God explicitly. Sophie does not encounter God in physical or sensate form either, but she knows Him.

Like Esther, Sophie deliberately defies Government and takes her chances - mortal chances. She also instructs or teaches men in what to do – something many Christians find challenging to this day.

Hadassah and Sophie share courage - and gumption.

The end of Sophie's life is described in detail by others[222]. What distinguishes her, as already mentioned, is her calm equanimity about death.

After praying with a Lutheran Minister, she has an unexpected last meeting with Hans and Christoph (they shared a cigarette, brief conversation, and farewell, in their last earthly encounter; n.b. the Stadelheim Prison guards took a substantial risk in allowing them this last moment together. It was a token of the guards' respect for them, and their individual admiration for the stand they had taken). Then, Sophie is first to be executed, walking to her death, apparently with a limp of unknown cause (but very likely the consequence of some kind of crass, cruel Gestapo attempt to prise information from her).

---

[222]  See e.g. Inge Jens (ed.) 2017, *At the Heart of White Rose*, pp.311-12, and A. Dumbach & J, Newborn 1986, *Sophie Scholl and the White Rose*, pp.159-161.

Her only audible regret is her lament that it is a sunny day outside, and that she cannot enjoy it long[223]. At 1701 (5.01pm) on 22-2-1943, this beautiful and outstandingly courageous, principled young woman is senselessly killed by the Nazi State and its minions. It may be apocryphal that in an act of petty spite and bile, the attending SS officers ensured Sophie was guillotined face up.

It did not matter to Sophie. Her trust and hope in Jesus is now present and eternal reality.

She stands with Jesus the Christ, counseling us: ***Honour Him***.

∞

---

[223] Even this is poetic – in German, Sophie says *'Es ist so ein herrlicher sonniger Tag und Ich muss gehen.'* With a slight flick of accentuation, this is a haiku. Amen.

# Epilogue

**Mary Magdalene-Bethany** did not need faith in the *unseen* to know and believe Jesus – she very empirically saw Him doing miracles and wonders over and again - blind people instantly regaining their sight, legalistic Pharisees backing off as they heard unwanted truth, the demon-possessed healed and cleaned. She walked the hills and tracks of Judea and Palestine with Him. She saw the dead breathe, and bright angels inside a tomb.

**Jehanne** observed and participated in miracles, communicated with angelic beings, great martyrs of the Kingdom, restored the Royaume to France, establishing the foundation of the modern Republic – and she spoke with a Voice which initially scared and then delighted her, a Voice who could save her soul.

**Sophie** related to Jesus in faith; this is the majority of Christians' experience today (2025 atow). She did not experience miracles or wonders as Mary and Jehanne did. Arguably then, she had the strongest faith of these three, embodying **John** 20:29a – she believed anyway, by trusting Jesus' printed narrative, by listening in prayer, seeing God's artistry in Creation, contrasting holiness and evil. Hers is the most abstract faith, and also the most familiar to us who are C21st Western Christians.

Each knew overt trauma and affliction.

*Mary* had been demon-possessed, was likely a slave used for sex, and was entrusted with sharing the initial news that Jesus Christ had actually risen from death. It is the most momentous news in history, trusted to a woman, a former slave, and a demoniac. It marks the starting line for the history of Christendom; first human witness to the Resurrection.

*Jehanne* knew that she had one year to fulfil her mission to defeat and disenfranchise the English occupation, and to establish authentic French government in France; after that year, she knew she could be killed at any time. France as we know it exists today directly because of Jehanne's strategic skill, fighting acumen, and total faith in Jesus. Without the French nation, there would be no USA today, nor a free Europe.

*Sophie* knew she had to educate and inform the German people in the reality of Nazi German warfare, and the Nazi State's appalling war on human rights. Certain death would ensue if she was caught disseminating criticism of Führer and State – she proceeded anyway. The contrast between the Christ and the Führer was galactically stark, and Sophie outlined the difference very clearly for Germany, regardless that very few paid attention.

Each of them had tasks/missions which would influence world history, and each continues to witness powerfully to Jesus Christ today. Very simply, they loved Him: 2000 years ago, 600 years ago, 85 years ago. Jesus was present and real to them; their commitment was absolute.

*'Jesus Christ is the same yesterday, today and*
*forever.'* – **Hebrews** 13:8 (NLT).

***Why would they take such colossal and seemingly reckless risks, endangering their lives in the process?*** Mary could easily have been caught and executed by the Romans. Jehanne and Sophie were both martyred, when they had so much for which to live! Why would they undertake such hazardous risks? And why were they unafraid of death itself? (Jehanne was not so much afraid of death, as by its manner, which is profoundly understandable).

Reader, may that question stay before us, until we see the answer gifted to us by these three beautiful and wondrous women. They were not just pursuing an ideal, a doctrine, or a theory. They were honouring their closest and most important relationship in real life and time, in what we call history: for Mary it was c.30 – 90 AD, for Jehanne it was 1412 - 1431, and for Sophie it was 1921 - 1943.

They knew *Who* they were obeying and following.

Truth is a *Person*, not an equation, system, consultation, discussion, meditation, mantra, theology, syllogism or dialectic. A Person.

God often appoints/anoints one unlikely disciple/servant to bring about disproportionate historical and universal change. Some of them we know about because they became famous, but many remain anonymous – celebrated only in Heaven... for now.

In the Bible, Gideon, David, Ruth, Hadassah, Josiah, all accomplished much for God from unlikely starting places, because they honoured Him and He lifted them up. Outside the Bible, Alfred the Great, Abraham Lincoln, Olaudah Equiano, John Brown, Anthony Ashley Cooper (Lord Shaftesbury), Harriet Tubman, William Cooper, Rosa Parks, Stan Dale – all very unlikely. Yet, God changed history through them.

**Mary**: a slave, a woman, a former prostitute, uneducated - someone who was regarded as beneath any value in either Roman or Israelite society.

**Jehanne**: a peasant, illiterate, a woman, a shepherdess, someone at the lowest tier of agrarian society in medieval Europe.

**Sophie**: a woman, a kindergarten assistant and munitions worker, a former member of the Nazi Girls League, daughter of a disgraced father, someone with no cachet and no prestige.

And they are *Great in the Kingdom*, Redeemed,
Called, Faithful, Great in Sanctity.

*'God arms me with strength;*
*He has made my way safe.*
*He makes me as surefooted as a deer,*
*Leading me along the mountain heights.*
*He prepares me for battle;*
*He strengthens me to draw a bow of bronze.*
*You have given me the shield of your salvation.'*
**Psalm** 18:32-35a.

Amen

∞

# Holy Grace Prayer

*Ravensbrück Concentration Camp* was a place in northern Germany where evil was cultured like a putrid laboratory infection. Innocent people were then subjected to this through the profane psychopathy of those who sinned against the Holy Spirit by calling what is holy, evil, and what is evil, holy.

Torture, sadism, malevolence, diabolic cruelty, murder – a perverse and disastrous litany.

There were many such places in the criminal states of Germany and Japan in the 1930's-40's, where innocents were proffered to a demented, wicked insanity. Evil is a type of insanity, all the more wretched because it is chosen, either by commission or omission. This choosing corrupts a person permanently; there is no forgiveness for calling the holy, evil. The Holy Spirit cannot be blasphemed with impunity[224]. So, are the evil most to be pitied? Can fruit come, even from this?

Ravensbrück's victims, mostly women, were liberated on 30/4/1945 – the same day that Adolf Hitler suicided. Ironically, the Red Army freed them - the Soviet Russian Army. Like Nazi Germany, Soviet Russia was a criminal State; its Premier, Josef Stalin, was another evil man like Hitler, Showa (Hirohito), and Tojo in Japan – all megalomaniacs. The Ukrainian 'Holodomor' of

---

[224]  **Matthew** 12:31-32.

1932-34[225], in which millions of Ukrainians were deliberately starved to death in induced famine, was like a prelude to the Shoah ('Holocaust'). Concentration camps like Ravensbrück, Belsen, and Dachau, each inflicted extremes of inhumanity upon their victims. Each camp recorded a history of unimaginable suffering. Piles of corpses had littered the camps. Each corpse was a son or daughter, a brother or sister, a best friend, a wife or husband, a father, a grandmother. At Ravensbrück, in May 1945, as the bodies were separated and carried for burial, a scrap of paper fluttered from a young girl's rags of clothing; a soldier picked it up and saw writing, and brought it to the attention of Russian Officers who in turn must have preserved it.

This young Jewish girl had prayed and written:

*'O Lord, remember, not only the men and women*
*of good will, but also those of ill will.*
*But do not remember all the suffering they have*
*inflicted on us; remember the fruits we have*
*borne, thanks to this suffering:*
*Our comradeship, our loyalty, our humility, our*
*courage, our generosity, the greatness of*
*heart which has grown out of all this,*
*And when they come to judgment, let all the*
*fruits we have borne be their forgiveness.'*

This is love - humility, faith, redemption, courage, grace. Sanctity.
A place for silence and adoration before God.

Mary, Jehanne and Sophie stand on this ground. Listen.

---

[225] In discussion with linguist and teacher Daria Volokh, February 2025. '*Holodomor*' is specific to the Stalinist famine inflicted on Ukraine in 1932-34, a compound proper noun ГОЛОД (lit. 'hunger') + МОР ('mass death').

# Select Bibliography

(N.B. All listed texts contributed, but not all are cited.)

## Mary Magdalene-Bethany.

Bible, *New Living Translation* 1996, *New King James Version* 1982, *King James (Authorised) Version* 1611.

A.W.Allison, H.Barrows et al. 1975, *The Norton Anthology of Poetry (rev.)*, W.W.Norton & Co. New York, NY.

W.H.Auden 1940, *Funeral Blues* (poem) in *Another Time*, Random House, New York, NY.

Australian Institute of Health & Welfare 2021, *New insights into suicide and self-harm in Australia, including potentially modifiable risk-factors*, aihw. gov.au 04Nov2021.

William Barclay 1970, *Bible Commentary: 2 John*, St Andrew's Press, Glasgow UK.

University of Bath 2008, *First Rule of Evolution Suggests that Life is Destined to Become More Complex*, Science Daily, www.sciencedaily.com/releases/2008/03/030817171027.htm.

Amanda Borschel-Dan 2018, *Anomalous blue-eyed people came to Israel 6500 years ago, DNA shows*, Times of Israel, 20 August 2018.

Jeffrey Bütz 2020, guest post on Dr James Tabor 2024, Taborblog: Religion Matters from the Bible to the Modern World, *Was Mary Magdalene the same person as Mary of Bethany?*

Paula Di Martino 2007, *Life After Loss: A Personal Journey... Surviving the Death of a Baby. A Story of Hope.* Google Books.

F. Barton Evans 1996, *Harry Stack Sullivan: Interpersonal Theory and Psychotherapy*, Routledge, Hove UK & New York, NY.

F. Mira Green 2015, *Witnesses and Participants in the Shadows: the Sexual Lives of Enslaved Women and Boys*, DOI:10.1353/hel.2015.0009, researchgate.net

Michael Haag 2017, *The Quest for Mary Magdalene*, Profile Books, London UK.

Dineke Houtman 2023, *What language did Jesus speak?* Protestantse Theologische Universiteit 11/05/2023, pthu.nl.

David Instone-Brewer 2015, *Autopsy of a Crucifixion*, Premier Christianity (magazine), www.premierchristianity.com, 12/03/2015.

Grenville J. Kent 2010, *Mary Magdalene, Mary of Bethany and the sinful woman of Luke 7: The Same Person?*, Journal of Asia Adventist Seminary, 13(1), 13-28.

S. Gregoire le Grand, *Homiliae in evangelia*, II, xxxiii, PL76, col.1239C, cited in A. Feuillet, '*Les deux onctions faites sur Jesus, et Marie-Madeleine,*' *RevThom* 75 (1975):361, n.12.

C. S. Lewis 1942, *The Screwtape Letters*, Geoffrey Bles, London UK.

Malachi Martin 1976, *Hostage to the Devil: the Possession and Exorcism of Five Contemporary Americans*, Harper San Francisco (1992).

Percy Bysshe Shelley 1818, *Ozymandias* (poem), in *Norton Anthology of Poetry*, p.667.

Anne Theriault 2020, *Unravelling the Myth of Mary Magdalene*, Broadview Magazine 16/03/2020, broadview.org

Dylan Thomas 1943, *And Death Shall Have No Dominion* (poem), Academy of American Poets, *poets.org* website.

M.I.Troya, G. Cully, D. Leahy, E. Cassidy, A. Sadath, S. Nicolson, A. Ramos Costa, I. Alberdi-Paramo, A. Jeffers, F. Shiely, E. Arensman 2021, *Investigating the relationship between childhood sexual abuse, self-harm repetition and suicidal intent: mixed-methods study*, British Journal of Psychiatry (BJPsych), doi:10.1192/bjo.2021.962

Sheldon Vanauken 1977, *A Severe Mercy*, Harper & Row, San Francisco.

Voice of the Martyrs, 01-04-2023, *The Imam Who Met Jesus*, vom.com.au

Dominique R. Wilson 2021, *Sexual Exploitation of Black Women from the Years 1619 – 2020*, Journal of Race, Gender and Ethnicity, 10-Spring, 123

## Jehanne Darc.

Bible, *New Living Translation* 1996, *New King James Version* 1982, *King James (Authorised) Version* 1611.

Lance Bernard 2001, *The Sword from Heaven: An Inquiry into Joan of Arc's Sword, Found at the Church of St Catherine de Fierbois*, stjoan-centre.com

Søren Bie 2024, *Transcripts* translated into English for *Trial of Condemnation (AD 1431)* and *Trial of Nullification (AD 1455-56)* of Jehanne Darc, www.jeanne-darc.info

Dietrich Bonhoeffer 1937, *The Cost of Discipleship* [German: *Nachfolge*], SCM Press (1959), London UK.

Crow M., Zori C., Zori D. 2020, *Doctrinal and Physical Marginality in Christian Death: the Burial of Unbaptized Infants in Medieval Italy*. *Religions* 2020; 11(12):678.https://doi.org/10.3390/rel 11120678.

Kelly DeVries 1999, *Joan of Arc: A Military Leader*, The History Press, Port Stroud, UK.

Joseph Freyaldenhoven 2022, *Angels in the Life of Joan of Arc*, Catholic 365, University of Dallas, Texas.

Mary Gordon 2000, *Joan of Arc*, Weidenfeld & Nicolson, London, UK.

C. S. Lewis 1963, *Prayer: Letters to Malcolm*, Fount (William Collins & Sons), Glasgow, UK.

Theresa Aletheia Noble 2020, *A Chapter that Changed My Life: Joan of Arc and the "One Thing"*, Wordonfire.org, 2024.

Régine Pernoud 1962, *Joan of Arc: by Herself and Her Witnesses*, Macdonald & Co., London, UK.

Régine Pernoud & Marie-Veronique Clin 1998 (trans. by J. duQuesnay Adams), *Joan of Arc: Her Story*, St. Martin's Press, New York, NY.

J. Phillips MD, Brian Fallon MD, Salman Majeed MD, Keith Meador MD, Joseph Merlino MD, Hunter Neely MD, Jenifer Neelds MD, David Saunders MD PhD, Michael Norko MD 2023, *Undiagnosing St Joan: She Does Not Need a Medical or Psychiatric Diagnosis*, Journal of Nervous and Mental Disease 211(8): p 559-565, August 2023. [DOI:10.1097/NMD.0000000000001654]

Christine de Pisan 1429, *Ditié de Jehanne d'Arc*, Joan of Arc: Documents (Prof. Leah Shopkow), Indiana University, dmdhist.sitehost.iu.edu

Qur'ān (Koran), [English trans. Marmaduke Pickthall 1930], Everyman's Library 1992, David Campbell Publishers, London UK.

William Shakespeare c.1590, *Henry VI Part 1*, in *The Complete Works of William Shakespeare* (1926), World Syndicate Co., New York, NY.

J.R.R.Tolkien 1977, *The Silmarillion* (Christopher Tolkien, ed.), George Allen & Unwin, London, UK.

Willard Trask 1996, *Joan of Arc: In Her Own Words*, B.O.O.K.S & Co. Turtle Point Press, New York, NY.

Patricia Nell Warren 2008, *What Did Jeanne d'Arc Look Like? Solving a Mystery: Gay Icons and History, Transgender and Intersex*, retrieved from Jeanne-darc.info, Articles and Essays section.

Ludwig Wittgenstein 1921, *Tractatus Logico-Philosophicus*, Routledge, Oxford UK.

## Sophie Scholl

Bible, *New Living Translation* 1996, *New King James Version* 1982, *King James (Authorised) Version* 1611

Alan Adelson & Robert Lapides (ed's.) 1989, *Łódź Ghetto: Inside a Community Under Siege*, Viking (Penguin), New York NY.

Hannah Arendt 1963, *Eichmann in Jerusalem: A Report on the Banality of Evil*, Penguin Random House, London UK.

Dietrich Bonhoeffer 1939, *Life Together*, (English translation by John Doberstein 1954) [German: *Gemeinsames Leben*] SCM Press Ltd., London, UK.

Dee Brown 1970, *Bury My Heart at Wounded Knee: An Indian History of the American West*, Vintage (1991), London UK.

Randall Bytwerk 1998, translation of: Joseph Goebbels '*Nun, Volk steh auf, und Sturm brich los!*' ('Nation, Rise Up, and let the Storm Break Loose'), speech at Berliner Sportpalast 18/2/1943, Calvin University, research.calvin.edu

Annette Dumbach & Jud Newborn 1986, *Sophie Scholl and the White Rose*, Oneworld Publications, London UK.

T. S. Eliot 1934, *Choruses from 'The Rock'*, in *Collected Poems 1909-1962*, Faber & Faber, London UK.

Anne Frank 1947 (1985), *Het Achterhuis: Dagboekbrieven 14 Juni 1942 - 1 Augustus 1944*, Bert Bakker, Amsterdam, Netherlands.

Viktor E. Frankl 1946, *Man's Search for Meaning: an introduction to logother-apy*, (English translation by Ilse Lasch 1959) [German: *Ein Psycholog erlebt das konzentrationslager*] Hodder & Stoughton, London UK.

Brooke Fraser 2006, *C. S. Lewis Song,* Track 6 in album *Albertine,* Sony BMG Music Entertainment (New Zealand) Ltd.

Sigmund Freud 1913, *Totem and Taboo: Resemblances Between the Psychic Lives of Savages and Neurotics,* (Internetarchivebooks), Vintage Press, New York, NY.

Richard Grunberger 1971, *A Social History of the Third Reich*, Penguin Ltd, Harmondsworth UK.

Denise Heap 2021, Center for White Rose Studies, www.white-rose-studies.org (website [Shopify]).

Adolf Hitler 1925, *Mein Kampf,* English translation published 1969 (intro. by D.C.Watt) under Hutchinson & Co. Ltd, London, UK.

Holocaust Historical Society 2018, *Hans and Sophie Scholl,* holocausthistoricalsociety.org.uk

Jake Johnson 2019, *Christianity, Rebellion and Sophie Scholl: The Final Days, The Idea of an Essay*: Vol. 6, Article 22, Cedarville University, Ohio. https://digitalcommons.cedarville.edu/idea_of_an_essay/vol6/iss1/22

Harper Lee 1960, *To Kill a Mockingbird*, Mandarin, London UK.

C. S. Lewis 1943, *The Abolition of Man*, William Collins & Sons (Fount Paperbacks), Glasgow, UK.

Alexandra Lloyd 2023, *The Arts, Culture, and the Evolution of the White Rose Resistance*, Oxford German Studies, 52 (1), 1-14. https://doi.org/10.1080/00787191.2023.2180945

Frank McDonough 2009, *Sophie Scholl: the real story of the woman who defied Hitler*, History Press, Stroud, Gloucestershire UK.

Anthony J. Nicholls 1968, *Weimar and the Rise of Hitler*, (2nd ed. 1979), Macmillan Press, London UK.

James Peron 2018, *The Three Trials of Hans Scholl*, The Radical Center, medium.com

Sylvia Plath 1962, *Tulips* (poem), *Norton Anthology of Poetry*.

Elvis Presley 1967, *How Great Thou Art* (Audio album) RCA, New York NY.

Ramet S.P. & Hassenstab C.M. 2023, *The Anti-Fascism of Hans and Sophie Scholl: Intellectual Sources of the White Rose*. In S.P.Ramet, J. Pirjevic & E. Pelikan (eds.), *Anti-Fascism in European History: from the 1920's to Today* (pp.103-121), Central European University Press, https://doi.org/10.7829/jj.4032515.10

Adrienne Rich 1971, *I Dream I'm the Death of Orpheus* (poem) in *The Will to Change*, W. W. Norton & Co., New York NY.

Alex Ross 2018, *How American Racism Influenced Hitler*, New Yorker Magazine, 23/4/2018 newyorker.com

Ernestine Schlant 1999, *The Language of Silence*, Routledge, New York NY.

Hans Scholl & Sophie Scholl (Inge Jens, ed.) 2017, *At the Heart of the White Rose: Letters and Diaries of Hans and Sophie Scholl* (translated by J. Maxwell Brownjohn), Plough Publishing, Walden, New York.

Inge Scholl 1970, *Students Against Tyranny; the Resistance of the White Rose, Munich, 1942-1943,* Wesleyan University Press, Middletown Connecticut.

William Shirer 1960, *The Rise and Fall of the Third Reich*, Pan Books Ltd, London UK.

Makayla Scharf 2020, *'Biological Soldiers': War and the Nazi Euthanasia Killings,* the Ascendant Historian 7 (1), 48-56. https://journals.uvic.ca/index.php/corvette/article/view20011

Spartacus Educational, *Hans Scholl* & *Sophie Scholl*, www.spartacus-educational.com (website)

Joseph P. Stern 1975, *Hitler: the Fuhrer and the People*, Flamingo (Fontana), London UK.

Hetty E. Verolme 2013, *The Children's House of Belsen* (3rd ed.), Werma P/L, Perth Australia.

Simone Weil 1951, *Waiting for God*, Harper Collins (First Harper perennial Modern classics Ed'n 2009), New York NY.

Cate Williams 2014, *Dance of Life* (Audio CD), Klenner Studios, Perth Australia.

Stanislav Zámečník 2002, *That Was Dachau 1933-1945*, Comité International de Dachau, Brussels Belgium.

# Acknowledgements/Thanks

It's a rare privilege to spend time with people like Mary Magdalene-Bethany, Jehanne Darc, and Sophie Scholl; women of extraordinary caliber, and overawing beauty and faith. Though they are not physically present, they are certainly very real. Each is inspiring, moving, strengthening and humbling; time spent studying and learning from them has been deeply edifying.

A variety of people have helped me with a generosity I cannot repay. Some of them are still alive, others not - some have discussed aspects with me, some have provided spaces and/or resources for researching and writing, some have just been interested, some I have met personally, some not. Thank you for your kindness, especially when it has been hard for you to take the time to share and to engage.

Thank you Dad, for trying to be interested when it was very difficult for you, and for repeatedly asking surprising and helpful questions; thank you Søren Bie; thank you staff at numerous Libraries; thank you Regine Pernoud, Grenville Kent, Inge and Elisabeth Scholl, Anne Frank, Hetty Verolme, Ansu, Tony. And the girl who prayed the Holy Grace Prayer… you are not forgotten - you are wondrous.

IHSV.